PRAISE FOR

How To Bury Your Brother

"Lindsey Rogers Cook has blessed us with this penetrating, page-turning mystery about that greatest mystery of all: family. *How to Bury Your Brother* is a deeply wise book about the secrets that families keep, about the dysfunctions that grumble just beneath the surface. A profoundly honest and insightful and beautiful novel."

—Nathan Hill, *New York Times* bestselling author of *The Nix*

"Brilliantly plotted and beautifully written, *How to Bury Your Brother* questions how well we really know the people we love—and whether it's ever too late to learn the truth. An unforgettable debut."

—Kristy Woodson Harvey, bestselling author of *Slightly South of Simple*

"Lindsey Cook is a radiant new voice in Southern fiction. The debut novel, *How to Bury Your Brother*, is both wise and captivating. Cook's prose rings true as she takes us through the journey of a sister coming to terms with her brother's death, family hidden stories, and her own role in all of it. This is a book, and an author, who will grab your heart and not let go even after the very last page."

—Patti Callahan Henry, *New York Times* bestselling author

"*How to Bury Your Brother* explores what happens when a lifetime of secrets pushes one woman to the breaking point. Both heartbreaking and hopeful, Alice's journey to find the truth about her brother's death uncovers more about her family—and about herself—than she ever bargained for. A must-read."

—Haley Harrigan, author of *Secrets of Southern Girls*

"The one thing Alice knows with certainty on the day of her beloved brother's funeral is that, somehow, she must find answers to the questions that have haunted her since the day her brother left home at the age of fifteen—even if the quest could destroy everything she thinks she holds dear. With *How to Bury Your Brother*, Lindsey Rogers Cook has penned a deeply felt novel that unspools the threads of secrets long buried beneath the seemingly sunny surface of one Southern family. Readers will find themselves immersed in Alice's quest, and rooting for her to discover the real meaning of home."

—Mary Kay Andrews, *New York Times* bestselling author

"*How to Bury Your Brother* is a beautifully crafted novel about the tethers of family, the wounds of dysfunction, and the persistence of truth. Lindsey Rogers Cook brilliantly uses the power of place to remind us of what we might find when we truly go home."

—Sarah Enderlin Healy, author of *The Sisters Chase*

How To Bury Your Brother

LINDSEY ROGERS COOK

sourcebooks
landmark

Published by Sourcebooks Landmark, an imprint of Sourcebooks
P.O. Box 4410, Naperville, Illinois 60567-4410
(630) 961-3900
sourcebooks.com

Library of Congress Cataloging-in-Publication Data

Names: Cook, Lindsey Rogers, author.
Title: How to bury your brother / Lindsey Rogers Cook.
Description: Naperville, IL : Sourcebooks Landmark, [2020]
Identifiers: LCCN 2019038808 | (paperback)
Classification: LCC PS3603.O5725 H69 2020 | DDC 813/.6--dc23
LC record available at https://lccn.loc.gov/2019038808

Printed and bound in the United States of America.
VP 10 9 8 7 6 5 4 3 2 1

For my first editor and grandmother,
Dr. Jennie Springer

"I might well say now, indeed, that the latter end of Job was better than the beginning."

—Daniel Defoe, *The Adventures of Robinson Crusoe*

PROLOGUE

Tuesday really would be the perfect day to die.

I tick through the other days as warmth spreads toward my knees and elbows, out to my fingers and toes like sunlight dancing on the river where I played as a child. It's the feeling I used to get listening to "Here Comes the Sun."

Saturday and Sunday, I never considered—why ruin anyone's weekend? Mondays are bad enough already. On Thursdays, my mother plays bridge, always has, a respite she'll need, especially this week, so that's out. Wednesdays—blah—something about the middle of the week, and that's when the band practices.

My life's most significant events seem, by default, to occur on Tuesdays. My own birth. My sister's. Several other happenings, less positive.

The record scratches and silences its melody. Bad timing—a problem I'm doomed to repeat in death as I have since birth, when I knocked on the world's door during an epic hailstorm that flooded Atlanta, only to draw out the labor, as my mother always liked to remind me, more than twenty-four hours. Maybe I was waiting for the Tuesday. Today, too, the Tuesdayness made me linger, gave this cosmic game of chicken more weight, and I stared too long at the pill bottle.

When I woke up from "the game" these past few times, I wasn't sure if I'd won or lost, but now God has handed me this answer, this sign. I reach into my shirt pocket, retrieve another pill, and swallow it with what is now gin-flavored, half-melted ice.

I flick my eyes to the record player spinning silently, and it makes me want to cry, just thinking of how, even with YouTube and the internet where anyone can make a record like this one, we still haven't found another Queen or Nirvana or David Bowie.

My hand grips the glass where it rests on the chair's arm. The condensation will leave a stain on the leather. *Sorry, Lila.* I smile, in case this Tuesday really is as significant as it feels. I don't need another thing to apologize for. If today she finds this worn-down body, I want her to see me smiling, without a tear streak on my face.

Pulsing starts in my chest, edging out the warmth. The tempo enters slowly, like "Hotel California," then progresses to "Beat It." When the banging in my chest hits Metallica range, I know. This is it.

A wave of anxiety rises in my throat—or is that something else? *Is this what winning feels like?* I swallow it down, along with the fear.

I look back to where I know the letters are and sing Nirvana's "All Apologies" in my head, the song that would be playing were it not for my shitty timing. The shitty timing that will no longer scar anyone I love. Not anymore.

I picture my letters, floating into the universe, down the streets I've walked so many times, into the nooks and crannies of my childhood. I picture the black ink of my words finding them, all the people I've let down, all the apologies I need to make, all the wrongs I need to make right.

But most of all, her.

Alice.

My life doesn't qualify me for a last wish or request, I know. But if it did, I would ask that those letters surround her like a shield, that she'd feel that protection, like I can feel her presence now.

She's calling me.

She says it's okay to go. She doesn't blame me for leaving. Not this time.

So I close my eyes,

and let go.

SUMMER 2007

The Funeral

CHAPTER ONE

Alice studied her brother's mourners through the window of the church. The large Gothic structure in the middle of Atlanta cast a shadow over them as they shuffled in their shined shoes, their black kitten heels framing hosiery that disappeared under tasteful black dresses despite the thick summer heat. Tears pooled at the corners of Alice's eyes while she watched them chatting with one another on the way to the door, as if they were heading into any other church service, rather than a funeral. None of them cared about her brother. Alice doubted they remembered his name. She blinked rapidly to stop tears from falling.

"Alice," her mother said. "Put it—"

"In a box in your mind," she finished.

Her mother nodded, pleased.

"Maura, give her a break," her father said. "I mean, look at her."

Alice removed her hand from her pregnant belly and accepted his offer of a handkerchief. She wiped her eyes.

"Now is *not* the time," her mother said.

She was right. Alice had allowed herself seventy-two hours to mourn her brother, and those hours were up—she glanced at the blue plastic sports watch her mother had asked her not to wear—two hours ago, conveniently timed to end before the funeral, so she could smile at all her mother's friends. The ones who hadn't considered the existence of Maura's runaway son in decades, who were only here to build up a type of social capital, so they could ensure that the same people would brave the downtown chaos when the ghost of death came for them. It was time to get the funeral over with, to say a final goodbye to the person she'd already spent a lifetime saying goodbye to, and then to move on with her life.

"Showtime!" said Jamie, in a faded gray suit and a cheerful purple tie. Her father's best friend helped Alice up from the window ledge, and she trudged over to where her mother had positioned herself in a type of receiving line by the door, ready for the sea of supposed mourners.

Before the first stranger entered the church, Alice rubbed her neck and prepared to straighten up into a posture her mother had forced her to perfect during her teenage years with a knuckle to her vertebrae. Lack of sleep wasn't helping her meet her mother's standards for looking presentable. Instead of sleeping, Alice had spent the previous nights cycling through familiar dreams of her brother, which all ended the same: "Please," she would beg. "Don't go." But he always did, slinging his guitar and duffel over his shoulder, the way he had the last time she saw him, and taking her childhood with him.

Closest to the door, Maura hugged the first couple. "Most people don't know how pretty a hand-cut diamond can look," she said, still holding the woman's wrist. "Have you lost weight?" she said to a man with a salt-and-pepper mustache.

Alice's father, Richard, offered each man, woman, and child a handshake. To his only living cousin, he volunteered "Harold" and a nod before his eyes returned to his shoes.

Jamie lingered behind, waiting for Maura to invite him into the family's line. Though he was close enough to the family that everyone at the church had forgotten he wasn't actually Richard's younger brother, Maura turned her cheek in refusal to his silent question. Instead, he trapped men in a conversation about his latest hobby—online gaming—as they finished talking to Alice. "These kids, you would not believe," he said, lifting his arms. He curled his fingers and darted his thumbs up and down in demonstration.

Her brother would have despised this scene. If he were here, he would have led her to the narrow staircase and up to the sanctuary's balcony, like he always did as a child on Sundays. They would invent fake nonsense conversations as they watched the people in their fancy outfits, Alice laughing so loudly their mother would give a stern look from below. Or they would talk, the scratchy carpet itching the back of Alice's legs, exposed in one of the ruffled dresses her mother always made her wear to Sunday school.

"What do you think heaven's like?" he had asked her once, as they tried to count the ceiling's intricate tiled diamonds. He couldn't have been older than twelve.

"Angels and singing," she said with a child's confidence. "And lots of animals. With wings."

"In heaven, I want to live in a high, high building where I can play guitar on the roof and look out at earth. And you can live next door in a tree house over the forest. And we'll see each other all the time."

She hoped he was there now, but the larger, practical part of her brain doubted. Doubted that vision of heaven was real, maybe that heaven existed at all. And even if it did, doubted that her brother had made it there. She let herself slump and allowed her mind to rest inside the familiar blanket of Jamie's chatter, ignoring her mother's spirited small talk.

Her father shifted toward her. "The eulogy. It means a lot, to your mother."

Alice nodded, and he reached a hand out, as if to lay it reassuringly on her shoulder, but pulled back at the last second and formed a fist at his side.

"He could never fight his demons," her father said. "It's better this way. For the family."

She stepped back an inch, as if off-balance.

Before Alice could reply, the cheek of her nine-year-old daughter thumped onto her stomach. Her father looked at Caitlin, then turned away.

Alice reached down to stroke her daughter's hair as her husband, Walker, strode through the crowd, standing six inches above even the tallest men, though they were all shrunken from age.

It's better this way. For the family.

Could that really be true?

"She's still pretty sensitive," Walker said to Alice, with no explanation for his lateness or the dirty Converses on Caitlin's feet that Maura was already eyeing. She tried to read his expression as Caitlin buried her head deeper into Alice's dress. Though her daughter had never met her uncle, his dying had launched the concept of death into the air, as if she had only realized this week that it existed.

Two old men stood trapped between Richard's handshake and Alice's side hug in an awkward limbo. She gestured at Jamie, and he danced over to take Alice's place in the line.

"You're not going to die next, are you?"

"No, honey, I'm *never* going to die. You can't get rid of me."

Caitlin wiped her eyes with the back of her hand, leaving pink streaks down her cheeks. "Promise?"

"Well, we'll die sometime," Walker said, leaning down to her level. "When we're old."

"But you're old now!"

Alice gave her husband a face that said *Let me handle this, idiot* but remembering what was to come, she mustered her last reserves of patience and morphed her expression into the same fake smile she'd used with the mourners. Better to hang onto what she expected would be their last hour of marital (somewhat) peace for weeks.

Alice leaned down to her daughter. "We won't die for a very, very, *very* long time. Okay?"

Caitlin nodded, and the family stepped forward to greet the next mourner. The receiving line continued.

"How did he die?" one of the mourners asked Maura, the question petering out at the end. Alice raised an eyebrow and awaited the reply.

"Heart failure. *So* unexpected."

Her mother always lied with a smile.

She would never tell the mourners the words that rattled in Alice's skull now. Like the game of Pong her brother had been so happy to get for Christmas one year, the two words bounced in an endless loop: *overdose, OxyContin,* and back again. They were the only words Alice had retained after her mother delivered the news to her in the church parking lot on Sunday, saying simply, "Rob is dead. Heart failure."

Then, to the only question Alice dared to ask: "His heart stopped beating when he overdosed on OxyContin. Is that what you want to hear?"

————————————

When, finally, the last mourner entered the church, Alice stepped away from Walker and her mother, now cheerfully introducing Caitlin to her Thursday bridge group. She walked past dozens of cross-shaped flower arrangements that threatened to collapse into the crowd—all addressed to her mother—until she reached a table usually cluttered with church flyers.

Her mother had decorated it with a row of pictures that showed the two Tate children growing up. At various stages of childhood, they climbed their tree house, canoed on the river, hugged a golden retriever, or squeezed into the driver's seat of one of their father's eighteen-wheelers with *Tate Trucking* in block letters across the side. Alice's cheeks burned with anger as she looked at their smiling faces. She longed to reach into the photo and pin him down there, to keep him from leaving, from dying.

Her eyes skipped over a photo of the young family in front of her parents' house, a place she hadn't been in years and hoped never to see again. She was sure her mother had brought the photo to torment her, as if her brother's death and the tension with Walker were just shy of far enough.

The next photo showed the family's annual trip to Amelia

Island, the trip the year before her brother left. Five years younger, Alice was small enough to perch on his shoulders. Her legs dangled down over his strong arms, and she wore jean shorts and the T-shirt she'd received a few weeks earlier at her fourth-grade field day. She looked right into the camera, caught in mid-laugh. His neck and smile hid his other features as he tipped his face to look up at her.

She remembered thinking a day at the beach with her brother was the most fun she'd ever had, the most special she'd ever felt, his eyes focused on her as if he wore blinders to the rest of the world, while her father would barely look up from his newspaper when she talked, and her mother would only correct her grammar.

Was the family better off with him dead, as her father suggested? No. The only better reality would have been for him not to have existed at all, to erase these happy memories from her consciousness. Pretending her brother never existed, that's how she'd chosen to live with Walker for the last decade, after all. The loss and loneliness of the years after her brother left were painful only because she had experienced the other reality, with him, the reality that had flooded back to her anew in each hour since his death.

Jamie sidled up to her in front of the photos. "He was such a cute kid."

She nodded. Paused. "Daddy said that even though it's hard right now, it's best for the family. That he could never"—she made air quotes—"'fight his demons.' Do you really think that's true?"

"Look at it from his point of view: Your dad, he'd been sent away to that terrible school, barely survived Korea. I shouldn't speak ill of your grandfather—Lord knows he saved me when I had nowhere else to go—but he was a real son of a bitch. I never saw him crack a smile in the five years I lived with them. You and your brother, when you were growing up, you had everything. Good parents, nice house, plenty of money. Your brother had all that, a perfect life, people who loved him, who adored him, and look what he did with it." Jamie spread his arms toward the pictures and the mourners.

It was true. Yet Rob had taken the pills to numb something inside, numb something Alice would never understand or know. When he took off, not bothering to call, not caring enough to worry about her, Alice assumed he was busy having the time of his life in Paris or London or Los Angeles. And she hated him for it. The pills, though, they introduced a new tinge to her many conflicting thoughts about her brother: guilt.

"Maybe I could have done something, found him or helped him in some way," Alice said, but even to her, the words felt hollow.

"He was so stubborn, that boy," Jamie said with the overly mature air he used when talking about "the kids," even though by age, he was thrown in between her father and her brother, truly belonging to neither generation. "He chose not to be part of this family anymore. He didn't care about you or Richard or Maura. He wasn't exactly—"

"There you are!" Alice's best friend and former college roommate, Meredith, kissed Alice on both cheeks before wrapping her in a long, tight hug, interrupting Jamie. Alice felt the threat of tears, so she stepped back and rubbed her hands on her belly, trying to ground herself.

"Are you feeling better about the eulogy?" Meredith asked with a look at Jamie, who met her eyes before walking away. Alice had always been jealous of Meredith's ability to dismiss someone with a look.

"No, I wish"—*Wish what? So many things*—"wish I *knew* who he really was."

"Well—" Meredith started, to contradict her, comfort her, assure her, but Alice didn't want to be comforted. She cut her off.

"I'm just glad it will be over soon."

Meredith shut her mouth.

Alice sat down on one of the benches that lined the church's hallway, and they sat, shoulders touching, for a few minutes in a silence her friend knew enough not to interrupt. Alice rested her head on Meredith's shoulder. She could close her eyes and sleep here for hours, just feeling her friend breathing and the baby squirming.

"I'm going to name the baby Robbie, after him," Alice finally said, raising her head.

She had been so scared that breathing a name into existence, as she had three other times, would cause the baby to disappear from her womb. She felt now that she would be able to give Caitlin a sibling as the universe yanked away her own childhood hero, a Faustian bargain.

"What did Walker say?"

"He said he doesn't understand why I'd want to and why I'm so upset, since Rob and I weren't close." *Pregnancy hormones* is what he'd actually said, accompanied only the first time by a small laugh.

Not close. Like a second cousin or long-lost aunt. Not that Alice could fault Walker. She'd said it herself at their first date, to dismiss further questions about her brother. "One brother. We're not close." Had barely brought up her brother while she and Walker had been together.

But she never believed it was really true, only knew that if she hadn't said those words—*not close*—she wouldn't have been able to smile up at Walker on their wedding day. She wouldn't have been able to laugh with him on the couch as their spoons went to war over the few remaining pieces of cookie dough in the ice cream. She wouldn't have been able to scream "She says keep holding on!" as he let go of Caitlin's bike.

To create those memories, she had to bury those of her brother, had to raise the stakes not to go back to the dark place of her young adulthood, not to go back to being consumed by someone who couldn't even pick up the phone to let her know where he'd gone. But, she knew she'd never be able to explain that to Walker.

Already, she could see the word *liar* floating between them. She'd felt the accusation from the moment Walker hugged her lightly when she told him the news of her brother's passing, gasping like an asthma patient and blasting snot onto his church clothes. His hands had tensed around her shoulders with the knowledge that he was missing some essential bit of information.

But had it been a lie? Alice wondered in the hours she spent alone, erasing and rewriting the eulogy, avoiding her husband and all the questions he had never known to ask, all the stories she had never told. *What makes someone close?*

Is it that you talk every day or every week or every year, or is it that their favorite sayings, the way they watched a sunset, how they licked their lips while concentrating on a book, or sang to you when you were scared, are coiled around your DNA like any other molecule that defines you?

The funeral director rounded up Maura, Richard, Jamie, Alice, Walker, and Caitlin and led them to another side room while guests filled the chapel. Her family squashed the room's new silence with anything but talk of the deceased. Maura summarized the plot of *Cats* for Caitlin, which they had tickets to for Saturday night at the Fox Theater. Avoiding Alice, Walker struggled for a conversation with Richard and Jamie.

"Hot today," Walker said.

"Grass is dying," her father said. The three of them stood with their hands in their pockets. "How's yours, James?"

Alice stared through the stained-glass window into the sanctuary. Through the lightest-colored glass, she could make out the brown casket with its regal gold trim in front of the white marble altar. Alice had gone with Maura to pick it out yesterday, trailing her at the funeral home while her mother scrutinized the various features of each, exactly as she would a new car. After Maura ran her hand along the cream silk inside one, she pronounced it "perfect" and ordered three, one for her, one for her husband, and one for her son.

"Don't you want one?" Maura asked.

"No."

"We'll all be matching. You'll be left out."

Alice shook her head.

"You'll regret it later," her mother had said before turning back to the funeral home's director without missing a beat: "So, you'll get these and coordinate with the home in New Orleans?"

"Yes, ma'am."

New Orleans, where her brother died on Tuesday, according to the funeral director. More questions Alice didn't want to ask. She was too afraid of what the answers would be.

A church usher led the family to the front pew as the organ began "How Great Thou Art," her brother's favorite hymn, at least when she knew him.

Sweat glistened on the pastor's forehead as he approached the podium. The same pastor who her brother had spent so much time imitating to her in church, laughing under their breath until Maura shushed them. The man had been old back then. *It should be him in the coffin*, Alice thought, before regretting it. She apologized in her head as he began with ten minutes of listing the family's résumé in the church: Bible groups Maura led, fundraisers she organized, instruction she gave at Vacation Bible School, how "we wouldn't have expected any less from a pastor's daughter." The pastor pronounced Richard a "true servant of God," mainly because of the checks he signed, Alice imagined.

The pastor launched into a generic speech about "trusting God's plan." Alice sighed too loudly, and her mother shot her a look. She'd heard the same speech three times before at other church funerals. It had prompted her to volunteer to give the eulogy in the first place, so that her brother could have something personal. No matter what her words would cost her.

She tuned out and memorized the funeral pamphlet in her lap. Her brother stared at her from the photo as a teenager, holding the acoustic guitar she couldn't separate from him in her memories. Underneath, *July 16, 1968–August 27, 2007* stood out in cursive writing with his full name: *Robinson Wesley Tate*. He hated being called Robinson. Their mother named both him and Alice after literary classics, but he got the worst of it. Not that anyone would dare tease him in school.

"Now," the pastor said. "Robinson's sister, Alice, would like to say a few words. Alice…"

She scooted out of the row past her mother. The preacher placed his hand on Alice's back and guided her to the podium, as if she might double over in grief, exhaustion, birth pains, or a mixture of all three. She straightened her dress, the largest of her maternity clothes, which had been stored in the deepest entrails of her house where they couldn't mock her with the inadequacy of her misshapen uterus. The fabric smelled like attic with a hint of squirrel droppings.

"Thank you for that beautiful service, Pastor Perry," Alice read from her paper. "On behalf of my family, I'd like to thank all of you for coming today and honoring my brother's life."

She skipped over the next line, which she'd found in a eulogy template online: *Rob was a son, a brother…* The list was supposed to go on…a chef or a father or a neighbor or a committed member of his community. "A child of God," the website suggested, but that, she had no idea.

"Rob was my older brother. I was always the deputy and coconspirator in his adventures. In the summers, we spent a lot of time at our father's warehouse, building things with all the empty boxes. Rob would start planning at Christmas. He would draw up a blueprint using butcher paper he took from school. Our friends would help, but he always put me in charge of the most important section. One year, we made Atlantis. Another year, the White House. They never looked much like the real thing, but we always had a lot of fun crawling through our creations."

Alice chuckled awkwardly, remembering the seriousness he'd brought to the project, the tingling in her stomach as he assigned the roles, fearful for a second that he would forget her, and the swelling of pride when he assigned her the biggest part, like always.

Alice's eyes found Walker watching her carefully from the second row, questioning. *Was this the same brother Alice acted like wasn't worth mentioning? The one she said she wasn't close to?*

A second too late, Meredith joined in with her own laughter to break the room's silence. Alice looked back at her paper.

"Rob was creative and smart like that. When he was still in elementary school, our mother ordered a set of encyclopedias so that we could look things up for school. Rob would start a volume and read it like a book. One year, he read the entire *B* volume. It seemed like he knew about everything: how baseballs were made, bullets, Brazil, bees. I was young at the time and didn't realize the pattern until he had moved on to *D*."

She paused and attempted to make eye contact with a few people in the audience, like she'd learned in college in a required public speaking class. A lady from her mother's tennis group gave her an encouraging smile from the third row. A man near the back snoozed with his head resting on the pew and his mouth wide open.

"I always felt safe with him, no matter how crazy his adventures got. In the house where we grew up, our closets were connected by a crawl space that I was small enough to go through. I got scared at night and would open the door and crawl through to find Rob in his own closet, reading or silently moving his fingers on his guitar with nothing but a flashlight. He let me sleep in his bed, staying with me until I fell asleep."

She could still summon it, the sense of security she felt as she drifted off in Rob's bed, her older brother still on the closet floor, quietly turning pages, the dog a few feet away.

She looked at her parents. Her father stared at his shoes. Her mother looked straight at her, not really seeing anything, with her head held a bit too high, probably regretting not pushing harder in her request to edit Alice's speech. Maybe not letting her mother help had been a mistake, but she knew what would have happened if she had accepted the help. Rob would become Robinson; her real memories would be turned into the version her mother wanted to present to the world, the one that had never existed. Alice looked over the rest of the audience and willed one person to cry, so she wouldn't have to.

"I had to take a lot of biology classes, and one of the first things you have to do is Punnett squares. A Punnett square determines the traits of offspring. For example, my parents both have brown eyes, but each have a recessive blue eye gene, so Rob got blue and I got brown. Since we learned of my brother's passing, I've thought often about those squares. The truth is, I wouldn't be who I am today—the ecologist, the mother, the friend—without him. My mother gave me her industriousness. My father gave me his levelheadedness. But I have Rob to thank for my passion, and for just a pinch of his rebellion."

She laughed again nervously at the reference to how the audience probably perceived Rob—as a teenage troublemaker with uncut hair.

Without trying, her eyes bounced to Walker again. He stared at her, and she could read his face clearly, as she could when he was caught off guard. Their eyes met, and in an instant, he checked his expression, wiped it clear. But, she had seen it—hurt. Betrayal. She could see him realizing: Alice *had* been close to Rob.

And she hadn't told him any of the stories, any of this chapter of her life. She could see him deciding that the tension between them during the last week was more than pregnancy hormones and bad communication; it was the exposing of a decade-long lie.

In an effort to get away from Walker, her eyes found the casket's polished wood. She opened her mouth to begin her next story, about how her brother took over the school speakers with his high school band to sing her "Happy Birthday" in the style of the Beatles. But she couldn't make out the words.

She pictured the adult inside the casket, resting on the flawless silk, the adult she couldn't tell one story about, the one she shared blood with, had thought she shared a mind with for so long.

We weren't close.

He was my everything.

Weren't they both true? The tears came, unstoppable. She blurted out "Thank you" and stepped away from the podium. As she walked to her seat, regretting not getting the casket and thinking her mother was always right, she noticed someone she didn't recognize lurking by the doorway. He was tall, and large, someone she would remember if she had seen him before.

When she plopped herself into her seat, Walker's knees shot toward Caitlin's and away from Alice's as if she were made of lava. She turned away from him to watch the stranger. *Who is he? Did he know the adult Rob?*

After the pastor read a few more generic Bible verses, Alice popped up from her seat next to Walker to go after the stranger. She half waddled, moving as quickly as she could, and dodged several of her mother's friends as they tried to praise her speech or tell her that she looked like she was "about to pop!" She reached the doorway and followed it to the side lot as an old minivan pulled out and drove away.

She stood in the open doorway, watching the space where the van had been, until Walker exited the front door with Caitlin on the other side of the parking lot. Though he didn't know he was being watched, he spun to look behind several times as he fast-walked to the car, pulling Caitlin by the hand. The earlier ease was gone from his stride, replaced by hardness and anger. Though his shoulders slumped from a level of sadness appropriate for a funeral, Alice knew grief over the dead had nothing to do with it.

She breathed deeply, filling the parts of her stomach and chest that already felt close to bursting, and thought of little Robbie. When he came, Walker would forget about today. The memory of her brother and his secrets would once again be hers alone to bare.

As the mourners filed out of the church, Alice found her mother in the bathroom. Crying.

"Are you okay? Mama, I think the service was great." Alice stared at her, unsure what to do. She reached her hand toward her mother's shoulder, but Maura shuddered away from the touch.

"It's the damn flower company!" Maura said, suddenly straightening up. "I said *no* orchids. And what do I get? Orchids! Of course." She scooped the flowers out of the vase and threw them in the trash can. Alice reached to stop the crystal from falling as her mother flung open the door.

Alice remembered seeing her mother cry only twice. The last time was two mornings after Rob left. Alice woke up to the sound of her mother ripping band posters off his bedroom wall, sobbing.

The first time was when Alice was about six. She remembered running around the house with Rob, chasing the dog, which— along with opening the decorative books on the shelf, doing crafts on the kitchen table, and the word *fart*—was forbidden in the Tate household. They ran around the main floor's loop, all three panting and giggling, until the dog froze at the sound of the garage door. Both Rob and Alice barreled into the dog, and the tangled group rolled into a vintage bookcase, knocking two delicate plates off their stands.

Maura ran in to survey the damage. When she saw the broken china, her face crumpled as tears ran down her red cheeks, bringing her mascara with them.

"Those were wedding presents! I *told you* not to run in the *house!*"

The dog ran off, but Alice and Rob froze, barefoot in the middle of a minefield, waiting to be dug out by the unfriendly forces.

When Richard saw the mess, he crunched in to retrieve Alice. Rob waited until their father left to find the dustpan before struggling out of the wreckage. As Alice trailed Rob up the stairs, watching blood from his left foot drip toward the carpet, they heard their father say, "That's why we shouldn't have all these damn antiques. Children need to be able to play in their own house."

But growing up in that house, the antiques were the least of their problems.

WINTER 2016

*8½ years
after the funeral*

CHAPTER TWO

Alice stood barefoot in the kitchen, stirring a gigantic pot of chili. The smell of freshly cut cilantro from her garden, still resting next to her on a wooden cutting board, mixed with tomatoes and the smooth air of a mild Georgia winter that flowed through the open windows.

She breathed it all in, trying to settle her stomach before dinner. She had barely eaten since a lawyer rang their doorbell a few days ago with the contract her mother had signed last spring, selling the house where Alice grew up and slating it for demolition two weeks from tomorrow. She didn't fear the wrecking ball. In fact, Alice had imagined it gliding into the too-quiet brick colonial like an eagle in flight, exploding the pain and loneliness of her childhood along with the Corinthian columns out front. Picturing herself stepping inside her parents' house, though— that's how she thought of it, never *her* house or "home"—sent her back to the fridge to pour another glass of wine.

She had entered the house less than a dozen times since graduating from the University of Georgia at twenty-two, and never beyond her mother's elegant parlor off the foyer. Since her mother left, the house had ticked as an unavoidable bomb in Alice's mind, one that she'd wanted to evade for another few months. "Procrastinating," Walker had called it.

Alice moved around the kitchen island, picking the last chili ingredients from among the scattered papers, mail, outdated report cards, dog treats, energy bars, pens, and spare change. As she walked past her open shelving crowded with knickknacks and frames filled with mismatched art, Alice prepared herself for tomorrow by mentally walking through the house of her childhood, with its pristine antiques and silver frames from Tiffany's.

The sound of a car on the driveway cut through the neighborhood's quiet, the reverent hush Walker had used to convince Alice they should buy the house, even though the stone facade and gated neighborhood were grander than she'd envisioned for the house where she would raise her children. She restacked items in one corner of the island, turned down the music, and switched it from Johnny Cash to REM.

Normally, she valued the quiet time to mince, stir, and drink wine before the family piled in, especially since she was never alone at work anymore. In the last few years, her tiny cabin on the lake had become a full-fledged research and outreach center, complete with donors to impress, research assistants to coach, and staff meetings to call. The Georgia Creekside Center was a dream of hers, a success, yet she couldn't help but miss the glorious early years as the founder and only employee, wading through the water with a teetering Caitlin. Today, though, Alice was eager for the family's noise.

"*Who's that?*" she said to Buddy. She walked to the door as the golden retriever slipped on the hardwoods with his enthusiasm.

"How was your day?" Alice asked her husband. But when he leaned in to kiss her, she couldn't stomach acting like normal, not today, and turned the other way as if to check the simmering pot.

In answer to the rejection, Walker ignored her question. "Isn't it a little cold for the windows to be open?" He walked over to shut them without waiting for an answer.

Without another word, he stopped at the fridge to grab a beer and went to sit on the gray suede couch in the living room. His tennis shoes, still muddy from running up and down the sides at Robbie's game, clunked to the floor, and the television flipped on.

After a hug from Alice, Robbie sat on the hardwood floor with the back of his too-clean soccer jersey against the dark island cabinets and Buddy propped under his thighs. He retrieved a cursive practice sheet from his backpack and started to draw the letters carefully.

Alice dialed Caitlin and struggled to balance the phone on her shoulder while opening a bag of shredded cheese.

"Where are you? I made chili. Weren't you going to come home earlier tonight so we could have Sunday family dinner?"

"I'm at Chelsea's. Maybe it's better if I eat here."

Alice sighed. "I feel like I haven't seen you." Since the day Caitlin announced she would apply to NYU and Walker forbade it, her waking hours at the house had dwindled to near zero.

"Will you come if I tell him not to bring it up?"

"Fine. Be home soon."

Finally, a crisis Alice knew how to solve.

Alice retrieved a beer from the fridge as a bargaining chip and walked to the family room. "If you keep this up," she said to Walker, "she's going to be living at Chelsea's pretty soon."

"We're not letting her live at her girlfriend's house." He turned his eyes away from *Mad Money*. "The farthest I'm willing to go is Duke. It was good enough for us, right?"

She handed him the beer, and he twisted off the cap.

"Promise me you'll drop it for tonight."

He nodded and looked back at the TV.

When Caitlin came in ten minutes later, she and Robbie set the table as he explained the intricacies of his teacher's post-marriage name change: "She was Miss Smith, but now we're supposed to call her Mrs. Hersch. Isn't that weird? Last week, she changed the name on her desk and everything."

Caitlin nodded. "Very weird."

The family sat at a dinged-up six-seater wooden table in the kitchen with Buddy at Alice's feet. Like most of the house, the room felt homey but a few years too worn, the walls a warm yellow that was no longer in style and made the entire room look dark. For years, Alice had put off Walker's pleas to work with a decorator to mimic the magazine decor of his colleagues. And since Walker's promotion to partner at a top Atlanta law firm a few months ago, he insisted a complete remodel was the only solution. She imagined her plants in their mismatched pots and the children's artwork gone in favor of stylized accessories, and her stomach twisted again, remembering what tomorrow held.

Alice and Walker joined hands, but Caitlin lingered before she grabbed her father's hand. He squeezed and smiled at her. Caitlin closed her eyes.

"Dear God, Our Father," Walker said, and on cue the family bowed their heads. "We thank you for the gifts we are about—"

The telephone rang, and Caitlin hopped up to grab it.

"It's Mimi," she said, bringing the still-ringing phone over to Alice. Alice considered not answering, but clicked the phone on for the last ring: "Hello?"

"Hello? With whom am I speaking?" her mother said, voice dripping honey, as if she had dialed a friend and a sweet-voiced child answered instead.

"It's Alice. Your daughter." She tried to mimic her mother's sweetness.

"What?" her mother said too loudly.

In the background, a nurse said: "Your daughter, Alice. You wanted to call and talk to her, Mrs. Tate."

"Yes. Robinson is going to check you out after third period. We're leaving for Florida at 2:00 p.m. sharp. I'll hold you both accountable if you're late, and we'll go on to the beach without you. Is that understood?"

"Yes."

"Yes what?"

Alice closed her eyes and tried to gather her patience. "Yes, ma'am."

"Good girl." Maura hung up.

Her mother had returned them both to this moment—the last shred of normalcy before everything with Rob fell apart—more and more frequently in the last months, as if Maura's brain was a speeding train that knew it was about to hit a wall, as if deep inside her subconscious, she remembered about the house and its sale and demolition, as if she remembered Alice would finally be forced to go inside. But the call was only another lapse in memory, even if it felt like a victory lap to the decades-long battle of stubbornness that Alice and Maura had fought over the house.

The battle over the house intensified every year. First, when Alice came to pick up her mother from the house, she would take longer getting ready as Alice waited in the driveway, to see if she would come inside to fetch her. When that didn't work, Maura doubled her standards for Christmas every year in a silent plea for relocation to her own home. The silver and lace tablecloth, tall burning candles, and crystal wineglasses waged war with Alice's scratched leather-backed dining chairs, but neither Maura nor Alice voiced the battle out loud. At times like those, Richard had always acted as the buffer between Alice and her mother. He died five years ago, but she still missed him.

"How was she?" Caitlin asked, while Walker spooned sour cream into his chili.

"Sounded like a bad day."

They ate in silence for a few minutes, forgetting the unsaid prayer. Robbie raised a full spoon above his bowl and let the chili splash back down.

"You know the rules," Walker said to him. "Eat or you're not leaving this table."

Robbie rested his chin on the table and eyed the full bowl.

"If you need me tomorrow, call my cell, instead of the Center. I'll be at Mimi's house all day."

"Why?" Robbie said.

"Since she's living at her apartment now"—that's what she and Walker called the nursing home—"I'm going to get all of her stuff out, so they can build a new house there."

"Why?"

"Because Mimi's house is old," Walker said.

"How long will it take?"

"Only a week." Alice hoped, although she had two before the demolition, if she needed more time to figure out what to do with her mother's endless collections and antiques. She had left

Grace, the Center's assistant director, with dozens of tabbed folders and lists of what would need to be done while she was gone.
The winter months were always the slowest because fewer school
groups traveled to stay at the on-campus aquatic camp. But Alice
wanted to prepare for their busiest months in the spring when the
professors she worked with would rush to analyze the year's data
in time for grant deadlines. She planned to call to check in every
day, even though she promised Grace she wouldn't.

"Mom, can I please be excused?" Robbie asked.

Alice nodded, and he stood up from the table. "But don't let
Buddy come," he said. "He'll walk all over my puzzle again."

She placed her foot on Buddy's fur to keep him steady.

They ate quietly for a couple more minutes before Caitlin and
Walker started into a heated discussion about something happening in the Middle East. "If people would stop blowing themselves
up," Walker said. Alice stopped listening.

She supposed forty-two was a little old to fear a house so much,
to avoid a whole section of her life. But dwelling on memories of
her time there created a sinking feeling in her chest as if her heart
was a hole with gravity strong enough to suck in her other organs.
She pictured the house—and the tree house where she and Rob
would play—alone on the empty street, lots cleared of old houses,
a vortex that inhaled the mailbox and bugs and their childhood
pets and her mother's hatpin collection, and finally, inhaled the
family itself, with only Alice left holding onto the edge—

"*Mom*, he's doing it."

"Doing *what*?" Walker threw his hands up in the air.

"Let's not fight tonight. We all agreed not to talk about NYU,
right?"

"It wasn't about NYU," Walker said.

"I said I think I want to major in English or creative writing and minor in women's studies, wherever I go, but probably at NYU, and he said—"

"I said I didn't think the job opportunities would be good for that, but even with that degree, she could still go to law school later. I really don't think the minor is a good idea; she shouldn't be broadcasting *it*."

"What's that supposed to—"

"I work in the corporate world. I know—"

"Ready, Dad, say it with me." Caitlin brought her hands in front of her chest. "Les"—*clap*—"bi"—*clap*—"an."

"No!" He glanced behind him to the wall, as if they were in a public restaurant. "No, that's not what I meant. I guarantee no one at my firm took women's studies. That's all I'm saying. Plus, I am paying for this crap, if you remember."

It wasn't completely true, but Alice didn't contradict him. Meanwhile, Walker reached for a piece of corn bread and took a large bite.

"Forget it." She turned to Alice. "I need to work on some stuff anyway."

"Love you so much, honey!" Walker called as the sound of Caitlin's combat boots on the stairs echoed through the house. He turned to Alice with a smile, as if the last thing he said was all that mattered. Upstairs, the music for the play Caitlin was directing at school seeped bass beats and electric notes down the stairs. Alice prayed the premiere on Saturday would be the end of the house-shaking vibrations.

"You just can't help yourself, can you?" Alice said.

"Guess not." He stood up, carrying his beer to the basement. Alice sat surrounded by half-eaten bowls of homemade chili.

As Alice brought the bowls to the sink, she attempted to convince herself that going to the house was a positive, as she always did with the things she dreaded most. Maybe it was coming at a good time since she could use some alone time to think. She could run over the other item on her procrastination list—her marriage— instead of looping again through a conversation with Maura from last Sunday's visit to "her apartment." She'd spent so much time with her mother in her head in the last week that Alice gave herself a pass for today's weekly visit.

That day, her mother was in one of Alice's favorite forms: a friendly stranger, not stuck in the past or unhappy at her confusion.

"Why would a young lady like you come talk to an old lady like me?" her mother said—teasing, friendly.

"Same reason you would want to talk to me."

"And why do you think that is?"

"It's nice to have someone to talk to. So you don't get lonely."

"Is that why you think old people like to talk to young people? Bless your heart! I'm not lonely. I have myself, and I'm the best friend I've ever had."

Alice laughed. Her mother was charming, something Alice could see easily now that had eluded her when they lived in the same house.

"We like to talk to young people to share our wisdom. It

makes us feel like all our pain was worth it, if only the next generation could learn from it. Of course, young people are always
too stupid to listen. I was the same way. What problem could you
use an old lady's pain and wisdom on?"

Did she dare?

"Well, one," Alice began, monitoring her mother's face
for any switch in mood. "I found out yesterday my husband
has been having an affair. He doesn't know I know. I..." She
guessed her mother wouldn't understand texting or the subtext
of an eggplant, then donut emoji, not to mention all the creative
synonyms for what Alice had only heard her mother refer to as
it. Alice pushed the words from her mind. "I found letters they
wrote to each other."

Her mother clucked her tongue. "Difficult, but nothing you
can't handle," Maura said.

Alice looked at her mother, hoping for a second that she knew
to whom she was speaking, if only to have the confidence her
mother had in her.

"Are you satisfying him?"

"Mam-ura!" Alice said, attempting to change to her mother's
name mid-exclamation.

"At least you haven't gotten fat. What color is that lipstick
though? It does nothing for you."

"It's ChapStick."

"Exactly." Maura smiled, as if her point had been proven.
"What will you do?"

Alice shifted in her chair, crossing her legs the other way.

She knew suddenly why she had chosen her mother, an unlikely
confidante for this secret: her mother's generation saw marriage as a

logical piece of machinery, a system of levers and pulleys that, with a quick repair, could run smoothly. Success was measured only in that the machine kept running; happiness was inconsequential.

"I don't know." Wasn't it a sign that she'd let that view of marriage seep into her own thinking, that she could utter these words—"I don't know"—so levelheadedly? That after seeing the texts, she had promptly left the room to take Buddy out and continue with her morning?

"Are there children?"

"Two. Caitlin is seventeen and Robbie is eight."

"Put it in a box in your mind, lock the box, and put it on the highest shelf." Maura looked directly at Alice, as if wondering if she had formed the right words to reflect the sentiment. "You understand what I am trying to say, don't you?"

Alice nodded. It was the advice she knew her mother would give, but why then had she wanted to hear it so badly?

They sat in silence for a few minutes.

"I like that name, Robbie. Is it short for anything?"

She watched her mother carefully. "No. Just…Robbie."

"How nice."

———————————

Alice started the dishwasher, and her mind came back to the empty, now clean(ish) kitchen. The memory of Walker's texts lingered though; the memory of reading them at the island joined the rest of the room's chaos and to-do's. She grabbed her house key and went to the garage to stare at Walker's pristine (leased) Audi, sitting innocently in the garage with its buffed shine.

She knew what she was *supposed* to feel as she constantly replayed the conversation with her mother: hurt, enough to burst into tears, or even better, rage. Like the kind she had seen last summer at the neighborhood pool when a wife, whom she recognized from the women's events she forced herself to go to for fundraising contacts, had marched over to her own husband, smoking cigars with a group of fathers and drinking a beer, slapped him in the face, and told him he deserved to be castrated. Alice wanted to summon that feeling, but instead, she felt nothing.

At first, she thought the feeling of rage would come once the news sank in. Yet, eight days had passed, and she still felt, if not *nothing*, then annoyance only for how utterly predictable Walker had turned out to be. As soon as she read that text from Brittani—"Still sore after last night! ;-)"—she knew what the rest would say, right down to the punctuation (or lack thereof). She knew where he would meet Brittani, how he'd conceal the affair. She could guess when and how the texts started, so accurately that she'd grown tired of reading after a few screens, not even feeling the need to scroll all the way to the top of the message thread.

She couldn't blame him completely for that, though, for his predictability was exactly why she had married him. Knowing what to expect meant comfort, safety, had allowed her to dive into him and blend herself effortlessly into his life without him asking questions about who she really was, about her past, or why this life would be appealing.

She circled the car once, the key heavy in her hand. One scratch down the door, the kind another car could do if parked too close—maybe that would free the anger and hurt, allow it to fill her. Maybe that's what would help her move to the next step, the action, the what next, not working long hours at the Center or spending extra time in her garden or walking Buddy, as she had since she'd read the texts.

She stood next to the car, miming opening a door, trying to map where the scratch would happen, how long it would be, how wide it would be, all the while imagining Walker's face when he saw it, how he'd first squint at a distance, wonder if it was just his Lasik acting up again. He'd gallop to the car, lick his thumb and furiously rub the mark, the beating in his chest growing thicker in his ears as he felt the indentation from Alice's key.

It was sad, really. Pathetic.

As she could play his reaction to the car, she could also play her remaining years with Walker in her mind like a movie. She knew that Walker would never divorce her, no matter what he told Brittani—"when her mother improves." Another thing that would never happen. Eventually, when Brittani grew tired of Walker's games and ended the affair, he would book an expensive Caribbean trip for Alice and him. He would make quick friends with another perfectly chiseled father of two. She would read research papers on the beach in her black bikini. They would settle back into their lives.

Caitlin would find a job. Robbie would go to college. Alice would continue to grow the Center, withdrawing further into the lake's serenity. Walker would retire, making a full-time job of watching sports, badgering his stockbroker, and playing golf. They would retreat to separate corners of the large house they shared as roommates.

Alice saw only two options in front of her: say nothing and let the comfortable, predictable future play out or tell him she knew and dare to ask the questions about what came next. Divorce, but what after? Her view of that path was hazy, foggy, and a sense of panic seized her chest as she thought of the blank space ahead.

She reached the key toward the paint, resting it there, feeling a type of reassuring power through her body at the pain she knew it would cause him. Just as she pressed in, ready to drag the key along the slope she'd mapped out in her mind, the door to the garage flew open and she jumped.

"Mom, what are you doing?"

She straightened. Caitlin stood in the doorway with a bright-green face mask globbed onto her skin, holding Alice's old hiking boots with the leather trim.

"Nothing, just… Nothing."

"Okay… Can I wear these to school tomorrow?"

Where had she even found those? "Sure."

Caitlin disappeared back inside, and Alice followed. It was 9:00 p.m. She should go up and make sure Robbie was asleep.

She shut the door to the garage.

She would use the alone time cleaning out her parents' house to let the choices settle in her mind and percolate. She trusted that by the time the wrecking ball swung, she would know what to do.

CHAPTER THREE

The next morning, Alice passed her mother's hair salon—which she always thought of as the dividing line between their two Atlantas—just as the morning air swallowed its first gulp of humidity. She could feel the day around her growing heavy as the chill whipped by her rolled-down window. In the passenger seat, Buddy curled deeper into himself.

She drove toward the neighborhood streets of her youth, where she had walked to school as a child. She followed the unexpected dips of the Chattahoochee riverbanks, trying not to think about where she was headed. When she finally glimpsed the river between the trees, she barely recognized it anyway. The full river of her childhood was low from years of less rain and brown from years of erosion, something that always surprised her, despite the clear downward slope of her graphs at the Center.

She stopped at the last turn before her parents' house, where the river's water stood almost completely still in front of her windshield. It was the same light where, instead of turning left to their neighborhood, a teenager drove his car straight into the water after a party one night when Alice was in elementary school. She had thought about him at the bottom of that river, ready to grab her foot and pull her down, too, long after Rob told her they already took out the body. Now, she wondered how it felt, jamming his foot on the gas, wondered if it had felt like flying when his car leapt off the last foot of dirt and pavement and dove into the water.

The brick colonial sat at the top of its long driveway at the end of a cul-de-sac, lined with perfect grass and tall magnolias, where she would climb even higher than the house as a child. She parked at the top, next to a sign giving notice of the impending demolition. She reached over to the passenger seat to pet Buddy as she studied the house from the front window of her Prius.

It was wasteful to demolish a five-bedroom house to replace it and the one next door with a ten-bedroom house, complete with a guest house, pool, and private tennis court. But as she stared at the second-floor window in the middle that used to be Rob's bedroom, with its polished glass and its pale-green shutters, Alice understood the demolition. Perhaps the house's loneliness seeped from the structure, casting an unmovable black shadow that could be felt by all who walked by, as it could by her.

Alice got out of the car, turning the unfamiliar key in her hand as she walked toward the wood-and-glass front door with Buddy ambling behind her. As she tried to unlock it, the door stuck from months of little use. She yanked it open and stepped inside with Buddy.

She paused as her eyes adjusted to the house's dark coloring. Almost-black hardwood floors coated the entire main floor, and a grand staircase in the middle split off at the top to the house's two quarters. Instinctively, she walked the circle of the main floor.

She passed her mother's perfume cabinet, with her parents' wedding invitation and her own in matching frames, one of the only differences she saw, as if her parents had frozen time when she left for college. Alice ran her fingers over the collection of crystal bottles that stuffed the cabinet. Her father brought each sparkling bottle home after a fight with her mother. As a child, she had coveted them so much that Rob stole one for her. Alice would dab the sweet-smelling liquid on her neck before bed, like she saw her mother do.

Alice walked through the dining room where her parents' best china was set on the twelve-seater table as if they expected a large dinner party to arrive any moment. In the kitchen, the oak cabinets—where Rob would organize all the items in the pantry in ABC order—were still the same. Applesauce next to beans next to cereal. Each time he found it out of order, he'd have to take everything out and start again. She remembered now that she would sneak in before he got home to put every-thing back the way he liked it. When she moved the items her mother had shifted, Alice's chest had swelled with such purpose at completing this simple task for the person who did everything for her.

Across from the cabinets, a breakfast den held a six-seater table where each morning, after Alice checked on her science experi-ments in the shaky tree house, she studied her purple youth Bible between articles her father read to her from the paper. "Listen to this," he would say to no one in particular, and Alice would snatch the rare offering of parental attention, enthralled by her father's lulling voice as he read the latest story on the price of gas. They sat there until Maura and Rob woke up, when their mother would make grits and eggs and read the children's daily vocabulary word.

But all of this stopped after Rob left.

Alice veered toward the closed door to her father's office with his mahogany desk that faced out the window as she finished the loop, avoiding the French doors that led to a screened porch overlooking the river. At the sight of them, the loneliness after Rob left washed over her.

The memory was so sharp of her hours, days, weeks, years sitting on that porch, watching the leaves change. How she could go days without talking to another person. How she could see the tree house from the porch's perch, longed so much to feel the sun on her face outside, to run in the grass, but instead remained a prisoner in the empty house. "Stay here, Alice," her mother warned each morning as she left the house, perfectly primped.

She walked quickly back to the front of the house and climbed the grand staircase, where she had seen so many debutantes take pictures, her mother instructing them how to pose, pretending Alice didn't exist since she refused to take part.

At the last step, Alice and Buddy stopped as she took off her shoes, ready for her mother's screams to do so before she stepped on the cream carpet. She turned away from her parents' closed bedroom door and walked down the hall, staring straight ahead so as not to make eye contact with the stately ancestors from her father's side in the wall portraits. She walked past the closest door to Rob's room, where Jamie lived after dropping out of college when Alice was young and again after his divorce, the only reprieve Alice got from her mother in the year after Rob left.

As she walked, Alice thumbed through a pack of green sticky

notes that the estate company had told her to stick on anything she wanted moved to her own house. They would clear out the rest before the demolition and sell or donate it. Her parents' entire lifetimes had been reduced to a stack of sticky notes, and green at that. "Tacky," her mother would have said.

She opened the door to her childhood bedroom. The smell hit her first—a hint of lavender from the little baggies of loose lavender in the house's drawers.

The walls were a light shade of pink she had always despised. A white bed stood centered in the room, which Buddy jumped on and quickly fell asleep. A desk and bookshelves crowded the right side, each packed full of books she had never opened.

On the left side, a white crib housed a collection of antique dolls. With their too-wide eyes and porcelain skin, they looked like something from a horror movie. Alice picked up the folded duvet from the bed and threw it on the crib to hide the creepy demon dolls. Every couple of minutes she jerked her head from the house's creaks, half expecting to see a ghost. Although she hadn't seen *him* since college, this was the exact place for him to show up again.

Alice opened the door to the bathroom and walked in front of the mirror, eyeing the door at the other side that would lead to the room she had stared at from the street.

She turned on the sink and splashed her face. As with a childhood bully that won't stop whispering insults under his breath, she could hear every step of her socked feet on the bathroom's tile, every drip of the faucet and patter of the water in the pipes. It echoed so loudly in her brain of the time after Rob left, when the dead quiet tingled in her ears, so different from before when

Rob would practice scales on his guitar until three in the morning, sending the music bouncing off the floors. So different from mornings with Rob as bumps reverberated through the house, along with his yells of "dang" as he hit his toes on the baseboards in contrast to the rest of the family's quiet. She missed that most when he left: those sounds that interrupted the polished quiet and gave it life, that reminded her she was where she needed to be, with him. She was home.

Alice shut off the water and went into Rob's room.

With only her mother's sewing machine on a bare table and spare dressers for supplies, the room looked soulless, but Alice saw it so easily as it had been before, with the record player and the KISS albums propped against the wall. Her brother's twin bed had nestled in the corner farthest from the door with the band posters above it, all but the sheet stripped from his bed and books stacked in their place, as if it were a desk, since he rarely slept there.

The neatness of it all depressed her: the bolts of fabric tightly wound, the measuring tapes hanging straight, a notebook over on the table with girls' measurements on it, the thread organized in a bin next to it in a rainbow. She walked around the room, opening and slamming the cabinets and drawers full of sewing supplies, if only to create some noise. All trash—or perhaps one of her mother's friends would want them. She didn't care.

You did this, she wanted to say to Rob. *You ruined this.*

She returned to her room and collapsed in the desk chair. The first day inside the house would be the hardest. She knew that. The sooner she started, the sooner she could leave and return to the solace of the Center, return to the roles she enjoyed—mother, friend, boss, conservationist—instead of the ones to which she was obligated. Daughter. *Wife*, her brain added, along with the conversation with her mother about Walker's texts. The ones she was supposed to think about at this moment, but instead, she only thought about how her mother used to refer to divorce only by the letter D, as in "Jennie down the street is getting a D."

When I get married, she remembered thinking, *I would never get a D. I'd only be happy to always have someone to talk to, just like when Rob was here.* Unlike with her brother, who would happily listen to her talk for hours about her love for Flemish rabbits—how could a rabbit even *get* that big?—she now knew that in the real world, being listened to always came with a cost.

She opened the first drawer.

Pencils, paper clips, blank scraps of paper, bouncy balls, erasers, and a highlighter littered the drawer. She shut it. One down.

Drawer two was full of miscellaneous paper. She took the stack out and set it on the desk—flipping through notes on Shakespeare, multiplication tables, and doodles of flowers. Easy enough. Then, another paper.

Dear Mr. and Mrs. Tate,

As I'm sure you are also, at North Atlanta Christian Academy we are concerned about Alice's behavior in the recent weeks. We are aware that Robinson's departure has affected her and want to help her as your family experiences this transition. We have scheduled appointments for her with our faith-based counselor weekly, which she will have during her homeroom. We find that in situations such as these, parental involvement is key. I encourage you to call the school so we can set up a time for you to come into the office to discuss.

God Bless,
Mr. Hopefield
School Principal

"Through him you believe in God, who raised him from the dead and glorified him, and so your faith and hope are in God." I Peter 1:21

She knew what her mother would have said, if Alice had shown her the letter—"Put it in a box in your mind." Rob, though, had always hated their mother's favorite directive. Alice remembered when she was in second grade, running the mile home from school, wiping the tears and snot from her face with the sleeve of her school uniform. When she flung the front door open, she finally rested with her hands on her knees and let the tears flow.

"Goodness."

Alice jumped. She hadn't expected her mother to be home.

"Well?" her mother said.

"Nothin'."

"Noth*ing*," her mother corrected. She crouched down in front of Alice. "What happened?"

"Tommy killed Ralphie."

Her mother gasped. "Who?"

"Ralphie, my snake."

"Oh."

Maura led Alice to the kitchen table. She poured a glass of

milk for Alice and more brown liquid into her own crystal glass. Alice looked out the window and tried to stifle her tears. She should have gone down to the river where she could be alone.

"Tommy, the Collins kid?"

Alice nodded. "He calls me—" She stopped so she wouldn't start crying again. "He calls me...lizard face. I never want to see Tommy again."

"Because he likes you, that's all. You're just going to have to put it in a box in your mind and forget it. Tommy could be your husband one day."

Alice crossed her arms. She wouldn't marry that dummy, even if humans were endangered and they were the only ones who could keep the species from dying out. Tommy didn't even know that snakes and lizards were different.

The door burst open again.

"Al?"

"In here!"

"Do they let children waltz out of that school whenever they damn well choose?" Maura reached up to rub her temple as Rob ran in.

"What happened?" he said, breathless.

He always treated a childhood insult as if it were a stab wound, and in some ways, it was. "Someone told me you ran away crying at recess."

Somehow, Rob always seemed to know when Alice had a bad day. She suspected that Rob's friend Edward got daily updates at lunch from his own sister, Hayley, at Rob's request, but on this day, Alice was thankful for the spying.

"You both go back to school, *now!*" Maura clanged the glass down on the kitchen counter.

"Yes, ma'am!" Rob said.

When he grabbed her hand and walked toward the door, Alice started to cry again. But then he winked at her. She relaxed.

"I'm going upstairs, and when I come down," Maura called from the kitchen, "you both *better* be down the street."

Unlike Rob, Alice would have been too scared to lie. But they all (even their mother) knew Maura would let Rob get away with anything. Rather than provoking jealousy, their mother's laxness with Rob was just another gift the siblings shared.

Once he shut the front door, Rob repeated: "What happened?"

She had introduced Rob to Ralphie when she found him two weeks ago and started keeping him in a box by the playground, told him about how they had played together at recess, how she had fed him worms, how he liked to lie in the sun and slither over her shoulder. But that was before Tommy stomped on Ralphie at recess. He had told the teacher he was only protecting Alice from a snake when she protested, but Mrs. Davis only thanked him "on Miss Tate's behalf."

"What did Mama say?"

"She said to put—"

"Put it in a box in your mind?"

"Yeah." Alice glanced behind her, ready for her mother's correction: "*Yes.*"

Rob sighed.

"Come on." He tugged her hand, then took off running.

Alice ran after him. He didn't glance over his shoulder as she would have done, but kept his eyes ahead, sure that she would follow him.

"Where are we going?"

Instead of answering, he sped up, and she brought her arms in and tucked her head to keep up. They ran down another street, past houses she hadn't seen before and out to another cul-de-sac, around a house that needed a paint job, through the side yard with its long grass, and out the back. They ran into the forest until Alice no longer heard the sound of the river.

"*Rob!* Where are we going?"

"We're here." Rob stopped abruptly and she barreled into him, though he didn't move an inch. She bounced back and landed on her butt in the dirt.

"You hear that?"

She stood up and brushed the dirt from the khaki skirt and long socks of her school uniform. Mama would be angry. "What?"

"Listen."

"I don't hear anything."

"Exactly."

"I don't get it."

"AHHHHHHHH!" He screamed louder than she had ever heard anyone scream, and she flinched and whipped around behind her. Nothing was there. She looked back at him where he was still screaming. She covered her ears.

"WHY ARE YOU SCREAMING?" she yelled so he could hear.

He stopped.

"Whenever I'm angry, I come here, and I scream."

"Why?"

He shrugged. "Try it."

"Ahhhh!" she said.

"That sucked."

She brushed the dirt off a tree stump and sat down.

Rob sat on the dirt, not bothering to protect his school pants. "Do you want to know a secret?"

"What?"

"The 'box in your mind' is stupid. This is better than the box. Try it." He stood back up and walked over to her. "What makes you *angry?*"

"Tommy killing Ralphie," she said immediately.

"What else?"

"I don't know."

"Come on, what else?"

"Uhhhh...."

"Close your eyes. Picture the 'box in your mind.' What's in it?"

"Tommy saying I couldn't play baseball because I'm a girl."

"What else?"

"Mama making me wear this *stupid* skirt to school when the other girls get to wear pants."

"YEAH? What about when she makes you wear those lacy socks to church?"

"YEAH! I *hate* those."

"Scream!"

"I HATE THOSE!"

"And what about Tommy?"

"I AM NEVER GOING TO MARRY HIM!"

"AHHH!" he screamed.

"AHHH!" she answered.

Rob changed his scream into a howl. "OW, OW, OW!" She laughed and stopped screaming.

"Okay, again," he said. "One, two, three. Go!"

They screamed together, long and loud until they both stopped and gasped for air.

"Feel better?"

She nodded.

"And one more thing: you can't put what you want in a"—he switched to a zombie-like voice—"box in your mind." She giggled. "You have to fight for what you want and stand up for yourself."

"How?"

"What time is it?"

She looked at her plastic pink watch: "Two." She had wanted the blue one. She should have screamed about that.

"Come on." Rob took off and she ran after him, following him back to the street and toward the school.

"No, Rob! I don't *want* to go back to school!"

He chuckled. "We're not going back to school." Even still, he ran toward the school.

"Okay, wait here," he said when he reached the spot between the high school and elementary school where they usually met to walk home together. He disappeared over the hill that led to the elementary school.

She waited, watching as the last bell rang at the high school and the kids started walking toward the road and back to their houses. Finally, she saw Rob, dragging Tommy by the sleeve of his uniform shirt. He released him when they reached Alice.

"What do you have to say?" he said.

"I'm sorry, Alice." Tommy looked at the ground.

"And?" Rob said.

"You're not a lizard face."

"And, are you going to do it again?" Rob's voice rose. "Are you going to mess with *my* sister again?"

Alice looked at Tommy. His eyes were wide now, fearful. She almost felt bad for him, for Rob's rage was as laser-focused as his praise. She reached her hand up to curl it around Rob's arm, a silent warning, for that was their pattern. He brought the passion, the storm, the fun; she brought the calming morning fog, the tame to his anxiety. She felt his muscles release their hold on Tommy. Tommy shook his head no.

"Good." Rob shoved him lightly on the shoulder.

Alice had drifted off to sleep that night thinking about boxes cracked open and anger spilling out, brainstorming what she would scream about tomorrow in the clearing. Ironic, then, that it was Rob himself who made her realize the wisdom in their mother's advice.

CHAPTER FOUR

Alice looked around the remaining items in the bedroom where she had dreamed of screaming that night so long ago now. The possessions made the room feel full, maybe even homey, to someone else. The dolls, the desk, the books, the flowered chamber pot in the corner, Alice had lived beside them through her childhood, but they were all her mother's. Nothing felt like it belonged to *her*, not then or now.

She stopped at the unfamiliar pictures on the bedside table. In one, a woman with short flapper hair stood seductively in a light-blue dress, some distant relation she couldn't remember. In another, a man looked seriously into the camera, a cigar at his lips—her father's father? Alice flipped over the frame and slid out the back. Two pictures fell out. One of the man and the cigar and one of her and Meredith, from their days rooming together in college. They were on a summer trip in Savannah, lying on the beach's brown sand in their bikinis, laughing.

She reached for the other frame and slid out the back, her mother's handiwork, no doubt. Another picture from college. Looking into the camera, Alice stood on a patch of grass, her clothes covered in dirt, holding a hoe, her face shadowed by a University of Georgia baseball hat that said Class of 1993. A man, tan with jet-black hair, looked at her, smiling, his hands in work gloves.

Jake.

Her stomach dropped. She slipped both photos into the small pocket of her backpack anyway.

Two rooms down.

She stood up to head to the next room, walking past the door to her closet. She remembered sneaking through the crawl space to the closet where Rob often slept, where he would never turn her away, would always listen to her dreams, how he'd distract her from her nightmares with long stories.

"Once upon a time, there was a young girl named Alice who lived with her brother in a tree house, high above the forest floor," he always began. The story was about how the siblings had to save the animals and their forest, but he was always meandering off the main story to talk about the family of chipmunks below who missed their daughter since she left for chipmunk college or the hawks in the sky who argued constantly about where they planned to fly in the winter.

"Where were we?" he'd say, ready to return to the siblings. But with him, it hardly mattered. They were together. By the time she sat next to him, she was already safe, already happy, and already her eyelids had become heavy again. And carefully, he'd pick his book back up until she heard only the sounds of the pages turning.

She decided to allow herself one indulgence before going to the next room. She went into her empty closet where she pulled the little door open to the crawl space in between her and Rob's closets. As she stuck her head inside, feeling the cool air from the attic above, her breath caught in her chest, and her heart jumped.

Against the side wall, lying on top of two boxes, she could just make out the outline of an acoustic guitar.

She carefully fit her shoulders through the small door and army-crawled toward the guitar with her feet dangling out the door. She lay on her back so she could pick up the guitar, angling it toward the light. She ran her fingers over the smooth wood. The strings stuck out randomly with all but one off the bridge. She blew the dust from the inscription at the base and squinted to see the initials in the light's beam—RWT. Robinson Wesley Tate.

Rob had left with this guitar; she remembered it so clearly. *How did it make its way back here?*

She moved so she could study the boxes without the darkness of her shadow. Taped to the front of one was a piece of her mother's stationery: *From the desk of Mrs. Maura Tate.* Across the sheet, her mother had written in large letters: *FOR ALICE, DO NOT DISCARD!*

Alice pulled her legs into the crawl space until she was propped on her knees, so she could see the top of the boxes. They were sealed with a packing label from New Orleans still unbroken across the top, addressed to the house, but with no name. New Orleans, where Rob died, and the date was in fall 2007, just a few weeks after the funeral.

She swallowed the fear down, the same fear that had stopped her from asking more questions after Rob's death. Her mother wanted her to find the guitar, these boxes, even if her mother had never wanted to know what was inside. Perhaps she was too afraid that it was her fault that she didn't do more, follow him, look more, a fear Alice knew well.

The boxes were a choice, presented to Alice alone.

She reached her nails to the end of the packing tape and picked off the tape, inch by inch, and opened the box's faded top.

Clothes. Jeans, sweaters, an assortment of T-shirts, socks, and underwear. She stacked the fabric item by item on one side of the box, then did the other side, to make sure she went through everything. She didn't recognize any of it. *Why would someone send clothes here?* She noticed she was holding her breath and let it out through her mouth slowly.

"Please don't be more clothes," she said to herself as she opened the second box. She yanked at the flaps, snapping them off from the tape and ripping the cardboard in half. A spiral-bound notebook, a folder of pictures from Walgreens, and a shoebox.

She opened the folder and slid the pictures into her hand. With the first, her eyes immediately centered on the two faces, a man and a woman, before she realized they were naked. Her head jerked back, and she heard herself say "ugh!" before she knew who had said it. She looked at the scene again—someone's poorly lit bedroom. The girl, who she didn't recognize, was on her back, sideways on the bed, her dark-black legs dangling over the side. The man was standing, looking at her, hard and naked and trim, his face barely angled toward the camera. Alice looked at the next one, where the man looked straight at the camera, this time from on the bed behind the woman, who was skinny and pretty with a long neck and cropped short hair. Alice looked at the face. It was him. She flipped through the other pictures, which were the same. She closed her eyes tightly, hoping to get this image of her brother out of her head.

Putting one hand over the lower half of the photograph to cover the naked parts, she studied her brother's adult face. The blue eyes and sandy hair were the same, but his face was longer, with a strong jawline, balanced by the same dimples from his childhood.

She opened the spiral-bound notebook, thinking perhaps it was a diary. The first page, written in cursive, said, "It's better to burn out than fade away." Again, "It's better to burn out than fade away." And again. She flipped to the next page. Again and again, the same sentence, each one meticulously written, identical to the next. She turned pages and more pages—still the same. She flipped to the back page. It ended on "than," the exact wrong amount of space required to finish the project.

She moved on to the shoebox. She lifted the lid to find a fountain pen in a case, a bottle of ink, and a stack of envelopes. She removed one. It was addressed, without a return address, in neat script by a practiced hand. She flipped through the sealed envelopes, questions in her head threatening to bubble over. She didn't recognize the first two names.

Then, a name she knew, her father.

She flipped frantically past envelopes addressed to her mother and Jamie, then another name she didn't recognize, until she was on the last one. It wasn't for her.

She laid them out in front of her.

Mr. Dylan Barnett
Ms. Lila King
Mr. Richard Tate
Mrs. Maura Tate
Mr. James Hudson
Mr. Christopher Smith
Mr. Tyler Wells

Seven envelopes with seven names, and he didn't have one for her. She didn't know what the envelopes were, only that she wanted one. The same childhood feelings of rejection after Rob left entered her chest, constricting it and quickening her breath. Her brother didn't leave her one.

Seven names and addresses, so close, in Georgia, except for Lila, and still, so many questions to which she didn't know the answers.

Alice found the envelope addressed to her father and examined the decade-old seal, which would no doubt pop off cleanly, glad its job was finally done.

She opened it carefully, unfolding the fancy paper inside with the same large, cursive script.

Dick:

"For there is nothing hid, which shall not be manifested; neither was any thing kept secret, but it should come abroad." —Mark 4:22

You could have prevented everything. I hope you carry this knowledge to your grave, and look your wife and daughter in their eyes knowing it's true.

Respectfully,
Rob

Daddy could have prevented what? Alice thought. Her mind went immediately to the image of her mother, lying in bed, ignoring the constant screech of the phone, after Rob left. Instead of attending her various activities, Maura read through the family's library, looking for Rob's loopy scrawl in the margins and his signature pencil tick marks from his habit of sliding a pencil down each page as he read. She separated those books into a pile that grew next to her bed until it was taller than Alice.

She puzzled over the verse. It was just like Rob to choose something from King James to make his obscure point. A tickle of her old rage at Rob ran up through her tense shoulders. Poetics and symbolism had always been more important to him than clarity.

As she sat there, rereading the open letter and ignoring the burning in her knees from her crouch in the closet, the unmistakable sound of rattling glass in wood rang out from downstairs. The front door.

She threw the letters back in the box, scrambled out of the closet, shooed Buddy out, and shut the door, hurrying back to the hallway, as if she were afraid of being caught trying to sneak into Rob's room as she had as a child.

Booted footsteps slammed into the hardwood in the house's foyer. "Alice? Aaallliiice," the voice called.

Jamie.

She had wondered how long he could stay away.

ROB'S LOST LETTERS:

Mr. Dylan Barnett
Ms. Lila King
~~Mr. Richard Tate~~
Mrs. Maura Tate
Mr. James Hudson
Mr. Christopher Smith
Mr. Tyler Wells

CHAPTER FIVE

As she appeared on the landing, he sang "There she is, Miss America," like always.

He continued the song as she walked down the stairs. She breathed deeply, trying to slow her heart rate, but her thoughts were completely consumed with the letters. Maybe the others would say more, maybe even why he left, where he had been. She adopted the calm facade she always used when speaking to parents about to leave their children for a week at the Center's summer camp, being careful not to betray the chaos she knew would come. She didn't want Jamie to know about the letters, not yet. Not until she knew what they said and what to do with them.

The song ended.

"I came to see if you needed any help."

He had offered to help three times before. And each time, Alice had said she wanted to be alone. Although she loved Jamie like a father (he had been around more than her own, after all), she had needed the space to think about Walker without Jamie's continuous monologue. Now though, she wanted only to grab the box from the closet and go, to reread her father's letter in the privacy of the Center's cabin and let someone else deal with her mother's various collections of china. And with Jamie helping, she could finish in half the time.

"Actually, I could use your help."

"Really?" He beamed back at her.

She nodded. "Everything seems pretty clean and organized here. I bet we can finish by the end of the day if we work together." She hoped.

Buddy carefully wobbled down the stairs, having given up on Alice returning upstairs. Or maybe his old ears had finally picked up Jamie's voice.

Jamie leaned down to pet him. "I should've brought my dogs! I didn't know Buddy would be here."

Alice smiled, but said nothing. All she needed was six prima-donna competitive border collies underfoot—who already got 80 percent of Jamie's attention (and the same of the trust fund her father left him).

"Well, why don't I start in Richard's office? See if there's anything related to the business we might need."

"Sounds great."

She watched him as he started down the hall with his hunched back and not quite steady footsteps before she walked to the dining room. The verse from the letter filled her mind as she looked at the china cabinet, table, and oversize buffet, wondering where to start: *"For there is nothing hid, which shall not be manifested."*

She opened the bottom drawer in her mother's china cabinet, expecting to find another set of perfectly stacked china with thin paper between each plate. Instead, it held a moldy roll, a set of three-pound weights, and her mother's diploma from Agnes Scott in a gold frame and was lined with what looked like every Christmas card her parents had ever received. *What the heck?*

She opened the drawer above it where her mother kept her

silver serving platters, stamped on the back with her social security number. She remembered her mother displaying the numbers proudly, as all the wives in the neighborhood had done, to ensure the silver would be returned if stolen. Instead, a few broken mismatched plates littered the drawer over one of the platters, next to a bottle of cough syrup, which had leaked onto the drawer's wallpaper lining. Dried red goo caked one side of a folder labeled *Financial.* Alice opened it, thumbing quickly through tax documents, a pamphlet from an auction in Atlanta where her mother had purchased an antique armoire, and random bills of money floating between the pages. Alice's heart began to race at her mother's hidden rebellion.

"Alice? You better come in here," Jamie said.

She ran into the office. "Oh no," she said as she entered the doorway.

Her father's desk still sat in front of the window, but meticulously labeled boxes covered every inch of the floor space, as though a hoarder with perfect cursive had secretly taken refuge in the otherwise magazine-decorated house. Pegboard covered one of the walls, the little holes used to organize a random assortment of pots and pans, rifles and canes. A vintage unicycle hung from the ceiling. Another wall held framed paintings and pictures that reached from the floor to the ceiling, like a puzzle with each space occupied, some by framed postcards.

Furniture protected by taped blankets crowded the room at different angles, and several mattresses stuck out against the organized chaos. A twenty-foot wooden table took up one corner, and a vintage train set sat on top, as if a child walked away for a glass of milk and planned to return. *How could her mother have even gotten all this in here?*

She jogged back through the kitchen, throwing open the closed door that led to what decades ago had been the maid's quarters. It looked the same as the office. The only difference was a twin bed stuck in the corner, the bedside table littered with tissues and a pair of her mother's reading glasses.

Alice opened a kitchen cabinet, then another, with Jamie and Buddy trailing behind her helplessly. Manila folders labeled with her mother's tight cursive stuck out of most every drawer and shelf, amid bowls, directions on how to work the coffee maker, sports equipment, and photo albums. Her mother had replaced the perfectly alphabetized spice rack with a collection of random cords and dozens of reusable shopping bags, neatly folded and wrapped with rubber bands.

She opened the fridge. It was stuffed with boxes of garbage bags and mismatched Pyrex and held a large crystal globe in the space where her mother used to keep several bottles of white wine. The globe read *New York 1939 World's Fair*. Jamie caught the door as Alice closed it and took out the garbage bags.

The important documents previously in her father's left desk drawer were scattered among different folders in various locations. A folder labeled *Certificates* Alice found under a couch cushion held her grandparents' death certificates, along with a Best Mother certificate Rob had made at school and her parents' birth certificates. She found a folder between a stack of mismatched plates labeled *Children* with a picture of Alice as Glinda the Good Witch and Rob as a sheriff on Halloween. Several pages of veterinary records followed the picture, as if the family pets deserved the same footing as the family children.

Alice realized she was wading through the wonderland of

her mother's decaying brain, all full of strange connections she couldn't understand. Every drawer she opened was stuffed with expired canned food, scraps of paper with bits of information— "memory aids," her mother's nurse would call them—and expensive-looking antique knickknacks.

When she had opened every cabinet and drawer on the main floor, she sat down on the only remaining cushion on the living room couch. Her whole body buzzed with overwhelming thoughts about how she would get the house ready for the estate sale company and then ready for the demolition, but above that came the guilt.

She should have noticed her mother was getting sick. She should have known before that call from the police officer when her mother ran her BMW off the road and wouldn't go with him because she thought he was a murderer. It seemed like her mother's decline had happened so fast and so sporadically at first, like one of Alice's graphs at the Center, all highs and lows, each more extreme than the last. Even after the crash—"fender bender," as her mother called it—she had snapped back to normal, yelling at Alice to drive her home "this instant" or she would be late for a luncheon.

She should have known before that next call. A police officer picked her mother up watering rocks with sugar water in the middle of the night in nothing but her nightie and took her directly to the hospital. But who did her mother call? Not her only daughter, but her housekeeper, who packed up some clothes, her most expensive jewelry in tissue paper, and her extensive collection of bathroom products and dropped them at the hospital.

The bags would make their way briefly to Alice and Walker's

house, then to the assisted living facility. The packing had seemed like a kindness at the time, but now, Alice realized her mother hadn't been trying to save Alice from the house's painful memories, but to hide the destruction she had wrought on the house as long as possible.

Jamie picked up a small stack of black-and-white pictures from the seat next to her, where Alice had thrown off the cushion after noticing a folder sticking out. He put the cushion back and sat beside her, still holding the photos.

When he didn't fill the silence, she glanced over at him and followed his eyes to the photos. The Tates were recognizable, posing in front of the large oak in her grandparents' front yard— they stood on the left, each with a hand on one of Richard's shoulders. He looked handsome in his army uniform. On the other side of the tree stood another family. A man stood behind his wife. A young woman in a fitted floral dress stood next to her mother, holding the hand of a little girl who looked about ten, in a black dress that must have been a school uniform. Jamie stood in front of the wife, smiling and looking straight at the camera, his little hands gripping backpack straps. He couldn't have been older than six.

"Is that them?" Alice said. "Your parents?"

Jamie only nodded.

Alice tried to think of something else to say or ask about them. The only thing she knew was that his sisters and parents had died in a car accident, that they were her grandparents' best friends and next-door neighbors, and that Jamie had ended up in their care. Before she could ask anything else, though, he slipped the photo into his chest pocket.

On the next one, he said: "This is your aunt Bennie, you know. Your father's mother's sister. She could never stand your mother. I thought when Richard said he was going to marry her that she'd never get over it."

Alice leaned over to look at the photo. "Is that the one who called Mama 'country'?"

He chuckled. "Forgot about that."

She plucked the photo from his grip and ripped it down the middle. She tossed the two pieces on the floor and smiled at him. "Good riddance."

He laughed.

"The house will be okay. We'll work on it together. It's mostly trash. It won't take as long as you think." Jamie put his arm around her shoulder, and she leaned in toward him.

As if reading her mind, he added: "If she hadn't wanted us to know she was having trouble, there would've been no way to know. She was always good at keeping up appearances."

"She got a dumpster," Alice said. "I remember her telling me that. She got a dumpster and she was cleaning out the house, getting rid of stuff after Daddy died. Downsizing."

"I remember that too."

He tapped her knee twice, and she stood up. He handed Alice a garbage bag, and she accepted it without comment. After picking up the ripped photo and dropping it in the bag, she went straight for the kitchen. The letter with her brother's writing was far from her mind.

CHAPTER SIX

Jamie was right.

Alice quickly adjusted to the new reality of the house and, in two hours, had become as efficient as an ant colony building a new home, ruthlessly sorting through her mother's clutter, singularly focused on each task. She stuck the scrapbooks and most of the folders in a box to take home and sort through later. She left anything that looked valuable for the estate sale company. Everything else, she threw away. She had already stuffed twenty black trash bags and stuck a green sticky note on the perfume cabinet in her mother's parlor. All without a peep from Jamie, as if the state of his friend's office had shocked him into silence.

When her hunger started to make a can of corn older than Caitlin seem potentially edible, she went back to her father's office to find Jamie. Inside, he had written "trash" or "sell" with Sharpie on many of the boxes and had his own little stack of folders on the desk.

"I broke a glass in here." He pushed her lightly out into the living room. She let him guide her, glad for the lessened effort for her to make it back to the living room couch where they had sat earlier.

"Lunch?" Her hand found its way to her growling stomach.

"Why don't you go pick up something and bring it back? I might be able to finish in there while you're gone."

She sighed in relief. She couldn't wait to sit in her car's silence and its (mostly) clean and uncluttered space. "If you're sure."

"How about the Varsity?"

The classic burger joint in downtown Atlanta was a little farther than she'd planned on going, but he could probably sense her desire for a break. She didn't protest. "The usual?"

He nodded.

"All right, I'll be back in, like, forty-five minutes." She stopped to pet Buddy on her way out, telling him to stay.

She climbed into her car quickly and drove a bit too fast out of the driveway and down the street, only stopping when she reached the stop sign, out of view from the house. There, she stared at the river ahead.

The house was an explosion, all the things her mother refused to talk about resurfacing in overflowing abundance. Even Rob's boxes in the closet upstairs. How long had they been up there? Since Rob died? Given the state of the rest of the house compared to the state of the sewing room, it seemed like her mother hadn't been on the second floor in years.

The words from Rob's letter rang in her mind, fighting with the image of her father in his army uniform, smiling and handsome. Which should she believe?

Writing off someone like that was just like Rob. He had always seen people as all good or all bad, whether they deserved the criticism or the praise. Maura was good, strong, sweet, and he was constantly loyal and defensive of her. Richard, on the other hand, was misguided, selfish, stupid. Jamie was the only one Alice knew who had switched from one of Rob's categories to the other.

When a car honked behind her, Alice turned left toward the

highway and the river disappeared out her rearview window. She rolled down one of the windows, with only the sound of the whirling air for company, and tried to let her mind sink into silence, if only for ten minutes. She looked over her shoulder to merge lanes onto the highway toward downtown. Her eyes stuck on the empty back seat, without her backpack, without her wallet.

She sighed and merged the other way, toward the off-ramp.

Five minutes later, as she passed the stop sign where she had sat minutes earlier, she screamed, relishing the violent vibrations in her throat, just as Rob would have.

When the house came into view, Jamie was in the driveway, putting a box into his car's open back seat. Intending to grab her wallet and head back toward lunch, she pulled up next to him and left her car running.

"Forgot my wallet. What's that?" she asked casually, pointing to the box.

His face was exactly like Caitlin's when Alice had caught her trying to sneak out a few months ago with the fire ladder through her bedroom window. He shut the door to his car, sending a waft of wet dog smell into the air.

"Some old Tate Trucking records. Think they would be good to have on hand, just in case. Lunch is on me." He pulled his old leather wallet from his back pocket, the same one her father had, engraved with Jamie's initials in the same font as her father's, and handed her two twenties.

Was Jamie being extra nice to her? It wasn't like him to pay.

He was terrible with money, and despite the aura of wealth from his house, his hobbies, his car, his dogs, he always seemed to be short of it.

"I don't want to drive without my license." Alice started toward the steps.

"I'll get it for you," he said. "Where is it?"

She ignored him and continued to the door. Her hand lingered on the doorknob as the house's familiar dread washed back to her. She twisted the knob, and the door bumped into another box.

"Alice...? Alice, wait."

She reached into the box and pulled out an oversize manila envelope that rested inside. On the black flap was a smudged word. She could make out her mother's handwriting, forming the word she would recognize second only to her own name: *Robinson*. A second, smaller envelope, unlabeled, hid behind in the otherwise empty box.

"Were you going to take this?" Her tone was clipped, like when she needed children to pay attention to safety instructions at the Center's aquatic camp.

"Look, there are things in this house I thought your mother threw away a long time ago that are private to your parents, things they wouldn't want you to see, that you shouldn't see."

As he continued, her mind raced ahead to invent causes for what was inside. Jamie and her father shared so much: the past of the trucking business, stock in the company to which they sold their shares, a trust from Richard's parents, who had officially adopted Jamie when he was twenty ("for tax purposes," Jamie always said, sadly). The papers could have been anything.

He finished a sentence: "I didn't want you to get hurt, that's all," and she jumped in.

"What were—"

He spoke louder, over her question: "I know you hate being here." She stopped talking. "All you've wanted ever since Rob left was to leave this house and never come back. You can do that. I'll finish. I don't mind."

"That's not true," Alice lied. "That's not what I… If there's something about… If there's something about Rob…" Rob's handwriting on the letters bounced into her mind, and her chest clenched with fear. Could Jamie have found the letters? Taken them?

"If you give me a couple of hours, I can get rid of this stuff. Then, you can go through all the scrapbooks, remember your parents in the way they would want to be remembered. I really think that would be best."

"This is my family. These are my parents, my brother. Not yours."

He stumbled back, and she knew she had wounded him. *Your family, your parents are dead*, she thought. He should have understood what it was like, to be left with nothing.

"Well, I think you know that I love you like my own daughter. And I know it's better for you, for your health, if you let sleeping dogs lie, if you let me take these. Or we can throw them out."

"My health?" she said, her voice rising. "Ever since Rob left, you and my parents were always protecting me. I'm a grown woman! I don't need it. Maybe I never needed it!"

"I think we both know that isn't true."

She prepared herself for what she knew came next—a reference to her running away after Rob left. She knew, of course, that her "trips," as she thought of them at the time, were why her parents and Jamie never brought up Rob around her, why her mother had limited her freedom so much, why the house felt so suffocating to her now, yet another pile of blame that her mother had heaped on her father that meant they never talked, never touched.

"We all thought you were dead," he continued.

"I know."

"You want to know why I'm protective? Imagine if you thought Robbie or Caitlin had been kidnapped or murdered."

She blushed. "That was a long time ago."

"Well, not to me."

She needed to end this conversation. The longer it went on, the more anxiety she felt about the letters. If Jamie had found them, if he knew about them, they'd be gone forever. If he felt this strongly about whatever was in the envelopes, he would have destroyed them. Her heart jumped as she smelled a hint of burning wood. Had Jamie burned something? Had he burned the letters?

"Walker's on the way here," Alice said. "He was going to help me go through the legal papers." Walker was not on the way over to the house, but she knew Jamie wouldn't stick around with Walker on the way. They had never warmed to each other.

As she finished the sentence, she stopped. She had evoked his name so easily when she needed it, even now, even after the texts. The ease of it made her tense. She saw Jamie looking at her and steeled her expression again. "I want you to leave. We'll talk about this later."

"I really do think you'll come to regret this."

"Leave the other box too!"

Alice watched as he turned and stormed off down the front steps and to the driveway. He set the box from his car on the hood of hers. As soon as she saw his car disappear out of the driveway, she raced up the steps to Rob's room, threw open the closet door, and dove into the crawl space between their bedrooms. The guitar and the letters were still there where she left them earlier. Her hand went to her chest in relief.

She crawled to open the door to Rob's closet and set the guitar down carefully on the carpet. RWT, the guitar reminded her.

She should go downstairs right now and read every single piece of paper in those boxes, she knew. Maybe even tear open the letters, recipients be damned. But Jamie's voice echoed uninvited in her mind: *You'll come to regret this.*

As she piled the letters, photos, and notebook on the floor next to the guitar, Jamie's words ticked back and forth in her head like her car's windshield wipers on a rainy day. The pressure built behind her eyes, images flashing so quickly she could barely grasp them: herself paddling alone in the canoe looking for Rob, them screaming in the clearing, the crushing longing she'd felt when she had been called to the principal's office one day.

She remembered now, she ran all the way there, knowing Rob would be in the office waiting, the prodigal son returned. She circled the entire room, saying "Where is he?" out of breath. But it was only the school counselor who, after seeing the display, changed her school schedule to allow for weekly "faith-based sessions" and handed her the note she'd found earlier in her desk, addressed to her mother.

She climbed out of the crawl space and into the closet.

Of course, she knew now that despite her childhood certainty, he was never there. He was not waiting on her. He might not have even been thinking about her, missing her at all. The missing "Alice Wright" letter was only further proof.

She jumped at her phone ringing in her pocket. Walker.

"Alice, where the hell are you? The school called me—did you forget to pick up Robbie? Are you okay?"

"Sorry, sorry. I…I lost track of time." She checked her watch. *Damn.* "I think I have bad service. I'm still at my parents' house. I'll leave now and get him."

As she gathered all of Rob's items in her arms, she spied two rolled-up posters in the corner, paper-clipped neatly and taped from where her mother had ripped them off the wall, as if she wanted to apologize to the Beatles and Kiss. Alice took everything to her car, along with the bracketed envelope with *Robinson* on it and the unlabeled one, moving faster than was perhaps necessary and hitting her thigh for Buddy to follow. After locking the front door behind her, confident Jamie wouldn't have another key, Alice put the last box in her trunk and drove away from the house.

She eyed the larger envelope again with its black letters— *ROBINSON*—and thought again of that girl who ran to the principal's office asking, "Where is he?" But what fresh pain would those answers unleash?

CHAPTER SEVEN

After a (belated) school pickup and basketball practice, Alice, Robbie, and Buddy pulled into the driveway at home. Walker sat in one of the rocking chairs on the front porch with a beer. By the time she parked, sent Robbie upstairs to shower, and placed Jamie's box and her backpack with the letters and the two envelopes in the hall closet, away from the family, Walker was waiting for her at the kitchen counter.

She let the silence stretch between them as she opened the fridge, took out a bag of chicken strips, and sliced red and green peppers, dumped them in a pan with a packet of fajita seasoning, and set the stove to simmer.

"I can't deal with stuff like today when I'm at the office. Not right now," he said.

She ignored him. "Selective listening," her mother had called it, Alice's ability to completely tune out what she didn't want to hear.

I should call Grace and make sure she watered everything, Alice thought.

She opened the kitchen cabinet and stood on her tiptoes to pull out a stemmed wineglass. Walker came up behind her and lifted it from the highest shelf with ease. He removed the rubber stopper from the bottle on the counter and poured a healthy glass, then slid it across the granite toward Alice.

She nodded at him instead of saying thank you, and he let another few seconds pass in blissful silence.

"A little early for dinner, isn't it?"

She eyed the clock. It was 5:45 p.m. "I didn't eat lunch."

"I thought you were going to let the estate company handle most of the house. Isn't that why we hired them? Now you forget Robbie and are too busy to eat lunch? You do remember the dinner party at Mark's tomorrow, right?"

She stopped. She hadn't. *Was she supposed to bring dessert?* "Of course, I remember. And the house is more complicated than I thought it would be."

Taking breaks to stir the food or sip her wine, she told Walker about her day out of habit, starting with the disarray of the house. She paused, considering how far in the story to go, how much to tell. As she mentally ticked through the pros and cons of openness, she reached up to run her necklace's pendant along its chain, the one with Caitlin and Robbie's birthstones that Walker brought to her in the hospital while her C-section scars healed.

It was all such a joke, she thought. The necklace, the way he kissed her with the baby in her arms like he would never be as happy as in that moment. As if that happy moment would last them through the next decades of their marriage, would forgive everything from the funeral and all the secrets of their pasts.

The last few months, the weight of keeping the affair a secret, a barely hidden one at that, didn't faze Walker, not like it would have Alice. Even as a child, Rob would have to coach her the entire way home when they planned to tell their parents a "story." She could always feel her palms sweating, even as Rob tried to reassure her with their secret look, right before they entered the door. He would blink at her rapidly, like cats did to say they loved you (something he learned in the C encyclopedia). Whenever she saw cats do it, she couldn't help but think of him.

"I can't believe he did that," she said, finishing the story with Jamie trying to take the "Tate Trucking" box, but leaving out the letters and the "Robinson" envelope. She turned back to stir the fajita filling.

"If your parents didn't want you there, let Jamie finish up. It'll be less work for you anyway."

"I'm their daughter!"

"Don't get all riled up. All I'm saying is"—he tilted up the beer bottle to finish the last sips—"if I died, I wouldn't want people going through my stuff either." He set down the bottle on the island like a form of punctuation.

"Really." She pictured his new large office at the firm on the coveted partners' hallway—a large mahogany desk, like in her father's office, with a third drawer that locked and a separate locking file cabinet. She actually had no idea what his new office looked like. But she knew it involved wood and drawers with locks, now that she thought about it. Of course, Brittani would be only a few hallways away, close enough for them to exchange smiles in between meetings.

"It's probably nothing, just some embarrassing stuff he doesn't think your father wanted you to know."

"What, like an affair?" She locked eyes with Walker.

He shrugged, betraying nothing. "Yeah, maybe."

I know, she thought. She turned over the possibility of telling him what she knew, feeling the power of it at his clever shrug, the sharpened blade of it that she could stab into his chest at the exact moment it would hurt the most. Every day she waited to tell, it got sharper, stronger.

"What's 'affair'?" Robbie said, walking in to stand beside Alice. She ran her fingers through his damp hair without taking her eyes off Walker until he broke the gaze to look down at Robbie.

"It's when someone that's married spends a lot of time with someone who isn't their husband or wife," Walker said.

"Like Mom and Aunt Meredith?"

Walker smirked at Alice.

"Go watch *Planet Earth*, honey," Alice said to Robbie. "Dinner will be ready soon."

She walked toward the closet by the garage and pulled out her backpack, with Walker following her.

"Where are you going? Alice?" he whisper-screamed.

"An affair's not 'nothing,' and neither is what I found in the house." She walked to the car with him following her and pulled out the guitar. She handed it to him.

"It's Rob's."

"Who's…?" Walker started, but then recognition crossed his face and his eyebrows knit with the old hurt and confusion that boiled up from the funeral. Alice was back at the podium giving Rob's eulogy. Looking back now, when her misty eyes had met Walker's look of betrayal, it was the first time they both acknowledged the true facts of their relationship—that they didn't really know each other, never had and didn't care to now.

As he did in the negotiations with other lawyers, Walker wiped the emotions from his face, leaving only a hollow, empty look that seemed more serious than his previous look of betrayal. Walker handed the guitar back to her without comment.

He turned, and they both saw Robbie and Buddy peeking from behind the door to the garage.

"Why don't we play a game of chess before dinner?"

"Really?" Robbie asked, his face all smile.

Walker nodded.

Alice stood with Walker and watched Robbie sprint down the hall and around the corner to get the chess set, showing more dexterity than in the last month of forced sports games and practices. Walker walked into the house and shut the door, leaving her in the garage holding the guitar. She leaned against her car.

She shouldn't have gotten Walker involved, even in the Jamie argument. Always the lawyer, he argued the opposition, and his default position seemed to be if you didn't engage, you couldn't be blamed. And with him, the Rob issue was still sensitive, would always be something that stood between them.

Although Jamie's concern for her "health" had sparked a familiar rage deep in her stomach, he had been right, in a way. Looking for Rob had only led her to pain and anger, never to him. Even when she tried to ignore him, not to talk about him, not to think about him, cutting off that part of herself cast a shadow over all the others. She had never been able to do what Maura did: two months after Rob left, like a switch, Maura returned to normal and never mentioned him again. The first part, the normal part, was something Alice could never get right.

Four months after he left, Alice said, as she had many times, that she missed Rob. As always when Alice mentioned Rob, her mother didn't respond. Alice repeated the sentence louder, and her mother walked out of the kitchen and snapped at her to "stop dilly-dallying and get ready for dinner." But Alice hadn't stopped;

she had pushed her. She ran after Maura and yelled, "Rob's coming back. For me! I know he is," and her mother, instead of ignoring Alice's constant reminders of Rob, like usual, turned on her heels and thundered as loud as she could, "THEN WHERE IS HE?"

Alice had stopped, shocked by the outburst. After her mother sent Alice to her room without dinner, she lay in bed and turned the question over in her head. It was a good one—then *where* was he?

As a child, she never wondered *why* he left. That much was obvious. She would leave, too, if she could. That came later, in adulthood, once she understood the enormity of what he had done by leaving on his own.

As a child, she had wondered, *Why didn't he take me with him? When is he coming back for me? Where could he have gone?* She decided maybe he was waiting for her to come find him. Maybe he was waiting for her to get the message, then they would leave together.

The first night Alice snuck out of her room, she went to the forest behind the abandoned house, where Rob had taken her years before to scream. He wasn't there. The next night, she went to the school, shining her flashlight around the grass where a tent could hide. The third night, she went to the riverbank where Rob taught her how to fish, where she had smiled so big as he clapped at the first fish she reeled in. Nothing.

When she had returned home from that unsuccessful attempt, she had opened the front door carefully, slipped off her shoes and tiptoed up the stairs using only the front of her toes, like her mother always told her to do when she wore heels (as if she ever would). There wasn't a moon and the house was pitch-black. She shuffled in the hallway with her fingers running along the wall, back to her room. She kicked something.

What could it be? Her mother had sent the dog and cats out-side weeks ago, after they annoyed her while she was lying in bed all day after Rob left. Even though the animals always liked the kids best, they had jumped up in bed every day to keep Maura company. Her head full of visions of intruders, Alice put her hand over the flashlight, as Rob had taught her, to damper the light and clicked it on. She froze.

Her father sat on the floor with his back to Rob's door, holding a bottle of something brown. His unfocused eyes looked at her as if he thought she might be a mirage. They stared at each other for a few seconds. His face was streaked with tears.

Ever so slowly, she stepped over his legs as he watched her silently. Looking back one more time, she opened her door, slipped inside, and shut it behind her.

Her heart beat through her chest as she climbed into bed. She stared at the ceiling and listened carefully for any stirs of her father moving.

Something she had heard at school gave her the next idea, one of Rob's old friends laughing about going out to one of the river's islands to smoke. She knew which island the kid meant. She and Rob had canoed there many times. Maybe Rob was camping there. It would be her biggest trip yet, but somehow, she knew he was there. She felt it.

She knew her father wouldn't tell about catching her, but even so, she took more precautions. She packed a few sandwiches and waited until later in the night before she finally set off on her journey. She made her way to a different shore of the river, where people docked their canoes in the water with rope. It was the first time she had been on the water since Rob left. As she pushed out into the frigid November water, she felt happy for the first time since he'd abandoned her, imagining their reunion again and again. "You figured it out!" he would say, beaming with pride, and she'd smile, knowing that she passed his test, the only kind of test that ever mattered to her.

Navigating the river from a distant shore, in the dark, wasn't as easy as she'd thought. Though she didn't feel afraid, she eventually gave up, sitting straight in the canoe, waiting to hit land and for Rob to find her. She drifted like that for what seemed like hours, time nothing in the darkness, until she finally heard the rustling of leaves and branches in the water. Thinking she must be close to shore, she grabbed the paddle. As she registered that the paddle to her right was stuck on a large tree and that she should shine the flashlight to see what lay ahead, something slammed into her forehead and she fell, peacefully unconscious, back into the canoe.

She woke up what seemed like seconds later, in a hospital bed with her mother staring at her face with weary eyes as her father had done in the hallway.

"Thank God!" her mother screamed, and she threw herself at Alice as she blinked. Before she could process anything else, Alice's first thought was that her life had changed beneath her yet again. When she returned home, seeing that Rob's bedroom had been transformed into a sewing room for burgeoning socialites, the scrapbooks full of happy childhood memories vanished from their shelves, she knew it was true. Rob was gone from their lives, and as far as her parents were concerned, he should be gone from their memories too.

But now, neither could make that choice for her.

In the garage, Alice turned on the light and read the reassuring word *Robinson* on the envelope she had stopped Jamie from taking. She weighed its thickness in her hand, feeling its heft. It scared her to think there would be so much that she didn't yet know. It also calmed her. The answers, they were here. They had to be. What kept him from her, where he went, the same answers she had sought that day on the river. But more than that, *why?*

In the house, Walker yelled, no doubt mourning another loss to Robbie at chess. She wanted to wait until she was truly alone to see what the Robinson envelope held. She turned off the light and went back inside to finish dinner.

After Alice cleaned up the plates and Walker put Robbie to sleep, they lay next to each other in bed with the lights off. Alice stared at the ceiling, thinking about the box Jamie tried to take, the unopened letters, Rob, his words to their father, all the mysteries of her life stirring together into one black hole of unknowns.

Had her mother sat in the sewing room, blinking as she focused on a stitch too late at night, wondering these same questions: What could she have done differently with Rob? Had she wondered what to do about her own husband? Had she ever wanted to pack up and leave her life behind, to go hide in a little shack on the coast, if only for a night?

Leaving was Rob's thing, though it was always her father's move, too, after a fight—a sudden business emergency in Memphis or a game of golf with Jamie that stretched from sunup to sundown. It was Walker's, too, with his monthly trips to DC, which for the last few months he'd no doubt spent tangled in the hotel sheets with Brittani. Leaving was always the man's play, not Maura's. Not Alice's.

Walker crossed the emptiness of their king-size mattress. The light stubble on his chin from his five-o'clock shadow tickled Alice's face as he kissed her earlobe.

Her body locked, and she struggled not to jerk her head away from his lips. She always hated how he responded to tension by reaching for her physically, at the exact moment she wanted to be away from him, at the moment she most wanted to sink into their roles as roommates and ignore the other parts.

"I'm really tired from all the stuff with Jamie today, okay?" She pictured the photo of Jake, zipped safely in her backpack, before hating herself for connecting her rejection of Walker with a man she had never refused. Was Walker thinking about Brittani right now? How *she* would have been the one to roll over, to kiss his cheek? Would things be different—warm, loving—if she were lying next to Jake instead of Walker? Would sex be something she looked forward to regularly, instead of a prescription pulled out in the worst moments of tension, a stint to keep the heart pumping when it was near giving up?

"Isn't the point of being off work to be less stressed, not more?" he said as if she were on vacation, instead of dealing with an ever-growing mountain of drama and deception. Walker rolled over so that his back faced her.

They lay in silence for a few more minutes.

Alice replayed her mother's advice from last week: "Are you *satisfying* him?" Maura had asked.

"Walker?"

"Hmm?" he answered, already half asleep.

"Do you think you can ever truly know another person, even someone you're close with? Someone in your family?" *Did I know my brother at all? Is it possible to feel you understand someone so deeply, yet know almost nothing about them?* She wanted to hear one person say it: *Yes.*

He turned to face her again. "What?" His voice was sharp with anger.

Too close to Rob, Alice thought. "Nothing," she said. "Never mind."

Silence.

"Tell me a secret," Alice said. "Something I don't know about you."

"It's almost midnight."

"Just a quick one."

"I secretly love green apple martinis, but I'm afraid to order them at bars."

She chuckled. "No, something else."

"The only fight I ever got into was in middle school because some asshole kid was calling my brother names. I went up to him on the playground and punched him in the face. He got knocked down and started bleeding all over the place, and we both got detention."

"What did your parents say?"

"My dad told me he was proud of me."

Alice considered this.

"Now, go to sleep." Walker rolled back over, and within thirty seconds, he was snoring lightly.

Alice waited a few minutes to make sure he was asleep before she got out of bed. She tugged on her robe to fight the house's winter chill and walked back to the garage. She climbed into the car's front seat, shutting the door quietly. The guitar lay across the center console. She turned on the car's overhead light. She found the large "Robinson" envelope and undid the brackets and slid its contents into her hand, a thick stack of black material.

X-rays. Their snap and bend—now familiar from her endless conversations with Maura's doctors—echoed in the car's small space. She held the first to the overhead light. On the side, *TATE, ROBINSON WESLEY* was printed in all caps followed by *CLARK STATE* and an address. It showed some nondescript chest, or perhaps she was supposed to look at the ribs, heart, or spleen. The X-ray shone with different shades of black and white like an abstract painting, the kind Walker liked to remark that he could replicate easily and question why they had to pay to look at art he could do himself.

When she reached the last papers, she gasped.

The block letters of *AUTOPSY REPORT* screamed across the page and contrasted with the neat, businesslike script of the form's author.

Name: Robinson Wesley Tate

Her eyes traveled over a simple diagram of a man's body. Pen marks annotated the black etching with various dots and symbols she didn't understand.

Narrative: White male, aged thirty-eight. Primary cause of death: heart failure. Opioid and alcohol located in system. Evidence of malignant neoplasm of the lungs, spread into tissue

and affecting liver and heart functions. Neoplasm of advanced
stage.

Her questions from the funeral about how her brother died
flooded back. The heart failure and the drugs she knew, but
her parents knew much more. She quickly Googled *malignant*
neoplasm on her phone, finding that it meant *cancer.*

She erased the image she'd had of her brother from the funeral
of desperation, a drug overdose, and replaced it with one of her
brother in a hospital, alone. As a child, Alice always felt Rob's
injuries more intensely than he did, and again, she felt that pain
in her chest, the feeling that her cells were turning against her, as
he must have felt.

The stamps on the X-rays hit her with the same wave of
loneliness and anger she'd felt in the years after he left. One said
2005, and the other held an address. Her brother knew his life
would end soon, a full two years before he died. And even worse,
the X-rays had been done less than a three-hour drive from her
house. Why would he drive all the way to some hospital she'd
never heard of in southern Georgia? And still not contact her?
And you didn't try to find him, her brain filled in, regret tensing
her shoulders.

Hoping the next would be better, Alice unbracketed the second
envelope and slid out a few sheets of white printer paper. It was a
contract with a private investigator, addressed to her mother but
with Jamie's information for payments and his signature at the
bottom. The contract was for six months, with an opportunity
for renewal, to locate a runaway, age fifteen when he left, sixteen
now, with brown/blond hair and blue eyes. Paper-clipped to the

front was a business card and a photo. The card was for a diner with the private investigator's name and phone number scrawled on the back in pen. The picture was maybe the last taken of Rob before he left. He looked serious in the school portrait, as if from many decades ago, before people smiled for the camera. On the back, it said, "Robinson Wesley Tate, age fifteen" in her mother's cursive.

Had her mother and Jamie looked for Rob? Her father wouldn't have participated or approved. With his elevated sense of duty, Richard felt that Rob was dead to him the second he walked out of the house on Amelia Island. "He'll come back when he's good and ready," he said. "He'll be back by Sunday" became next week, next month until eventually her parents stopped talking about Rob. Then, after Alice's canoe trip and the hospital, her parents stopped talking altogether. *You could have prevented everything*, Rob had written. Could this have been what he was referring to? Their father could have looked for Rob, could have paid, could have not left Rob to his own devices, as he instructed Maura to do?

As a child, Alice thought her mother felt the same way, but from the crying at the funeral, the carefully taped posters and the letters in the crawl space, she realized that was wrong. Her stomach swelled with gratitude toward Jamie, that he would keep a secret from her father. If he didn't want Alice to know he had helped Maura, Alice understood. It hadn't worked, after all, had only ended in disappointment for them and for Alice now. At least someone in the family had done something, though, while Alice stood by depressed and idle. She should call Jamie and smooth things over tomorrow. Thank him for helping look for Rob. Maybe Rob's letter to Jamie or to their mother would explain why they couldn't find him.

Alice took the letters out of the backpack again and ran her fingers over the seal of her mother's. She would take it tomorrow, hope her mother was having a good day, and if not, she'd open it anyway. She would.

For now, though, she zipped everything into the safety of her backpack and went back to her bedroom. There, she tossed and turned for three hours before finally realizing what should have been obvious from the start—she wouldn't be able to sleep. The figure of the man's body—her brother—from the autopsy, with his x's and o's, burned in front of her eyes when she closed them.

CHAPTER EIGHT

By six o'clock the next morning, Alice had already walked Buddy around the neighborhood's two-mile loop, pulled all the weeds in her garden with the aid of the headlight she'd bought for night fishing, thrown out the expired items in her pantry (and there were many), listened to some lectures from an ecology researcher that she had downloaded two months ago, and texted Grace that she would take the Girl Scout troop scheduled at the Center for later in the real morning hours, before she caught herself checking the digital clock in the kitchen four times in a ten-minute period. She racked her brain for another task. Anything to keep her distracted from the figure of the man on the autopsy report with his markings of pain and sickness. She finally made French toast and bacon, Robbie's favorite breakfast, and carried it up to his bedroom on a plastic tray.

"*Captain Planet* marathon!" she said when he rubbed the sleep out of his eyes. She turned on his TV, and they sat on his bed, an hour earlier than he normally woke up, and ate the French toast and bacon, both doused in syrup. As the opening started, they sang the *Captain Planet* theme song about thwarting pollution.

"This is so cool, Mom," he said, in his Pokémon pajamas.

She smiled at him, a little guilt behind her lips for waking him up early for her own selfish reasons and burrowed deeper under his covers.

Two hours later, Caitlin and Robbie safely on their way to school in Chelsea's car, Alice pulled into the parking lot of the little log cabin on Lake Lanier that acted as the office for the Georgia Creekside Center, with Buddy in tow. The sun reflected off the lake, giving it the appearance of sparkling.

She opened the passenger door, and Buddy trotted to a folded comforter waiting for him by one of the rocking chairs on the cabin's front porch. She watched as he walked in a circle twice, yawned, and fell asleep. She heard the boat knock lightly against the dock in the back as the wind made the lake restless, just under the surface.

She hunched against the wind as she approached the cabin, letting her shoulders slump. Staying away for a week had been a test all involved knew Alice couldn't pass, but she had expected to last more than a single day. After all, the Center kept her up long hours, caused plenty of hair-pulling over finicky donors, and offered little in the form of salary. The cabin's roof leaked, and the juxtaposition of the alarming data she collected with the inaction of many Southern politicians depressed her. But she knew the work mattered. And the little cabin had always been her refuge, the part of her life that was hers alone, a dream she'd sketched out in silence at Duke, then breathed to life with her ingenuity and a few pen swipes from Walker's checkbook for the startup cash. Today, she needed that escape.

Grace had returned her text in the morning with a bug-eyed emoji that radiated judgment, saying she would come in the afternoon instead. Alice would have Girl Scout Troop 1298 of Birmingham, Alabama, to herself.

The screen banged against the door as Alice went inside to start more coffee. The Center didn't have heat, only a space heater in the corner, so she kept her favorite North Face jacket tight around her as she waited for the coffee. She studied the map they kept tacked to the door, with all of Georgia's waterways outlined in black. It morphed into the figure from the autopsy. The coffee maker beeped. Only an hour of silence to fill before the girls would pile in—excited, screaming, giggling, uncomplicated. Then, this afternoon, Alice would visit her mother with the letter. She would read more of her brother's perfectly looped words. She only hoped these would be happier.

Alice warmed her right hand over the steaming coffee as she used her left to make a list of everything she could do to take up the hour. After she could think of nothing else, Alice called Buddy in for a treat. He trotted behind her as she fed a struggling mouse to the snake and climbed on a step stool to dump fish into the tank of Bentley the turtle, the Center's mascot. She filled the boat with gas and lowered it into the water. She collected water samples in different areas around the Center, then sat at the computer to record all the measurements and check the water-quality data Grace had input yesterday.

She shook her head at the lake water levels, and Buddy's ears perked up at the tsks. Through the window over the desk, Alice saw a long expanse of mud with trees and limbs where the lake's shore had receded in answer to Georgia's years of drought. The graph provided the only proof at first because the sinking was so slow, you could hardly notice it. The homeowners along the lake always seemed to wake up one day in anger, months or years from the true start of the decline, and wonder how the lake got so low, so dirty, while they had been concentrating on the everyday struggles of their lives. Like life, she thought, you think you have all the time in the world, and then you wake up one day and your life is caving in around you. It seems sudden, but you consented to the avalanche each day, as the stones moved inch by inch.

Measurements entered, she poured herself another cup of now-lukewarm coffee with a little milk before sitting back at the desk. She stirred the coffee with her finger and watched the white of the milk until it disappeared into the black coffee. This is the last cup, she promised herself.

Still ten minutes to go. In search of anything else to fill her thoughts but Rob's autopsy, the evil word—*cancer*—echoing in her brain, she fished out the pictures from the zippered pocket of her backpack. She stared into the eyes of a younger Alice, standing next to Jake.

They looked so young. Alice looked happy, the regret and loneliness from after Rob's disappearance replaced with gratitude and surprise that she'd found someone like Jake, the same happiness and ease that was absent from her wedding photo with Walker, the same emotions she'd recognize next in the picture of little Caitlin on Alice's chest at the hospital. Jake looked into the camera with a wide smile, without a trace of the coy guardedness visible in most photos of men that age. How naive she was, completely unaware of the power she had given Jake.

By the time Alice applied for college, her mother worried, no doubt, that Alice wouldn't find a husband at all. Her mother invited the first "eligible" boy over for dinner two days after Alice turned sixteen, and she didn't stop until Alice packed her bags for college. Each time, Alice crossed her arms and stared at her plate as if she could set it on fire. In reality, it wasn't the boys who irritated her (though they did), it was the *Leave it to Beaver* routine her parents, even Jamie, put on for them, as if the dinners weren't the only time they ate as a family in all the years since Rob left. Not acknowledging the truth, that after Rob disappeared, they ceased being a family. He had somehow been the glue holding everyone together.

When Alice packed up her bags for the University of Georgia, her mother rationalized the choice over Georgia State (where Alice could live at home) because it would be "the perfect place to find Mr. Right." Not wanting to harm her chances of escaping the house at last, Alice only smiled and said, "Maybe," though her real plan was to spend all her time studying science and none of her time preparing for an MRS degree.

There was one problem with that plan, though, and his name was Jake O'Connell.

Alice first saw the problem while walking back to her dorm from her freshman literature class. The problem sat with his back against one of the trees that shaded the Quad, where a group of fraternity boys played football. He wore faded blue jeans and a green T-shirt from one of the agriculture clubs, Birkenstocks lined up next to him. He caught her staring and winked. They waved at each other without speaking for the whole semester.

Alice thought it was the perfect relationship. But everything changed the next semester when she walked into her resource conservation class, drew *South Korea* from a hat, and went to sit under the proper sign, next to a window. She watched the students running to class before they were late.

"Hey," said a male voice as a face popped into her field of vision. She jumped.

"Sorry! I didn't mean to scare you. I... Hi. I'm Jake." The boy from the Quad extended his hand, smiling a quirky smile that showed slightly crooked teeth, surrounded by a neatly trimmed beard.

Two years older, Jake was a junior, studying international affairs with a focus on environmental policy. This class was his life goal, and he debated passionately for South Korea. So passionately, that by the end of the class, their group won the competition. And because of the half-study, half-make-out sessions that filled Alice's semester, she ended it with an A and a boyfriend.

Her sophomore year, with many nights of whispered secrets behind them, Alice told him her biggest, about Rob, that she had never told anyone. It would forever intertwine the two men in her mind.

That night, Jake and Alice lay outside on Myers Quad, trying to point out different constellations, or if they didn't know their names, making them up with ridiculous stories for how the stars were named.

"Sometimes, I think I see him." She had told Jake about Rob, about her family, about how she had been sure he would come back for her. About the night she ran away and the years-long ripple effect that left her mother more protective than ever. Jake propped up his head with his hand to look at her.

"What do you mean?" The streetlamps lit his outline just

enough for Alice to fill in the rest of his expressions from memory.

"I'll be sitting in a room and think I see him outside the window." She chose her words carefully. "I'll be walking downtown and think I see him walking in front of me, be at the Grill and think I hear someone say his name. I know it sounds insane. I don't even know what he looks like anymore. I don't know if I would recognize him, but I can't stop seeing him."

Jake didn't try to speak, so she continued, the words spilling from her mouth.

"When I had trouble sleeping sometimes as a kid, he used to tell me I shouldn't be scared because angels were always watching us, taking care of us. Sometimes, I wonder if that's what he does now, with me, from wherever he is. Is that crazy?"

"I don't think it's crazy." Jake used his other hand to brush a strand of hair off her face. "I think it makes perfect sense."

They kissed. She felt the wetness of tears as their faces rubbed together but didn't understand why she was crying.

"When we find him, you can ask him yourself," Jake said. It was all part of their plan for after her graduation—to find Rob. To build a life together, one that included her brother. Even then, as Jake rubbed her arm trying to reassure her, Alice had to close her eyes to stave off the panic. Unlike when she went looking for Rob in the canoe, with so many years between them, she feared what she might find, how she would feel, what she would say. She felt the prickle of anger, of blame even then, the rage that he would take off without even a sign for her.

She felt what would surely be Jake's coming disappointment too. Jake seemed to have the solution at the ready, so sure he could fix her, by only locating Rob. But Alice knew her real self was beyond the repair even Rob could bring, and it was only a matter of time until Jake found out too.

———————————

Alice heard the honks of a bus and loud songs from open windows as the girls celebrated their arrival to the Center. She put the photo back, next to the letters that threatened to wreak the same havoc if she let them. She called Buddy, her chest still buzzing, a warning of coming trouble, like how she could feel from the heaviness of the air on her skin when it would storm. She shook it off. Together, Alice and Buddy exited to the front porch, where the girls were already filing out of the bus.

She walked down the steps yelling "Good morning!" as the last girls leapt off the bus steps and gathered with their parents on the lawn in front of the cabin.

"I can't hear you. I said, 'GOOD MORNING!'" They thundered back the greeting at her—still young enough to revel in this often-practiced routine.

"Welcome to the Georgia Creekside Center. My name is Alice, and I'll be your guide today, and this is Buddy. Since we'll be learning about Native Americans, you can also call us Flying Creek and Chief Barkerton." Alice whispered "speak" to Buddy, and he let out several barks as a testament to his true name. The girls giggled.

After a quick orientation for the girls and their chaperones, they pulled canoes from the dock, furiously snapped life preservers, and chatted excitedly. Three girls and one adult climbed into each canoe with their paddles. Once everyone was on the water, Alice climbed into her own canoe with Buddy in the front. As she threw everything in her dry bag, her phone screen glowed 9:15 a.m. She had about an hour on the lake before she needed to meet Meredith for their weekly brunch, then she would read her mother's letter and accept whatever it unleashed.

She paddled out to join the girls. "Today, I'm going to tell you the story of the Muscogee tribe. Because they settled around Georgia's rivers and lakes, Southerners called them the Creek tribe..."

The girls smiled at the lake and the adventure and leaned in close to listen.

As she always had, Alice lost herself in the water. She let the gentle rippling of the lake eclipse the tumbling music in her head of Rob and Jake, the figure of the man's body, memories of too many whispered secrets. As her paddle disturbed the water, these thoughts floated away and her mind calmed.

CHAPTER NINE

Meredith placed the first page of the autopsy report on the table in front of Alice. With a long intake of breath, she started on the second page. Alice watched her friend's face turn from surprise to worry before she noticed Alice studying her.

They sat in one of the tattered red leather booths at the Grit, Athens's famous vegetarian diner. Colorful paintings with papier-mâché fingers stuck out at 3-D angles decorated the light-green walls, where beneath, paint peeled randomly. The spot was less than a mile off the University of Georgia campus where they first met as assigned roommates. Now, when Meredith wasn't in New York or on book tour, they met there every Tuesday at noon.

A college-aged waiter with tattooed arms brought their coffee.

"Be a dear and bring us something stronger than these. Do you need to see my ID?" Meredith said.

While Meredith moved on to the contract with the private investigator, Alice sipped the cup of coffee she'd promised herself she wouldn't have. She was getting jittery. She bounced her foot as she looked away from Meredith's facial expressions and focused on possible meanings of the painting on the wall opposite their table. It had two boobs with huge nipples sticking out, decorated with magazine covers showing women in swimsuits. Caitlin would have liked it.

"You found these in the closet?" Meredith said.

"I found *the letters* in the closet. Jamie had the big envelopes. I don't know where he found them, but I think in my father's office. There were papers everywhere." Alice had already given her the *Reader's Digest* version of the state of the house and her argument with Jamie.

Meredith flipped through the letters, looking at the fronts and backs, inspecting them closely from all sides as if she were Nancy Drew. The hipster waiter's hovering broke her gaze.

She stacked the papers and letters to one side of the table and waved her hand at the waiter. "Well, go ahead, honey. We don't have all day."

He set down a cowboy omelet and a vegetable platter, along with two Bloody Marys.

Once the waiter left, Alice asked, "What do you think it means?"

"What do *you* think it means?" Meredith countered. One of her favorite tricks—returning a question with a question, something she had done countless times at author events, when people asked her why her characters acted like they did. It wouldn't work today, though, because unlike the audience members, Alice had no theories, or rather had so many that none seemed worthy of being voiced aloud.

"I don't know."

"Only one way to find out. Open the rest."

"Daddy's was different since he *can't* read it. They aren't addressed to me." Alice said it matter-of-factly, but her chest panged with the reminder. There wasn't one for her. She bull-dozed over the feeling. "And what if he didn't want them sent?"

"What if he did?"

Alice didn't ask the obvious next question—if he meant to send them, then why didn't he? Because she knew Meredith would give her the response her brain had already filled in, that she didn't want to say out loud: What if he had died before he could send them? And besides, neither theory would explain how they ended up in a box postmarked for her parents' house anyway.

"At least Google the names, for Christ's sake."

"I don't need to because I'm not opening them." Even a Google search would release secrets she wasn't sure she wanted to know. "Besides, I'm pretty sure that would be mail fraud," Alice said, trying to lighten the conversation a little.

"Did you really just use mail fraud as an excuse? I think you'll be…" Meredith's eyes stared at the top of Alice's head, and she trailed off, no longer fully paying attention.

Alice turned behind her to see what her friend saw. Nothing there. She looked again at Meredith, whose eyes had narrowed. "What, do I have something…?" Alice patted the top of her head until she heard a crunch. A leaf.

Meredith ducked her head under the table and back up. "Nice shoes," she said, referring to Alice's muddy hiking boots. "You went to the Center this morning?"

Alice took a big drink of the Bloody Mary, nodding over the glass.

"So, you find letters written by your dead brother, his autopsy report, and proof that your mother and Jamie were tracking him down, and you go to the Center, even though you're off for the first time in years?"

"I went out on the lake with the cutest group of Girl Scouts.

There was this one girl, she was shy, but you could tell she was really listening, you know? And of course, Buddy was a hit like usual." She glanced out the window where a group of college girls was petting him as they walked to class. He tried to follow them but stopped when his leash went taut.

"Hmm." Meredith picked up her fork and poked at her omelet.

Alice waited. Meredith said "hmm" again. Alice spread her napkin into her lap.

She couldn't remember a time when Meredith had *hmm*ed before saying something Alice actually wanted to hear. The *hmm* usually warned of trouble before the bomb hit. The *hmm* said "Do you want my opinion, or should I let it go?" The *hmm* said "I want you to be happy, but if acknowledging what I'm about to say is too painful, I can wait a year or ten because I'll still be around."

Meredith *hmm*ed through the favors Alice did for professors and bosses. She *hmm*ed through group projects that turned out to be anything but. She *hmm*ed through Alice's wedding; she often *hmm*ed through dinner with Walker, when they actually invited him (and he actually decided to join them). More than anything, the *hmm* said what Alice already knew, deep in her subconscious where she only let dreams penetrate.

Finally, she gave in.

"Why are you *hmm*ing?"

"I'm *hmm*ing because you are fucking ignoring the situation."

Alice scanned the restaurant, like she always did after Meredith cursed. She wanted to make sure she didn't need to apologize to any young children or old ladies on her friend's behalf. She relaxed a little, seeing that the patrons looked like college students still nursing hangovers from the night before.

"Ignoring. The. Situation." Meredith punctuated each word with a movement of her fork.

"What situation am I ignoring?"

"The situation that *your family* kept this from you. For years. When I met you, you were still so upset about Rob leaving. Doesn't this make you angry?"

Alice pictured Rob screaming into the clearing that day, telling her to scream what she was most angry about. Rob was wrong, though, she reminded herself. And that was Rob, the child. A Rob of the past. She didn't know the real Rob, the adult Rob, and he hadn't *wanted* to know her.

"They thought they were doing the right thing. And my mother left the boxes for me! I went to the Center because I just needed a break after Jamie and the house, my mother, all of this"—she gestured to the papers still laid between them— "Walker. To deal with something...logical. For a few hours. Before I go visit my mother with her letter."

"Walker? Is there something going on with him...other than the usual?"

Oops. Alice stopped.

She wasn't ready to tell her friend about Walker's cheating. She knew Meredith—always a woman of action—would expect a decision to be made. And saying it out loud, seeing the look on her friend's face, would make it worse.

"No." Alice spooned a heaping portion of black beans into her mouth and chewed. She changed the subject. "When I was in my room, I found an old picture of us and one of Jake."

Alice took out the pictures and showed them to Meredith. Meredith smiled at them both. "Good times."

"Wonder what he's up to now." Alice moved the food around on her plate, trying to decide how much more to eat.

"Probably only a Facebook search away. Want to try it?" Meredith twirled her iPhone between her fingers.

Alice had used Facebook when it first came out, friending some high school and college classmates with whom she had fallen out of touch. But since the newness wore off, she had let her page languish, preferring to let Grace and the interns handle the Center's website and social media. She knew Meredith was somewhat of a Facebook celebrity though.

"Umm… Let's not. With everything going on with my mother and Caitlin applying to colleges and the house, it's not a good time."

Meredith shrugged with exaggerated nonchalance and clicked the phone off. They ate in silence for a couple of minutes, both drinking their Bloody Marys and spreading jam on toast. Even though Alice hadn't told her friend about the texts, she could feel it between them as they ate, as if Meredith either knew or sensed a difference in her attitude with Walker, could feel the tiptoeing. But as always, Meredith was patiently determined, letting it sit between them until Alice was ready. Her friend was satisfied to fight a war of attrition, to wait, listen, and understand. Alice liked to think that quality was one of the reasons Meredith had accomplished everything she'd talked about on those nights they lay awake discussing dreams in the dark across their lofted beds.

Meredith continued her well-paying day job at a large consulting firm for years out of college, but at night began writing novels, her real dream. Her third book skyrocketed to the top of the bestseller list and made her sexy books a feature on every housewife's bedside table. Meredith quit her job and traveled around the country to shake hands with women who left their husbands, bought a vibrator, had a threesome, or whatever other activity they'd never imagined themselves doing before they started reading her books. The *New York Times* had recently called her "the voice behind a collective sexual awakening."

Now, Meredith split her time between an apartment in New York overlooking Central Park and her house outside of Athens in Oconee County, where she lived on the lake. She restored the property over the years, turning the barn into a hanger for her two vintage planes. She shared it with her current live-in boyfriend, Christian, who was twelve years her junior.

"I thought I was done with this, with Rob."

Meredith watched her.

"When I started dating Walker, I didn't want to think about Rob anymore. And even after he died, I gave myself a few days to remember him, but that was it, and I stuck to it. But, Rob and I... I loved him. So much."

"Then why not remember him? Why not think about all the good memories you have with him?" Meredith asked.

Alice locked eyes with Meredith.

"You know why. You were there before. With Jake." Unlike their laughter over the pictures she found, this time, Alice struggled over the name.

Meredith pushed her plate forward two inches to signal she was done eating, as if the statement had soured her appetite. "Yes, I was there."

Alice did the same.

"Mere, that and after Rob left were the worst times of my

life. But I just want to know what happened to him. More than anything."

Robbie, she thought. The only thing she had ever wanted more. The little boy who took so many years to stick.

Meredith caught the waiter's eye and gestured toward Alice's empty coffee. He came over to fill it, and they both watched in silence as he poured it and walked away. Alice took a sip.

"What if I read these letters, and I don't find out anything? What if they're all like my father's, nothing but some poetic wild-goose chase? Or worse, if I find out something terrible… If I find out it was my fault, if I could have done something, if he expected me to come. What if I find out he's not the person I thought he was?" She choked on the last words.

"Oh, honey." Meredith reached out and put her hand on Alice's.

"I can't do that again. I can't go to that bad place like I was in college. I have Caitlin and Robbie now." Alice slumped into the side of the booth by the wall where she could hide her face.

"I'm here. You won't. You're strong. Stronger than you know. Stronger than you were then." Meredith paused. "I have a sense you'll find what you are looking for," she said, smiling at Alice. Alice laughed, wiping the last tear from her cheek.

It was a joke with them: the "senses" Meredith felt that Alice never really believed in. Meredith sensed Caitlin would be a girl when Alice was pregnant the first time—this she held as all the necessary proof of her skill. Granted, it had been a fifty-fifty shot.

"I hope you're right."

They finished their Bloody Marys and paid the bill. Meredith drew a heart on the receipt and wrote "Stay hot!" Alice shook her head when she saw it. She knew Meredith only did it to cheer her up.

As she put everything back in her bag, she left out her mother's letter. She carried the letter with her as she untied Buddy and they got in the car. She fingered the seal as she drove home and dropped him off, then knocked the envelope's sharp edge against her thigh as she drove to her mother's "apartment." She would find out what it held. Today.

CHAPTER TEN

St. Margaret's Care Facility pretended not to be the type of place where you dropped off your memory-challenged mother. With the bright windows shaded by navy awnings and the flower boxes with the dusty millers spilling out, it seemed like somewhere you might vacation for a long weekend in the fall, or at least that's what the guilty children told themselves as they drove away from their ailing parents.

Alice practiced what she would say to her mother as she signed in. She would read the letter to her, if it was a good day. Hopefully, it would be.

Inside, cushioned benches and iron sconces lined the hallways. St. Margaret's didn't look like a hospital, but its scent mixed stale urine, the heavy musk of clothes that have been in storage, and the sharp, clinical smell of a doctor's office. Alice hated it.

Entering her mother's room reminded Alice of a game she used to play in the summers with the neighborhood kids. A "king" stood next to the pool with his or her back to the water while the other kids floated on one side of pool. The object was to swim to the other side without being tagged by the king, who could turn around three times and jump in the pool to tag a prisoner. Once someone reached the other side without being tagged, they could sneak up to the king and push them in the water to dethrone them. She preferred to watch Rob pumping his fists from the sidelines, feeling the pride of his victory as if it were her own; he lived for his time as king. Unlike him, when it was her turn to be king, every muscle in her body tensed as she waited for the coming attack or flipped around, ready to dive into the water and race to tag her peers.

Visiting her mother felt like that. Alice never knew if she would turn around to no attackers and calm waters or turn around to a battle underway and need to jump into the fray to defend her crown—the one she didn't want to begin with.

Maura lay on her hospital bed, designed to look like a real bed. The television mounted in the corner of the room blared the shopping channel. Alice wasn't even convinced her mother could see without her glasses, but Maura stared without blinking and didn't move in response to Alice's knock.

"Hi, Mama. How are you today?"

Maura turned toward her, an urgent movement in slow motion.

"Alice. I'm your daughter." Alice inched closer to the bed.

"I know who my own daughter is. I'm not an idiot," her mother snapped at her, crossing her arms and turning her head away. A good sign. The sickly sweet days were the worst.

Alice sat in the chair by the bed, moving an open copy of *Our Town*, which Caitlin must have left when she visited on Sunday. "How are you?"

"Terrible. The people here are insufferable," her mother said.

"What happened?" Alice asked, happy for a conversation in the present. Alice had never thought she would so crave her mother's ridiculous complaints as she had for the past months.

"Yesterday, at breakfast I was with the girls, all of us eating off god-awful trays—is there no more dignified way to serve food? Anyway, they settle on a discussion of grandchildren, as they always do, and the main lady, Jean, she asks what my grandchildren call me. I say 'Mimi,' and then they go around the table and every one of them—do you know what they say—Granny! Granny! Who on this godforsaken earth would want to be called 'granny'? I can assure you, I have nothing in common with such a person."

"You'll find something in common with them. What about Karen. You like her, don't you?"

"She died."

"Oh," Alice said. "I'm sorry. Do you need anything?"

"One thing: I need you to go to the Fur Vault and pick up my mink coat. I'll need it for church on Sunday, as the weather is getting cool."

Alice sighed. It was the end of winter, not the beginning (and never mind that Maura didn't need a fur coat in the mild Georgia winters—ever). Alice had forgotten about the long brown coat that she had loved to pet as a child, walking behind her mother as they climbed the steps to church. Or at least she had loved the soft fur before she found out what died to make it. She made a mental note to remember to pick it up. Even if her mother eventually forgot the request, Alice didn't want to leave a coat that could be sold for a semester of college tuition.

"You need to remember to take it back in the spring. Even if I've expired, it needs to be returned for the insurance. You'll remember that?"

Alice smiled, another good sign. While Rob was Maura's favorite topic on bad days, on good days, her own death was her favorite. Memory was funny like that, Alice had learned. Like how some days Maura couldn't remember Alice, but could apply an eight-step skin-care routine, as she had nightly for decades. The bottles were lined up on the bedside table even now, although if anyone asked how she kept her skin so youthful, she always claimed the secret was only Vaseline and good genes or "luck."

"Yes"—her mother glared at her—"ma'am." Maura turned her head back to the shopping channel.

Alice decided to test the waters, to flip around on the ledge and see what awaited her.

"Mama, I've been at the house—"

"*What*? Stop mumbling. You know I *hate* it when you mumble."

Louder now: "I've been at your HOUSE."

"Okay, I heard you. It's my memory that's the problem. Not my ears."

"I was wondering...about those pictures in the upstairs hallway. They're all Daddy's relatives. I want to make sure I keep any important family pictures." Alice glanced at her mother who half watched the blurs on the shopping channel. "Are there any pictures of your family? Anywhere?"

Maura looked at Alice, and for a second, Alice thought she wouldn't respond. Maura turned back to the blurs in the corner.

"Not of which I'm aware."

"What happened to them?"

"I suppose I threw them out."

"But you never get rid of anything." After her hours of wading through the house yesterday, Alice knew this for a fact.

Maura shrugged.

Alice knew her mother wasn't proud of her rural background. Her father preached at a small church in Arkansas, or so Alice had pieced together over the years.

"They are dead," her mother said. "Soon, I will also be dead, and there would be no use for such sentimentality. You've never met them anyway."

"That's true. I never met them."

Her mother turned her head back to the shopping channel.

"In the house, I found something. Mama, can you look at me?" She turned. "Do you remember those boxes in the closet upstairs? The ones you left for me?"

Her mother looked in the distance, and Alice could see the gears turning, shifting through her brain's clutter.

"Rob's?" Alice prompted.

Maura's eyebrow twitched. The tides shifted, as they always do—frantically.

"Why isn't he with you? Where is he?" Her mother's voice rose, and she looked left to right as if searching for her son.

Alice was trapped in this conversation, forced to dive into the water and attempt to beat her opponent. She tried reciting the response she had practiced many times. "He can't be here right now. But he loves you, and he is going to come by later." Usually it was enough.

"He's not coming because he's mad at me, isn't he? He hates me. He hates his own mother. I should never have told him to stay away. I know I deserve it, everything I've gotten."

Alice continued her script before her brain processed what her mother said: "He loves you. I promise. He's not mad... What do you mean you told him to stay away? When?"

"You're trying to protect him, aren't you? You hate me too. My only children hate me. What did I do to make my only children hate me, God?" She looked at the ceiling, throwing her arms up, questioning. "All I've done is try to be the best mother I can be and do what I thought was right."

"Mama, no one is mad at you." Alice reached over and put her hand on top of her mother's. Her mother jerked her hand away. "What do you mean though? Can you explain it to me, please?"

Ignoring her, Maura turned to Alice before lacing her hands together in a begging prayer. "Please. Please. Please. Let me call him. Let me call my son. Please let me—I have to tell him the truth. I have to tell him I want him home. I always wanted him. He'll come visit then."

"All right! All right, Mama. You can call him, but he probably won't answer, okay?" Alice picked up the phone on the bedside table and dialed the number, handing it to her mother, hoping it might elicit some sort of explanation.

"Thank you. Thank you."

Alice watched her mother's tear-stained but happy face, tightening her grip on the bottom of the chair. A beat passed before her cell phone vibrated in her jacket pocket. Eventually, it stopped, and her mother's smile sank.

"He didn't answer. I'll leave a message, though, and he'll call me back."

Alice played the automated voicemail in her head. "You've reached 6-7-8…" The emotionless machine voice was unaware of the situation.

"Hey, it's Mama. I miss you so much, Robinson. Please come

home. Alice is with me and she misses you. We both want you back. We'll do whatever it takes to get you back. I'm sorry. I take full responsibility... The guilt is on my shoulders. I drove you away, like Alice probably thinks. She's right, you know."

She hung up the phone, satisfied. "Now, we'll wait for him to call back."

"Excuse me for a minute."

Alice stood up, taking her backpack with her. She walked like she did in college after one too many beers, wanting to appear normal, calculating every step, wondering if it was too long or too short, too light or too heavy. When she reached the hallway, she sank down to the floor and took out her phone.

One new voicemail.

She swiped, and a screen full of voicemails of the same number appeared. She brought the phone to her ear and listened to the desperate, yet cheery sound of her mother's voice on the other end until the message ended.

Alice looked at the drooping garlands, which still snaked around the railings lining the hallways even though Christmas was several weeks past. It had been Alice's first Christmas without her mother, and the family, plus Jamie, had crowded around the dining room table without Maura's lace tablecloth, eating off mismatched plates and bowls, with paper napkins and plastic containers instead of Maura's usual formality. The scene had so depressed Alice that she went downstairs to find a silver goblet, if only to have a little of her mother's flair. She always despised it—the endless polishing of those silver forks! But without her mother's touch, Christmas hadn't been the same.

Alice would never say that to her mother though. If she hadn't realized she had been left for Christmas, Alice certainly didn't want to bring it up. After Alice brought her here in the summer, her mother didn't speak to her for so long that she began to forget the sound of her voice. She would sit in the chair by the bed while her mother watched the shopping channel and try to remember. How thick was her accent? Did she actually say *story* for *lie*, or did Alice make that up? Did she really say *warsh* for *wash*, the only betrayal of her rural Arkansas roots? Until one day her mother had turned to her and gossiped about the neighborhood drama like normal. She never knew if the choice was intentional, or if her mother simply forgot to be angry.

After a few minutes, a hello came from the end of the hall, and Alice looked up to see a nurse rolling her mother's friend Karen to the sunroom in a wheelchair. She pulled her legs closer to her chest as they passed and smiled at the nurse.

"Hello, Mrs. Mays," she said, and Karen frowned. Not dead after all. Typical.

Not for the first time, she wished Rob were here to share the burden, to tell her she was doing the right thing with their mother. Alice unzipped her backpack and took out the letter, staring at the words on the envelope. "Mrs. Maura Tate." Who had she been kidding? She couldn't read the letter to her mother.

Alice slid a finger under the flap. It revealed the back of a photo, where "Robinson Wesley Tate, age thirty-nine" had been written lightly in pencil. She took the photo out. In the picture, Rob sat alone on the steps of what looked like a church. His hands rested on the acoustic guitar, not in a playing motion like the photo from the funeral pamphlet, taken in his teenage years, had shown. Instead, his arms draped over the top, his body shielded behind the guitar's own, as if he crouched behind for shelter. He was skinny, the plain black T-shirt he wore engulfing his shoulders, far removed from the pictures she found in her parents' basement where he looked strong and stocky. She stared into his blue eyes, the same, but with hollowed skin surrounding them. He smiled, putting on a brave face, but he looked sick, the cancer Alice read about in the autopsy already turning his body against him.

She unfolded the yellowed paper that was behind the photo in the envelope. The same large script that decorated the front of the envelope covered her mother's letter end to end, a neat, loopy, and loose cursive, much different than her mother's tight letters.

Mama,

I think about what you must have thought when you were a newlywed, pregnant with me. Perhaps you walked through the house, rubbing your stomach and basking in the glory of God's creation. Perhaps you painted a nursery or watched as someone else did it. Perhaps Richard was even happy, thinking of his coming son—of the baseballs they'd throw, of the driving lessons he would someday give him and the company he would pass on, like his old man, of the day they would drink his first legal beer at a bar, toasting glasses and joking about women.

Then, I came along of course and fucked everything up. For both of you.

Even now, thinking about the call that will come to the

house, how you'll get the news of my death, I'm happy, thinking of his reaction. Will he feel responsible? Or will he thank God the great scar on the Tate family has finally been erased? Will he cry? Comfort you or leave for Memphis, slamming the door behind him, like usual?

I digress.

What I wrote to say is this—I'm sorry. When I ran away, I was ashamed, of the person I was already and the person I was becoming. I knew I had to get away from it all. Leaving you and Alice was a cost I didn't want to bear, damage I didn't want to inflict, but when I walked out onto the beach that night, it had seemed so temporary, and I never imagined I wouldn't see you again.

I called, waiting to hear how much everyone missed me, waiting to hear that I had won, shown Richard a lesson that I could be on my own, that he needed me. When you picked up the phone that day, I expected to hang up like normal, to wait until you or Alice, or even Richard, said "Hello?" just to hear your voice to tide me over.

Was it my breathing that gave me away? That day, that call, is still one of the darkest days of my life. I've never forgiven myself that because of me, because of looking for me, Alice was put in danger. Perhaps you don't remember, but you yelled that I had ruined everything, that I should stay away and go if I was going to go, that it was better for her and better for you. I'll always remember that thwack of the phone as you slammed it down before I thought of something redeeming to say. I don't say that to pile on blame, quite the opposite. You were right.

As the years inched by, I only became more afraid to show

you everything your golden child had become. It was always better to have the weight of your disappointment than to show my scars without shame.

I wish I could go back and explain everything away, but the truth is too much now, so I'll rely on meaningless platitudes, something I know you hate. Can't help it here, though, I'm afraid.

I know you blame me. I'll certainly accept it.

I know you blame yourself, for that call and for whatever else. I won't accept that. Please, allow it to rise out of your own body; let the unseen black fog seep through the air, and I'll swoop down and breathe it in deep. Because I don't blame you, for anything. My cowardly absence has allowed you to carry blame though. That was wrong.

Love,

Robinson

Alice folded the letter delicately, so if any tears escaped, they wouldn't drip on it. Then, she shook her head and sighed. Why did it matter if she damaged the letter? Her mother wouldn't read it. She couldn't understand the message, even if Alice tried to tell her.

Her first thought was of Rob holding the phone after her mother slammed down the receiver. Alice closed her eyes. She saw it so clearly now—her mother trying so hard to get him back had been the thing that kept him away.

Could it be true? A piercing in her chest caused her to slump on the floor.

She was wrong, Rob. It wasn't best for me. You were best for me. Strangely, her next thought was how much her mother loved her. Telling Rob to stay away, worrying so much after that night she ended up on the river, and getting so worked up with anger that she had yelled at Rob, who Alice knew her mother wanted back home more than anything.

What had Maura's "golden child" become, though, that Rob was so afraid of showing?

He had died from an overdose, sure, but could that really be it? Not for the first time, worry about Rob's death filled Alice. Rob clearly felt so much blame and responsibility, for her and for their mother, felt so much disappointment that he was the "scar" on the family.

Did Rob commit suicide? The letter seemed so dark, but surely Rob had some good times in the two decades they'd spent apart. She hoped.

Her chest tightened, too, remembering the anger she'd heaped on him, concentrating as if she could send him messages, as she thought she could as a small child. *This is your fault.* Had part of him heard?

The letter also said that Rob hadn't seen their mother again. But she had tried to find him, something he didn't seem to know about. At least if he did, he didn't let on in the letter. There was one person who would know if they found anything. She took out Jamie's letter and peeled herself off the tile floor.

Reading the letter had hurt her; writing it had no doubt hurt Rob. It showed their mother's own pain. That pain wove their family together, even hundreds of miles apart, across memory and time and death.

Even through it, Alice smiled, because he was the same. The Rob who wrote the letter was *her* Rob. The one she remembered.

ROB'S LOST LETTERS:

Mr. Dylan Barnett
Ms. Lila King
~~Mr. Richard Tate~~
~~Mrs. Maura Tate~~
Mr. James Hudson
Mr. Christopher Smith
Mr. Tyler Wells

CHAPTER ELEVEN

As Alice drove toward the school pickup line, she dialed Jamie.

The phone answered on the first ring. "There you are," he said cheerily. "I was hoping you would call."

She paused, thrown off by his unexpected pleasantry after their argument. Before she remembered the speech she had rehearsed—she understood why he had felt the need to warn her about the autopsy but still didn't agree with his methods—he barreled on.

"I'm sorry about yesterday," Jamie said. "I was completely out of line. I hope you know that I was only angry because I love you like my own daughter. I don't want to put that in jeopardy. You can do whatever you want with the house, and I won't try to interfere. I hope I can still come to Caitlin's play?"

"Of course!"

"I'm so embarrassed for how I acted. I tossed and turned all night, worrying you were mad at me. I didn't even eat breakfast this morning I was so upset."

"It's okay," Alice said, fighting her typical impulse to apologize herself when an apology was given to her. "The house was a surprise for me, too, and we were both…caught off guard."

"Yes, and I'm sure what you found was a shock too. The only reason we decided not to show you the autopsy after Rob died was that we knew it would be too upsetting. I'm sure that was hard for you to see."

"It was." The figure from the autopsy flashed in her mind as she stopped at the light, and she thought back to the hollowed skin around Rob's eyes in the photo from her mother's letter. "But I'm glad I got the chance to see that you and Mama looked for Rob. Thanks for helping her. I'm sure it meant a lot."

"We tried, Lord knows we did. Your mother, well, angels couldn't have done it better."

"And Daddy didn't know?"

She wished, no matter how unlikely, that Jamie would say her father helped, had changed his mind, had proven Rob wrong. If only Rob could have seen their father the night she tripped over him and his bottle of whiskey while sneaking back in the house. He would have understood how much Richard loved him, even if he wasn't always good at showing it.

Jamie sighed.

"I still feel guilty about that, but I can't say no to a woman in distress. She had already talked to Richard about it, and he didn't want to be involved, didn't want her to do anything either, but your mother wouldn't stop. Credit goes to her. It was only a loan from me. I only wish it had ended differently."

"Me too." Ended with Rob coming back to Alice, coming back to the family. Ended with Rob knowing their mother had searched for him, hadn't wanted him to be on his own, had missed him and didn't mean what she had said in rage after Alice ended up in the hospital. If only.

Alice looked at Jamie's letter, where it sat in the passenger seat.

"How did the rest of the day go?" he said. "Find anything else of interest?"

The light changed to green, and she looked away from the letter. There would be a time to give him his letter, to discuss what Rob had written to their parents, but not until she knew what to do with the letters addressed to people she didn't recognize.

"I'm pulling in to pick Robbie up now, but I'll call you later in the week and give you an update on the house. Bye."

"Wait… My offer's still good, if you need it. About cleaning out the house."

The last-ditch offer made her remember the shocked tone of his voice when she caught him with the box. She hung up, wishing she hadn't heard the last part of the call.

As she pulled into the elementary school pickup line, where it already wound out of the school and down the street, the word *loan* stuck out. A loan until after Richard died, when Maura had control of the purse strings absent his precise balancing and calculations. After everything Jamie had done, he deserved that, at least. She made a mental note to make sure her mother remembered to pay Jamie back. With interest.

She unlocked the car, and Robbie climbed in the back seat.

"Where's Buddy?" he asked as he buckled his seat belt without her having to ask, as he had since he was small. He was her little rule follower, so different from his namesake, "the great scar on the Tate family," as Rob had called himself.

"I went to visit Mimi today, so I had to take him back. We'll see him when we get home." She glanced at Robbie in the rearview mirror as she pulled out of the school parking lot. He looked quietly out the window, probably deep in thought about the school day. She didn't question him, but let him sit, allowing her own thoughts to fill the silence.

Growing up before Rob left, Alice had been so much like Robbie, a rule follower, content with silence, quiet at school. But, after he left, she had inched closer and closer to her brother, adopting his world labels, rebelling, sulking, sneaking out to find him, and refusing to take part in any of Maura's activities that she had submitted to with a frown with Rob around. Meanwhile, even separated from her, he had inched closer to Alice, writing his letters, hiding his fears about their mother on the highest shelf in his brain, as he had cautioned Alice not to. By the time he wrote the letters, the siblings seemed more alike than ever, as if opposite magnets drawn together by a force more powerful than either. The knowledge, although sad, made Alice smile, to think that she'd had an effect on Rob, even apart, as he had on her.

A few hours later, Alice shifted from one uncomfortable black heel to the other on the front porch of the Welshes' stone mansion. She was about to fish her mother's letter from her bag to read it again when the new Mrs. Welsh came to the door. Kayla opened her mouth in a wide smile and waved frantically with one hand as Alice approached the door. Alice waved back, returning the exaggerated smile and the jerky motion with her hand.

"How are you?" Kayla leaned in and touched her cheek to Alice's. "We were afraid we'd have to start without you!"

"Sorry, the sitter was late." Alice stepped into the oversize foyer.

"Can I take your bag?"

"Nope! No...I've got it." Alice swung the bag behind her back. Kayla narrowed her eyes in confusion at her and the bag.

"Thanks though." Alice smiled.

As they passed the stairs to the basement on their way to the kitchen, Alice heard the television and the laughter of Walker and Kayla's husband, Mark, Walker's best friend. They had met in undergrad at Emory and remained close.

"I think we're about twenty minutes away from dinner. The chicken's almost done." Kayla peeked nervously at the food in the oven. This was the first get-together at her house since Mark married Kayla, the twenty-seven-year-old fitness trainer he had run off with. Alice had been friends with his first wife, Helen, but after the divorce she moved to North Carolina with the kids to be near her parents.

As Alice watched Kayla pour wine into the newly mono-grammed glasses, she thought she should help toss the salad or set the table, as she normally would. But she wanted to talk to Mark about the X-rays. After she thanked Kayla for the wine, Alice disappeared down to the basement. She heard Kayla ask how much butter Walker liked on his lima beans as she descended the stairs but didn't turn around.

"Lady on the premises!" Mark called. He beat his hands on the wooden bar like a drumroll. Walker turned from the couch in the other room and raised a vintage whiskey glass in greeting as he watched her hug Mark.

They talked about the kids briefly, and how Mark's were adjusting to the new school—"They're fighters, I'm telling you"—before Alice asked if she could get his opinion on something. She gestured toward the now-empty playroom next door. He nodded and followed her.

"I know you're not this type of doctor, but I was wondering if you could look at these." Alice pulled the X-rays from her bag.

"Hmm. What'da we have here?" he said. He glanced at them for a moment. "You stealing people's medical records?" He laughed, but her cheeks flushed.

"No, um. They're my brother's, I think."

"Oh." He studied her for a second as he took a pair of reading glasses from the pocket of his starched shirt. In the other room, Walker said "You've got to be kidding me!" at the TV.

Mark held the black sheets to the light. Alice stared at each one as he did, trying to see what he saw.

"You know, I'm an anesthesiologist." He looked at her and she nodded. "But I'd say these indicate a pretty advanced stage of cancer. You can see it here," he said, running his finger over the blotches on the black. "In the lungs and spreading into other areas. I can't remember... Is that what he died from?"

"I'm not sure." She glanced at Walker looking at the TV and felt Mark's eyes on her. "I also have this." Alice retrieved the autopsy report from her bag.

He whistled as he read the numbers on the blood analysis chart. "What?"

"There's a lot in his system."

"Could that be the normal dose, if someone was...if someone was terminal?" She tried to remain distant, imagining herself as a doctor on a medical show, asking about a John Doe patient.

"The opioid could be from a legal prescription of pain medication. It's likely he would be prescribed that if his cancer was advanced. But the amount in his blood here is way over the legal dose. About four times more." He looked at her. "Combined with alcohol and a half a bottle of Tylenol, could be a lethal."

Mark was looking at her, studying her facial expressions with too much interest. She rushed to fill in the silence.

"Clark State." She pointed to the name and address on the X-rays. "Do you know any doctors who work there? Is it a good hospital?"

His brow furrowed, then he shook his head no.

"Clark State *prison*," he said. "Not hospital. One of my buddies volunteers there. They always need medical help."

Every muscle in her body went rigid.

A *prison*.

Rob was in prison.

"You okay?" Mark touched her arm.

She waved him away, unable to form words.

The intercom crackled, and Kayla's voice rang out in her singsong: "Dinner's ready, darlin'."

Mark flashed Alice a pitying smile and called Walker to come upstairs.

The dining room was freshly painted, a color so dark it looked black, with a large gold mirror hung above a china cabinet. Kayla and Mark sat at opposite ends of a long iron table with Alice and Walker on either side in monogrammed gold and maroon velvet chairs. Something about all the empty chairs and staring at herself in the mirror doubled Alice's loneliness.

As Kayla droned on about the table and the house, Alice tried to put together all the pieces—the cancer, the drugs, the amount, what she heard from her parents at the time, the letters meant for her mother and father...her brother behind bars. True, Rob had an intensity to him, even as a child, an affinity for disobeying the rules, but she didn't believe him capable of doing something truly terrible.

Walker stared at his dessert knife, brooding. He had been happy this morning when she said she planned to go to the Center instead of the house. But she could tell from watching his shoulder blades while she climbed the stairs behind him that he'd listened to more of her conversation with Mark than she thought.

"So, I called them," Kayla said. "I called them and got some guy in India—you know how it is—and I said, 'Let me talk to your manager,' and he put me on hold and someone else picked up and I explained the situation, that we were meant to have a dinner party here this week, and if they didn't get this table here by then, they might as well cancel the order, and not only that, but that I had a three-million-dollar house to fill and I would never order from them again unless they got that table here!"

Mark erupted in laughter. "Look at this girl. Knows how to get what she wants, that's for sure."

Walker chuckled.

"Alice, I don't know how you do it," Kayla said, and Alice whipped a bit too fast back to the conversation.

"Do what?"

Kayla spread her arms, gesturing to the expanse of stuff and house and space around them. Alice tried to focus on her, but a vision of the dining room as it had been before distracted her, the floral wallpaper with those blue jays on it halfway up, and below, the cream walls smudged from the hands of Caitlin and Robbie and Helen's three children, playing and running, happy. Exactly the childhood she'd wanted for her children, the one that had been taken from her. Now though, with Helen and Mark's divorce, the house was quiet; the water glasses, crystal.

"I feel like I'm working three full-time jobs decorating this house. I'm working with a designer, but even then, there's so much to do. On top of that, cleaning, cooking, grocery shopping—we have people helping, but the agency sends people who've never done this before. They have to be watched so closely, you know. And trying to meet our new neighbors, go to Women's Club events. I'm trying to learn to golf so Mark and I can play. And to think what it'll be like when we start having kids."

Walker wouldn't want more kids with Brittani, Alice dared to hope. Their screaming matches over the shots, the hormones, the cost of multiple rounds of IVF were the only time in their marriage they had been willing to come at each other, instead of retreat to separate corners. If he hadn't wanted that, surely he wouldn't want another baby at his age, but then again, that was with Alice and her misshapen uterus, not with Brittani's likely perfect one and fresh eggs. She pushed the capers off her chicken.

Kayla pursed her lips into an air-kiss to Mark across the table, and he returned it.

"And you, on top of all that, with two kids and volunteering with those schools at the lake, it's so sweet."

Walker gave Alice a look as if to say, *I dare you.* But the dinner was bad enough already without another fight about how what started as a "hobby," alongside her "most important job" as a mom, had become a full-fledged career, with employees, a seven-figure budget, and partnerships with universities. She didn't correct Kayla.

"I know how you feel." Alice took a long sip of her wine. "It's a lot."

Alice pushed the thoughts of X-rays and prison and children out of her mind and listened closely so she could remember what Kayla said; she wanted to tell it to Meredith later. Any interaction could be deemed worth it if Alice laughed about it with Meredith afterward.

"I try to talk to my friends, but they don't understand. They do their jobs and they're done, and they go to bars or to eat out or whatever. They don't know what it's like managing a house, you know?"

"That must be hard," Alice said. She did the math in her head—calculating how much older she was than Kayla. It felt like several generations. But really, it was nothing to do with age. Alice had heard this conversation dozens of times at the Women's Club events she sometimes convinced herself to attend to make connections with new donors for the Center.

"And on top of that"—everyone turned to Walker as he joined the conversation—"she has a new project too. Why don't you tell them about your little project, sweetheart? I'm sure Kayla would love to hear about it."

How many drinks had he had? Alice tried to place his slurring, almost satirical tone on a spectrum she'd come to know well since Robbie entered school and Caitlin began high school. Ten? Twelve?

"Oh yes! I would *love* to hear about it," Kayla said.

"Well, it's a genealogy project," Alice said. Walker let out a "Ha!"

"I wish I had time to do that. My mother did a big project about five years ago. She went all around the country to local libraries and courthouses. One of my ancestors is a Native American princess. You wouldn't know it, of course, with how pale I can get," Kayla said.

"My father sent off for military records when I was young too," Mark said. "Found out one of our ancestors was a 'damn Yankee'! I swear, I didn't even know 'damn Yankee' was two words till I was about fourteen."

Kayla and Mark laughed together, while Alice stared and Walker brooded.

"What are you finding, Alice?" Kayla said.

"I've just started really. I'm in the documents phase right now, mainly gathering pictures and records in my parents' house."

"Exciting," Kayla said.

"You know what else is exciting?" Walker said with exaggerated enthusiasm. "Alice thinks we should let Caitlin apply to *New York* University for college!"

Kayla looked at Mark, questioning, as Walker muttered "I'm done" and pushed away his plate. He disappeared back to the kitchen. Alice heard the jingle of his keys and shot Mark a look. He stood up to follow Walker.

"Do you think it was the chicken?" Kayla said.

Alice didn't answer.

She looked at herself in the mirror, hair down and curled like Walker liked, her lips outlined in red lip liner and filled in with red lipstick, all in an effort to erase last night's tension, to keep things calm a little longer. She hadn't dressed up this much since the last function she attended with Walker. She felt unlike herself, like someone else inhabited her body and said things like "bless his heart!"

She was a liar—and had always been—with Walker, from their first date. Rob and Jake had hollowed her out, and Walker had met merely the shell left behind. Although the shell was only inches deep, he had never thought or cared to question what it had held before.

Her children, however, didn't deny who they were. Caitlin's personality had surprised Alice, that always-questioning girl, a tomboy in her youth, directing boys and girls in play as she did now at the high school. How did she raise such a child, so willing to buck convention, when Alice's habit was being quiet and doing what was expected? She figured it was random—nature, not nurture—but then with Robbie, it had happened again. She was raising a quiet, contemplative boy who seemed to ignore the pressure to fit in, even from his father, a boy who was happy to slump and drag behind his team members in the four organized sports teams in which Walker enrolled him each year.

Her children gave Alice the courage to question her own choices, so slowly she had let the foundation of her marriage crack. Through the cracks, her real self, the one she had buried after Rob and Jake, came through. Inch by inch, Walker and Alice stepped apart and Alice stepped closer to herself.

That's why she didn't blame him for the texts, not really. Finding them was almost a relief, to know that he felt the distance between them too. That he cared enough to do *something*; it was more than she could say for herself.

But she was doing something now, was untangling her

mistakes and the pain she had put off with Rob, daring to relive the choices she had made and, for the first time, admit why.

––––––––––––––––

Alice said goodbye and thank you again to Kayla and left the house, as she heard Mark reassuring Kayla that she hadn't done anything wrong and that Walker "was having a hard time at work." Alice opened the door to her car. Walker slumped in the passenger seat with his head resting against the window. She decided to let him figure out how to get his own car home in the morning.

Walker looked up as she slid into the driver's seat. She started the car, and Walker laid his head back on the headrest and closed his eyes halfway.

She drove in silence to the end of the Welshes' street and took the left onto the parkway that led to her neighborhood. The route felt so empty without kids' chatter in the back seat and that old country song Walker liked to sing with them after a few beers.

"If you let her go to New York…" Walker lifted his head off the headrest and turned toward her. "If we let her go to New York, she won't come back."

Alice stared straight ahead at the road, empty except for one truck in front of her—a teenage couple huddled together while the boy gunned it at every light, probably trying to make curfew. She stopped at a red light.

"I don't know if that's true."

"It's true," Walker said. "You know she'll like it better there. You know. She won't come back. She'll call you, but she won't call me. She'll be gone."

He slurred his last words slightly: "You know. Let's just make her stay, keep her here."

Walker laid his head on the cool material of the seat belt, which fell an inch, then locked itself and he rested his head there, letting it sway with her turns.

She watched him at the next red light as his breathing slowed and his face relaxed. She longed to teach him the lesson he hadn't yet learned, the one she knew all too well: You can't make someone stay if they don't want to. Even your child. Your brother. Your friends.

She reached a hand to run through his soft brown hair with the slight curl at the end that Robbie had inherited. The light turned green, and she let her hand drop.

CHAPTER TWELVE

Robbie was asleep, and Walker ambled to the bedroom, leaving Alice to pay the babysitter and turn off the house's many lights. After, she sat on the family-room couch in the dark and stared at the black television. She didn't turn it on, but let the thoughts in her head fight with one another. Even with last night's lack of sleep, she didn't feel ready to go to bed.

"Come on," she said to Buddy, and he sprung from where he had laid his head in her lap and followed her to the garage. She opened her car's passenger door and he climbed in.

Alice let the full moon guide them to the little pond by their house, the same one where Walker had lost thousands of golf balls over the almost twenty years they had lived here. A few minutes later, Alice sat on the dock, barefoot, and listened to the eerie quiet, interrupted only by splashes in the water and the sound of Buddy sniffing in the grass behind her.

She fished in her backpack for the picture of Jake, realizing then why she had brought it. She let her head rest on the dock's rough boards. The moonlight lit the faces in the photo, but her eyes still squinted to make out the details: the mud on their clothes, the garden behind them where they had been planting vegetables that would be used at the on-campus day care.

The photo showed one of the last times she'd seen Jake, only days before she had dropped him at the airport.

She remembered how they had woken up in his apartment, like they had so many times over the last two-and-a-half years, how they'd dotted each other's faces with sunscreen and spent a few quiet hours digging in the dirt. Later, they'd ended up back in his apartment, where they'd soaped the caked-on dirt from each other's bodies. The urgency of his kiss was the only betrayal of what the week would bring.

While Alice finished her senior year, Jake would spend a year in Ecuador, implementing a professor's research on the impact of agricultural-based interventions on community engagement, which he had already spent the year after his own graduation working on in Athens as a research assistant.

"We'll only be apart nine months," he said, standing with her at the airport gate a few days later. "I'm going to find the best apartment, with a view of the beach." They planned for her to come to Ecuador after she graduated, to be with him for a few months until the research ended.

Throughout the next months, Jake's letters glowed with the excitement of another continent. He wrote stories in his tiny, slanted script detailing the generosity of the community, about once-hungry children who kicked soccer balls with him, about a baby cow he nursed back to health and his adventures traveling South America with members of the research group. He sent a whole letter about a trip to the Galapagos Islands, which inspired him to get a tattoo of a tortoise. The letter included a picture of it—a large thing that wrapped around his right calf, its shell colored with the yellow, blue, and red of the Ecuadorian flag.

The letters became a war inside Alice, splashed on the page.

As she read them at the lab desk where she examined plants under a microscope with only the fluorescents' humming noisily above her for company, Alice fell more in love with him. Her boyfriend *cared* about people, spent months helping create something, was adventurous enough to permanently ink his body. Someone Rob would like.

When she wrote back, though, she struggled to imagine herself in the country Jake called "the most beautiful place I've ever seen," rather than in the lab, with her plants, near Meredith and the rest of her friends and everything familiar. She didn't want to write that latent anxiety had begun to tick in the back of her brain. She didn't want to explain how that blow to the head when she ran away in the canoe had lodged it in, how it haunted her whenever she stepped off her parents' plan for her life.

Instead, she wrote about the conference prizes she won for her research on the evolution of sunflower species, about what Meredith and the rest of their friends planned for after graduation, about how nights over a few beers became easily sentimental as graduation neared, as life reared up to fling everyone to different corners of the earth.

As the date for graduation came closer, Alice counted the weeks until she would fly to Ecuador and see Jake, until everything would be right, feel right, when they were together again. She was counting on it. She pictured it in her mind to steady herself—her getting off the plane in Ecuador, a well-tanned Jake picking her up in a dirty Jeep Wrangler, a little box in his pocket that would assuage her fears, a far-off gem she'd never heard of, that he purchased from a healer promising a long, happy marriage. Never mind her mother's dream of Mr. Right and her own dream never to fulfill it.

She imagined how they would spend a perfect summer together at the beach and white-water rafting through the Amazon, then fly back together, holding hands the whole way, choose a graduate school together, maybe out west where Jake was from. He would like that. They'd find Rob. Then, they'd all three be together, be happy.

One night, two months before she was set to leave, she was walking back from a friend's house downtown when she felt someone staring at her. The streets were emptier than normal. It was bad weather, and still early, and most of the students were napping before the night's festivities. She turned to the left, acting as if she were adjusting her backpack strap, to see if he was friend or foe. When she looked, though, her brow furrowed in confusion, and she found herself staring. A man, older than most of the college crowd, stood on the next street. He wore a gray band tee that blended into the drizzly sky. His dirty-blond hair was shaggy, too long, and looked like it needed to be washed.

"Rob?"

She crossed the street, accidentally stepping in front of a car.

The driver slammed on his horn, and she turned to look at the sedan as it stopped inches from her. When she looked back to the sidewalk, her heart racing, she could only see the blur of the man's high-tops as he rounded the street corner.

She tucked her elbows and raised her knees high as her legs pumped hard, trying to chase after him. He turned down an alley. Seconds later, she skidded around the same corner, hydroplaning with her sneakers on the wet sidewalk. It was empty.

She walked back to her apartment, lost in thought: *Could it really have been him?* As she went over every millisecond in her head, she grew more sure that he was here to find her, to undo his past mistakes, to beg her forgiveness for leaving her alone in that terrible house.

She went back to the street corner at different times, looking for the man in the gray band shirt. But he wasn't there.

A week went by, until 8:00 p.m., the night Jake promised to call. She grabbed the phone on the first ring.

"Jake?"

"It's great to hear your voice."

"I know calls are expensive." He had only called a dozen times since he left. "And that this call is to book my flight to Ecuador, so I want to get it out of the way that I can't come right now."

"What? Why? Did you not tell your parents yet?" She hadn't, but that was secondary.

"It's Rob. I think I saw him." Talking as fast as she could, she told Jake about the man she saw downtown, how she had chased after him and how he had disappeared. She knew Jake would understand. "I have to stay, so he knows where I am. So he can find me."

"Al... Al..." He stuttered, like he did the rare times he was really scared, but hearing Rob's nickname for her only made Alice more confident in her decision. "How do you even know it was him? It could've been anyone!"

"But he *ran*."

"Maybe he ran because there was a strange girl chasing him!"

"No, that's not... No. If your fellowship isn't over after I talk to Rob, I'll come then. Otherwise, I'll see you in August. It's not much longer anyway. We'll be fine."

Jake sighed. "Alice, they offered me a permanent position: director of sustainability. I'll be here for two years, maybe three. Help get an infrastructure in the local communities. They need me."

Alice felt like she was choking on her tongue. She simultaneously couldn't breathe and forgot how to talk. He wouldn't say yes, not without talking to her. Right?

"I know you're going to love it here! They need a research assistant to gather water samples and said you can do it. The apartment is perfect."

Alice's vision of herself in the airport, the ring, grad school out west, it all poofed in her head, leaving only blankness, a rootless uncertainty that lasted years rather than the blip of a single summer. She paced with the phone still in her hand, the cord trailing her like a leash.

"Alice? Are you there?"

Was she? She felt empty. The wind whooshed through her chest. Her body was merely an outline of matter, hollow in the middle.

"Yes," she managed to croak. She sounded like a demented frog. "I can't leave! Tell them no, tell them you have to come back. Tell them something came up."

"I've been working toward this for years. This is a big deal. You should be happy for me!"

"I can't come to Ecuador for three years." Silent tears raced down her cheeks and fell onto her T-shirt. "What about Meredith? What about my parents? What about grad school? What about finding Rob, like you said?"

What about me? she thought.

"I promise, when it's up, we'll come back. We'll find Rob,

like we planned, we'll move anywhere you want, go to any grad school, we can even live with Rob if you want to!"

"I. Can't. Come," she said through tears.

They went back and forth like that, yelling at each other, apologizing, arguing, until Alice heard knocks in the background. She pictured Jake sitting in a little phone booth, a line of men knocking against the glass.

"Alice, I have to go now. I love you."

"How can you *say* that? Don't say that!"

After the line went dead, she threw the phone against the wall, drank half a bottle of rum and crawled into Meredith's bed. She didn't wake up Meredith, but instead watched each second tick on Meredith's Marilyn Monroe clock. With each, she became less sure it was Rob that day.

Tick.

She had thrown away her relationship with Jake over a mirage, a hallucination.

Tick.

She was mad. Mad at Rob. Mad that he left. Mad that he didn't come back for her, that he never would.

Tick.

Mad that he didn't *want* to see her, because if she knew anything about Rob, it was that he *always* did exactly what he wanted.

Tick.

Mad that her mother was right that day when she screamed, "Then where is he?"

Tick.

He was off, having the time of his life, like he planned, leaving

Alice to torch her own, over and over, trying to find him. Each drop of resentment she amassed for Rob, she drained from Jake, until she knew he had always been too good for her.

Tick.

It was good that he figured out who she really was now, because he never would've been happy with her anyway, like Rob wasn't happy at home with her. Jake would have left too.

Tick.

Then, blank.

Alice sank into her sadness and shame. She remembered nothing tangible from that month, only knew that she became a feral thing, animalistic, like a neighbor's cat that was so bent on its own destruction, it would attack its tail like a predator, causing open sores.

Alice's next memory was several weeks later, when she woke up to Meredith yelling at her. That morning, Alice remembered with perfect clarity.

"Get up!" Meredith had yelled. She shoved Alice into the shower with her clothes on. The cold water felt like darts that somehow all hit Alice in the temples.

"Let me out!" Alice screamed. She jumped to each side, attempting to step out, but Meredith blocked her. They screamed at each other like that, both wet, both breathing heavily.

"Do you *know* what happened last night?" Meredith yelled. Something Alice had never seen burst inside her. Meredith cried openly, not bothering to hide her tears as Alice would. "Some guys I don't even know brought you home passed out at 3:00 a.m. I was so worried about you! I called everyone. I went downtown to try to find you." Meredith sank down next to the toilet and wrapped her arms around her legs. "I can't handle this anymore."

Alice turned off the faucet and stepped out, soaking with the frigid water. Meredith handed her a towel.

"Just *enough*. Enough! Okay?" Red from crying ringed Meredith's dark-brown eyes.

Alice nodded. Seeing her friend so broken pieced something back together in Alice. It *was* enough.

Later, when Alice emerged from the bathroom in her robe, Meredith had a cup of coffee, two Advils, and the faculty phone book waiting for her. She pointed to the book and ordered, "Beg. We're walking across that stage together," then disappeared into her bedroom. As Alice made the calls, it amazed her how much you could mess up your life in so little time.

She called her professors and worked out makeup assignments. She scheduled meetings with her adviser and the other professors in her major about the future. The director of her lab offered to put in a call to Duke, and two weeks after Meredith's intervention, they were planning a post-graduation trip to the beach. She blinked, and she was at Duke, taking summer classes for her master's program.

By that time, any thoughts of Rob were locked in a box, deep in her brain where she knew it was dangerous to go, so intertwined with her past and her resentment, with Jake and their plans and her life's glaring failures. Meanwhile, her body marched forward with the rest of her mother's plan for her life, like a researcher grabbing for the next hypothesis after her primary one had failed.

A year and a half into her program at Duke, with many more hours logged alone in the lab, a man touched her elbow as she walked out of the graduate library.

"I see you at the library a lot."

She stared at him, confused about whether he was trying to

mug her or ask for directions. He was tall, and her eyes were in line with his Duke Law sweatshirt.

"I'm taking you out this Friday. I'll pick you up in front of the library."

"Oh, I…" Alice stammered, without forming a complete thought.

"Alice, right? My buddy's girlfriend lives down the hall from you. It's Walker, by the way," he said and turned, jogging off with his bag over his shoulder.

She showed up at the library as instructed to find his polished BMW, the type that would have made her mother proud. Sitting in the front seat as he drove, Alice allowed her brain to switch to autopilot.

At the restaurant, she sipped the wine he ordered and nibbled on her salad, exactly as she knew she was supposed to. When he asked her a question, she found the words—her mother's words—effortlessly on her lips. And when he poured more wine in her glass and asked casually, "So, do you have any siblings?" it felt like the most natural thing to say, "One brother. We're not close." It felt so easy to lock the box in her mind that she had packed when she left UGA, to split herself forever into two Alices, and to exist only as the one her mother had nurtured for decades. It felt so right to tell the truth to Walker and to herself: *My brother and I aren't close. We're nothing but strangers now.*

After reading her mother's letter, though, Alice longed to reach into that moment to say *He remembers you. He believes he's doing what's best for you.* Would that knowledge have changed what happened next?

The young Alice would never have been able to grab the perfect dress for visiting Walker's parents in Birmingham without even trying it on. This Alice chatted mindlessly with the girl-friends as Walker smoked cigars on the porch with his friends, chuckling along when one of the women followed a complaint with "but that's our boys for ya." This new Alice allowed herself to be absorbed by Walker because even though she knew she would never love him with her whole self as she had with Jake, she knew her heart would never again be broken.

She wouldn't repeat her past mistakes. Walker was safe. He would never have the same power that Rob had, the same authorization Jake had to destroy her, to promise her stupid little dreams about Rob that would never come true, then turn on her when she started to believe them.

On the dock, Alice strapped her feet back into the heels she hadn't thought to change out of.

She again pictured Rob, on the other side of the phone call with her mother, when she told him to stay away after Alice came back from the hospital. He had stayed away. She had changed the course of his life, their life together, without even knowing it. And hadn't he done the same—wrenched her off the course of Jake and toward Walker with nothing more than a misplaced doppelgänger?

She remembered how, as a child, one glance at Rob's face could alter her mood for the whole day. The days of his lost-in-space expression, the blank sadness that made her constantly scan the house for anything that might nudge him further down into one of his dark moods. Her own anxiety would build up in her chest, turning over a joke or a story that she prayed would cheer him up. And he threw away his own days at school or the playground with one helpless look from her, rushing to her side.

And even now, he reached out of the grave, calligrapher's pen in hand, into Alice's life, bringing her back with his letters.

She couldn't say she regretted any of it, the haphazard connections, made and missed, that led her to this spot on the pond. Marrying Walker had made her children possible and made the Center possible. For she had only thought of the Center six months into their relationship, when she had dared to dream again. With Walker, her dreams focused on work instead of on rings and weddings and children, as they had with Jake.

She only wondered, if Rob hadn't left or if he'd come back, what would her life—her children, her marriage, her job, her friends, her family—look like? It was a hard question, one that Rob would never be able to ask of his own life and the many directions that never were. If things had been different, if she hadn't gone to the hospital, what *would* he have done? It was only a fluke of timing that he called then. Imagine the call coming a week sooner, Alice safe in her bed. Again, Maura would hear the breathing on the phone, but this time, she would beg him to return, and he would.

Maybe he would be with his family in a house in the suburbs right now, a mama's boy, ever-present at the nursing home, weighed down with his mother's favorite books, teaching Caitlin and Robbie the guitar, laughing on Alice's front porch with her deep into the night.

She could never know.

She put everything in her backpack. As she grabbed her phone, though, she hesitated. She opened the browser and decided to answer the one question she could. She tapped until the letters slowly formed into something she knew. "*J-A-K-E O-C-O-N-N-E-L-L.*"

The circle ran around its loop as the search results loaded painfully slowly. Alice rested her finger on the lock button in case she decided to make the screen go dark. There would probably be nothing. Not everyone was searchable on Google.

The first result was a Facebook profile. She clicked.

His profile picture showed a tanned man sitting on the side of a creek, holding a fishing pole. He wore sunglasses and a hat and had a beard, but she couldn't make out his features with the zoomed-out photo. It was the only picture she could see since they weren't "friends." She clicked "About."

Jake O'Connell. Lives in: New Orleans, Louisiana. A pang hit her chest. New Orleans. Where Rob had died, where the boxes came from. Where Rob's letter to Lila was addressed.

Her eyes skipped over "Works at: Environmental Solutions" and centered on "Relationship Status: Single," and a smile spread on her face before she checked herself. Emboldened, she hit the back button to go to Google and clicked the next result.

"Environmental Solutions" sat in the left-hand corner of the page with a blog reel down the center. She clicked "About Us."

A picture of a man in a suit filled her screen, and her eyes bore into him. He looked different, polished, but she still saw the same playfulness in his deep-brown eyes. In her mind, he remained the twenty-year-old in his muddy Birkenstocks and cargo shorts, but they had both grown up.

Jake O'Connell founded Environmental Solutions in

the wake of Hurricane Katrina to develop solutions to watershed management issues in the Southeast. Drawing on a career of sustainable farming in Ecuador, Jake explores connections between the environment and the people who live there. He works for the people, representing them and the New Orleans environment to lawmakers in Washington, DC.

Alice clicked off the website and went back to the Google results. The next was a news article in the *Times-Picayune*, "Services for Kellen O'Connell."

A bar appeared at the top of her screen. A text from Walker: Qhere arw yiu???

She ignored it and waited for the website to load.

Kellen O'Connell was a happy toddler, his parents said, despite his challenges. Jake and Christie knew their son had a rare disease when he was six months old. They are both genetic carriers for an infant lung disease that affects about eight babies born in the United States each year. In lieu of flowers, the couple requests donations to Children's Healthcare of Atlanta.

She closed the browser and called Buddy. The panic of picturing herself in that position caused her heart to thud in her chest.

Took Buddy out. Be back in a second, she texted Walker, and stood to go home.

CHAPTER THIRTEEN

When Alice woke the next morning, Walker had already left, no doubt up from bed in a productivity streak that always followed nights of heavy drinking. He could never sleep past 5:00 a.m. after too many drinks. When they were dating, often after a night out with Walker's friends, Alice would wake to coffee, eggs, bacon, blueberry pancakes, and Walker's tiny kitchen littered with abandoned plastic bags from the twenty-four-hour grocery store.

This morning, though, she climbed out of bed and circled the main floor once, listening for any stirring in the house with her shoulders tense around her ears. Hearing nothing, she continued toward the kitchen where she expected to find Walker at the coffee maker. She brainstormed justifications and arguments, accusations and reactions to last night as she went. Instead, she noticed his running shoes gone from their place in the front hall, next to the muddy heels she'd worn last night to the dock. She found her phone in its normal charging spot with a text from Walker: Ran to Mark's to get car, then headed early to the office. Her shoulders relaxed.

She retrieved her backpack from the car and quickly, before she lost her nerve, flipped through the five remaining letters to find the closest address. She punched it into her phone's GPS. As she expected, it wasn't far away. If she hurried, she could probably get there and back in time for her appointment to pick up her mother's coat at Macy's.

After seeing Robbie and Caitlin off to school, including a promise that Alice would come pick up Caitlin before she went to the Fur Vault—"I can make time for something as crazy as *that*," her busy daughter said—Alice pulled on jeans, brushed her teeth, washed her face, and threw her hair up in a ponytail. In ten minutes, she had climbed in the car with Buddy in the passenger seat, a to-go coffee in the cup holder, and the letter addressed in her brother's cursive to Dylan Barnett in her lap.

Twelve turns and thirty-nine minutes later, the five-lane road whittled to four, then three, then two, until Alice's car kicked up gravel on a dirt road. The GPS remarked, "Your destination is on the right." Alice drove past a white ranch-style house next to a gas station. She inched her Prius up to the curb and scanned the house's three windows for life. A television glowed in the right window. Buddy eyed the house suspiciously before lying back down next to her. For the first time this morning, she allowed herself to question the wisdom of the trip: Were these people murderers? What if Dylan didn't live here anymore?

She glanced at the unopened letter in her lap. Mail fraud or not, it felt like an invasion of privacy to rip the delicate cream paper and the melted red of the fancy seal.

Alice looked at the house again as a truck pulled up behind her. An orange and blue Fisher-Price slide, a little Flintstone-style car with an orange roof, and about ten other toys littered the house's overgrown lawn. Surely, she wasn't in danger if there were children in the house.

The truck honked, and she turned down the next street to

park. She cracked the window and told Buddy to "stay." When she reached the black wooden door, she stopped. What to do now? Ring the doorbell? Knock? Leave the letter? No, that would defeat the purpose of coming. She wanted to talk.

She knocked on the door and stood back. She moved her wedding band up and down as she waited for the door to be answered. Nothing. The television blared what sounded like cartoons through the door. She pounded the door with a closed fist.

The television muted.

She fumbled for the letter as a man opened the door. He wore a white undershirt, carpenter jeans, and a five-year-old child in a princess nightgown around his thigh. Alice estimated the man to be about her age, perhaps a few years younger. His hairline receded slightly, but he had a friendly face. He began to ask "How may I—" then stopped. The man, with the girl standing on one of his booted feet, took a few steps backward, clearing the way for Alice to enter the house.

"Sorry to bother you," Alice began. "I'm—"

"I know who you are."

Alice looked at the girl for confirmation of some sort, but she only stared up at the visitor with big green eyes.

"Rob's sister, right?"

Alice smiled. Dylan was still here! She had never thought that she and Rob looked alike, but maybe they did more than she realized. Alice nodded in confirmation, before clearing her throat: "Yes. Alice."

"Dylan," he offered.

He took another step backward and gestured theatrically with his arm for her to "come on in."

She glanced back to the direction of her car, then followed as Dylan walked into the kitchen, where the countertops peeled up in the corners to show the wood underneath.

"Can I get you something? Water? Coffee? A Coke?"

"Sure, coffee," she said. "Thanks." She watched him carefully to try to get a read on the stranger.

"Sit down, sit down!" He pulled a wooden stool from the island and patted it twice. He whispered something to the girl, and she scurried down a hallway between the kitchen and living room, with more toys scattered across the carpet than in the yard. Somewhere down the hall, a door closed.

"I have to admit, I'm surprised to see you." He took a seat on a mismatched stool on the other side of the island.

"Well, the reason I came was to give you this." She slid the letter across the island. He took it, reading the name off the front before he turned it over and ran his hand over the embossed seal. In the back of the house, the sound of cartoons clicked on again.

Recognizing her purpose, Alice continued. "It was in Rob's things when he died. They've been in storage, but when I took everything out, I found letters he wrote. From reading my mother's letter, it looks like they were written shortly before… before he died." She still had trouble admitting her brother was dead, that he was gone forever, as opposed to gone for now, as he had been most of her life.

"Do you mind?" he said, holding up the letter.

She shook her head no.

He slipped his finger under the envelope flap, waiting for the seal to release. He tugged out the folded papers and a photo.

He looked at it, smiled, and set it down on the table in front of him, facedown.

Not wanting to intrude, Alice looked away and sipped the coffee from a mug with a small handprint on the side that dripped paint from its fingers. As Dylan carefully unfolded the letter on the same fancy paper as her mother's and father's, with black cursive writing that bled lightly through to the other side, Alice couldn't help but steal glances at his face and try to guess at the contents. A slight smile, then a crease on the forehead, serious now, then a deep breath in and an exhale. He put the letter back in the envelope as Alice's patience hit an end. The buzz of questions made her feel like she shouldn't drink more coffee.

"Did you read this?"

"No, no, of course not."

"Could've mailed it."

Under the table, her hands returned to her lap and she fiddled with the wedding band.

She waited. He waited.

Finally, Alice said, "I'm hoping to find out more about my brother. We weren't…in touch."

"Oh, well." He flipped the photo over and slid it toward her. "We were friends a long time ago."

Alice's eyes scanned the photo for Rob's presence. She saw him in the middle of the foursome of guys sitting in chairs in a circle, guitar cases, amps, and beer bottles scattered at their feet.

"That's me." He pointed to a younger, skinnier version of himself wearing jeans and a T-shirt. "That's Rob, of course. That's my cousin, Michael." He pointed to a young man who couldn't have been older than Caitlin. He moved his face closer. "You know, I don't really remember who that is," he said of the fourth man in the photo, who looked older than the rest. "Oh, wait, that must be the manager of the 40 Watt."

A jolt went through Alice's body.

"What was his name?" Dylan looked toward a water stain on the top corner of the ceiling. "Leeee… Liam, Luke. I think it started with an L. I think—"

"The 40 Watt in *Athens*?" The college town housing the University of Georgia—and Alice for four years of her life. Her mouth hung open.

Dylan nodded.

"Rob was in Athens." She stared at Dylan, willing him to answer the nonquestion, a classic trick of her mother's that Alice trained herself over the years to counter with silence instead of a fumbled reply.

"Was that a question?" He laughed nervously. "Yeah, we were in Athens together. He was always close to the vest with his personal life, but I assumed you knew. You know what they say about assuming."

Yes, she knew.

Like Alice had assumed that when Rob left the family on that trip to Amelia Island, he had boarded a train to New York or San Francisco or a plane to Berlin or Barcelona or anywhere far away from their parents and her and their life together. Instead, he had been in Athens, had been in prison in Georgia, and eventually had died in New Orleans.

"When?" she managed to force out.

"I got there in ninety-three, I think, and he was there a couple of years before me."

In college, Alice had thought she was going insane, seeing Rob, seeing what she thought was a ghost of her previous life. But the entire time, he had really been there, and Alice had really seen him. She had seen him on the street that day, before she broke up with Jake. She was sure of it now. It wasn't a vision. It was her brother.

"Why?"

She volleyed the question to Dylan, but her brain buzzed ahead of his answer. Rob came to Athens for her, she thought, she hoped. He came when he knew she would be there. It was too coincidental otherwise. But, then why wouldn't he talk to her?

"When I got to Athens, he was deep in the music scene there. He dealt for all the biggies. I guess you could say he used the 40 Watt as a kind of office. My cousin Michael and I, we thought he was the coolest… You know how it is when you're young and stupid."

She had been to the black-floored music club with the colored Christmas lights dangling from the ceiling. It was right downtown, across from campus, near where she had eaten with Meredith yesterday. She could have seen him dozens of times. He could have seen her. He could have seen her when he was there… dealing, her brain finally registered. Dealing drugs. Maybe he'd even gone to prison for it. But that was a line of questioning she wasn't ready for.

"How did you know I was his sister?" Alice said. "Did Rob talk about me?"

"We've met before," he said as if that explained it.

"No, we haven't." Alice looked him up and down. She hadn't seen this man before in her life; she was sure of it. She stood up from the stool, ready to leave if necessary. Dylan was lying and she didn't trust him, even if he was Rob's friend.

"Sit down, I'll prove it to you. In college, you lived in a purple house on Pulaski Street, didn't you?"

She sat back down. Nodded.

"It's innocent, I swear," he said and put his hands up. "I helped Rob bring you back home one night when you weren't doing so hot, to say the least. I don't think I would remember my mother's name in that state."

Alice clenched the mug so hard, she burned her fingertips. Her mind rushed to make the logical connection that would verify what he claimed: that not only had *they* met, but that she had met *Rob*. That he stayed in Athens and knew where she lived for years.

"This must sound crazy," Dylan said.

"What happened?" Alice tried to quiet her mind and concentrate on his voice.

"Michael and I were hanging out and got a call from Rob to come meet him at some place downtown where we knew the frats hung out. He was the kind of guy…" Dylan started to say, then folded his hands and his voice trailed off. "Well, if he called you and said to come somewhere, you went."

"We got there, and he was drinking a beer at the bar, sticking out like a sore thumb. We figured he was dealing something to those rich bast"—he glanced up at her before correcting—"guys. Anyway, we thought he was there meeting someone he needed backup for. But when we got there, he pointed to a booth in the back and said that the girl—you—was his sister and that he wasn't leaving the bar without you."

Alice lifted her hand to give him a hurry-up motion, but

forced herself to listen, stay still, and remember every detail. Her stomach churned from the anxiety, the coffee, and the lack of breakfast.

"Rob, he tells us that he's going to go talk to the assholes you were with, and that no matter what happens, Michael is supposed to take you back to the car. Now, we thought he was being a bit of a drama king—he was always talking like that—so we went along. We all go up to the table, Rob in front, and he says 'Alice?' and you let out kind of a groan. One of the guys with you, he says something like 'What are you doing, man?' and Rob says, 'Nothing, I just came to get my friend.'"

Alice's cheeks burned, and she reached her hand up to fan her face.

She felt the darts of that cold shower and the shame of making Meredith cry. She remembered standing soaked with cold water on her clothes as Meredith yelled about how some random guys had brought Alice home passed out. The only time Alice had ever blacked out in her life, her lowest point after seeing Rob, after the breakup with Jake.

This had to be that night.

"Well, they kind of laughed at that and told him to fuck off. He turned around"—Dylan stood up from his stool and turned, miming the movements—"like he was going to leave, and for a second, I thought it was over, but then he winds back and punches this guy right in the face! Wham!" Dylan's own fist hit his other hand. "I didn't have time to think. Adrenaline kicked in! Oh…sorry, excuse me, didn't mean to get so worked up." He sat back down.

He looked at Alice, and she nodded quickly that it was fine.

She stared at her nails and the white lines usually clouded from the dirt at the Center to try to calm herself down.

"It wasn't much of a fight. We run out basically carrying you after a few punches and get you in the car and Rob's driving. I don't know where we're going, but you fell asleep on Michael's shoulder as soon as we get in the car and it's weirdly quiet. Rob's driving like a madman, fidgeting, turning the radio on and off. He finally parks the car and carries you to the door like a baby."

"We get to the door and knock, and another girl answers, and she starts freaking out, asking us all these questions that we didn't know the answers to and yelling at us like we're the ones that did something wrong. Rob's all clammed up and doesn't answer anything, just walks past her and lays you on the couch and walks back out. Michael, he was always quick on his feet, he starts explaining how he was in one of your classes and that's how we all know each other and that he just saw you and helped you home."

Alice remembered Meredith yelling that Alice should be glad that she had someone in her class to take her home and warning that it may not end up as well next time. Alice had gone to class the next few weeks wondering who they were. Of course, she never found out.

"When we got to the car, we asked Rob what the hell had happened, but he told us to never talk about it again, and...we didn't."

Her toes clenched in her worn Converses. The only time she had talked to her brother since she was eleven and she couldn't remember it because of her own stupidity. As soon as she plucked that thought from the sea of chaos in her mind, every muscle tightened with another line of thought: What the hell was Rob thinking? He had hung out less than a mile from her for years, didn't say anything, and then decided to swoop in to play hero at her worst moment? He had actually *run* from her that day she saw him on the street. She had left Athens at the exact moment he might have contacted her, just as she'd told Jake she wouldn't. She brought the mug to her lips with both hands, but realized the coffee had chilled and set it back on the counter.

"Here!" Dylan said, leaping from his stool. "Let me heat that up for you."

She stared at each of his movements as he whisked the mug away and beeped in the numbers.

When she was in elementary school, Alice had thought Rob could hear her thoughts, that she could summon him by only thinking his name, like a bat call into the dark night for a hero. He always seemed to be there when she needed him. She would think "Rob, I'm bored," in class and there he'd be outside the school window making faces at her through the glass until she laughed, and the teacher screamed, "Robinson Tate! Go back to your classroom *at once!*"

Her mother would be ready to pull the most lace-filled and constricting dress from her closet for church, and Alice would think, "Rob would hate that." He'd barge into her room, singing "I'm ready!" grab her least-hated dress from the closet and throw it at her, and take their mother by the hand with a question about last week's sermon, smirking at Alice out the door as he went. Whenever he materialized, she felt a wave of calm and reassurance. *Rob is here. He'll know what to do.*

Had she needed him that night in Athens, summoned him with the old childhood connection she never felt break? Or was he on the periphery waiting to jump in, waiting for the call he knew would come?

Before the questions could become overwhelming, Dylan sat back down, staring at her as she looked off into the distance, thinking, wondering. She wanted to sprint from the house, go back to her car, and lie with Buddy for the rest of the day. *You wanted to know what happened*, she reminded herself. *You wanted to know who Rob really was.* She cleared her throat.

"Was the letter about all the good times you had at the 40 Watt?"

"Um, no." For once, Dylan was short on words.

"Do you mind if I ask what it was about? It's just, there weren't that many letters, only seven. I'm guessing the people he chose to write to must have been really close to him."

Closer than I was to him, her mind filled in.

"I don't know if I would say that." Dylan looked down and ran his thumb over the letter's seal. "We didn't talk after I left Athens."

"Well, what would you say?"

"It's an apology letter."

"Something to do with a girl?" Alice tried.

He laughed at that. "No."

It was quiet. His head bobbed back and forth, considering.

"I just don't know if I would want my sister to know everything about me."

"Look, I know my brother wasn't perfect. No one is."

"He didn't need to apologize," Dylan said, looking down at the grout in the floor tiles. "Michael, my cousin, we went to Athens together. We didn't have much family. Anyway, he got caught up in some bad stuff. I guess Rob felt responsible for pressuring him, but truth was that if Rob hadn't dealt to him, he would have found it another way, eventually. People like that always find a way."

He stopped talking and cleared his throat.

"How is he now?" Alice said quietly, afraid of the answer.

Dylan ran his hand over the front of his head where there was no longer hair before dropping it back to his side.

"He pops up every once in a while." He looked at Alice with a sympathetic smile, as if she should understand. "I regret it, too, for not watching out for him enough. He was so young, we all were, I guess. But regret, it will eat you up and create a hole you can't fill, you know?"

Alice looked at Dylan for a few seconds before he broke the stare. "I know what you mean."

They sat in silence, both looking at their hands until the creak of a door swinging on the hinge tore through the quiet, and the little girl puttered back into the kitchen.

"Daddy, you promised when SpongeBob came on that we could play. That's what you said." She crossed her arms and pouted, ignoring the visitor.

"Well, munchkin." He scooped her up into his lap and enveloped her in his arms like in protection from a bomb. "I did say that."

He looked back at Alice. The girl, nestled comfortably in her father's arms, stared at Alice as if noticing her for the first time.

"I never got into that stuff," Dylan continued. "Didn't like the feeling. But I got busted on a drunk-driving charge in '96. Ran into a grocery store. Thank God no one was hurt. Rob and everyone else had pretty much scattered by then anyway. It was a wake-up call for me. I got my GED. Went to school after. Got my darling Katherine." He kissed the top of the girl's head and put her back down.

"Go turn it on," he said to her. "I'll be right there. But then you've got to get ready for Granny's and eat lunch." The girl jogged into the living room and jumped up on the couch. She fished for the remote from between the cushions.

Alice stood up. "Thanks for everything, Dylan. You have no idea how much I appreciate it."

"Don't mention it." He started into the living room, but then turned back to her and spoke more quietly. "I know what it's like not to know what happened to someone close. If there's anything else I can help with, let me know." He pulled out a business card from his wallet. A wrench decorated the upper-right corner, above Dylan Barnett and his phone number.

"Thanks," she said. But the little girl dragged her father to the couch by his hand. He stooped to oblige.

Alice let herself out the door and back onto the lawn. Rob *had* been in Athens. Rob *had* come back for her. The undelivered letters burned a hole in her backpack, radiating heat up her back. Like Rob must have felt when that first pill slipped down his throat, she had gotten a taste of something she liked, and the only thing she wanted now was to burn through the rest of her stash.

As soon as she closed the car door, she pulled out her phone and typed in the name from the next letter in her stack—Tyler Wells. The first hit was for a news story.

He was in prison for an armed robbery.

ROB'S LOST LETTERS:

~~Mr. Dylan Barnett~~
Ms. Lila King
~~Mr. Richard Tate~~
~~Mrs. Maura Tate~~
Mr. James Hudson
Mr. Christopher Smith
Mr. Tyler Wells

CHAPTER FOURTEEN

By the time she got back on the highway, Alice needed to speed to get to the high school and pick up Caitlin so they could make their appointment at the Fur Vault. She had spent the last few hours investigating the rest of the letters. Christopher, she couldn't find anything about. When she called the PI's number on the back of the business card, it was disconnected.

But she knew so much more now than she had a few days ago.

Rob had written to Dylan. To Lila, who Alice learned was a singer. And to Tyler. Who was a convicted armed robber. One loop in her mind overshadowed these discoveries though: Rob had been in Athens.

All her new knowledge changed nothing—Rob was still dead. She still didn't have her own letter. Her parents and Jamie had hid things from her. But, somehow, the fact that Rob was in Athens changed everything. Rob hadn't abandoned her, even after their mother had said to stay away. He had helped her. She had really seen him that day on the street.

As silly as it seemed, Rob had earned back her trust, even from the dead. And now she trusted his plan with the letters, trusted she was meant to deliver them. That they wouldn't fail her. That *he* wouldn't fail her. Not again.

I trust you, she had said to herself an hour ago, when she'd

stopped to FedEx a letter to Tyler in prison with the fastest possible shipping, asking to visit him to talk about Rob. *I trust Rob*,
she reminded herself again now, even as the thought that Rob had
hung around with...criminals...sent a chill down her spine.

But then, what did that make Rob?

When she parked at Macy's Fur Vault in Atlanta, Caitlin
hopped out of the car and waited at the door. Alice set her questions aside and fast-walked to keep up with her daughter.

A huge smile lit up Caitlin's features as she threw open the
door with dramatic flair and stomped her combat boots on the
carpeted floor.

The counter and its surrounding decorations were grand, but
not modern. Alice wondered if a lack of renovation or a purpose-
ful decision to stop the aging of the outside world had motivated
the decor choices. An expensive-looking maroon carpet, with
a black design that looked like the patterns on a turtle's shell,
covered all but a foot of the hardwood floors. Uncomfortable-
looking cream couches spread throughout the waiting room with
a few old women on them and one restless young man. In the
corner, an attendant dressed in black manned a rack of furs for
purchase and a full-length mirror. A woman modeled one, not
bothering to look at the price tags. Alice imagined her mother sitting on the couch with a cup of black tea in a bone china teacup.
"Two lemon slices, two tea bags, if it's not too much trouble."

Alice looked at her daughter, standing in the middle of the room,
seemingly scanning each object, cataloging it in her brain. Caitlin
and Rob were so much two sides of the same coin. Both were
slightly detached, in their own universe, and perceptive to a fault.
But while Rob had studied the world, taking note of everything that

didn't meet his expectations, Caitlin studied it as if she were an alien, fascinated by every inefficiency favored by humans. If Rob had been in Athens, could he have been in other areas of her life? Could he have seen Caitlin? How she wished it were true.

"Good afternoon, Mrs...?" the woman behind the counter said, extending her hand for Alice to shake. She wore all black with a severe-looking turtleneck, bright-pink lipstick, and the largest glasses Alice had ever seen. She might be one of the most glamorous women in Georgia, Alice thought. Knowing her mother and her friends, Alice knew a lot of contenders—a type of glamour that had ended with that generation. Alice grew self-conscious of what she was wearing—jeans she purchased at Target and a T-shirt from a "Clean the River" event the Center hosted several years ago.

Alice took the hand but gestured with her other. "Oh, no, I'm...I'm here to pick up my mother's coat."

"That's not a problem. Fill out this form, and we'll get it for you."

Alice looked at the form. Did she know what kind of fur it was or where it was made? How many coats did her mother have here? When was the last time it had been glazed? Alice didn't even know what that word meant, outside the context of doughnuts or paint. They wanted her mother's social security number?

"My mother's very sick. I'm not sure about some of this." The woman shrugged and waved Alice to the couch.

Caitlin materialized next to Alice. "I'd love to ask you some questions," she said, pen posed on a notebook she produced from her bag.

The woman looked back at Alice with wide eyes, as if she had never seen anyone so young in the Fur Vault and feared she might be an animal-rights protester.

"How old are you, dear?" The woman behind the counter smiled at Caitlin as if she were six.

Caitlin mimicked the woman's sweetness and said, "How old are *you?*"

"You can go ahead, ma'am," Alice said to the woman in line behind them, and tugged Caitlin to the couches.

They sat down. Alice filled out the paperwork, while Caitlin sat, pen poised over her notebook but writing nothing. When Alice placed the half-complete paperwork on the counter, the woman didn't move toward it. Alice sat back down and sighed.

They both watched the clipboard, until Caitlin moved to cap her pen and fold back the top of her notebook. "If I get in, I want to go," she said. "I know how Dad is, that he takes time to get used to things. But if I get in, I'm going." She paused and her voice shrank in confidence. "Do you think he'll come around?"

Alice patted her daughter's hand, then put her arm around her and kissed the top of her head like she used to do when the kids were toddlers. "We are so proud of you. Your dad is too. And if NYU is where you want to go, we will find a way to make it work. I promise."

Caitlin's body slumped a little, the question hanging over her now answered. She pulled away and thanked her mother and said, "Love you." Caitlin retrieved her phone from her purse and began typing furiously. No doubt telling the good news to Chelsea, who had already applied early action to Columbia.

"Mrs. Maura Tate?" the attendant called, holding the paperwork and the coat in a black garment bag. She unzipped it for their inspection, and Alice ran her fingers over the soft fur as she had as a child. The coat was beautiful.

Alice folded the papers she apparently needed to send to the insurance company, retrieved a check from her bag to pay the annual storage fee, and started signing the many forms reclaiming responsibility for the coat. With the manager's full attention, Caitlin retrieved the notebook from her bag.

"How many coats do you have stored here?"

"About nine thousand."

"What happens if someone dies and never picks up their coat?"

"We keep it."

"Really! For how long?"

"Forever."

"Really!" Caitlin said without looking up, as she scribbled furiously in her notebook. "But what if someone stops paying?"

"We still keep it. Then, if they ever want to pick it up, they pay the storage fees."

"What's the longest you've had a coat here?"

"Twenty years."

"Whoa! Do you think it will ever be picked up?"

"Eventually. It's much easier for us to contact relatives now, with Facebook. We used to have to run newspaper ads."

Caitlin flipped a page over in her notebook and muttered something unintelligible under her breath.

Alice pushed the finished paperwork toward the woman, who took it and walked away from the counter without glancing back at Caitlin. They turned to leave with Alice carrying the coat. It was much heavier than she remembered.

"What do you think they look like? All those abandoned furs, waiting to be worn, up in that warehouse—the ghosts of Old Atlanta." Caitlin stopped and wrote that in her notebook, before returning it to her purse. She pointed toward the mirrors. "Can I try it on before you bring it back to Mimi?"

Alice held the hanging bag while her daughter slipped into the coat. It was a funny image, her clean face, long wavy hair, and the boots peeking from under the coat. Coats usually weren't that long anymore, and seeing the length of it reminded Alice of a little girl playing dress-up. She laughed, and Caitlin fluffed her hair. She drew the coat around her and turned side to side in the mirror. "Butler, bring me my cigarette case."

Caitlin's hands slipped into the pockets to admire it like that, and she stopped turning. She brought out a piece of paper and inspected it. "Hmm," she said, handing it to her mother and returning to look at herself in the mirror one last time.

Alice took the paper and looked at it. It was a stick-on badge with her mother's picture on it, folded in half and stuck together. On the top, it said *VISITOR* and under that *Clark State Correctional Facility*, the same prison name as on the X-rays.

Blood rushed to Alice's cheeks, and she raised a hand to feel the heat emitting from her forehead. Her mother knew Rob was in prison when he was *there*, not only after he died. She had visited the prison. At *least* once. And she hadn't told Alice.

The date on the badge only deepened the betrayal. In 2005, around when the X-rays were taken. Maybe her mother knew about Rob's illness or went because of it.

But Rob's letter made it sound like they hadn't seen each other again after he left the family.

The visit had to be related to Rob, though, because who else did Maura Tate know in prison?

No one.

CHAPTER FIFTEEN

"Are you insane?" Meredith wanted to know.

A few hours later, after Alice dropped off Caitlin at school and the coat with her mother, who was thankfully asleep, she watched the Breakers in a life-or-death match against the Wolves. Fans screamed from the sidelines, huddled under their blankets. One coach screamed at his players to "HUSTLE!" from the darkness beyond the spotlights. The referee strolled lazily up and down the field as angry fans called her a hack or worse. It was youth soccer, and as always, the stakes were high. The nine-and-under league took no prisoners.

Alice and Meredith briefly halted their conversation to stand and cheer for Robbie as he received the ball at midfield before quickly kicking it out of bounds.

"*I* don't think I'm insane," Alice said.

"Why didn't you Google him? Or ask me to go with you? He could have been a serial killer for all you know. Someone else could have lived there—a demented person."

"I took Buddy!"

"He's quite the guard dog." Buddy looked up from Alice's feet at the mention of his name, yawned once, and fell back asleep.

"Well, nothing bad happened. Dylan was nice. And very helpful."

Meredith gave her the side-eye from the bleacher.

"Okay, you're right," Alice said, caving. "I researched some of the other letters this afternoon anyway. It won't happen again."

"Good. So?"

Alice caught up Meredith on what had happened with Dylan.

"Do you remember that night when they brought me back?"

"It was so long ago," Meredith said. "And I was worried about *you*, not taking in every detail of the guys you were with."

"I know."

"Sorry."

"It's okay."

They both watched Meredith's boyfriend, Christian. He kicked a soccer ball in a corner off the field and dribbled it around some of the siblings on the team, laughing. He saw them watching and waved at Meredith. She smiled and passed Alice the flask with red wine that she had been sipping.

"You know, for the longest time, I thought I was seeing ghosts or hallucinating in Athens," Alice said. "I would think I saw Rob. But he was there the entire time and didn't find me. I don't know why he never talked to me."

"I'm sure it was nothing you did, hon." Meredith put her hand on her friend's back. "And you could have told me. That sounds like a hard secret to carry around."

Alice looked at Buddy sleeping at her feet. She took a breath and worked up the courage to tell Meredith her current secret, about Walker.

"Mere."

She looked at Alice.

"There's something—"

The whistle blew for halftime, and the players half walked, half jogged off the field toward their parents. Alice waved off Meredith, the courage gone.

"Did you see me, Mom? Aunt Meredith! Did you see that?"

Alice reached to brush some dirt off Robbie's face.

"Yes, sweetie. It was amazing."

"When is Dad coming?"

"I think he'll be here soon, okay? I'll check."

She kissed him, and he wiped off his cheek before running back to eat orange slices on the sideline with his team. Although she couldn't hear the speech, the coach walked back and forth in front of his troops, gesturing wildly and clapping his hands at random intervals. Soon the team gathered for the cheer.

Alice texted Walker: It's halftime. Where are you? She stared at the bubble with the little "…" in it that seemed to stretch on for hours. Sometimes, she wondered if he did this maliciously— typing random letters and backspacing to give the appearance of responsiveness.

She clicked her phone screen off and threw it back in her lap.

"I tried the number from the PI's card today too," Alice said.

"And?"

"Disconnected."

The game resumed and immediately the other team scored.

"What about the other letters?"

She filled in Meredith on her research, including her request to visit Tyler in prison.

"Fuck," Meredith said.

Alice shushed her. "We're at a children's soccer match."

"Right, yeah." Meredith glanced at the women next to her. "Sorry. How do you think Rob and Tyler met?"

"Maybe in prison or maybe they knew each other before-hand... I don't know. I called to try to get information about Rob's medical records and what prisons he was in and when, but they wouldn't give me anything. The only proof I have Rob was even in prison is those X-rays."

"Why? You're his sister for fuck's sake."

They watched the soccer team run up and down the field, screaming at one another "Here! Here! Here! I'm open!" then panicking when the ball came to them. Robbie trailed the team as players ran up and down the field, kicking grass as he went.

"Can I try?" Meredith said.

"Can you try *what*?"

"Let me try calling for you."

"They're going to tell you the same thing they told me," Alice said. "They can't release anything without the form, which has to be signed by the person themselves or their designated contact, and it's anyone's guess who that is. It's protocol."

Alice said in her head what she knew Walker's response would be, if she told him: "Your tax dollars at work!"

"Protocol blah, blah, blah." Meredith made a talking motion with her hand. "You know I love you, but maybe a little more drama might help the situation."

After some bargaining on how demanding Meredith would get—Alice had been with her to the Apple Store and didn't want to release that havoc again—Alice handed over the number and Meredith dialed.

"Hello! This is Mrs. Alice Tate Wright. May I ask to whom

I am speaking?" Meredith said into the phone as Walker walked up.

"How's he doing?" Walker pointed to Robbie.

Meredith gestured to a corner away from the bleachers. Alice's stomach lurched, watching her walk away with the phone and free rein to say whatever she wanted. Alice tracked her as she paced, talking, and gesturing with one hand.

Walker waved his hand in front of Alice's face.

"Alice—*hello?*" he said. "I said, 'How's he doing?'"

She looked back to the field. "Fine."

"Has he touched the ball at all? How were his dribbling and his blocking?"

"He had it a couple of times," Alice said. "He looks like he's having fun."

"Great," Walker said, a bit sarcastically, before striding to the other sideline to the team's bench. She watched as he talked with the coach for a few minutes before pacing up and down the sideline along with the team. As usual after a disagreement, neither of them would bring it up, and eventually, the increased tension would stop.

Alice's eyes flicked from Meredith to Walker and back again, each animated in their own way.

She noticed one of the other mothers nodding toward Walker. She held her breath. When she heard "right under her nose," her cheeks reddened. They were talking about her, she knew. Her and Walker.

On the sideline, Walker yelled, "Be aggressive! That's your cover, Robbie!" when a boy from the other team passed the ball a few feet away from him.

The other team's parents clapped when the boy dribbled to the goal and scored. The mother who had been talking about her yelled, "You'll get 'em next time!"

Alice concentrated on the players' movements. The mothers all knew. They must, if she knew. Alice was at the game, dressed, productive, smiling—she didn't want their pity. Yet, she could feel it anyway, beaming from the other side of the bleachers.

Robbie trapped the ball, and with Walker screaming at him to do so, he passed successfully to the forward. The forward scored.

Alice stood up to cheer, and Robbie ran over to the sideline and Walker, who high-fived him with both hands. "That's called an assist!" Walker yelled happily, flashing a thumbs-up to Alice. She could feel the other moms' eyes on her as she gave him a thumbs-up back.

Soon, the game ended. The teams lined up to do high fives and say "Good game."

Alice woke Buddy and gathered her stuff as Walker walked over to her, carrying Robbie's soccer bag.

"Rick scheduled a meeting for tomorrow morning, so I'm going to go to DC tonight instead."

Alice wondered how much Brittani and last night's fight factored into his early departure. But she didn't say anything. There was no point. She looked over her shoulder to see if another mom had heard. "Okay, we'll grab something to eat on the way home then."

Walker said goodbye to Robbie and leaned in to kiss Alice on the cheek before walking in the direction of his Audi at the other end of the field. One of the moms gave her a small wave, and Alice spun around and fast-walked to her own car before she started a conversation. "Come on, hustle," she called to Robbie as he ambled behind her. After hearing what the mothers said behind her back, she didn't want to fake a pleasant conversation. Especially if whatever she said would only be reported to the others via a group message of which she'd been conveniently left off.

"Alice. Aaallliiice!" Meredith sang, jogging over with Alice's phone. Alice jumped. In her rush to avoid the other mothers, she had forgotten about Meredith.

"So, you're right that they wouldn't give me anything without the paperwork," Meredith said, smiling. "But…I got the name of the designated contact. If you talk to him, he can call and get all the information and give it to you."

"Who is it?"

"Someone named Edward Lee Davis," Meredith said, and Alice's face dropped.

"What! What's wrong?"

"Nothing. I, um… I know who that is. We grew up together."

CHAPTER SIXTEEN

The game had been away, on the other side of Atlanta, and as she pulled out of the parking lot, Alice didn't turn toward home, but instead, in the other direction. Walker wouldn't be there to meet them, and she didn't think the address from Christopher Smith's letter was too far. She only wanted to drive by.

"Mom, where are we going?" Robbie said.

"Just a quick detour, but we're going to grab some food first. What do you want?"

"Chick-fil-A?"

"You got it."

Once Robbie had nuggets, fries, and his headphones plugged into a movie, Alice punched the address into her GPS. She was right. It wasn't too far from where the game had been, another thirty miles north.

As she drove, she ate a large portion of waffle fries, licking the grease and salt off her left hand before she returned it to the steering wheel while chanting in her head: *Edward Davis! Edward Davis...EDWARD Davis?*

Maybe Edward didn't know he was Rob's contact. That seemed more plausible than Edward agreeing to it. But even that theory wouldn't explain why Rob would put his name down in the first place.

She didn't know much about her brother's adult life, but she felt sure of this: Edward (never Ed) and Rob had absolutely nothing in common.

But as children, the two of them, along with Alice and Edward's sister, Hayley, had everything in common. They had their car rides, crammed into the back seat, giggling as they double-buckled the seat belts. They had their summers at the river. They had made-up games and songs and families. They were childhood friends, thrust together by a shared street address and eventually pulled apart by all the differences age brings out.

When Rob left, the seams holding his friendship together with Edward had already frayed. Edward had turned into a "suit," having won freshman class president during the school year. Alice and Hayley had little in common by that time either. Alice was determined not to spend any time inside. Hayley was determined not to spend any time outside her Cotillion dresses.

They and their families stayed on Christmas card lists and wedding invitations. Alice still saw Edward every few months because his firm did the accounting for the Center, her mother, and Alice and Walker. Another reason the name surprised Alice. If he did know about Rob, he had kept it a secret for more than a decade, smiling at her with his annoyingly perfect teeth through every interaction.

Her clearest memory with Edward though—the one she thought of every time she went to his office, even during the years when she tried to push all reminders of Rob deep into her stomach and away from her heart—was one day at the river. Nothing that happened that day set it apart from any other summer day with Rob. In fact, it reeked of ordinariness. The day stuck out in Alice's memory because of what happened later.

It was her last clear memory before her life with Rob began to shift. The last summer day she could remember passing with their friends the way they had for years, the way she thought would last forever.

The Last Summer Day began like any other. Maura, Rob, and Alice sat at the table in the breakfast den while their father finished his coffee in his office. Rob mixed his eggs and grits together on his plate into a breakfast mush while Alice pushed her food apart.

Maura nibbled on the last of the five strawberries she ate each morning from a floral teacup and opened her notebook to the ribbon to read the children's vocabulary word for the day. *Capricious, C-A-P-R-I-C-I-O-U-S: adjective. Changing quickly in mood or behavior, based on an idea, desire, etc., that is not possible to predict. Fickle, unpredictable, unsteady, inconsistent.*

The children agreed that they would be home for dinner by sundown. Rob retreated to his bedroom, promising he would meet Alice by the river in a couple of hours. Alice left to retrieve Hayley from down the street, and they rode bikes around the neighborhood's loop, then to the riverbed to skip rocks.

An hour or so later, they heard honking and turned to see Rob at the wheel of Richard's Jeep, a brand her father always bought because it was an "everyman car," the canoe strapped to the top. Edward pumped his fist at the pair from the passenger seat.

"Rob!" Alice screamed in delight. She loved canoeing, but normally, they only went bird-watching with their father on quiet trips or sometimes with Jamie. "What are you doing?"

"I thought I would give you ladies a lift upstream," he said. Two weeks ago—two years before the trip she would never forget—they had returned from their annual trip to Amelia

Island, where the adults had allowed him to drive the car around the small neighborhood.

"What if Daddy finds out?" Alice asked. Hayley stared, wide-eyed and smiling.

Instead of answering, Rob pulled the car onto the dirt and pushed the canoe off the top. It clanked to the ground. As usual, Alice trusted him, believed in his crazy plans and his ability to execute them. At his instruction, they pushed it through the mud to the water, climbed inside, and began paddling to the little island in the middle of the river. While paddling, Rob broke into a chorus of "Jailhouse Rock," his best Elvis imper-sonation. The girls sang along between laughs and splashed their captain during the slow parts. Edward stole nervous glances at the houses on the river.

When the song ended, Edward interrupted the album. "Maybe we should turn back." He nodded toward the approach-ing gray clouds.

Rob pointed the paddle at him, and Edward flinched at the water that flicked off the end: "Are you with us or aren't you?"

Edward nodded.

"Good, Eddie, good," Rob said. They all knew he hated being called anything but Edward, but he simply turned to look at the approaching island. Alice relaxed. The trip and the song resumed.

When they neared the island's shore, the girls jumped out, nearly tipping the canoe, and swam to the island, the cool river water dripping from their hair as they stormed the beach.

"Explorers!" Hayley said, requesting one of their most favorite games.

Rob tied the canoe to one of the trees sticking out of the water and approached the beach, picking up his walking stick, which sat on the beach where they left it from the last trip, as he came.

"You be Robinson this time," he said to Edward.

"Then who are *you?*" Alice said suspiciously. Rob was always the best at being Robinson Crusoe. Duh.

"I'm a cannibal!" he screamed. "And I want to *eat you!*"

Hayley yelped as Rob stalked toward them like a zombie with his arms stretched high like claws.

"Quick, explorers!" Edward said in a stuffy accent. "We must reach camp before he takes us!"

They all ran off, screaming and giggling, into the island's trees, which they knew so well.

When the sun lowered in the sky, Rob and Edward paddled the canoe back. Back on shore, they tried to lift the canoe on top of the car, but they couldn't reach far enough. While pushing, Alice tripped in the mud and scraped her knee on a rock. Blood trickled down her leg. Eventually, with Rob pulling from the top of the car, they secured the canoe and headed home to get showered before their mother's return, laughing at their day of mischief as they climbed the staircase.

When their mother called them for dinner, Alice came down in loose shorts and T-shirt. Her mother was fresh from the beauty parlor. Curls branched from her head like a tree's leaves.

"Good evening, Mama," Alice said.

"Robinson!" Maura called again.

Richard appeared from his office, and all four sat at the table. Out the window, the gray clouds morphed into a vicious southern storm. The summer rain pounded down like a baptism, the thunder boomed and shook the glass in its frame as the window filled with a godly light. Alice watched the storm while Rob successfully defined *capricious*.

She rose to put her dishes in the sink.

"Alice Tate. What is that on your knee?" Maura walked over, bending down to inspect the blood that dripped down Alice's leg like the chips in a game of Plinko. Her mother clucked her tongue.

"It was my fault," Rob said.

Surprised by the lie, Alice's eyes darted to Rob's face. *Rob, don't*, she thought at him, willing him to hear the message.

He refused to look at her, trudging on with his story: "I pushed her, out by the river."

"Robinson!" Maura said, and looked at her husband, shocked. "Did Alice—"

Pop!

Alice saw her father's hand sling across her brother's cheek, dissected each movement of Rob's face as it spun away from her from the force.

"I will *not* raise the type of man to hit a woman. Go upstairs. Now!"

Rob turned to go, his eyes only on Richard as he did, refusing to look at Alice. Her cheeks burned as if she had been slapped. He wouldn't provoke their father so much if he knew that watching him getting slapped was worse punishment than getting slapped herself.

"Come here, sweetheart," Richard said, and she went to him, zombie-like, as if she were underwater, weighed down with the air's new heaviness. He pressed a napkin into the cut. "Did it hurt?"

"We've talked about this," Maura said. "If you keep scraping your knees, they will scar. When you get older and you want to wear a nice cocktail dress, you'll sit down at a dinner party and your knees will be scarred. That would be embarrassing, wouldn't it?"

Richard withdrew the napkin, and Maura walked over to Alice. Her mother's imagined portraits of her later life made Alice wish she would never grow up. She stared at the floor, waiting for the moment when she could follow Rob upstairs.

"Wouldn't it?" her mother said.

"Yes."

"Yes what?" Maura grabbed Alice's chin and tilted it up to look her in the eye. Her mother stared with her crunchy curls, waiting for an answer.

"Yes, ma'am."

"If you can't go down to the river without bloodshed, then maybe you shouldn't go at all. Now, get a Band-Aid for that knee and get ready for bed."

"So unlike him," her mother said as Alice left the room.

An hour or so later, Alice came down to get a glass of water. The dinner plates were cleared and replaced with teacups. Their mother and Rob sat close together, talking about Greek mythology or the symbolism in *Grapes of Wrath* or the etymology of the word *capricious*. Maura barely looked up from her open book as Alice filled her glass and walked out. Rob looked up and winked. She smiled.

By the time the southern storms gained their full force the next year, Rob had retreated deeper into himself, and while Alice could sometimes draw him out, those days at the river were over. And while Alice couldn't see them then, the gray clouds that would drive her brother away just before his sixteenth birthday had already started rolling in over him.

And he'd already begun setting up his poles as if readying to get struck by lightning, just to see how it would feel.

CHAPTER SEVENTEEN

She pulled into a small driveway, and her headlights shined on the sign for "Woodland Cemetery." She checked the address again. It was right. What could that mean?

Alice thought about going in, but the gates looked locked. She glanced behind her. Robbie slept in the back seat with his headphones on. She already felt guilty for bringing her tired child to a cemetery at night (and feeding him fast food), so she wasn't about to leave him in the car while she checked out a creepy graveyard in the dark. As she drove home, she listened to Robbie's soft snores from the back.

When she arrived home, Alice carried Robbie to his room and lay down in her own, the bed now empty with Walker out of town. Instead of searching "Christopher Smith" as she had earlier that day, she tried his name and "Woodland Cemetery." It was a hit, on the records for who was buried on the grounds. So he was in the cemetery after all. And had been since 1997.

Alice went out to get the letter. She opened it carefully, without ripping the paper. It was different though. While on the same type of paper as the other letters, it unfolded to the size of a poster instead of the letter size of the others. A huge decorative cross, done in fountain pen ink like the others, dominated the page.

"What the hell, Rob?" Alice said to no one.

She leaned in to look at it more closely. The strong pen marks without any wispy lines reminded her of the sketches he'd do as a teenager, always without the aid of a pencil. By age twelve, he'd filled an entire book with drawings of Jamie, the only person who'd sit for him more than once. Even Alice had grown tired of constantly being accused of moving, even though she was holding her breath.

She went to her jewelry box and pulled a paper from its bottom drawer, the only relic she had left of Rob, which had escaped her mother's Rob cleanse because it was in Alice's school locker at the time. She liked to look at it in class, instead of paying attention, flipping back and forth between her textbook and Rob's paper.

The drawing looked like her. Even as a child, she knew it did, but something was different in the face, harder. The Alice in Rob's drawing was strong, defiant; her lips full of a skeptical pout, her eyes narrowed.

Looking at it now, it was her expression she noticed. She hadn't looked at the drawing since his funeral, and before that, since leaving UGA for Duke. The remembering always hurt her. But now she wondered why she hadn't taken it out, hadn't framed it, hadn't kept it near always. For Rob had drawn that strength so clearly, reflected back at her, the strength she always thought belonged to him alone. Was it possible he felt the same way, that it belonged to *her* alone? Or did he draw it this way because he knew what would come next?

They had been on their way to Amelia Island when he drew it.

Rob and Alice sat in Savannah, where their mother always forced the family to stop on the way. They had all eaten lunch and bought fudge at River Street Sweets. After giving a time (and a budget) to Maura, Richard disappeared with Jamie. Their mother told Rob and Alice to sit on the pier and wait for her. She handed Alice a sheet of times tables saying that she expected three pages complete before she returned. Rob sat next to her while she filled them out, reading *The Picture of Dorian Gray*, his summer reading book for tenth grade. She remembered that was the book because she would read it over and over again after he left, looking for clues, wondering if it was something in the book that caused him to flee from her. She wondered now why he had been so diligent in reading if he knew he would leave before school began again.

"I *hate* times tables," she had groaned.

"Let's do something else, then."

"But Mama said I have to do these."

He motioned for the paper and she handed it to him. He bit his lip and began filling it in, using blocky letters that looked like hers, instead of the slanted ones he normally used. In ten seconds, he had already done more than she did in the last ten minutes. She looked out at a red-and-white riverboat as it chugged down the river, studying the way the water churned through the paddling wheel.

"Okay, done. I've got a game for you."

She looked at him, smiling. The week had been one of his worst; he barely talked to her on the long drive that morning. The game, the times tables, showed it was over. The trip could return to normal. Everything would be fine now, she had thought then.

He took out a sheet of paper from his school notebook and ripped it in half haphazardly, presenting them both to Alice to choose one, as if it were a cookie they were sharing.

She pointed to the bigger half of paper.

"Interesting choice." *Had she chosen wrong?* "Here's the game.

You draw me, and I'll draw you, then we'll swap, and we can keep
them forever to remember this exact moment."

"I suck at drawing. Why don't you draw us both? It will be better!"

"Because those aren't the rules of the game," he explained,
patiently, firmly. She saw his point. She liked rules.

She took the paper, and he spun around from her, looking right
at her where she couldn't see his paper. She did the same so that
their feet lined up toe to toe, almost touching on the pier's bench.

Although she couldn't remember what her own drawing of
him looked like, she remembered the stress of making it. How
she'd erased and redrawn Rob's eyes, trying to get them right,
trying to make them smart looking, trying to put the feeling that
she got when she looked at him into the drawing, trying to make
him understand, trying to will him to stay happy, to let the rest of
the week with their parents and Jamie progress peacefully.

Even with the erasing, she finished before Rob.

She waited, until finally she got so bored that she picked
the math worksheet back up, working backward through the
problems he solved. Meanwhile, he looked rapidly from her to
the paper, making a stroke or two only every minute. When she
saw her mother approaching, loaded down with shopping bags,
she leaned over to look.

"You can see when I'm done!" he said, teasing.

"Fine!" she said, laughing. "Then you can't see mine either."

"ROBINSON! ALICE!" their mother yelled. "I *know* you can
hear me!"

Rob grabbed Alice's hand to pull her up from the bench, and
they jogged over to their mother, still smiling, and headed back
to the Jeep to continue their trip.

After tucking the drawing safely back inside her jewelry box, Alice returned to bed. Another question she could never ask him.

She picked up Christopher Smith's cross again. It might be another dead end, but she had one last-ditch idea.

She looked at the clock. It wasn't even 10:00 p.m. She found Dylan's card and dialed the number. He answered on the first ring.

"Dylan? It's Alice. From this morning?"

She explained about the letter and asked if he recognized the name.

"Doesn't ring a bell."

Alice leaned her head back and hit it on her bed's wooden headboard. She rubbed the spot that hit.

"Well, thank—" she started to say.

"But, let me ask around a little bit and see if I can find anything else, okay? I want to help you. Why don't you give me a few days, and I'll call you back?"

"Really? That's great!" Alice said. They hung up.

She went to bed feeling hopeful. Things were finally happening. Alice felt like after decades underwater, she was breathing air again.

ROB'S LOST LETTERS:

Mr. ~~Dylan Barnett~~
Ms. Lila King
Mr. ~~Richard Tate~~
Mrs. ~~Maura Tate~~
Mr. James Hudson
Mr. ~~Christopher Smith~~
Mr. Tyler Wells

CHAPTER EIGHTEEN

She arrived at Edward's firm at 8:30 a.m. and told the secretary that she needed to see him.

Ten minutes later, he strutted into the lobby from the back hallway in a slim-fitting gray suit with slicked hair. He shook the hand of another man in a suit and patted him on the back as he left.

"Alice, hello." He waved off the hurried explanations of his secretary. "I didn't know we had an appointment today."

"I was hoping you could squeeze me in, for something... personal."

"I see. I thought it might come to this." He said something to his secretary, who disappeared down a hallway.

Did Edward know? She briefly wondered if Dylan or the prison had called to warn him before shaking it off as too unrealistic. Although, after finding out yesterday that Rob had lived in Athens for years, and after seeing that picture of her mother on the prison badge, Alice told herself not to assume anything else.

"Come with me," he said.

Alice and Edward walked to his large corner office, with a view of Atlanta. In the distance, Alice could make out the green of Centennial Olympic Park in one corner, where her father had bought Caitlin and Robbie their own bricks on their first birthdays to match Alice and Rob's, where Jamie would take Alice and Rob to play in the fountains.

Edward walked to his desk to retrieve a metal canister of water before sitting in an armchair at the end of his desk area and gesturing for Alice to sit on a couch across from it.

The secretary came back in and handed Alice a plastic water bottle and Edward a file. Before Alice could say she didn't need water—she hated drinking from plastic, too wasteful—the secretary had disappeared, walking faster in her heels than Alice ever could. Edward made *tut, tut, tut* and *mmm* sounds as he flipped through the file, Alice presumed to let her know it wasn't her turn to talk.

He slammed the file shut with flourish. "So. From our side of things, it's fairly simple. We'll send these files over to your attorney. They make clear what assets belong to whom and which are shared. Of course, we'll be as helpful as we can, but I can't promise any favorable treatment on your side."

"What are you talking about?"

"Well, I know we have, shall we say, a history together? But we—the firm, I mean—must remain objective. Think of us as your financial mediators, similar to the mediator you may see to resolve the arrangement for child custody. You are using a mediator, aren't you? I really, personally, recommend that route." He clasped his hands together with his fingers under his chin and whispered, "Keeps things from getting too nasty."

Alice's cheeks burned the same way they had at the soccer game last night. Alice glanced at the clock. In DC, Walker would be sleeping in with Brittani, probably discussing their room service order before the "early morning" meeting he would attend at eleven.

"Eddie." She saw with pleasure that he still winced at the nickname. "I'm here to talk to you about how you're listed as Rob's designated contact with the prison." A scared, knowing look crossed his face, like Jamie had when she found him trying to take the boxes. So, he knew.

She stood up. "What *the hell* is *that* about?"

Edward stood with his hands in front of his chest. "Alice, stop, okay? Honest mistake."

"What's an honest mistake? You're saying you didn't know about Rob being in prison?"

"No. My mistake about your, um, divorce." He did air quotes around the last word.

"Forget it." *She* wanted to. It was the first time someone had said the d-word out loud to her, and she wanted to clear the air of its existence. "What about Rob?"

Edward gestured to the couch for her to sit again, and she did. He returned to the checkered armchair across from it.

"What about him?"

She glared again. Edward glanced at his watch.

"I have a meeting with a client in ten minutes."

"Then make it quick."

"He called me a long time ago from prison and said I was his one phone call and that he didn't want any of y'all to know. I brought him some things—toothbrush, clothes, books, other things he asked for. I went down there a few times to make sure he was all right. The prison called me when he was transferred. I sent him some money and tried to help him get things squared away. I would have told you, but he asked me not to. I only told your mother when I noticed him getting sick."

"When he got cancer? What did she say?"

"Yes, but I didn't know that's what it was then. She said, 'Thank you for letting me know,' didn't ask any questions, and that was it. I never heard anything else about it. I never told Rob I told her, obviously."

But her mother had done something about it, Alice knew. She had gone to the prison. If she hadn't seen Rob (which his letter made it seem like she hadn't), she must have been there for something related to what Edward had told her about Rob's health.

"Did you talk with him about anything else?"

"He called me, or they did and told me what he needed, and I brought it or sent it to him. He called me to say thanks shortly before he died. That's it. He never really wanted to *chat*."

"Sounds like you were a good friend." Although she'd have done that and more if Rob had given her the chance. If he had trusted her instead of Edward.

"I like to think so." He leaned back in his chair and crossed his legs.

"Call the prison and get all his records sent to me."

"Speaking as a friend"—he crossed his legs the other way—"are you sure that's wise? He would have gotten in touch with you if he wanted to."

His words stung, but his arrogance pissed her off. In that moment, she hated him, even more than when he had assumed she wanted to talk about a divorce.

"I'm forty-two years old," she snapped. "I can decide for myself and my family what is a good idea and what isn't." It felt good to say this to someone in her bitchiest voice. Like the welling of satisfaction that day at the playground when Rob had dragged Tommy back to apologize to her after he killed her snake. The way Edward looked at her, though, made her think in his mind, they weren't talking about Rob anymore.

"I'll get the stuff sent to you." He took a deep breath, then checked his watch again. "I really have to go now." He stood and ushered her to the lobby.

"Wait, one more thing: Jamie mentioned he gave a loan to my mother. I need you to look and see if she cut him any checks after my father died and let me know how much. I want to make sure Jamie got what he needed."

Edward grabbed her hand to shake it and then, upon second thought, patted it twice with his other hand. She held the plastic water bottle the secretary had given her awkwardly with the other hand.

"I'll ask an associate to check right now. It will be okay. Everything will be taken care of." He looked away from her and toward the waiting faces in the ugly chairs. "Mrs. Daily, nice to see you."

She stormed out, letting the ankle boots she had put on for this occasion slam as hard as possible onto the carpeted floors. Even if Edward had helped Rob, he was still a suit. The type of person Rob hated.

When she returned to the car, she sat in the driver's seat and opened the water bottle. She'd recycle it, at least. She sipped slowly, breathing in between sips.

The bottle was only halfway empty when her phone rang, showing the number for Edward's office.

"Mrs. Wright?"

It was a young woman, not Edward.

"Yes?" Alice said. She took a gulp of the water bottle.

"Glad to reach you. As requested by Mr. Davis, I've examined your mother's accounts. The amount paid to Mr. James Tate comes to $223,000."

Alice choked on the water, coughing and beating her chest as she struggled to swallow.

Her throat burned. "Are you sure? Couldn't that be something from the will or something like that?"

"This is in addition to the sum your father left for him in a trust. Is there anything else we can do for you today?"

Alice hung up.

She had never hired a private investigator and didn't know how much they cost, but the contract with the PI had been for six months. The amount paid to Jamie was way over what she had imagined. What could the money be for? Something with the business? Then why wouldn't her father have paid? Why would her mother have waited to pay Jamie until her father's death? Was it possible that her mother had forgotten how much money she owed and paid too much? Surely, Jamie wouldn't have accepted it.

Riding her wave of anger from Edward's office, she dialed Jamie.

"Alice!" he answered. "How are you feeling today?"

"I'm at Edward Davis's office and—"

"Oh, Edward! He did turn out to be such a gentleman, didn't he?"

"And I asked him to pull some numbers from Mama's finances, so I could make sure that she paid you back."

She waited to see if he would jump in again, but the line was quiet.

"And he told me how much she paid you."

More silence. Alice could hear barking in the background.

"It's much more than I…expected, for the private investigator."

He didn't respond. So, he was going to force her to voice the question. She struggled to put it into words that didn't sound accusatory: "It's just… It's weird…to me. I wondered… What was it for?"

He took a long intake of breath.

"Your mother didn't want to give up. We paid that private investigator off and on until the day we found out Rob was dead. Several times we thought we were close, only to have him vanish again. Your mother kept up hope though. I'm not sure how much it totaled to"—Alice narrowed her eyes at that; she imagined Jamie had that number tattooed on the inside of his eyelids, with his terrible money-managing habits—"but paying thousands of dollars every year, essentially a salary some months, for more than twenty years, plus expenses, it adds up. And interest, which your mother insisted on, but I told her it wasn't necessary. Your mother said over and over again, 'Spare no expense.' And believe me, this guy took that to heart."

"Why didn't you say that when we talked before?"

"I didn't want to embarrass your mother. I imagine after Rob died, she wasn't too proud that she spent so much with nothing to show for it. I don't think she would have wanted you to know that she dipped into the family money, your inheritance, Caitlin's college fund, money for her medical bills, things like that. Money you could use to…strike out on your own."

Alice froze.

"I know *I* would have left What's-Her-Face way earlier if I had the money."

Rebecca, Alice said in her mind. *Your ex-wife's name is Rebecca.*

He continued. "There's a lot of other stuff she could have used that money for, you know?"

The phone rang again in Alice's hand and she jumped. She pulled her ear away as Jamie continued.

"It's Caitlin's school on the other line. I've got to go."

"I'm with the dogs, so I can't really talk more anyway. But call me back if you have anything else, and I'll see you on Saturday."

She clicked over to the other line.

It was an administrative assistant from the school. Could she come in today? Whenever she had time.

"I'll come right now," Alice said.

She thought about texting Caitlin and asking about the meeting, but Caitlin had already earned detention twice for texting. Besides, this was the fifth time the school had summoned Alice this year for some award or reading or some such. While she understood parents valued transparency, there was such a thing as overcommunicating, like the three meetings last year to discuss her daughter's "special needs" and what kind of "support" she may need as one half of the school's first gay couple. "Mom, there are like twenty others. We're just the only ones who kiss in front of the General," Caitlin had said with an eye roll. The General was the students' nickname for the straitlaced ex-military principal, who was at least seventy-five.

Alice decided to go straight to Hilltree High School.

CHAPTER NINETEEN

An hour later, her ankle boots clicked on the high school's lino-leum floors as Alice made her way to the teenager slumped over the visitors' desk.

The shock that Edward knew he was Rob's designated contact and the amount her mother had paid to search (unsuccessfully) for Rob didn't occupy her mind, although that would have been enough to process. Her mind stuck on the feeling that everyone knew about her and Walker and the true state of their marriage, except for her and Walker. Edward even thought she came to his office because of an impending divorce.

The teen at the counter didn't look up as Alice wrote her infor-mation on the visitors' sheet. She grasped the pen, but the letters on the page swirled. *Divorce.* She shook the word out of her head.

The teen looked up to see what was taking so long and tapped twice on a red-flashing clock next to the paper to indicate the time and date.

"Ah," Alice mumbled. She copied the numbers next to her name. The teen spun the clipboard to face himself, sending the tinging sound of metal on fake wood echoing off the scuffed floor and cement-block walls.

Alice drummed her fingers on the desk as he typed her infor-mation into a computer. She replayed the glances from the other mothers on the sidelines at the soccer game last night. Was it a sense, or had Edward, Jamie, and the soccer moms actually seen Walker around town with Brittani?

Money you could use to strike out on your own, Jamie had said. It seemed so…big. A blank slate that she wasn't sure how to fill.

She took the name tag from the teen and looked at the type, briefly confused at the block letters: *ALICE TATE.*

"Oh, umm," she began, about to say that her name was Alice Wright, not Alice Tate, but she didn't want to admit she had written her maiden name by accident. "It's fine." He had already gone back to stealing glances at his phone. She proceeded to the administrative office, where the secretary told her that she wouldn't be meeting with the General today, but with the new vice principal, Dr. Garcia. After a few minutes, a trim man in a baggy suit came out with his hand outstretched.

"Ms. Tate," he said, reading from her name tag.

"Nice to meet you." Alice shook his hand. "I'm Caitlin Wright's mom." Again, she decided not to correct him. What was one person thinking she was already divorced?

They walked through a hall lined with gold-plated awards and framed pictures of the football team until they reached a small office at the end with a simple desk, a world away from Edward's large mahogany bookshelves stuffed with leather spines.

Dr. Garcia perched himself on the edge of his desk, while Alice sat in a rickety metal chair that seemed to have been plucked from a classroom. "I'm sure you're wondering why I called you so suddenly today."

Alice readjusted in the chair, feeling the harsh plastic through her jeans. She looked up and nodded.

"I got news this morning, not two hours ago, that Caitlin got the scholarship." He smiled wide and stretched out his arms, as a magician would to reveal a disappearing rabbit.

"I'm sorry? What scholarship?"

"The Emerging Women Writers Scholarship, at NYU."

At the look of uncertainty on Alice's face, Dr. Garcia's demeanor changed.

"Oh, my apologies. I thought…" He shifted his position on the desk. "The nominating form required a parent signature. Caitlin said she told you."

"What is it?"

"The program is very prestigious. Students need to be nominated by the school districts themselves. Mrs. Lyons, the theater teacher, recommended Caitlin, and I met with her and decided to submit her name. Her application went to the top! Let me just…" He crossed over to his filing cabinet and leafed through files inside, extracting a stack of papers from one. He flipped to the last page and handed it to Alice. "Is this your signature? Alice…Wright?" he looked up at her, and his eyes flashed to her name tag.

Alice glanced at the signature, written in little loops, but not in her handwriting. She reached up to massage her temple with her right hand. She could feel a visual migraine starting at the edges of her eyelids. She smiled up at him.

"It is! Yes, I remember now. I just… My mother is very sick, and I've been a little scatterbrained recently. I'm sure you understand."

"Of course." His smile returned. "I called you in to tell you the good news and because we want to honor Caitlin on Saturday during the first night of the play. We'd love her family to be there as well."

The oranges and greens marched across Alice's eyelids.

"Is something wrong?"

Alice's hand dropped from her temple. "No! I'm surprised, that's all. With it being so…competitive, we knew the chances were slim. Her father and I had discussed her staying in-state."

As it had so many times the last few days, Jake's name popped into Alice's head. How much easier parenting with him would likely be. How proud he would probably be if *his* daughter had such high ambitions, how undisturbed he would be by her not wanting to live the same life as her parents. Living a different life from what you knew growing up was a goal Jake and Alice had shared, once upon a time.

"This scholarship is full ride: tuition, room and board, some spending money, everything. It's only given to the three most promising young female writers entering the creative writing program. We are very proud of her, as I'm sure you are too. We'd hate for…" He stopped talking and checked his watch. "Perfect," he muttered. "May I show you something?"

Alice followed him, still holding the application. "Sure."

As they exited the office, she jumped a little when the bell rang. Unlike in her own high school experience, when people easily overlooked her, hitting her shoulder and sending her a step back, these students parted like a sea for the adult with the name tag and Dr. Garcia, parted like they had for Rob when she'd walked with him through the hallways, as if he had an invisible aura of protection around him.

Couples dropped their clasped hands and separated from

embraces. A group of large boys clad in their letterman jackets whirled on their heels as if in a choreographed dance and turned down another hallway. Nerds huddled around a locker, peering at something inside, then turned toward Dr. Garcia and Alice and slammed the locker closed.

The bell rang again as Dr. Garcia opened the door to the theater's light booth. "Is it okay if we watch for a minute, Mrs. Lyons?"

The theater teacher stood up from her chair. "I was about to go get a seat in the front row anyway."

Alice and the vice principal stood side by side in front of the glass screen high above the theater's stage, watching the students in their performance-week frenzy. Caitlin cued a scene and the actors began. She weaved in and out of them, stopping to adjust their positioning. She jogged to the back of the theater, below the light booth, and yelled directions from the back. The students laughed together as they said their lines. After a few rounds of the scene, Caitlin asked them to go back to put on their costumes.

Alone onstage, Caitlin said a line from memory. She jogged to the other end of the stage in Alice's gray Converses, playing the part that answered and muttered the lines, scribbling a difference in blocking on a legal pad.

As Alice watched, her cheeks flushed. She replayed the conversation with Caitlin yesterday at the Fur Vault and their conversations with Walker about NYU. Why hadn't Caitlin told her? Alice couldn't ignore the feeling that everyone knew something she didn't—about Rob, about Walker, about her daughter.

Alice broke her staring contest with the stage to look at Dr. Garcia, who watched her too closely. She worked to clear her face of clues and plaster on a smile. In situations like these, she missed Walker. If he were here, he would tell Dr. Garcia to mind his own business, all the while using a smile and tone that, for people who didn't know Walker, convinced them he was on their side instead of against them. It had convinced her, too, at first.

Alice opened her mouth to speak, but Dr. Garcia spoke first. "She's extremely talented."

"She is."

"And she's well-liked by the teachers and the students," he said. Alice shut her mouth. "I have no doubt she'll do well at NYU. I urge you and her father to give it some thought, and if you'd like to come back and talk more, I'm happy to." He crossed to the door. "Shall we?"

They walked the empty halls, back to the front of the school, and Dr. Garcia continued. "Mrs. Lyons says that Caitlin has a feeling for the audience and the stage that's as natural as she's ever seen. We think her performance of the poems she submitted for the scholarship really set her apart."

Alice half listened to him. As they walked, her eyes darted to the application still in her hands and her fake signature on the parental guardian line. Walker would explode if he knew about the forgery.

"Now, I'm sorry to excuse myself," he said when they reached the door, "but we have a faculty meeting in a few minutes. We are so, so pleased about Caitlin's success. She is such a treasure, but of course, you know that."

"Yes, she is," Alice said, relieved for a remark she could easily agree with. "Thank you for your time." She tried to hand the application back to Dr. Garcia, but he waved her away.

"Feel free to keep that. We have copies. See you on Saturday."
He turned around and left.

Alice hurried to her car, flipping the application back to the first
page while she crossed the parking lot. She read, starting with her
daughter's name written in the messy handwriting that had earned
her low grades in penmanship in elementary school and notes from
the teacher about how Caitlin refused to correct her pencil grip.
She had always been so stubborn. Like Walker. Like Rob.

Alice looked up every few seconds to ensure she was still
headed in the right direction. Her eyes bounced over the address,
GPA information, and courses taken, until she flipped to the
recommendations. She skimmed praises from teachers about
Caitlin's stage presence, intelligence, willingness to help others,
and creativity. On the second-to-last page, Alice found it: the
submitted work that set her apart for her "performance."

She got in her car and blasted the heat.

"Little White Lies, A Poem by Caitlin Wright" and a URL
were the only things on the otherwise blank page. Alice found her
phone and punched in the URL, squinting to get the numbers
correct at the end.

A YouTube link for "Little White Lies," posted a few months
ago. Alice noticed the views first—367,261. This many people
knew something *she* didn't about *her* daughter.

The video finished loading and started to play.

Claps and whistles reverberated through the car's small space.
Caitlin stepped into the light wearing jeans and a simple black
top Alice recognized from a back-to-school shopping trip the
previous August. Someone yelled "Go, girl!" and a voice Alice
thought belonged to Chelsea screamed "Cait-lin! Cait-lin!"

Caitlin drew her hand across the crowd to silence it, then closed her eyes. The audience waited quietly, and she let them, a slight smirk on her face. She had practiced for and anticipated this moment. Alice could see the passion in that smirk.

Caitlin took a breath near the microphone so that the sound filled the room and Alice's car, prompting the audience to take their own breath.

I grew up skipping along the Atlanta streets.

I grew up cheering in a too-short skirt with ribbons in my hair for men represented only by numbers. I grew up with a chill in the air bouncing around in the straw-lined back of a tractor on Halloween. I grew up diving headfirst into lakes and rivers and oceans, fighting against the burn to open my eyes underwater.

These things, I inherited from my parents and their parents before them.

The most valuable thing I inherited, though, was my ability to lie.

Light chuckles escaped from the audience, no doubt primed to participate, maybe by the spirit or a few beers before the performers came on. Someone in the back yelled "Okay!" and Caitlin took another breath.

Down South, we don't call it lying though. That would be too negative, that wouldn't be godly! Oh, no. In the South, we call it "telling stories."

"Oh, no!" someone in the back yelled and Caitlin smiled, speeding up now like a train picking up steam, the crowd egging her on.

We Southerners have told stories since we settled on this stolen land, which a story says we conquered for God, bless our hearts. We told stories through slavery and through the War of Northern

Aggression and through civil rights. We told a story called The Birth of a Nation. *We tell stories so well, we call them history.*

We've told some stories so many times they're already worn out— the wife who ran into a doorknob, the child with the cigarette burn he must have gotten from a punk at school, the daughter who went to live with relatives for a year and came back quiet and twenty pounds heavier, the son who needed nothing more than prayer and some private time with the church chaplain.

"Woo!" someone yelled. And again, another "Go, girl!"

From a young age, children are taught that mothers and fathers tell stories differently.

Fathers concentrate their stories on the past and the future. They tell stories about where they've been—my father's phone constantly abuzz from work texts that cause him to run off to the office and come back smelling of perfume.

"Damn!" yelled the audience, and Alice felt a tremor in her chest like she'd been stabbed.

Even before technology, he learned from the storied tradition of men before him who left too early, came home too late, and drank too much, telling stories so that they didn't remember what they had done.

They tell stories of the future. We teach our Southern gentlemen at a young age to promise the world so that they can get what they want in the present, because the future is a long ways away.

The present requires a different type of story though. In the present, men tell their stories in the form of questions they don't bother to ask:

Caitlin bent into the microphone, almost whispering the next lines.

Are you happy?

What do you want?

Does this feel good?

The crowd erupted in claps and *ooh*s. Caitlin grabbed the microphone with both hands.

Outsiders say the South is a matriarchal society, so it's fitting that Southern women are the true masters at telling stories. Their daughters pick up this knowledge like rules passed down in a sacred book.

Mothers concentrate their stories in the present. They move around money to pay for the new washing machine, stealing funds out of a family cashbox in which they themselves invested half. They use the lie of makeup and a smile to make things neat so that questions aren't asked.

Southern women are so good at telling stories that they tell them effortlessly, even to themselves.

This too shall pass.

It's just a phase.

He needs this.

It's my fault too.

They tell the lie that it's not worth it to make a fuss, that it's easier to keep quiet, to keep their darkest fears locked in a box in their mind that only God can find. Southern women think our stories make us happy, when really, they're more than little white lies. Because those lies keep us—

The crowd couldn't be silenced as the stomps and shouts and whoops punctuated each line that her daughter labored over. Caitlin allowed the noise to fill the white space.

Those lies keep us quiet.

Gagged.

Silenced.

Complacent.

I would like to say the cycle ends with me. But I know this skill of telling stories has been mixed with my blood as much as the smell of hay or the taste of grits cooked in bacon grease or the fierce rain of a summer storm beating against my skin.

Or maybe that's just a story I tell myself.

Caitlin took a step back from the microphone and bowed. Claps and snaps filled the room, and someone in front of the camera stood up, blocking Alice's view slightly. She could just see Chelsea running onto the stage and catch Caitlin smile as they kissed. The crowd cheered harder, right as the video went to black.

Alice let her phone fall into the cup holder.

She felt naked, exposed, as if Caitlin had seen right into the core that she had worked so hard to hide, had found the box she'd hid in her mind and had opened it, cataloging every pain but sneaking out before she was caught.

This must be what my mother feels like, she thought suddenly. What it feels like to lie in that hospital bed with no control over the secrets and bad memories tumbling from your subconscious.

Alice leaned her head on the steering wheel and let the car's heat blow into her face. When her eyes started to water, she opened them wide to let in air, to keep tears from falling. She lay there with her head on the wheel until students began filing out for their free period. Then, she turned on the car and used her last gallon of gas to get to the station.

When she got home, Alice sat on the front porch steps with Buddy until the sky turned from blue to orange to pink and finally faded to black. Buddy, having given up on fetch hours ago, lay on the cement. Alice ran her bare foot over his coat, feeling the soft fur between her toes. The beer next to her was warm and half-full by the time headlights flashed at the top of the hill.

Buddy perked up his ears. When screams of little boys poured from the open car door, he ran to Robbie.

"Mom, can we order Chinese food?" Robbie yawned as he approached the house. *It's exhausting being a kid these days,* Alice thought to herself, as she leaned down to pick up his backpack.

They ordered food and ate it on the couch while watching *Inspector Gadget,* their tradition when Walker left town. What would the tradition become if they divorced?

"Since Dad's out of town, do I have to go to practice tomorrow?"

"Remember what Dad said—after this season we can talk about stopping if you don't like it. Your team's depending on you though."

He looked at Alice with droopy eyes, and she reached to put her arm around him. He leaned his head in toward her chest.

"But after school and practice tomorrow, you get to go to Caleb's, remember?"

He looked up at her. "And watch *Star Wars.*"

"Right."

Alice put him to bed in her and Walker's room. While he tangled himself in her covers, she turned on the evening news quietly, intending to stay awake until Caitlin made it home from rehearsal. She should say something to Caitlin, she knew, but she didn't know what, couldn't explain the exposure she'd felt watching the video and didn't want to burden her with it. As she always did when Walker was out of town, Alice fell asleep almost immediately, though, with the soft glow of the TV as a night-light.

She woke to the sound of Buddy whimpering. He lay at the foot of Walker's side, where Robbie slept.

She leaned over to Robbie and brushed the hair off his sweaty forehead. He was always a hot sleeper. The red numbers on the alarm clock glowed 3:12 a.m. She stared at the ceiling for a few minutes, then left the bed. Buddy perked his head up. "Stay," she whispered, and he lay his head back down on Robbie's ankle.

Alice crossed her arms against the cold as she walked through the house and then up the stairs. She stepped lightly on the carpet with only the sound of her ankles cracking to cut through the house's slumber. When she reached Caitlin's door, she pushed it slowly, silently with her fingertips. Caitlin lay on the bed, the covers tucked under her chin with her hands, and three textbooks, her computer, and her phone scattered around her body like a halo. The floor was littered with a hyper-organized chaos of office supplies: index cards lined up in a row or joined in a web with masking tape, pictures ripped out of magazines, and piles of pens organized by colors. Alice could never understand Caitlin's need for order. Her outfit for the next day was hung on the closet doorknob with the shoes tucked underneath.

Alice sat in the chair opposite the bed. She pictured Caitlin in the video and tried to reconcile the little girl breathing before her with the confident, strong woman on that stage.

Caitlin could do what she couldn't, could show her scars

without shame. She didn't have a box in her mind like Alice, like her mother. Didn't have secrets like Rob, that she'd have to write down in a letter only after she died. *She was right on the video*, Alice thought—the tradition would end with her, and it made Alice smile with pride.

When Alice felt herself beginning to drift off, she stood and walked to the door. She would talk to her tomorrow.

"Mom?" Caitlin mumbled. "What're you doing?"

Alice crossed over to the bed, stepping carefully to avoid the papers on the floor. "Just making sure you got home okay." She leaned down and brushed the hair out of Caitlin's face, feeling the cool of her forehead.

"Rehearsal ran late. They can't get a scene right. Peter keeps forgetting his lines," Caitlin said with her eyes still closed.

"It'll be okay, go back to sleep."

Caitlin turned over to face the other wall. Alice watched as her breathing slowed again.

When Alice returned to her bedroom, she couldn't fall back asleep. She scrolled through CNN on her phone, then checked her email.

An email from the Georgia Department of Corrections told her that an inmate had completed her visitation application and that she could come during visiting hours. She read through the list of rules and went back upstairs to Robbie's room, where she retrieved clothes for him and packed his overnight bag for Caleb's so the morning would go faster. Even with her anxiety about the visit, she knew she wanted to get it over with, to see Tyler. *Tomorrow*. She wanted Rob to lead her to the end of this search, and hopefully to an answer on what to do with her own family.

She stood in front of her closet in one of the rare times when she fretted about what she would wear. Perhaps her mother had been onto something with the fur coat. Were you supposed to dress in your Sunday best to go visit prisoners? The dress code they'd emailed Alice was only slightly less restrictive than Caitlin's impossible school dress code: no hats, no revealing necklines, no skirts above the knee, no flip-flops, etc. She opened a drawer and ran her fingers over her folded T-shirts before giving up and returning to bed for another hour of sleep.

CHAPTER TWENTY

With the kids off, Alice set out toward the prison on the monotonous highways that decorated Georgia's map like the scribbles of a particularly artless child. She should be visiting Rob, not Tyler.

When Alice arrived at Clayton County Prison in jeans, a light-blue blouse, and ballet flats she fished from the back of her closet, she realized she probably didn't need to worry about her wardrobe as much as she had. She studied the building, one of the ugliest she had ever seen, through her windshield as she parked.

The off-white structure reminded her of a building made entirely of Legos because of its harsh, square appearance. Little slits littered the stone like scars on a human body. Nothing but dirt surrounded the area, until fences twisted with barbed wire rose quickly, encasing the fortress.

She parked and walked to the entrance. As she passed two guards, complete with full body armor and large rifles, she held Rob's letter to Tyler in front of her like a shield. She nodded at one of the guards as she passed, but he stared ahead, not acknowledging her. Maybe these guards were like the ones who stood at Buckingham Palace and couldn't react to other people. *Seems peaceful*, she thought, *knowing your reaction should always be to stare ahead, seeing everything but not really seeing it, like a kind of meditation.*

In the visitors' center, a large woman sat behind glass. Without looking up at Alice, she demanded, "ID."

Alice fumbled with the backpack's pockets. Her fingers thumbed uselessly through endless stacks of the heavy personal credit cards she shared with Walker, business cards for the Center, her loyalty cards to Home Depot and Kroger, and receipts for soil and wood from Lowe's and another for glue sticks she'd bought for Robbie's class.

"Sure, let me just… It's right here. I just need to…"

She thumbed through another zippered pocket. Nothing. She reached for her wallet, before she realized it was useless since she rarely returned her cards to it. After a little more digging, she remembered she'd put her driver's license in her pocket that morning to make it easily accessible for this very moment. She smiled apologetically at the woman and placed it in a little metal box that snapped shut and disappeared.

Alice twisted her wedding band up and down on her finger.

"Who are you here visiting?"

"Tyler Wells," Alice said.

"Checks out," the woman said, still without looking up. "Smile."

Alice did as the woman told her without realizing why the command came until the flash of light made her close her eyes. As she blinked back spots, the box's snap reverberated from the walls and she jumped. She smiled again at the woman behind the desk, who still refused to look at her, before she slid out her license and the sticker with her picture on it, just like her mother's. The technology at the Georgia Department of Corrections had apparently progressed little in the last decade.

After stuffing her bag and everything else into a locker that reminded her of high school, Alice proceeded to the last door where a guard who looked about sixteen waited with a wand like the ones used at the airport.

He asked who she came to visit and then went to retrieve him. But a few minutes later, he returned to say Tyler already had a visitor and that she would need to wait until they left.

Defeated, Alice walked back to the locker and sat on an unadorned bench next to it to wait her turn with Tyler's letter balanced on her knee. She looked at the address, as she had done many times before coming here. Tyler hadn't been in jail when Rob wrote this. He lived in a suburb, like she did, not far outside Birmingham. Did he have a job, a normal life? Would he get to go back there? Did he have a family? Did they miss him? Did they know he was here? Or like Rob, did Tyler prefer to avoid those who loved him most?

A buzz rang through the waiting area and the doors opened. A woman and a teenage boy exited. The woman looked down at the floor and rested her hand on the boy's shoulder as they walked. The boy looked about fourteen. He smiled briefly at Alice as they approached a locker on the other side of the room. He unlocked it and handed his mother the key. After taking out the belongings, he laid each evenly spaced on the bench in such a way that the routine must have been developed over many days like this one. He slipped the key back in the lock, turned it, and shut the locker with the exact right amount of force to close it but not to create an echo of sound in the jumpy room. He turned and smiled at Alice once more as their eyes met before the pair disappeared out the second door and down the corridor from which Alice came.

Rob had been like that, she thought, even until the end, even amidst his dark moods. She remembered how a week before their final trip together to Amelia Island, their father had taken off for Memphis after a fight with their mother. The next night, at exactly 5:00 p.m., Rob rose from his perch on the couch where he had been strumming his guitar, mixed their mother a drink in one of the nice crystal glasses, and brought it to her without comment. Maura only nodded and took the drink in her hand, gulping before she even took the first sip. Or, hours before he left, Alice had sat outside at dinner with the family, listening to her father and Jamie laugh about someone they used to know. Before she even realized she had rubbed her arm, Rob had popped up and retrieved her jacket, draping it over her shoulders against the beach's chill. He was like that, able to anticipate their needs before they could, even as something seemed to shift inside him, a change in the family's tectonic plates felt by all.

It started with the guitar.

The tension had probably been building longer, since that day at the river with Edward and Hayley, maybe even before that. Were there glimmers that morning at church when he asked Alice about heaven? Either way, it was the night with the guitar that stuck in her mind now, the winter before he left.

She had been asleep in Rob's bed. As usual, she woke with confusion, unable to remember if she had fallen asleep there, or in the closet and Rob had carried her in, or in her room, only to sleepwalk into Rob's.

Whack, the sound that jolted her awake.

She wasn't scared, would never be with Rob. She walked to the back window. He stood on the awning where she sometimes found him in the middle of the night. He gripped the neck of an electric guitar that Jamie had given him for Christmas the month before. (Alice had gotten a chemistry set.) When he first unwrapped it, Alice had noticed how striking it was, and it was even more so against the dark night sky—red and black, the sides curved up harshly toward the neck like devil's horns, with a dash of white on the otherwise perfect paint. Rob looked out to the river; he didn't see her yet.

He raised the guitar over his head and brought it down with force until the base smashed into the copper awning, sending an icy puff of breath up against the winter sky.

Whack.

Alice looked to the left and right, worrying their parents would run in before she remembered that Daddy was out of town and Mama was at some sort of party where you "buy" tables. "You'll come with me one day soon," she had told Alice as she walked out the door in her evening dress and white gloves.

Whack.

Whack.

He brought the guitar down again, but it was resilient, and despite the torture, only half the strings had snapped.

Whack. Whack. Whack.

She could see the muscles through his shirt as he raised it again above his head.

Whack, whack, whack, whack.

He started heaving, and his shoulders jumped up and down as if he were sobbing, even though Alice couldn't see his face. He slammed it down with all his force until the neck finally broke. He sat down on the awning next to the broken guitar.

"Rob?"

"Yeah," he said, like he'd known she was there all along.

What's wrong? she started to ask. Or *Are you okay?* But, she faltered, stopped and started, for she wasn't sure how to get him to confide in her, didn't have the language she needed to express her questions. He was always the keeper of *her* secrets, the defender in *her* nightmares, the explainer to *her* confusion. Never the other way around. She was starting to recognize his dark moods more, but they were only that, an inexplicable darkness with no known causes, like any other storm.

She stepped through the window, onto the awning that shaded the first-floor window, and picked up the neck of the guitar. Alice raised it over her head and grunted, slamming it down into the copper as hard as her forearms could. So hard that she lost her footing because of the force. Rob grabbed her pajama shirt and pulled her back toward the house, just as she thought she would go over the edge.

She sat next to him, heart beating in her ears because of her brush with such a fall. They stared at the river in the distance, lit by the moonlight.

Eventually, he stood up. With a sniffle, he wiped his face on his sleeve. Then, he picked up the guitar's base and neck in both hands and threw them over the edge of the house. They landed with a crack next to the porch, and Alice watched as the base rolled a few feet down the hill.

"Let's go back inside," he said. Once he stepped in through the window, he patted his acoustic guitar, laying innocently on the carpet, a gesture of care toward the remaining musical soldier.

The next morning, neither of them mentioned the destroyed

guitar. Stupidly, Alice assumed that meant that Rob would go back to normal.

––––––––––

"You can go in now," the teenager playing dress-up as a guard said to Alice.

She stood and walked to him, but as she approached the door, he moved to block her path.

"Ma'am, nothing can go in with you."

Briefly distracted by the guard stepping in front of her, then calling her "ma'am," it took Alice a second to realize the statement referred to the letter.

"It's just paper. You can check it if you want."

"Nothing can go in with you," he said, before adding: "Ma'am."

"Okay, one second."

What could she do with it? She could put the letter in the locker and mail it to Tyler, but then she wouldn't know what it said, and she didn't want to come back here.

With one last glance at the pristine seal, she turned over the envelope and ripped off the flap. She yanked out the paper. The motion sent something flying, and she glanced back at the guard, who still stared ahead. She wondered what would happen to her for littering in the jail, or was it a prison?

Exactly halfway down the page and centered on the paper with such precision Alice wondered if Rob had used a ruler, sat one simple sentence—

Be good.

Unlike the others, it wasn't signed.

She turned the letter over, expecting something else on the back. "Be good?" Alice stood puzzling over what it could mean and became a little afraid at the prospect of going inside.

She bent down to pick up whatever had fallen out of the letter. They were little googly eyes, the type she had used in crafts as a child, and with her own children. She picked them up, one by one, collecting them in her hand, and threw them away. What could they mean? Some kind of inside joke?

"Ma'am, are you ready?"

"Yes, yes," Alice said.

With one more glance at her brother's handwriting on the letter, she slid it through the slot of a nearby trash can and watched it disappear into the darkness.

ROB'S LOST LETTERS:

Mr. ~~Dylan Barnett~~

Ms. Lila King

Mr. ~~Richard Tate~~

Mrs. ~~Maura Tate~~

Mr. James Hudson

Mr. ~~Christopher Smith~~

Mr. ~~Tyler Wells~~

CHAPTER TWENTY-ONE

A female police officer wanded Alice again, gave her a thorough pat-down, and read more rules—no hugging, no kissing, no holding hands. The visit could be stopped at any time by the guards for any reason. Alice nodded in agreement, and the guard eventually showed her to a metal table in a room full of metal tables and families talking under their breath.

A woman bounced a baby on her knee. A man in orange rested his hand on a table separated by an inch of impenetrable space from the hand of a woman in a pink floral dress. Women littered the room in their best dresses, decorating the drab decor and the men in uniform like colorful candles on a plain birthday cake.

A guard escorted a hulking man in orange to Alice's table. He must have been over six foot four. With his bulk, he towered over the guard but allowed the guard to escort him into his seat. The orange of the jumpsuit and his dark hair framed his acne-scarred face.

"Alice," he said in greeting, with a simple nod at her. She smiled at him, unsure how to begin. He sat straight with both feet on the ground, before changing his mind. He fell over the table, letting his arms bang on the metal, eliciting a snap from one of the guards. He slid his arms to the edge and used his hands to push himself up, shifting to one side of the too-small chair. When he stilled, he looked back at her.

"So."

"Right!" Alice said. "Like I said, my brother sent you a letter."

"Okay," he said in argument, the same way Caitlin spoke to Walker when she didn't agree but didn't want to argue either. As if to say, *Okay. For now.*

"Well, Rob and I were really close when we were kids, I mean, we weren't those types of siblings who don't like each other or fight a lot or anything," Alice said, picking up speed with every sentence as Caitlin had on the video, until she was short on breath. "But then, when I was eleven, he left, and I never knew why. I always wanted to find him, always hoped we would get back in touch, but we never did, and then I found out he had died. And my parents threw this funeral for him, this terrible funeral with all their friends, and I decided to talk because no one else—"

"I was there. I know how it was."

"What?"

"I was there."

"You were the man, the man who left after the eulogy, weren't you? I tried to talk to you, but you were gone."

He nodded and shrugged, as if to say *your loss.*

She paused, unsure of where to go next.

"Why didn't you send the letter?" he said.

"I brought it. It's...it's in the locker room." She could fish it out of the trash if she needed to, although that would probably be some sort of security violation. "I read it."

"You read my letter?" His voice rose a bit, with an edge to it that made her want to apologize and explain.

"Well, they wouldn't let me bring it in. I've never been to visit...here...before. I told them they could—"

"What did it say." Less a question than a demand.

She looked at the clock on the wall and wondered how many minutes she had until a guard would usher Tyler away. She dreaded being cut off before she got anywhere with him, but half desired the rescue from his curt attitude. "It was very short, shorter than most of the letters and—"

"What did it say?" His hand morphed into one giant fist on the metal table, and she watched the veins in his hands bulge through the skin, imagining the fear that the people in that gas station must have felt when Tyler barged in with all his intimidating bulk and demanded the money from the register.

"It said 'Be good.'"

Tyler's face froze, and he withdrew his hands and legs until it seemed to Alice that he occupied half the space he had before. Nothing happened for a few seconds, then a pipe burst inside his face. The strong jaw trembled, and his shoulders curved in on themselves. One tear threatened to clang onto the table, and before Alice could react to it, a stream came. She looked from left to right at her surroundings, unable to decide on the proper response. The man at the table next to them saw the scene in a glance and then positioned his body with his back to Tyler as if refusing to acknowledge what he had clearly seen. A guard at her three o'clock glared at them, and Alice feared that he would approach them and tell her to leave.

Tyler wiped his face with the back of his hands and leaned his face down to drag the side of it along his shoulder like Alice's childhood cat did when she gave herself a bath. To his right, Tyler caught the eye of the guy next to him and mumbled, "Fuck you looking at." The man's head snapped back to look straight ahead.

After thirty seconds, Tyler changed tactics and stopped trying to hide. He rested his hands on the table and looked down at them. He allowed the tears to roll down his cheeks until his face gave the appearance of rain streaks on a dirty car.

"Are you okay?" Alice reached to touch Tyler's hand. He didn't acknowledge her right away and she wished she hadn't said anything, because obviously, he wasn't okay. She never had been good at saying the right thing in these situations. She caught the eye of a guard who shook his head in warning. She remembered the no hand-holding rule and moved her hand away from Tyler's.

"It's—" He took in a breath like a balloon filling with air that seemed to raise his frame over a foot. It deflated. "I wasn't good."

Alice nodded as if she understood.

"The people that left before you came in, the woman and the boy? That's my wife and kid—one of them." He wiped off his face with his massive forearm and straightened out again.

"I'm the reason Rob was in prison." He spoke faster now, the story tumbling out. "I'm the reason. Me. You can hate me. And when he got sick when he was in, I couldn't help but think, you know, if he was out, he would have had better doctors and shit and they could have made him better and he wouldn't have died."

Could it be true?

A pressure filled Alice's chest as she waited for him to explain, waited for him to say why Rob had been in prison. She said a silent "please" in prayer that it would be something that wouldn't forever alter her opinion of her big brother and childhood hero.

"We were both into some not-good stuff, and then one night we got caught. We heard the cops were coming and everyone took off. Somehow Rob and I got trapped together. We decided that the best bet was for someone to run at the cops and the other to get away. Rob said I would be the one to run. He said I needed to go back to my wife and kid, and he said make it worth it; be good. I remember that, 'Make it worth it. Be good.' So, I ran, and they took him."

"I cleaned myself up like I said I would and got a real job. For a long time. My wife took me back in and my kid forgave me; we had two more. And then when I heard about Rob getting sick and so close to when he was getting out, I came to visit him, and I felt so guilty when I saw how sick he was. He just looked so bad right at the end, and I knew that they did it to him, in this place—that's what they do—and I knew it was my fault. I would have… I don't know, I thought I would have made it okay. People don't mess with me, and I can be on good behavior. Rob couldn't do no good behavior. But I let him run to them anyway."

Alice's eyes drifted down to her wedding ring, and she twirled it on her finger.

"He must have known that I'd end up like this, that I'd end up back here. Even if he didn't want to think it, he had a lot of people that cared about him too. I didn't want to say anything to my wife because we didn't really talk about that part of my life. Then it started, a few beers, some shots, a little coke, a few calls to my old buddies and jobs here and there. I thought I could control it, but I couldn't and I ended up back here. His sacrifice was for nothing. I didn't even do the one thing he asked me to do. All he asked me to do was go to some house and to put these stupid eyes outside on the mailbox."

She snapped back to Tyler as he continued, "That's all I had to do. It wasn't even a big deal. I did it for a while, but once I got in here, I couldn't. I couldn't even fucking do what he asked."

He banged his head on the table, and one of the guards

approached. He looked from Tyler with his head resting on the table to Alice and then said it was time for her to go. Alice stood up in a daze. Tyler started walking away.

"Wait! Tyler! Where did you take the eyes? What house?"

"65 Ringgate Lane, Marietta!"

Alice's fingers clenched so hard that she felt her nails dig into her palm. Jamie's old address. Why would Rob have wanted them left at Jamie's house?

As she exited the dark building, Alice's eyes burned at the harsh sunlight. She fast-walked to the car, spinning her backpack around and unzipping it as she went. She dug out Jamie's letter, held pristinely in the laptop section of her bag, uncreased with its regal calligraphy and seal. Even though she made sure to control her pace—running in a prison parking lot probably wasn't a good idea—the weight in her chest felt like she was running a marathon. After she climbed into the car, she tore the envelope, not taking care to make sure it remained intact. As she snatched the paper out, little googly eyes exploded in all directions throughout the car.

She unfolded the letter, reading:

Dearest Jamie,

Fuck you.

Always watching,
Rob

Alice finally saw the connection with the eyes from their child-hood crafts together as a chilling, if not creative metaphor. The many times Jamie stayed with her and Rob, when he lived at the house off and on, they made sock puppets often, using eyes like these. Rob always did have a flair for the poetic, even as a child. It was second only to his skill at hyperbole.

Alice's mind returned to the money from yesterday. Especially with Jamie's history, she had suspicions about his explanation yesterday, but now she was sure he was hiding something. Maybe even something more than an inflated bill or charging her mother too much interest.

She took out the card with the PI's name and number written on the back. Yesterday when she called, the number had been disconnected. This time, though, she called the diner on the front. Someone who sounded like a teenager answered, and she crossed her fingers and asked to speak to Clay Geoffrey. He put her on hold. Could it be? Maybe Clay used the diner as an office or worked there or went there frequently. Maybe he was there right now and would know more about Jamie and her mother and the search for Rob and why Rob would have been angry. If he was still searching for Rob up until the funeral eight years ago, he might even still be working today.

A woman with a smoke-stained voice answered: "You calling for Clay Geoffrey?"

"Yes," Alice said eagerly, hopefully.

"I don't know how to tell you this, but Clay's been dead for thirty years."

Thirty years?

If Clay was dead, that meant Jamie hadn't been paying him

since Rob left. Thirty years would have been only a few years after Rob disappeared.

Alice muttered "Thank you" and hung up. Suddenly noticing she was freezing, she rubbed her hands together to warm them and reached up to crank the heat. Her hand shook as she turned the dial.

A rush of images flew past, the sprawling ranch Jamie purchased after her father died, the designer dogs running along the acreage, the new cars with their shiny rims. She knew with a ferocity so strong she would stake her life on it: Jamie hadn't given the money to the PI. He'd kept it. He had lied to her mother and lied to her.

Jamie's money—from the business, from Richard, from Richard's parents (his adoptive parents)—had always come in a trust because of his lack of talent with money management, part of the reason he had so frequently landed at the Tate house. He had lost his fortune more times than Alice could count: a failed marriage, failed businesses, his countless expensive hobbies and careers, including one as a poker player. Even if he felt he needed the money, stealing money from her mother when she thought it would go to look for Rob would be a new low, one that would surely elicit a response from Rob if he knew. Could it be that Jamie had even agreed with her father not to continue looking for Rob, had arranged with him so her mother would think she was paying?

As she pondered the possibilities, she saw a text from Edward saying that an intern had dropped off the prison files at the Center. *Thankfully he didn't send them to the house*, Alice thought, before realizing the reason he didn't: Edward knew she was hiding this from Walker. And he was right. Her cheeks darkened again.

She reached for her too-hot Nalgene water bottle in the cup holder and drank from it to calm herself before getting back on the highway for the two-hour drive back to the Center.

ROB'S LOST LETTERS:

Mr. ~~Dylan Barnett~~
Ms. Lila King
Mr. ~~Richard Tate~~
Mrs. ~~Maura Tate~~
Mr. ~~James Hudson~~
Mr. ~~Christopher Smith~~
Mr. ~~Tyler Wells~~

CHAPTER TWENTY-TWO

The package sat on the porch when she pulled into the Center with Buddy, just as Edward had said it would.

The Center's lights let out an irritated buzz when she flipped them on, which joined the crickets' chirps and the rustle of the water outside. With the large windows, which let light spill in during the daytime, and the night tours and fishing that usually kept the workers outside in the nighttime hours, the lights weren't used much.

She lifted the box, surprised by its weight, and brought it to the large table in the center of the cabin where they held staff meetings. She walked a few circles around the box, which caused Buddy to bark. She shushed him, and he lay back down. She had been expecting something like a large folder. This would take longer than she had anticipated. She grabbed a beer from the fridge, ordered food from her favorite Indian place, and then sat in front of the box to drink a few sips before standing to put music on the stereo. It was too quiet.

She couldn't exactly call this night fun, but the prospect of sitting at the Center on a Friday night with only Buddy, knowing that her family was accounted for, made her feel something akin to pleasure. Caitlin would be in the final dress rehearsal for her play tomorrow, until the actors finally complained enough to be released. Robbie was excited about spending the night at Caleb's. Walker was still in DC (with Brittani), but she didn't want to think about that.

Alice cut open the box an inch at a time to ensure she didn't damage any of the documents and placed the rubber-banded files in separate piles on the table. They were unordered, but she lined them up on the table chronologically, according to the labels on top, which were written, scratched out, and rewritten from over-use. At the bottom of the box was a large bag, labeled "personal effects" in Sharpie with a few books inside.

She stood over the mass of documents, briefly frozen with everything to process. The sheer amount overwhelmed her. To take the edge off, she sat down and sipped from her beer until it was empty.

The stereo changed, and Miranda Lambert sang out from the speakers about mothers and daughters and broken hearts. Alice felt a little chill. She took the shuffled playlist as a sign she was on the right path. She would finish the journey her mother had set off with the box of letters she left for Alice in the closet. With each one she delivered, Alice felt more and more like the house's clutter was not just because of her mother's mental failing. It was a challenge. A challenge she would finish for both of them.

She found a yellow legal pad and a marker and set them both on the table on top of the files. She uncapped another beer. She pressed Repeat on the song and turned it up several notches, allowing it to fill places in her chest that felt empty.

At the top of her legal pad, she wrote "ROB" in all caps.

As Alice stared at the blank paper with her marker posed, the image of the funeral pamphlet came to her mind. She pictured it so clearly, Rob on the front with his guitar. The line under the image came into focus. She wrote on the first line of her paper "Born: July 30, 1968," then skipped to the last line: "Death: August 21, 2007."

Alice looked at the space between the two lines. What else? Her mind flashed back to the morning car ride before that night at Amelia Island when Rob left. She sat in the back seat of her father's Jeep, next to Rob. He looked out the window expressionless, as he had since he got into the car after a prolonged and teary (on her part) goodbye from his girlfriend. A goodbye their mother had watched, scoffing, "It's that girl, putting ideas in his head," without specifying what the offending ideas were.

Her father drove with his perfect ten-and-two hand position and sighed, loud and long, at something her mother was doing. And then Alice remembered what she was doing. Her mother was reading the text from *The Little Prince* out loud, pausing every few minutes to ask Alice questions. Her summer reading assignment for sixth grade. She counted back. Rob would be in tenth grade. He was only fifteen. How old he had seemed to her then. She wrote "Left home: 1984."

Then, Dylan. She wrote a few lines down "Athens, Georgia." Dylan thought everyone had left by the time he was arrested, and Rob probably lived there at least a year to be that established at the 40 Watt before Dylan and Michael showed up. She wrote "~1991–1995" next to "Athens."

And Tyler. That had only been a few years after. The first folder, from his arrest, was in 1998. She wrote "Arrested (Tyler): 1998." Then, the date from the X-ray: "Diagnosis: 2005."

She picked up the 1998 file. It began with his intake form:

Robinson Wesley Tate, a 165-pound male, picked up at 1333 Peachtree Road in Atlanta. The police report filled in gaps she could have guessed at: the police received calls from neighbors that the house contained a drug operation, and after three controlled buys by a confidential informant, they got a search warrant and planned to go bust it one night. They thought the force may have a leak, because when officers arrived, none of the reported people living there were home, but most of the drugs, scales, and other supplies were left behind. Police followed someone else who escaped on foot (Tyler), but they couldn't find him and settled on arresting the only person still in the driveway. Rob didn't resist but nodded when they read him his rights and sat in the back of the car silently, not answering any questions. He never asked for a lawyer.

She thought of Tyler, how he had so narrowly escaped, according to the report. First, Rob went into detox. She read through reports of the drugs in his system, which were extensive and diverse. His mug shot showed him standing in front of the camera, but his eyes were soft, as if looking at a loved one. Tattoos: three, a sparrow on his right shoulder blade and two filled in triangles, one on each calf. She wondered what they meant. He was sent to the county jail for holding, couldn't meet bail, and then was charged with several drug charges with intent to distribute. Because of a prior marijuana charge and the quantity and variety of the drugs in the house, his possible sentence stacked to twenty-four years in prison. He accepted a lesser charge for ten years (less with good behavior and parole, they told him) and pleaded guilty.

The food came eventually, and she nibbled on it as she progressed through the files. There were accounts of his various jobs in the prisons, of a fight early on, of his transfers to different prisons and units. In yearly reports from the guards, they regarded him as intelligent and friendly, but unpredictable. He spent most of his time in the library and became de facto librarian. Once, when the library closed, he went on a rampage that sent him to solitary confinement for a week, after which he spent two weeks repeating lines from what they eventually realized was *Moby Dick*.

There were records for every visitor. Alice's interest was piqued when she saw that Jamie requested visiting rights, but Rob denied them. If Rob knew Jamie had basically stolen money, she didn't blame him for denying visitation. Edward Davis's name showed up constantly, and as angry as she wanted to be at him for his presumption over her marriage and for keeping Rob a secret from her, she couldn't help but feel some tenderness toward him for visiting so often and sending her brother what he needed. Lila King, from the letter addressed to New Orleans, showed up several times in 2003 and 2004, before his release, and Tyler's name appeared a few times, once with his wife. The list didn't include her mother's name.

The prison transferred Rob to the hospital in 2005 after he started complaining of a weird pain in his chest. At first, no one would listen, just another prisoner trying to get out of his usual duties. Then, an abrupt change. Three letters came from state congressmen and one arrived from the mayor. Copies of the letters—as well as letters her mother sent (in triplicate) to the hospital's manager dedicated to the prison patients—were included in the file with a note from the hospital's president, calling for Rob's examination and the hospitalization.

Alice's heart swelled for her mother, jumping into action,

despite the reaction she'd given Edward when he told her about Rob's illness. But her mother apparently never saw Rob. And it seemed from the files and the letter to her that Rob didn't know about their mother's involvement with his treatment. She pictured her mother barging into the prison that Alice had tiptoed into. Maura would have gone straight to the warden's office with her fur coat and demanded her son be given the treatment he needed, all the while making veiled threats using the names of her friends through her carefully lined red lips.

Finally, the hospital examined Rob. After, things went downhill fast. The court had already scheduled his release but moved it up once doctors determined he didn't have long to live. The prison released him to Lila King in summer 2006, and he made plans to move to New Orleans. After an appeal to a judge, he got his parole transferred to Louisiana. His warden had written on behalf of his release. Rob checked in for his parole hearings until he was too sick, at which time local police would check in with him at home.

She wondered as Tyler did how things would have been different had Rob not been in prison. She rewound the whole scene in her head. First, she played it with him out of prison, perhaps at some house in Atlanta, their mother again swooping in to help, but this time Rob would receive the best medical care, improve, beat the illness, call Alice weekly to update her on his progress. Then she played it with their mother yelling at the prison warden, with the story's end already decided.

When she finished the files, she let Buddy out and back in before she lay down on the couch. She understood why Rob didn't come back, why he didn't want to "show his scars without shame." But she still didn't know why he left. Maybe she never would. For the first time in decades, Alice forced herself to remember one of the worst nights of her life, the last night they were all together, the memory she had worked the hardest to forget.

CHAPTER TWENTY-THREE

Until the last trip, the Tate family's annual pilgrimage to Amelia Island was Alice's favorite time of year. It was better than Thanksgiving, because Mama didn't yell at her about not ironing the tablecloths fast enough. It was better than Christmas, because they didn't have to go see Daddy's random family members who always remarked how pretty Alice looked in her dress, then said nothing else to her, all the while having animated conversations with her male cousins. It was better than the other weeks of the summer because she got to go to the beach. It was better than her two weeks at sleepaway camp, because Rob was there.

Despite all this excitement, when they pulled into the beach house's garage after their stopover in Savannah, Alice was a mess of nervous chatter. Once everyone got back to her father's Jeep, Alice had hoped Rob would work more on the drawing and let her see it, but instead, Rob had clammed up again. Sensing this, Alice peppered her family with questions, hoping to break through the car's tension, until Mama told Alice to stop talking because she was giving her a migraine.

They always stayed in a cottage encased in shiplap, painted in a seafoam green that looked like the reflection of the ocean in the morning light. To Alice, the house had always looked like a doll house, one that had been trapped between two large hands and squeezed until it grew too tall for its width. Despite its tall, narrow look, it was the only house on the cul-de-sac.

The car pulled into the bottom garage that acted as the first floor of the house, and Jamie pulled up behind them in his own car. The ignition turned off, and for a moment, everything stayed deathly quiet; no one moved. Richard stared into the windshield as if he were still driving. Rob looked out the window as if scenery still passed in front of it.

"We're here!" Mama finally said, breaking the spell. Daddy opened the door, and the family piled out.

They fell into a routine practiced through their many years at the house. Mama went to the grocery store to buy provisions. Richard and Jamie retreated to the porch with cigars. Alice busied herself with opening all the windows in the house as Rob opened and shut cabinets.

"Are you looking for the cards? I brought some. I can get them." They always played games together when they were here. In the small confines of the beach house, they were forced to be a family. She could pick up the smell of Daddy's cigar and his and Jamie's laughter over the soft waves of the beach.

Rob didn't answer but continued his determined search with the kitchen cabinets. He yanked the cabinets open with such force that the doors bounced on their hinges, then slammed them shut. Alice was close to telling him that *she* was getting a migraine, when he stopped and trotted to the window she was in the process of forcing open.

"It's stuck." She leaned into the window, caked with years of paint and sea salt.

He ignored her and pulled her to the old couch by the arm.

They sank into the overstuffed cushions that enveloped Alice like a hug, nothing like the stiff antique furniture at her parents' house. She looked up to admire her favorite thing about the room: the light above them, which Mama referred to as "tacky." Pelicans danced around the brass encasing the light. At night, the holes projected little pelicans on the wall. Alice's earliest memory was here as a toddler, sitting between Rob's legs and looking at those pelicans on the wall.

"Listen, Al," Rob began. Her attention snapped back to him. "I..." He started, then shook his head and thought better of it. She stared at his hands bouncing on his knees and how much they had grown in the last few years, how much larger they were than hers now. Calloused skin dotted the tips of his fingers from playing his acoustic guitar.

"Something might happen, while we're here," he said slowly. "I might...go away for a while."

"What do you mean?"

"Leave the house."

Her chest constricted like it did right before the plunge down the wooden roller coasters at the pier where the whack of the cart on the track synchronized to her heartbeat.

"Why?"

"I can't explain it right now."

Alice's favorite two weeks of the year threatened to slip away from her. If he left, they would all leave. Then she would be trapped at home, listening to Rob and Daddy yell in the house like she had for the last six months, followed by her parents yelling at each other and shushing one another every few minutes when it got too loud.

They didn't realize she could hear everything from the crack underneath their bedroom room, which was two inches too large, could hear every argument about how Rob needed to learn to respect his elders, needed to stop skipping school, needed to get his act together and "get serious" now that he was in high school, needed to learn so many things about how to be a "gentleman," and maybe the boarding school where Daddy had gone was the place to do it. Plus, the kids could use some space—it wasn't "normal" for siblings to be so attached, and wasn't he a bad influence on Alice?

"You can't leave! You'll ruin everything!" She started to cry, and Rob hugged her. She refused to hug him back and her arms protected her chest, acting as a barrier between them.

"One day, it'll all make sense. I promise. I'll explain everything when you're older."

"I'll be in *sixth* grade this year! I am older!" She stomped her foot on the scratched hardwood.

"You're my favorite person, Al." He stood up and headed back to his room, leaving half the cabinet doors open. "Don't forget that."

She screamed behind him, "Rob? Just stay for a few days, please! There's nothing fun at home! Rob! Rob!" She heard the door shut, but she didn't go after him. She buried her head in the pillow, crying with frustration and confusion, breathing in the familiar mildew-and-salt smell of the couch. Eventually, she heard a car pull into the garage.

Mama came up the stairs, carrying a load of groceries as Alice sat up from the damp cushion. She stroked the impression of the cushion's seam on her cheek with her hand, feeling the indentation as a sign that this was real.

Mama set the groceries down on the counter and glanced at her from the kitchen. "Were you crying?"

Alice looked at her through wet eyes as a type of confirmation.

"*Why* are you crying?"

Alice was sure Mama's next statement would be "Don't be difficult."

"I can't explain right now," Alice said, trying Rob's phrase on for size.

"I asked. If you aren't going to tell me, that's fine, and you can just quit your woe-is-me act and help me with the groceries. I'm going to ask you one more time: Why are you crying?"

Despite Mama's insistence that she was going to ask only one more time, Alice didn't sense the issue would be dropped. And she wanted it dropped.

"It's hot," Alice said lamely. She was never a skilled liar. That was Rob's job—to invent the excuses and make sure she and he were on the same page before their parents came home.

Mama raised an eyebrow but went back downstairs for another load of groceries. After four more trips, she unbagged them and set everything on the counter, as if each item was on display. Alice watched with one of the cushions hugged into her body.

After a few minutes, Mama approached her and handed her an apron and a vegetable peeler. Without words, Alice rose from the couch and wiped her face on the apron. The fabric touched the floor as she tied it around her. She piled the potatoes in her arms and carried them to the sink. As she began to peel, Mama tsked three times with her tongue before she resumed her own chopping.

That night, after Mama came in to tell her to turn the lights out for the second time, Alice lay in bed in the dark and tried to stay awake. She thought about tiptoeing to Rob's room and tapping at the door. She wanted to say sorry for yelling earlier, but she was still mad that he might ruin the trip. *So selfish of him,* she thought, as she crossed her arms under the covers and tried to memorize the cracks on the ceiling. Plus, if she wanted to creep down to his room, she would have to wait for the adults to go to bed since Rob always slept in the basement. She could still see the porch lights on from her open bedroom window and hear her parents and Jamie talking. They were discussing the latest fight with his then-new wife, the one Mama wouldn't let Alice meet because "there's no sense in getting attached." The conversation bored her.

She tried to stay awake. With one finger out of the covers, she drew squares, circles, and rectangles of the shapes in the room, tracing each lightly with her hand in space. She counted how many items were in the room—143. She didn't say her nightly prayers. She knew if she did that the devil would put her to sleep because he didn't like prayers. She knew this because Jamie had told her.

Alice practiced the songs she'd learned that year at camp, determined to remember them when school started in August, so she could teach them to her school friends. She sang under her breath: "Miss Suzie had a steamboat, the steamboat had a bell— *ding ding*! Miss Suzie went to heaven; the steamboat went to— Hello, operator…" When she reached the end, she started again, and each time she progressed through the song a little slower.

When she heard a loud sound, she sat up in bed and realized she had fallen asleep. What time was it? Only pitch-black darkness and the sound of the ocean came through the window. She flicked on the lamp on her bedside table to look at the clock and saw it was 1:00 a.m. Afraid her parents would see the light, she turned it back off and went quietly to the door. She cracked it open.

"Shh," Alice said quietly, to no one. Everything was still. She crawled on hands and knees on the carpeted floor that separated her door from the landing and lay on her stomach, hidden behind the wall. Her head peeked through the railing at the living room and kitchen below.

Light filled the room and she drew back slightly behind the wall, blinking as her eyes adjusted to the light. She heard footsteps in the living room below. Daddy stomped across the room in plaid boxer shorts and no shirt. When he reached the stairs, he flipped on the light and she saw him disappear down them.

Alice briefly considered a retreat to her room with the desk pushed in front of the door. She was probably strong enough. What if the sound she'd heard was robbers? She tried to play the sound back in her head. Was it a bang and then a shatter, like if the window were broken? Was it a prying, then the sound of metal on wood, as if someone had broken in through the door? Was it a bang and then a soft thud, like if something had fallen off a shelf, hit something on the way down, and then hit the carpet? She couldn't remember.

Since Rob and Jamie always slept in the basement's two bedrooms, they were there. And now Daddy was in the basement as well. She thought the sound had come from that side of the house, but she couldn't be sure. Daddy kept a rifle propped up beside his bed in their house, but he didn't have it here. She tried to form a plan. If the robbers came up the stairs to the living room, what would she do?

Mama was no doubt still asleep in the master bedroom. Daddy always commented that she slept like a log and that Rob and Alice would need to wake her up if the house caught fire. She slept deeply, because according to Mama, she had a bad ear, but Alice thought it had something to do with the pill she took after dinner.

Now, Alice heard Daddy's loud, tense voice, the words muffled by the distance. She inched her chin along the carpet closer to the opening, but still couldn't hear what he said. She heard Rob too. They went back and forth for a few minutes, then it was quiet. She heard a door open and shut. A car started. No robbers then.

While Alice prepared herself to go down the steps, so she could better hear the commotion, she heard footsteps on the stairs up from the basement. She lightly clicked the door shut, raced back to her bed and pulled the covers up to her neck. She shut her eyes tight as she heard a car pull away.

Behind her eyelids, the level of darkness changed. Someone had turned on the hall light. Rob. She knew from the way he turned the doorknob—slowly, not trying to wake her, with less urgency than the situation required. The bed moved as he sat at the bottom. He was leaving and something told her now that it was more than just leaving the beach house.

If she opened her eyes and said goodbye, he would be gone, and no goodbye could ever be good enough. She kept her eyes closed and became very conscious of her breathing. In, one Mississippi, two Mississippi, three Mississippi. Out, one Mississippi, two Mississippi, three Mississippi, hoping that he would stay until morning, waiting, then stay forever.

He sat there for a few minutes, and she felt the bed tilt slightly a few times, as if he had moved his hand to touch her shoulder, then thought better of it. But after thirty-two Mississippis, he leaned over to her bedside table, and she heard papers rustling.

Then, he stood up and let out a small huff as he lifted something from the floor. Alice opened her eyes to watch him walk with his duffel and acoustic guitar case to the door. She opened her mouth to call his name, but no noise came out. He shut the door behind him, and he was gone.

Alice heard the small flick of the hall light turning off, and it was dark again. Another door opened and shut before the house fell silent. She reached over to the bedside table. Even in the dark, she knew he had switched his drawing with hers.

As a child and young adult, before she had slammed the door to Rob's memory, she played this scene thousands of times in hundreds of variations. Each time, she willed herself to be brave, to open her eyes, to hug her brother and to tell him to stay. Alice returned to that day, that moment in particular when she feigned sleep and her brother watched her. It was in that mistake that she would find years of blame.

She picked up the bag of books labeled "personal effects."

The first was *A Confederacy of Dunces*. She had never heard of it. On the first page, she saw "From the library of Mrs. Maura Tate" written in her mother's usual neat script. She started reading, twisting the book to read her brother's notes in the margin and around the corners as her mother had done so many years ago. Eventually, Alice fell asleep and dreamed random dreams of cluttered bedrooms, odd hats, and New Orleans.

Alice jolted awake when she heard the jostling of keys in the door. The sun streamed through the windows.

When Grace opened the door, Buddy sprinted out into the yard, and Alice jumped. They both took in the scene: the papers scattered on various surfaces, the Indian food containers, the beer bottles, the crumpled yellow papers that covered the tile in the kitchen.

"Well, good morning!" Grace said.

Alice rubbed her eyes and glanced at her watch: 8:00 a.m. How late had she stayed up last night? She could lie back down on the couch and sleep for several more hours.

"Coffee?" Grace pretended everything was normal and didn't pause to read any of the papers. She went to the coffee maker and busied herself with scooping in the grounds precisely, filling the water, and preparing them both mugs. She stood in front of the coffee maker with her back to Alice, swaying her head to a little melody only she could hear.

Alice stacked all the papers and files together and placed them back in the box with the books on top. She put the legal pad, now cluttered with her notes and the timeline, in her backpack. Next, she recycled the beer bottles and took the remnants of last night's Indian food to the compost. When she finished, Grace turned to her with two coffee mugs.

"Want to sit on the porch?"

Alice nodded, and they brought their mugs to the rocking chairs on the back porch.

Grace drew her legs in to her chest and rested her mug on one knee. She leaned over to blow it. "I just love the water in the winter, don't you?"

The gold necklace with her Korean name that Grace always wore glittered with the sunlight, and Alice absentmindedly reached up to drag the necklace Walker gave her with the kids' birthstones along its chain. She wasn't wearing it though. "Yes."

They both looked out over the water as they sipped their coffee. Alice studied the water and replayed last night. Her mind pictured the end of her notes where she had written New Orleans and circled it several times. She knew what she had to do next: the last letter, where the prison released him, where he died, where Lila King still lived.

And, from a distant place in her mind, she added: *Where Jake lives.*

By the time she made it back to the house, Caitlin had already sent Alice six different texts with things she forgot that she wanted dropped off at the school, where she would be holed up practicing until the play opening that night. Unusual, but Caitlin had inherited her mother's habit of lapsing into forgetfulness when under pressure.

Alice grabbed another cup of coffee and sat down at the computer in her house's little office that the kids used for their homework. She brought the timeline and the last letter. As she had days before, she Googled *Lila King*. This time, though, she searched for something different.

She passed the links for Lila King, a journalist at the *Washington Post*; Lila King, a teacher in California who recently won Teacher of the Year; Lila King, who died in Massachusetts at the age of eighty-seven, according to an obituary. Alice scrolled until she found Lila King, the singer, listed on websites for several bars and restaurants where she played. Most were in New Orleans, but some were scattered throughout the South. Alice couldn't locate any listings for that week.

She would go and find Lila, deliver the last letter. It seemed to make so much sense to Alice, especially while sleep deprived and a little hungover. Since she didn't know how long it would take her to find Lila, she booked a one-way ticket to New Orleans for that night, after Caitlin's play, when Walker would be back in town to watch the kids. She knew Walker would not take *that* well, wouldn't take any mention of her brother well. But as Jamie would say, it was time to fish or cut bait.

She walked into the bedroom and paused at the bed to kick off her shoes and jeans before she climbed in. She just needed to take a short nap. With her eyes closed, she ran through everything she needed to do before she left for New Orleans.

Talk to Walker, obviously.

Call her mother's nurses to tell them she would be out of town for a few days and wouldn't be visiting tomorrow. Text Grace that she'd be out of town for a few days. Get out of carpool duty for Robbie.

Buy flowers for Caitlin's play tonight. Deal with Jamie. Gather all of Caitlin's requests.

Sleep.

CHAPTER TWENTY-FOUR

Alice dreamed about New Orleans.

She meandered the streets of the Big Easy as if tugged by some unknowable force. She knew she should find her hotel, but the thought floated by without judgment. She was lost but walked uninhibited. Even without a map or her phone, she felt at peace. Alice wandered up a never-ending street and ducked into the different plant-filled courtyards as she went.

The street was empty, and but for the sounds of twangs, trumpets, and a jazzy saxophone that begged for her attention, absent of human players. As she listened to pick out the different instruments, her mind focused on the sound of a single acoustic guitar.

She turned at an intersection and saw him: Rob sat on the curb with his guitar, fingering out the notes in the careful way he did as a teenager. She stood there and watched him, as she considered what to say. He looked up, and the music stopped.

"Al! You found me!" He set the guitar down and stood up. She ran toward him. Healthy, he ran to her with a smile on his face. He had let his hair get so long!

She ran faster to reach him, but on the other side of the street, Rob slowed to a light jog. His hair lost some of its shine, his face grayed and his muscles shrank, and he morphed into the Rob from the photo in her mother's letter. The frail, shell-of-Rob Rob. Seeing this, Alice broke into a sprint, and her mouth fell open in a pant as she scrambled to reach the other side of the expanding street.

"Al!" he cried. "Alice! Alice!"

She ran faster: "I'm coming!" She tucked her head like she learned to do in PE and pumped her arms. Like she had run after him that day in the woods, when he'd told her to scream what she hated. Her calves burned, and she glanced at her feet, only to realize that she wore the sky-high heels with the red bottoms that remained untouched at the back of her closet from a bygone wedding anniversary.

"Alice! Alice! ALICE!"

She woke up with a gasp for air, as if she had just surfaced from a swimming pool.

"Are you asleep?" Walker said. "It's 2:00 p.m."

She was still in her bedroom. She looked at the clock on the bedside table and saw that Walker was right about the time.

"Yeah, sorry about that." She raised her hand to brush her hair from her face. It was wet with sweat. "I fell asleep at the Center last night, and I…just didn't sleep well."

Walker frowned.

"I came to drop my suitcase, but I've got to go into the office for a few hours. Meet you at the school?"

She nodded. He turned to walk out.

"Walker!" she said, remembering New Orleans and the information she had to deliver about Caitlin's scholarship. He jumped, and then turned back. Seeing his expression, Alice's resolve dulled. She made a quick calculation in her head: him finding out tonight would be better than finding out now because his window for reaction would be smaller. Or perhaps she just didn't have the energy to get into it now.

"Glad you're home," she said. He cocked his head, and she smiled.

"Thanks," he muttered and walked out.

From there, Alice popped out of bed and started her flurry of activity.

———————————

Three hours later, Alice returned for her second visit this week to Hilltree High School with Caitlin's stuff and Robbie in tow, and with plenty of time to make the 6:00 p.m. opening curtain.

"Wait a second," she said to Robbie, as he tried to scurry off with a friend and a deck of cards as soon as they entered the school. She hugged him. "I've got to go out of town tonight, so you're going to be with Dad, okay?"

"When will you be back?"

"In a few days."

He nodded, and she kissed him again on the cheek, telling him to "Be good for Dad" as he ran off again, wiping his cheek on the way.

As Alice made her way to the lobby, Dr. Garcia spotted her and charged toward her. "Tonight's the night!"

"Yeah, tonight's the night," Alice said. The night she would leave for New Orleans, the night she would come clean with Walker. The night she would choose not to tell any more little white lies.

Seeing Meredith in the corner, carrying the bouquet of flowers Alice had asked her to pick up, Alice excused herself. "I need to talk to you," she said.

"Oh?"

Alice eyed Christian as he lingered behind Meredith. She turned around and asked him to get some sodas. He smiled and ran off nearly as fast as Robbie.

"So, I've decided to go to New Orleans," Alice said. "To track down Rob. I'm on the last letter, and something feels *right* about going there to finish this. To find out the last piece."

"Then you should go," Meredith said, nodding, but with her eyes narrowed. "When?"

"Tonight."

"And how did Walker feel about that?"

Alice grimaced. *Why was Meredith always so damn direct?* "I haven't told him…yet. I was hoping you could check on the kids some, make sure Walker and Caitlin don't start World War III while I'm gone."

"Of course."

Alice took a breath to ready herself to say out loud the thing she had kept from Meredith for weeks. "I think it will be good to think about things. I…I found…" Better to just come out and say it. "Walker's cheating on me."

Meredith's face softened, but she caught herself quickly when Alice waved her hand in front of her body, as if to say it wasn't worth discussing. Meredith simply reached out to rub Alice's arm. "Oh, honey."

"I don't really want to talk about it," Alice said, crossing her arms and pushing off Meredith's touch.

Meredith nodded, changing the subject: "New Orleans, huh?"

"Yup."

"Haven't been there in a few years."

"I haven't been there since…that time." That time the three of them—she, Meredith, and Jake—had driven all night one Friday to make it to the Halloween parade on a whim.

"I bet not a lot has changed," Meredith offered, and Alice took it to mean that not a lot had changed with Jake, from the way Meredith looked at her carefully as she said it. So, she knew he lived there too. They had probably been friends on Facebook this whole time.

"Maybe," Alice said, without additional details.

Alice saw Jamie exit the bathroom and head toward the theater. Meredith followed her eyes, and Alice tugged her behind a wall as he passed.

"I thought y'all made up?"

"We did, but I think he may have stolen money from my mother, a lot of money. Or not *stolen*, but not kept on paying the PI. I don't think he's—" Alice said as the bell sounded to indicate the audience should take their seats.

Meredith and Alice found seats on the end. As a group of elementary schoolers sang "Catch a Falling Star" in a type of opening act while the audience settled, Alice's phone vibrated. Walker: He would be a little late. Could she save him a seat? She briefly considered saying she had already turned off her phone, but texted him the seat number anyway. As bad as it would be to sit next to him as Caitlin's announcement blindsided him, she worried what he would say without her there to police him.

Soon, the lights turned off and a teacher appeared onstage to announce the high school's interpretation of *Antigone*, directed by Caitlin Wright. An actor walked onstage with heavy Gothic makeup and a purple mohawk.

Alice didn't remember what the actors said. After an intermission in which she stayed in her seat and tried to avoid Jamie, the play continued. Alice sat straight, trying to make out Caitlin's arm motions from the orchestra pit or the side stage. When Walker sat down, he leaned in and kissed her on the cheek, before watching for a few minutes. After that, he typed on his phone, angling it slightly away from her. She noticed him texting Brittani. Of course.

"Work," he whispered to her. She watched him text, thinking he had everything situated, everything figured out. She couldn't help but smile, watching him. She felt powerful, knowing before he did that he would have a terrible night, maybe one of the worst in his life. Knowing what the next hour would bring, how he would feel his life caving around him—a feeling she knew well, but he had yet to experience.

In what seemed like a flash, the play ended, and the clapping began. They all stood as the actors bowed. After they introduced the students and clapped for them, Dr. Garcia took the microphone. "And I'd also like to honor our fantastic director, Caitlin Wright, who completely reimagined *Antigone* and what it could be in the twenty-first century."

Caitlin stood and waved each hand, like a presidential candidate, instead of bowing like the actors. Alice clenched and unclenched her toes and eyed Meredith with worry. Meredith looked back at her and mouthed *What?* Alice shook her head and held up a finger. *Just wait, you'll see.*

"And she'll get to continue to use her gifts next year at New

York University. We're truly honored to announce that Miss Caitlin Wright has won the Emerging Women Writers Fellowship and a full ride to NYU!"

In a second, Alice saw several things. The first was Dr. Garcia's large claps and plastered-on smile that looked like he was about to take his own bow in front of the district superintendent. The second was her daughter, briefly shocked, then frozen in place as Dr. Garcia approached her for a side hug. The third was Walker's warm breath on her ear as he leaned in and hissed, *"Did you know about this?"*

He had never been able to whisper. Alice had teased him about it when they first started dating, but after she had told him enough times about his volume, she realized he didn't care if people heard him.

On the stage, the spotlights caught Caitlin. She was looking at Alice, or Alice felt she was. Alice watched the emotions play across her sweet daughter's face—the surprise, the happiness, then Caitlin checked those positive emotions and replaced them with another: fear.

"Alice." Her shoulders jostled under Walker's hand and she turned to face him. "Did. You. Know. About. This?"

She nodded once, not really listening, and turned her head back to the stage.

She looked again at her daughter's face, the one she knew best in the world, the confidence from YouTube gone now. She wondered if Caitlin was watching her mother the same way, studying Alice's reaction and imagining she could hear her mother's thoughts.

Little white lies, Alice thought with a laugh. She thought back to the funeral when she'd made promises to what would become

Robbie, still in her stomach then. Caitlin had tugged at her dress, asking why her parents were fighting. Her daughter, who she still tried to protect, took it all in. Alice realized that now. Caitlin had absorbed every facet of their lives like a little sponge. An overwhelming wave of emotion rose up inside Alice that she struggled to identify—pride.

Dr. Garcia had her daughter's hand and they were posing for a picture that wouldn't turn out well, Caitlin staring dumbstruck beyond the frame.

Alice stood. She heard Walker say her name again, but she heard it without identifying it, like as a child at the river, deep underwater, when she listened for Rob singing Elvis from the canoe.

She clapped and felt the stinging of her hands. Meredith stood up beside her, pulling Christian up by his sleeve. The rest of the auditorium stood now, and Walker followed. It wasn't until Alice saw her daughter crying that she realized she was crying as well. She mouthed, *I love you. I'm so proud of you*, and watched Caitlin nod back at her.

Walker leaned in toward Alice. "We'll talk about this in the car."

She nodded. It was time. To talk about everything.

She watched as Walker approached the exit door amid the claps, hoots, and whistles for his daughter. Through his button-down, she could see the muscles in his back tense, as if he wanted to turn to see if Alice was following him but didn't want to give her the satisfaction.

Alice scooped the flowers off the floor, along with the bag with Caitlin's stuff still at her feet. "Can you take Robbie to dinner and then drop him home in an hour? I need to talk to Walker," she said to Meredith.

The rustling had started as the audience looked for their purses and finished cans of soda, ready to leave. Alice marched up the mostly clear aisle to where her daughter stood on the side, still stunned while people crowded around her and patted her on the back. Alice glanced behind her to where Meredith and Christian were looking in the crowd for Robbie, and to where Walker had strayed from the door and now stood halfway between it and her.

Alice pushed through the crowd around her daughter and hugged Caitlin, kissed her on the cheek, and smelled her hair, like she always did when she was a baby, breathing her in. In her arms, Caitlin shook, really crying now.

"I'm sorry, I'm sorry," she said. "I signed your name. I shouldn't have. I didn't know they were going to do that."

Alice pulled away and wiped her tears, turning Caitlin away from the crowd toward the wall so no one could see her. Caitlin didn't care though.

"I wish you would have told me, but it's okay. We're so proud of you."

Caitlin turned, looking for Walker.

"He'll come around. I'm going to talk to him. It will all be okay." She hugged Caitlin again, dropped the bag at her feet, and handed her the flowers. Then Alice released her daughter back to the crowd. She smiled at everyone waiting to tell her daughter congratulations and backed away, leaving Caitlin with her many admirers.

Alice felt a hand on hers with a slight pull—Walker. "Come on." He gave his daughter a small wave as he turned around.

Alice walked through the auditorium of well-wishers, stopping every few minutes as people told her how magnificent it all was and how they always knew Caitlin was destined for something special. Alice thanked them, and Walker smiled along too. In between, he began a halted conversation.

"You knew about this."

"I just found out. And I was waiting for the right time to talk to you about it."

"It doesn't matter," Walker said, loud enough to make a passing young couple stare, "because she's not going." He flashed a smile in their direction.

"She's going."

"Well, I'm not paying for it."

The card Walker had never pulled, even through years of funding the Center. He slapped it down in front of her with such ease that Alice realized it had been there, all along, at the front of his mind, even if he didn't voice it out loud.

"You're not the only with money." When her father died, he had quietly left a trust to "Alice and her children," as opposed to "Alice, Walker, and their children." As if Richard had known her marriage would fail, like everyone else apparently. Something she and Walker never discussed after their meeting with Richard's lawyer five years ago. "And besides, it's a full ride. It will be cheaper than UGA even."

Walker and Alice trudged forward in silence.

He leaned in again: "You made me look like an idiot."

"I made *you* look like an idiot?" She mouthed "hello" at another mother in Robbie's class and waved to her youngest child.

"Yes, you made me look like an idiot!" Walker punctuated the statement with the bang of his hands on the metal push bar on the school's exit door. They walked back side by side to the dark parking lot.

"Can I ask you a question?" Alice turned toward him as they stopped at her car. "Do you think I'm stupid?"

"What?" Walker said, surprised.

"Do you honestly think I don't know you're having an affair? Do you really think you're that smooth, that I couldn't see something so obvious that half the neighborhood knows, that your own daughter knows?"

Walker put his hands up in surrender as if this was the most ridiculous accusation he had entertained in his two decades of lawyering.

"I don't know what you heard or what Caitlin *thinks* she knows," he said, in a stilted voice she imagined played well with clients who were about to lose their fortunes. "But I don't know what you're talking about."

She felt a rush of sadness for him as she took in his features and the practiced look meant to signal confidence and slight frustration. She still wasn't mad, even now.

The ache of failure permeated her chest. This was who he turned into and who she turned into. Who they had made each other. And for all the effort she had put in, to accommodate him as he adjusted to Caitlin coming out in ninth grade, and the rapid growth of the Center in the last decade, and the increased demands from Maura on Alice's time—to all of the excuses she made for him and patience she gave him, he had answered with betrayal.

He was the one throwing his life away, the one who wouldn't realize it until he woke up one morning, without his wife, without his kids, without his dog, without the quiet comfort they had built around him. He was the one who would wake up and realize that he had ruined his life, while she would wake up tomorrow and feel hers beginning again.

"I'm leaving," Alice said. Walker flinched.

"Alice! What? Jesus Christ. Just wait a second!"

"For a few days," Alice interrupted. "To think. About things."

"This really isn't necessary."

"Just stop pretending. I've read some of the messages. You were texting her just now, in the theater."

"You read my texts?" he yelled, before he remembered the setting for their argument. He turned to smile in case someone was listening on the other side of the parking lot. He gestured to the car, and they both climbed into her Prius, with her in the driver's seat.

"You *read* my texts?" he repeated.

"Yes, I read your texts and you're cheating. Guess that makes us even." Her voice dripped in sarcasm. She crossed her arms over her chest.

She hadn't planned to read her husband's text messages. She wasn't one of *those* spouses. Just a glance to an illuminated phone on the counter was all she had needed to know. Hidden in plain sight, a lie he hadn't bothered to tell. Somehow the lack of effort he took to mask the affair intensified the betrayal, as if she didn't deserve proper lies.

"Fine. Okay? It's true. But she loves me. She actually treats me like she likes me and wants to be around me, wants to tell me things." He glanced toward Alice to see if the reference stung her. It had. She blushed.

"It just… It got out of hand," he continued. He grabbed her hands and held them over the center console, tracing the lines of her palm like he used to. He looked up at her with his head slightly bent, as if shrinking himself below her. She recognized the gesture from her studies of dominance in wolf packs during her conservation biology classes. "Let's just talk this out," he said. "Please."

She pulled her hands away and twisted to buckle her seat belt. Out her window, she saw the cars lining up toward the exit. People flooded out of the high school. She cranked the engine and drove a few rows over, then stopped in the aisle at Walker's Audi and pointed to it, signaling him to get out.

"You'll follow me?" he said, one hand on the handle, his face looking back at her. She stared ahead through the windshield at the dusty paw prints that clouded her view, left by the feral cats that lurked around the Center.

"No, I'm on the last flight out tonight." She turned her body to glance at her duffel resting on the back seat. He followed her eyes. "Meredith will drop Robbie off at home in an hour, and Caitlin's going to the cast party and then to a friend's to sleep."

She turned back to the windshield and tapped on the steering wheel twice with her fingers, as if to signal the conversation's end. Out of the corner of her eye, she saw his face looked briefly shocked, but she didn't turn toward it. With her left hand, she flipped the locks from muscle memory and the car clicked with the new freedom. He jumped at the sound.

"Where are you going?"

She shrugged. "I've got a few things to take care of."

"How long are you going to be gone?"

She shrugged again. She traced the seam on the back of the steering wheel with her fingertip.

"You're not serious?" She looked at Walker's face now. It made sense. For him, this seemed completely out of nowhere, when for her, she had built to this moment for the last decade as they stepped further and further apart.

"I'm serious." She released her seat belt and leaned over him to pull the passenger door latch. It sprung open.

"What do you expect me to tell the kids?"

She looked him right in the eye. "What do you think *I* tell them when you're with Brittani?"

"There's someone else, isn't there? You're getting all high and mighty with me when you're doing the same thing behind *my* back." He pointed to his chest and his finger crumpled against his heart with the force of it.

"We'll talk when I get back."

"I really think we should talk now!"

They both knew their talks went nowhere, neither willing to get into the ring, neither willing to show their scars. It was why they fought so infrequently—they didn't know how to cut each other, didn't know where to twist the knife because of all the unknowns between them. He could never hurt her as Rob had, as Jake had, as Caitlin's video had. The safety had drawn her to him, but to get what she wanted, to let her desires and hopes and dreams and fears out of their locked boxes in her mind, she had to leave that safety behind.

"Problem?" She and Walker both turned to see Jamie, approaching Walker's open door.

Alice's heart jumped again. She had to get out of here. Her calm facade eroded with the introduction of another adversary.

"Just get out!" She pushed Walker's shoulder, trying to encourage him to get out of the car. He finally climbed out to stand with

Jamie. As she leaned over the seat again to shut the door, her heart raced. She had more energy than she had had in a long time. She was *doing something.* She smiled.

She threw the car into reverse, as Walker and Jamie looked at her, with different shades of surprise. She backed out of the spot, skidding her wheels, and flipped to drive. Then, on second thought, she braked and rolled down her window.

"I'm onto you too, buster!" Alice said, pointing at Jamie wildly as she drove away. He wouldn't steal money from *her* mother without some consequences. Wouldn't call off the search for Rob without her finding out about it. And as much as he probably thought he would get away with it, he wouldn't. She wouldn't let him.

She chuckled to herself as she exited the parking lot, remembering their faces. By the time she reached the highway, though, and the adrenaline had worn off, her heart raced for a different reason. She knew there was no going back from what she had just done.

CHAPTER TWENTY-FIVE

Alice drove along the highway through Atlanta to the airport, watching the buildings dotted with light rise against the black night. As always, her Prius rattled slightly when the speedometer rounded seventy miles per hour. Usually it didn't bother her. Tonight, though, she needed the speed to add miles to her distance from home.

Her flight to New Orleans took off at 11:35 p.m., so by the time she checked in, only a few people waited in the security line. A college-aged girl in an oversize T-shirt, Chacos, and a backpack the size of her body explained anxiously to the TSA employee checking boarding passes that she was going backpacking. He looked her up and down as if to say "Duh." A young couple wrapped and unwrapped their limbs around each other and pointed to each other's wedding rings. "I'm traveling with my *husband*," the woman said before they exchanged giggles.

Alice held her boarding pass in front of her and looked up at the ceiling. She heard the light buzz of her phone vibrating in her backpack, as she had for the entire drive. She wouldn't look at it until she buckled her seat belt on the plane, she promised. It would be Walker.

She busied herself with finding her gate, changing out of nice jeans and a button-down blouse into leggings and a pilled sweater, and filling up her water bottle. Alice riffled through her backpack to retrieve the final letter one last time. Her eyes settled on the words *New Orleans* as if to verify that they hadn't disappeared off the page in her absence.

She boarded the plane with the letter in hand and stroked the seal with her thumb as she walked down the aisles to a row that remained clear thus far. She sat down and immediately took out her phone: twelve missed calls, thirty-seven text messages. Before she could stop herself, Alice let out a groan that made the man across the aisle glance at her, then turn away. Her eyes skipped over Walker's text thread and missed calls from him and Jamie.

Alice opened a text from Meredith: Dropped Robbie off with Walker after dinner at Waffle House, his choice :-)

She texted Caitlin: Have fun at the cast party! Let's talk tomorrow. She thought about telling Caitlin about her trip but didn't want to worry her on her big night. They could talk tomorrow.

She turned the phone off and lay back in the seat, with the letter still in her lap. Alice had never been afraid of flying but as the plane took off, she played all the things that could go wrong with this trip in her head, beginning with the plane crashing. Lila could be gone. Maybe she wouldn't find her.

The flight attendant reached Alice's row, and she ordered a rum and Coke and eagerly handed over her credit card. She rested the drink on her knee and felt the cold seep through her leggings until her skin felt prickly from the ice. She closed her eyes.

How many people heard her and Walker's display? Were parents chatting about it right now over wine, how all wasn't well in the Wright house? How Alice Wright had snapped? When she realized she didn't care, a new calmness washed over her. This world had never mattered to her, as if she had always known she was a temporary visitor to the country-club-going, high-heeled Kayla Welshes of the world.

Alice played her and Walker's future life together again. This time, though, with the secret out in the open, pretending seemed impossible. The vacation to the Bahamas that he would propose if she agreed to stay became forced, his arms crossed. Unlike her previous vision of the trip, now, with the weight of what happened between them so visible, neither would be able to overcome it. By saying it aloud—*cheating* and *affair*—she had violated some pact between them.

Surely Walker wouldn't prolong the divorce or make it more difficult, both because of his reputation at the firm and because of the children. But Alice had heard plenty of stories, passed around the neighborhood as the mothers sat by the pool, of once-sweet husbands who as soon as they heard the word *divorce* became vicious and amassed a team of lawyers to fight for custody of children they hadn't spent time with when they lived in the same house. The point: no matter how a man treated his wife when they were together, how he treated her when she wanted out remained a mystery. Would Walker be Dr. Jekyll or Mr. Hyde?

It was past 2:00 a.m. by the time Alice made her way to the hotel in the French Quarter that Meredith had booked for her. With her clothes and shoes on, she lay down without unmaking the bed. With all the pillows at the top of the bed, Alice's feet hung off the end. She kicked off her sneakers.

Outside her window, the music swirled around the hotel. It came from all directions like a call and response with one saxophone answering to a set of drums blocks over, which was answered in turn by a breathy jazz singer below. She closed her eyes. She thought one happy thought as she tumbled into unconsciousness—

Rob would have been happy here.

When she woke, the room was so dark that Alice lay still for a few minutes, questioning her location, the day, the time, if this was a dream, and if any of these questions mattered. Her hand fumbled on the bedside table in an unsuccessful hunt for the lamp. Finally, with her hands as a barrier in front of her, she inched to where she thought the windows were and opened the drapes. It was still dark outside, but she examined her surroundings for the first time by the light of the streetlamps. She found her backpack and retrieved her phone: 5:23 a.m. In Georgia, one hour ahead, Buddy would be pacing the hallway in front of her bedroom, waiting for his morning walk.

She was tired still but knew she wouldn't be able to fall back asleep. Alice ambled to the bathroom to splash water on her face, and as she did, her stomach rumbled. She searched the fridge but found only miniature bottles of wine and vodka. She would have to go out, but what could she find this early?

Then she remembered she woke up in New Orleans.

She dressed and trudged down to the lobby where the morning was still a continuation of the previous night. A woman yelled about the toilet in her room, and people staggered in and out, some dressed in costumes or masks, some obviously drunk. Alice walked out into the dark morning and headed toward the nearest lights.

A few determined tourists still meandered in the streets,

holding one another as cars scooted past them. The street performers, so active on her drive into the city, had dwindled to one
man sitting on the curb, breathing into a saxophone. The sways
that accompanied each note resembled a metronome clicking
back and forth lazily on its base.

She found an all-hours café and ducked inside to a booth by the
window. A waitress took Alice's order, rolling her neck at the same
time. "Bloody Mary?" she wanted to know on the second rotation.

After ordering coffee and the breakfast special, Alice laid the
map from the hotel on the table. She had stared at the cross
streets for Lila's address so many times on her phone that her
finger found the intersection easily on the map. It didn't look far.

She sipped her coffee and watched the last of the late-night
patrons leave the diner. Her tired-looking waitress talked to
another in a crisper uniform before she left. The new waitress
came over immediately and smiled at Alice before refilling her
coffee. Outside the window, the street cleaners took over the
sidewalks from the flashy night creatures, the air eerily devoid of
its normal jazz.

Alice was beginning to fold the map when the name of
another street caught her eye: Iberville Street. She looked from
right to left as if she expected to get caught before she retrieved
her phone and went to Jake's website to check the address again.
It was only a few blocks from her hotel.

Three plates arrived, and Alice breathed in the foods that
accompanied her childhood, mixed in with the Louisiana Creole.
Her mouth watered as she picked up her spoon to scoop a bite of
cheesy grits. Thinking of all the mornings with her parents and
Rob at the kitchen table, Alice stirred her grits, eggs, and the bits

of sausage until she ended with a slush that might as well have been churned through the blender. She stirred until she caught the eye of a man in a suit who sat down with his coffee. She straightened and spooned a bite of the mush into her mouth.

As she buttered and spread honey on her biscuit, Alice rehearsed the conversation she would have with Lila in her head. Would she think Alice was crazy for traveling to another city and dropping in on her unannounced? Would she even want to talk about Rob? Could she be the woman from the nude photographs that Alice had found in the box at her parents' house? Another part of her felt a desperate clinging. She knew Lila was her last chance to learn more about Rob. Whatever she learned today would be the most she knew about her brother, likely for the rest of her life. After she talked to Lila, he would truly be gone.

Alice paid her bill and left the café, walking toward Mid-City and the cross streets on Rob's last letter. By the time the sun warmed the asphalt in earnest, she was approaching the turn for Lila's street. In contrast to the French Quarter's five-floor-high houses with wraparound porches and only an inch between the houses, these spread out in a more residential area. Chained fences lined a few houses, and a man sitting in a rocking chair on his porch waved to Alice as she passed.

She walked in the street now, because the block didn't have a sidewalk, and she counted the houses as she passed, looking for the correct address. He could have died here. She remembered the liveliness of the city last night, with the music, which seemed to come from every direction, and the streetlamps with the light bouncing off the discarded purple and green beads that still decorated the trees. Now on Lila's street, Alice pictured her brother trapped in one of the little houses, with no view and no music to give him comfort, instead of seated on the curb with his guitar, strumming alongside the jazzy street performers.

Alice passed a fenced-in yard, decorated with signs that announced *Private Property* and *Beware of Dog* and glanced behind her to the man on his porch.

The houses skipped a few numbers, and seeing the street number from the letter, she froze. Alice approached the gate of a purple wooden house with a small porch and reached her hand to unlock it and let the latch down silently. She walked on a stone path, decorated with pieces of colored glass stuck into the cement, which interrupted a sprawling yard with weeds that poked out at random intervals of brown and green. As she looked down, so she could navigate the collapsed-in first step, Alice jumped. Out of the corner of her eye, she had seen a man in the window.

She hunched herself over and shuffled to a bush next to the steps to peer in the window. The man paced back and forth in the parlor off the front door, appearing in front of the window every few seconds. She held her breath as she watched his figure. He looked around her height, with hair down to his shoulders and a trim, but stocky build. He concentrated on a book folded over the spine so it could be held in one hand and tapped what looked like a pencil on the side of his head with the other as he walked.

Alice turned away and bounded up the steps to the doorbell. She rang it three times. Then, on second thought, she opened the screened door and knocked hard on the wood.

The doorknob turned in her hand and the door opened. As the light from outside streamed into the hallway, Alice could see him clearly for the first time. She had dared to hope it was Rob, this whole journey some twisted joke or perhaps a plot to fool her father or someone else, a brief jump in logic she hadn't even realized she made until the breath deflated from her chest at the bemused expression on his unfamiliar face.

"Hello?" he said with a smile.

Rob is dead, she reminded herself. The pain felt new each time she remembered this. This is what she wanted from New Orleans: Rob alive. The ability to say to him, it's okay. I forgive you for leaving, and to ask his forgiveness in return for not looking for him more, for not hugging him that night on Amelia Island and telling him not to go, for not asking him what was wrong that night he slammed the guitar. An impossible task.

"Sorry. I, uh, thought you were someone else." Her hands found her backpack straps, and she wrapped her thumbs around them.

The man, who she guessed was about thirty, younger than Rob would be if he'd lived, shifted his hold on the book in his hand.

"Okay, well?" he said, taking a step back, as if to shut the door.

"Sorry! I'm actually looking for Lila King. Do you know if she lives here?"

"You thought I was a woman?"

"No, I didn't think… Never mind. I'm Alice."

"Ben."

She extended her hand and shook his.

"Do you know her?" she said.

"What is this regarding?"

"So, you do know her," Alice offered.

"I'm her cousin. Can you just wait a second? Was she expecting you? I can call her, if you want? Are you a fan?"

"No. I'm...Alice. I'm... Can you tell her that Rob Tate's sister is here?"

"Oh, Rob?"

She nodded. "You knew him?"

"Yup." He punched numbers into a flip phone before he placed it to his ear. He gave her a one-second finger, and the door slowly closed as Alice inched backward to get out of the way. The lock clicked.

Alice looked at the door for a moment, confused, before backing up the rest of the way and letting the screen door slam in front of her face. She looked down the street to where a dog barked in the yard of the "Beware of Dog" house. How long should she wait before knocking again? After a few minutes, as she planned to walk to the end of the block and back, the door opened.

"Sorry about that, Alice. Yes, she wanted me to tell you that she's out for the day. Could you come back tomorrow, in the afternoon? She'll be here then."

"Sure, I—" Before she could ask anything else, the door shut again. This time, though, Alice turned and walked down the steps and back from where she had come. She replayed the interaction in her head, trying to make it seem like a positive. She had found Lila King! She still lived in the house! Tomorrow afternoon wasn't too far away.

As she walked the three miles back to her hotel, she called Grace to see if she needed anything that could be done remotely. "You just take care of yourself. You're on vacation!" Grace told her. She called Caitlin to ask about the cast party and tell her she went out of town and would be back in a few days. "You know how your father is," Alice said. "He'll get used to NYU. Just try to stay out of his way while I'm gone."

Alice called to check on Maura. Another subpar day, the nurses told Alice, before putting Maura on the phone. How much Alice wanted to tell her mother everything she found so far, wanted to tell her about New Orleans. "When I die, I want to wear the pearls," her mother said. "The biggest ones. I'll take them to my grave, so Robinson's catty wife can't have them. She's been eyeing them, you know."

At least in her mother's world, Rob was alive and married, maybe happy.

"I'll make sure of it."

She almost called Meredith but knew her friend would likely ask about the conversation with Walker. Alice decided to call and check on Dylan instead, to see if he had an update on the mysterious Christopher Smith. His letter had no words, only the cross, but Alice knew that for Rob, sometimes art could say more than words.

"Was going to call you today," he said. "I found someone who I think knew Rob through an old buddy of mine. I'm trying to meet up with him in the next few days. I'll call you back, all right?"

She thanked him profusely and hung up. The phone, with no one left to call, knocked lazily against her thigh as she walked.

By the time Alice reached the French Quarter, it was almost lunchtime. She took out the map to find one of the restaurants the man at the hotel's front desk had circled for her. Instead, her eyes lingered on the cross streets for Jake's office.

She picked one of the places and walked there. It seemed

like everywhere she passed, people were sitting down to Sunday brunch. Although the time zone only differed an hour from Atlanta, the timing seemed infinitely different. People moved slowly through the thick air.

She selected one of the circled places in the same courtyard as a famous beignet stand and picked up a *USA Today* from a street vendor on the way inside. She chose a table outside, where she had a good view of the slow-moving line for the sugary treats that looked one hundred people long.

After turning down her second offer of the day for a Bloody Mary, Alice took out the crossword. She ordered a sandwich, but expected it to take a while to arrive, as things seemed to here. She filled in the boxes with a pen but kept having to reread the clues.

Finally, she took out her phone. Taking a deep breath, she found Jake's website again and dialed the number. It's Sunday, she reasoned. No one will answer. Maybe she would just listen to his voice on the voicemail message, like she used to in college when she would call his phone and hang up when she knew he wouldn't be home.

Each ring echoed through her body; all the while, she told herself the call was nothing. Finally, a male voice picked up. "I told you already. Just meet me there with the truck at two. That's all. Can you do that or not?"

"Um. Hello?" Alice said.

"Oh! I'm sorry. You've reached Environmental Solutions, this is Derek. How may I help you?"

"Is…Jake there? Jake…O'Connell?"

"Of course. May I ask who's calling?"

"It's Alice. Alice Wright, actually Alice Tate…" Was she back to Alice Tate now? "Yes, Alice Tate. He knows who I am. We're… old friends… We're—"

She heard him scream "Jake! Some chick named Alice is on the phone for you!" The line went blank.

Alice briefly considered hanging up. She tapped the pen against the paper and watched the newest tourists join the line for beignets. A family with three young children slumped in the middle of the line, while the youngest child screamed. The middle child stared off at a juggler, not even noticing the screaming, deeply entrenched in his own world. It made her think of Rob. He tapped his sister on the shoulder to look, and she immediately stopped crying.

"Alice?"

"Jake?"

"Alice Tate?"

"Yes." She wondered if he could hear her muffled voice over the noise of the courtyard.

His tone changed to pleasant and he said, "How nice of you to call! How are you?"

"I'm in town actually, and I was wondering if you would want to…" She paused, as she had never planned on getting this far. *Hang out*, she almost said, before panicking and finishing, "Get dinner."

"Really?"

She nodded before realizing he couldn't see her. "Yes."

"Oh. Okay." The line was quiet. "I mean, yes." He cleared his throat. "I would like that. Good."

They arranged to meet that night at a place he recommended near her hotel and hung up. She sat staring at the phone in her hand until her sandwich arrived.

CHAPTER TWENTY-SIX

When Alice left her hotel to walk to the restaurant, the French Quarter was still very much alive, despite the lack of a moon, which darkened the sky to black. A pack of bridesmaids pulling along a woman in a veil, stumbled through the streets, with their drinks in hand. Fanny-pack-wielding tourists in varying levels of drunkenness lined up outside some of the restaurants, distinguished by nothing except for the lines outside. Light poured from the psychic shops Alice passed, and voodoo dolls rested on backlit displays in store windows.

She breathed in the dampness of the place, the humidity even in winter, devoid of Georgia's winter crispness. Perfect weather for a night out, she thought, feeling comfortable in a cardigan and her favorite striped chambray dress, which she had stuffed into her duffel at the last minute.

Since she left the hotel with plenty of time, Alice paused to listen to the street performers as she passed, picturing her brother among them. She loved to imagine Rob here playing with the fellow guitars and trumpets and drums.

When she reached Burgundy Street, she had to double back because she'd missed the restaurant. It had a black door that blended into the wall with a small sign and little lights outside, in the deep part of the French Quarter, where the street performers played with a different type of soul, absent the tourists and their cash-stuffed wallets. Alice checked her watch—still thirty minutes early, enough time to compose herself, to think about what she would say to Jake after all these years, and why she had called him in the first place, why she grabbed this dress off its hanger at home.

Just two colleagues meeting for dinner, she promised herself. No different from her hundreds of meals with grad students and donors. Alice heard a *hmm* in her head from her internal Meredith. She shushed it.

Alice told the hostess she would have a drink at the bar while she waited and was ushered into the room. The tiny space looked like a French courtyard with brick floors, brick walls, and a frosted-glass ceiling. About fifteen small tables lined the sides of the room, and a spiral staircase led to a loft where a group laughed over wine. Drooping plants hung from chains hooked from the ceiling over a small fountain in the middle. Lit by candles on each table and a light over the bar, the restaurant was so dark that Alice's eyes had to adjust before she could spot a seat at the corner of the bar.

Seeking some of her courage, Alice ordered Meredith's drink—a gin martini with a lemon twist. Her fingers fidgeted with her wedding ring. Walker would never think to take her to a place like this. A saxophone player emerged from the corner and started to play love songs. Two people from the loft inched from behind the table and began to dance on the stairs' small landing. The couples at the tables surrounding the fountain and the bar leaned together over their plates. It smelled heavenly—red wine mixed with seafood and spices.

Her drink came, and Alice drank half in a few gulps. Why had Jake selected this place? Did he expect something more than just talking? Did she? She pictured the Jake from her college days, mixed with the suited man on his website, and she felt a little dizzy. He would be so different now. *She* would be so different, different than he expected. He might even be…disappointed.

What if he got the wrong idea and tried to kiss her? How fast would she pull away? Immediately? After two seconds, maybe just to see what it would be like. She wondered how the affair between Walker and Brittani had started. Maybe just like this, a dinner they both promised themselves was for work.

She put a twenty-dollar bill on the bar and stood up to leave. Calling Jake was a mistake.

Her heart raced as she rushed back through the tables with the couples. A man who had been whispering in his date's ear or licking it, it was difficult to tell, looked up as Alice bumped their table in the haste of her escape. When she reached the hostess stand, she froze.

"Alice," Jake said. "Was just looking for you."

He approached her, and she found herself still frozen as he took her in from her shoes up, resting on her eyes. She had let her hair air-dry, and it fell to her collarbone in gentle waves, the kind Walker hated. "You're ready?" he would have asked. She had swiped on mascara, but no other makeup. She hated the feeling of eye shadow and foundation, like a film over her whole face that took three washcloths to remove.

"You look sensational." Jake leaned in to kiss her on the cheek. She smiled. The fear of seeing him in his business suit disappeared. He wore a plaid button-down that was wrinkled along the buttons, as if he dried it on the line instead of in the dryer, like he used to do. He wore a pair of khakis, but Alice noticed a dash of mud on the knee and relaxed a little. Jake's eyes followed hers, and he saw the spot, saying briefly, "Damn." He reached to brush it off, then met her eyes again and shrugged.

She laughed. "You look good too."

He smiled at her.

"Shall we?" He held out his hand, and the hostess walked ahead. She led them to a table just under the loft and went around to pull out a chair as Alice sat down, still in a daze. A bottle of wine appeared, and a waitress filled her glass. Did he come here often? Maybe with other girls? The Jake she knew would never make a habit of expensive dinners out with dates (or otherwise).

She remembered from Athens how much Jake enjoyed food. After growing up in Arizona, he loved Southern food in the way many Southerners loved Jesus. Instead of church on Sunday, he would drive Alice all over the state, visiting little BBQ shacks or diners that allegedly had the best grits in the South. At the time, Alice admired his passion for newness, how he embraced Southern food so deeply. He always saw change as an opportunity for adventure, instead of fearing it, like she did. She admired it until that passion had taken him to Ecuador, until it convinced him to stay.

"I'm glad you called," he said, leaning in slightly. "It will be great to catch up."

"Well, I'm not in the area often. I saw in the alumni magazine that you lived here. That article on your new business? Sounds fantastic."

She lied. She had called the alumni office multiple times, asking them to please not send her any more magazines, because she didn't read them and they were a waste of paper. She had seen the profile in his Google results, which she'd memorized, and the article struck her as a good excuse. "How is it going?" she finished with a question, glad that her turn to talk had ended.

"Amazing!" He launched into a discussion of the plant life in the watershed and the resilience of the environment, one that didn't steer away from the more technical topics, and she smiled. She hadn't talked about this type of ecology since undergrad. He paused, asking her opinion on the success of different plants in wetland restoration projects and she gave it readily, happy to be in a safe zone, with her business hat on. He asked her about herself, and she returned his formal tone as she told him about the problems with local riverbank erosion and the education she did with the local kids. The day's appetizer special arrived, fish with "rum-drunk" pineapples and hearts of palm, and they ate, still talking shop.

The work conversation reached a lull while they waited for their entrees, after a waitress whisked away the appetizer plates and poured another round of wine.

"So, how are you otherwise? Husband? Kids?"

She told him about Robbie and his love of puzzles and chess, to which he flashed a sympathetic smile because of the name's connection. She plowed past it though. She boasted about Caitlin and her scholarship, which he said sounded like a great opportunity.

"You and your husband must be so proud."

"Walker," she offered, twisting her ring. "Yes, well…I am."

Jake raised his eyebrow.

"He, umm, he prefers her to stay closer to home."

"I can certainly understand that. Sounds like mother, like daughter." He offered a smirk, a reminder of their plans to find Rob, to travel to South America, to settle down out west. The plans that she hadn't told her parents about because she knew they wouldn't approve, like they hadn't approved of Jake.

"So, what about you? How's Paula?"

"Best sister there is. She came to stay with me after"—he gulped a bit—"after my divorce, and she never left." He met Alice's eyes with a smile that made her feel pity for him.

"Sorry, about your divorce."

"It was a hard time. We had some obstacles we just weren't ready for. She moved back to Connecticut afterward, and she has a family up there now, a kid with her new husband."

Alice watched the wine he swirled in his glass circle like a cyclone. "She's happy, she deserves to be happy. I have the new business. I'm happy. Things ended well."

Alice wanted to reach across the table and grab his hand, and say, "Tell me about Kellen," to relieve some of the burden of what she read about, of Jake losing a child so young. But, she forced herself to wait until he brought it up, in case he didn't want to relive it with her, in case they weren't as close as she felt they still were, even after all these years, in case closeness was a measure of time instead of a measure of impact. She still wasn't sure.

Instead, she said, "Remember Meredith?"

"Of course. I have a few of her novels."

She laughed. "No, you don't."

"Yes! I read them!" He winked at her, just like he did when she first saw him that day on the Quad in Athens. "I thought they were good. Never doubted her for one second, back in college."

Alice shook her head, still laughing. She would have to tell Meredith that she had another fan.

"I wanted to support." He stole another glance at her. "Nothing like old friends."

Their entrees came. After being unable to decide about the menu, Alice had ordered the last special the waitress advertised, and was glad she had. Jake hadn't ordered but had just said, "Bring me whatever you think I'll like," and it looked like he ended up with some sort of crawfish creation. He stirred his food and slurped the concoction from the spoon, smiling with the warmth.

"Good?" she prompted.

"Absolutely delicious. Would you like some?" He offered his spoon. She hesitated, but leaned forward and tasted it. It *was* fantastic.

Alice noticed the waitress lingering. Jake saw her too.

"Do you like it?" she said.

"Love it," he said. "Thank you."

The waitress eyed Alice, who retreated a little from the embarrassingly intimate position the waitress caught her in, eating from Jake's spoon.

"Zoe, this is Alice. Alice, Zoe," Jake said, as if his mother had caught him on a secret date and demanded he introduce the girl to her. The waitress bent down to shake Alice's hand. "Zoe works at my foundation, part-time, but this is her real passion. She's an excellent employee though." Zoe smiled. "I like to come here and see the thing that takes her away from my plants."

She offered "Nice to meet you" and then left. So, that explained his comfort at the fancy restaurant.

They finished their entrees in silence, different from the quiet dinners she shared with Walker; where every pause seemed like an opportunity for him to plot what point he would bring up next; where the silence made her worry what soon would occupy it. With Jake, the silence felt comfortable and relaxing. Although maybe it was the round of drinks that had just been poured, the empty bottle whisked away, and another set down in its place.

The plates gone, Alice centered her wineglass in front of her and ticked her wedding band on the rim, the one she hadn't taken off since her hospital stay with Robbie. She watched the reflection of the little diamonds in the clear glass. When would she take it off— when the divorce went through? Before? It felt heavier than ever.

"Do you remember those nights on the Quad?" Jake said. She looked at him, but he'd already looked down again, rolling up his left sleeve. As he rolled up his right, she saw "Kellen" in cursive letters on his wrist, and she couldn't help but remember that first tattoo he had written about and been so proud of, that colorful tortoise on his calf. The last letter before their breakup, she remembered with a pang.

"We were so young." He looked up and smiled at her. "Happy though."

She looked away. Why was he doing this? He had been the one to sign on for years, without her. He had changed their plans and broken promises. But she didn't want to say that. She had blamed herself at the time, but she had been right about Rob. It was him that day, must have been him. She had been right, and Jake hadn't believed her, had left her, had continued his life without her, even while claiming he loved her.

The waitress corked the rest of the wine, and the bill didn't come.

"If you have time, I'd love to show you the greenhouse. We've got some different varieties in testing, to see which will help stabilize streambanks. I think you would really like it." She looked at him, considering. "I'll drive you back to your hotel after," he finished.

It would be nice to not have to walk back in the dark, and from an academic perspective, his group's attempts to counter invasive species interested her.

Alice nodded, and they stood. He walked in front of her with his hand slightly behind his body, and she struggled not to grab it, not to become the person she used to be, so close now.

CHAPTER TWENTY-SEVEN

When he let her into his truck and she spied the gearshift, he laughed a bit, and then said, "Difficult to break old habits, I guess."

She watched his right hand as he drove, the stick moving as if it had a life of its own. She remembered the rides in college, when Jake's hand would find hers, if only for a second, before the engine groaned and begged for his attention.

All at once, Alice's head swirled from the wine. As they pulled into his office, she wondered how she had gotten so tipsy and couldn't remember the last time she had let her guard down, always with the wordless expectation that she would stay mostly sober in order to deal with Walker later.

In Jake's company, she had let herself uncurl, but still so many secrets lay between them. She would tell him, she promised herself, the real reason why she had come to New Orleans.

He walked across the stacks, pointing out different genetic varieties of plant species, and she bent down to examine the leaves and the measurements on the clipboards that detailed the experiment. The operation was impressive, and normally, she would have been glad to study them and take notes for Grace, but not now.

"Jake." She heard herself call his name, before she realized she would.

He turned, surprised, then seeing her face, he came over and stood in front of her. The words were so close, but as Jake approached her and brushed a hair off her face—tucking it behind her ear as he used to do, a small gesture of intimacy that Walker never did—they no longer seemed important. He waited. He would stand there, mere inches away from her, and stare until she gave him an awkward smile and averted her eyes.

She didn't break the moment though. She still stared, seeing the other life she could have lived deep inside his dark eyes; the other Alice she could have been, or maybe still remained, somewhere.

She inched her face a little closer.

Alice didn't think about Walker. Instead, her daughter on the video entered her mind, with the strangers clapping, performing her deepest secrets. Alice's choices had led to that, her children, the Rob-like passion, but now, she needed to remember the lesson her daughter had never had to learn—that the secrets she kept weren't actually hidden. Remembering, her chest clenched again. She felt wetness on her face and realized she was crying, but Jake didn't look away. Maybe he saw a vision of a forgotten part of himself.

"I should have remembered that red wine makes you sad." He chuckled and leaned over to wipe a tear from her cheek. "Do you want me to take you back to your hotel?"

She remembered all the nights they spent just like this, where he would kiss the wetness off her cheeks and they would fall asleep, wet and happy and intertwined.

"Jake, the reason I came here… It wasn't actually to meet with a donor."

He waited, perhaps expecting something else, maybe something about her marriage, she realized.

"It... I..." As she searched for words, the sound of her phone rang out, bouncing off the walls, and they both jumped. As she reached into her pocket, Jake stepped back, the closeness no longer. She looked at the number. Dylan, calling back, like he'd promised. She thought about not answering it, but she didn't want to wonder all night about what he had discovered about the cross Rob drew for Christopher Smith and, maybe, what he'd found out about Rob in the process.

She answered, mouthing *One sec* to Jake. She cleared her throat before bringing the phone up to her ear.

"Hello?"

"Alice! I'm in the car, driving back from Atlanta, and I've got some news," Dylan said, talking fast with excitement. "So, I went to Atlanta and talked to a couple of people who worked with Rob and Christopher when they knew each other."

With the phone to her ear, Alice walked a little farther from Jake, who busied himself with the soil samples and tried to look nonchalant.

"Everyone I talked to seemed to say the same thing—that Rob wasn't doing well after he left Athens and came to Atlanta. He met Chris there. Chris OD'd, and it hit Rob hard. He was practically on the street, couldn't hold down any type of work and was stealing to get the money he needed. Then one day, he just disappeared."

She glanced back at Jake, before arching her body over the phone to respond, "Disappeared how? Did anyone know why?"

"The only thing I could find out... Bear with me because this is pretty out there, and keep in mind that this guy was high as shit when this happened, according to him even. But, I'm telling you anyway because I think—"

"Dylan!" she said too loudly.

Jake's head snapped to look at her with a confused expression. Alice and Jake's eyes met, and he bent down to pick up a spot of soil on the floor.

"It isn't a good time. Can you just tell me what you need to tell me?"

"Yes, sorry. Well, I talked to a guy who said he was in an old apartment where a bunch of them hung out. Late at night, someone starts rapping on the door saying 'Hello? Is anyone in there?' They thought it might be some kind of police officer or something, because everyone normally just came in, so a bunch of the guys left. Some just stuck around, though, too messed up to know what to do. Anyway, the guy comes in, and get this, he had a flashlight and went around the room, shining the light in their faces, saying, 'Rob Tate? Rob Tate? I'm looking for Rob Tate.' Eventually he finds him, and he picks him up and just carries him out of there over his shoulder. And none of the guys ever saw Rob again."

Alice's mind filled with possibilities: her brother had been kidnapped!

"Did he say anything else?"

"The only other thing the guy I talked to said was that he was sitting on the floor, where the guy's leg was eye level, and he remembers the guy having a huge tattoo on his calf that was a turtle? I think he said 'colored turtle,' or something like that. I wrote his number down if you really want—"

Alice's eyes moved down Jake's back, hunched over his soil samples, until she reached his calf. Even through his pants, she could almost see that stupid tortoise tattoo from the Galapagos, the one he'd sent her a picture of in that letter. It had to be.

Her fist clenched, and the nails dug into her skin, until she felt little welts with her thumb.

"Alice? Alice? Hello?" Dylan said in her ear.

She let the phone drop.

Jake turned quickly at the sound, then seeing her face, his features turned to worry. He rushed over to her.

"Alice, who was that?" Jake looked at the phone on the floor but didn't lean down to pick it up. "Something about your mother? Was it your husband?" He looked again at the phone and back to her. "What happened?"

A tide of anger overwhelmed Alice, like the worst red tides at the beaches she and Rob played in as a child, the shore so overwhelmed with dead fish that she thought it was blood changing the color of the water. Of course, he would think it was Walker.

"You!" Alice said, not pausing to apologize for the spit that flung from her lips with the accusation. He stared.

Forgetting about the phone entirely, she turned to leave. Jake picked it up and trailed her, only an inch or two behind her shoes, so close, she thought, that if she stopped, he would barrel into her.

"Alice! Please just tell me what happened! At least let me drive you to the hotel. I thought it was going well, us, together, here."

He stopped walking when she left the building and stepped off the curb. He wouldn't follow her anymore, and his words stung her. He would think it was *her* fault, that she left because of Walker. It wasn't her fault though. It was Jake's, and she wanted him to know it. Had *always* been Jake's.

She spun on her heels, the words tumbling out of her.

"It was going well, Jake! I was so naive, though, to think you were different." All the anger of the past few weeks spilled to the surface, all the things left unsaid, she heaped so easily on him. "You're not different. Everyone has a secret life. My kid! My husband! My mother! Rob! YOU!"

"I don't know what you're talking about," Jake said, pleading.

"You know why I'm here? I'm trying to find out what happened to Rob. He's dead, has been for a while, and I'm finally doing what I should've done a long time ago, what we agreed to do a long time ago. And I find out you were *there*, you found him. That's what the call was. *You* were *there*. You were looking for him. Without me. And you found him, and then he disappeared...?"

Jake's hands were up now in defense, and he tried to calm her down, but it only made her want to scream at him because it reminded her of Walker in the school parking lot.

Her heart raced, but this was so different from the stilted, shushed, transactional arguments she had with Walker. She felt angry, so angry all of a sudden, but alive, yelling at Jake, seeing how he reacted, feeling the power she had over him that she would never have over Walker. How much her words cut him. How focused he was on what she was saying. How he waited for her to twist the knife, trying to anticipate her next move to stop the fight before it got worse, instead of Walker's approach of trying to out-logic her, to win, to make her feel stupid, to keep quiet so the other parents didn't hear.

"I was going to tell you tonight; I swear I was. I—"

"Do you expect me to believe that?" she thundered.

"Alice, please just listen to me, just wait."

"Wait for what?"

"I'm trying to tell you! Be quiet for a second, goddammit!"

She stared at him, trying to catch her breath.

"I realized I was an idiot. After we broke up, the funding dried up in a year." He ran his fingers through his hair. "I messed up so badly, not talking to you first, choosing to stay over what we had. I wanted to come back and to beg you to take me back, but I thought I needed a grand gesture to show you how much I loved you and cared about you. I know it sounds so stupid now."

Alice stood, still frozen.

"I tracked Rob down. It took me almost six months, but I found people who knew him and knew where he was. My idea was that I would bring him to you and y'all would hug, and you would take me back."

Alice felt her face soften a little and willed to keep it scornful and rage-filled.

"I found him in some house in Atlanta. He was completely strung out," Jake said. "I didn't think it would be that bad. I took him to the hospital and stayed with him a few weeks while he recovered. I told him who I was, and he begged me not to tell you he was there. He didn't want you to see him like that, didn't want to hurt you anymore than you already were, and I understood, but I told myself I was just waiting for when he got better, and I would convince him. When I came back one day, he was gone. He had checked himself out. I went back to where I found him a couple of times, but they said he was gone. I knew you were at Duke, so I went there, and I was going to tell you. I went to the environmental science building and waited for you to get out of class. You were with Walker, and I saw him kiss you. You just looked happy. I realized I was stupid all around, thinking you would wait for me when I told you not to. I was so embarrassed that I left."

Her eyes fixed on the ground in front of her. "You should've told me."

"I know." He stomped his foot. "I know I should have. I'm so sorry." He approached her again. "I should have told you the truth about us. I should have told you I never stopped loving you, Alice. I was young. I was hurt. I was a coward. But I think if I've learned anything in the last twenty years, it's that life isn't long enough to throw away chances like that. Chances like this."

She looked at him and they were both crying now. She fell into his arms and kissed him, and he was surprised at first, but then kissed her back. The wetness of their faces mixed in with the sweat from the greenhouse air and the spit of their lips against each other. They left his truck, and he hailed a cab and they sat, kissing in the back like they were nineteen again.

CHAPTER TWENTY-EIGHT

When Alice woke in the morning, the light streamed in through the open windows onto where she lay in Jake's bed. Jake's arm was slung casually across her body, and her left side touched his chest and stomach. The previous night rushed back to her: the dinner, Dylan's call, the way Jake had betrayed her, her kissing him, the hours she'd spent in Jake's arms talking about all the things they missed.

He flung open the door to her as he had done the first time, welcoming her into the deep entrails of his brain as if he were welcoming her home. He told her about Kellen with tears in his eyes, relayed how his marriage deteriorated while he traced the curves of her hip with his fingertips. Still tipsy on wine and drunk with passion from their shared kiss, their secrets, the way his tongue danced up her inner thigh, Alice had told him about Walker, the texts, the NYU video, the fog that had descended on her as she marched through a life she couldn't remember piecing together. The types of conversations she never had with Walker.

Now, though, in the light, her sureness, her confidence disappeared. Every detail of him—his warm breath on her neck as he slept, how every part of his body seemed to curve toward her, the way she noticed in the light that everything in his bedroom, the IKEA dresser, the walls, the bedding, were shades of gray, as if Jake assumed his decorating would succeed if he stuck to one color—it all made her want him more, and that desire scared her.

Outside the windows, even the sky looked gray, like it threatened to storm. Her eyes fell on her dress where she had sloppily discarded it, the cardigan sprawled next to it with the sleeves inside out. *What time was it?* She started to scoot out of Jake's hold, but at her stirring, he opened his eyes and smiled. *Dammit.*

"Good morning, gorgeous. Whatcha doing?"

"Do you know where my phone is?"

"Oh, um." He stretched his arm over his head. "Around here somewhere." He climbed out of bed, leaned over to grab his boxers off the floor, and slipped them on. Alice wrapped the sheet around her chest.

"Found it." He walked over and handed her the phone. She clicked it on: 8:23 a.m. Still, they must have slept for only a few hours.

"I'll start coffee." He leaned in to kiss her once on her left cheek, then her forehead, her right cheek, her lips, and her nose. She remembered the ritual as part of her college years. She wondered if he had done the same thing with his wife. Was he only playing house? Content to share a night together and say goodbye at the airport, as he had done so many years before?

He walked out of the room and shut the door.

Looking at the phone, she saw four missed calls from Walker. After his text yesterday morning—"If that's how you want it, fine. Mature."—Alice had expected the silence to last a little longer, like the days it normally did after a disagreement until they both pretended the disagreement hadn't happened. She sighed.

"Everything okay?" she texted Caitlin.

Caitlin texted back suspiciously quickly for school hours. "Great. Chelsea drove us to school. Ordered Chinese food last night with Aunt Meredith. Enjoy your trip!"

After washing her face and putting back on her crumpled dress, Alice walked into the eat-in kitchen of Jake's one-bedroom apartment. Behind the couch, a large bay window opened to iron railings that looked out onto a street she didn't recognize.

Her head hurt, from the wine and from the thoughts about Jake and Walker and her marriage that she had been pushing to the far reaches of her brain and had finally set free. She pressed her index finger into the temple. It was time to go to Lila's, to finish this.

"Headache?" Jake asked. She nodded, and he fished a bottle of Tylenol from the kitchen cabinet.

Jake shook two pills from the bottle. He produced a glass and filled it with water from the tap before setting it next to the pills on the counter. A small offering, pushed toward her. Walker didn't even know where she kept their Tylenol.

"Still take your coffee with cream and sugar?"

She nodded yes at him before thinking and drank the water down. She took her coffee with only skim milk now, but she let the inertia of her past habits propel her forward. How would her mother define insanity in those little daily quizzes at the kitchen table? Doing the same thing over and over again, but expecting a different result. This man in front of her, now in his cargo shorts with abundant pockets and a T-shirt, looked so similar to the boy she once knew, the keeper of her secrets, with whom she would sit in coffee shops, drinking her coffee with cream and sugar.

She sat, and Jake placed the warm coffee in her grip. She left her hands on the sides of the mug, allowing the warmth to sting her fingers, concentrating on the sensation and the smell of the cup, instead of the tumult in her brain over what to say next.

"I should go back to my hotel, shower, call Walker back."

His face fell immediately. "Oh."

"If I don't, he'll just keep calling, and I don't want him to say anything to the kids."

Jake nodded, but looked away. Did he judge her for being in a relationship where she had to worry about her husband puncturing the lie she had fed about a business trip to their kids, if she didn't respond? She stared at the tan coffee in the mug, straining to see something under the surface, like in the muddy Georgia waters of her youth.

She stole glances at Jake, who pecked at his laptop as she sipped her coffee, seemingly trying to ignore her, to give her the necessary time to process. How easy it would be to make him happy. She would only need to stay here, to sip her too sweet, too milky coffee, to sink back into their past life.

"Where are we?" She walked to the open windows with her coffee cup to admire the street. "It's beautiful."

"The Garden District." He popped up from the bar and over to the window. "I moved to the neighborhood with Christie when she was pregnant. I used to take Kellen to that park," he said, pointing to a patch of green. "And after…everything, I left the house, but couldn't leave the area."

They stood, looking out on the street. A group of tourists ambled down the block on a tour, and a couple pushed an old-fashioned pram on the other side.

"Anyway, I can take you back to your hotel." She heard the clink of keys disappear into his pants pocket.

"That would be great."

"Then," he said, slowly, carefully, "I thought maybe we could eat lunch, show you a little of the city before you go see Lila?"

She considered this, his face so expectant and hopeful. "Okay, sure. Let's do it."

They took a cab back to his office, picked up his truck, and then he drove to her hotel. They sat with the engine off, both trying to decide how to leave things. Finally, she leaned over the center console and kissed him goodbye, lingering long enough for his hand to reach around her back.

"See you soon," she said and turned around to walk away. She didn't look back until she shut the door to her hotel room.

The room had been tidied, and she glanced at her belongings, folded in neat little piles that reminded her of Walker and the kitchen island's clutter he so despised. She plugged her phone in without looking at it and turned on the shower, letting the room fill with steam before stepping in. She normally didn't take long showers—too wasteful—but today she let the water run down her back as her mind grew blank, even just for fifteen minutes, to get the guilt from Jake's touch off her body, and the fear that she wouldn't see him after today. When she emerged, a towel twisted around her wet hair on top of her head, she sat on the bed in the hotel robe and called Edward. He answered on the first ring.

"Could you pull some of the documents together that we… that you mentioned when I was in the office?"

Of course, he didn't get the message right away. She threw in a few more words: *assets, college fund, inheritance, shares in the Center*, and finally, he showed mercy and promised to send her an email with information tomorrow. "And thanks, Edward. For everything you did for Rob. I know it probably wasn't easy."

They hung up, and she sat on the bed for a few minutes. She leaned back and traced the lines on the ceiling with her eyes. Outside, she could make out the clinking of mimosas and Bloody Marys as the brunch crowd carried on downstairs, even though it was Monday.

She decided to let herself off the hook with Walker. Instead of calling, she texted him that she would be home tomorrow and that they would talk then. Alice dressed, this time in a blouse, cardigan, and jeans with her Converse sneakers. She dialed Meredith.

She told Meredith about Lila King. "Her letter is the last one I have," Alice said. "What if it's nothing? What if she can't tell me anything else?"

"Maybe she can't. But maybe, that's just what you need."

Alice paused, thinking about this.

"None of what happened to Rob is your fault, honey. If that's what you're looking for—another way to blame yourself—you aren't going to find it."

Meredith had told her this before. Each time her friend said it, part of Alice wanted to ask her to say it again, to repeat it until the thought snaked its way into Alice's subconscious. But, another part of her wished Meredith wouldn't say it again, embarrassed that her friend could so easily see the need still hungry in her chest even after all these years.

"I went to dinner with Jake last night."

"What!"

"And we slept together."

"What!"

The confession briefly shocked Meredith into silence before she followed up with "How was it?"

"He's picking me up for lunch in a few minutes, actually."

"That good, huh?" Meredith laughed, and Alice let herself laugh, too, briefly allowing the warmth of her night with Jake to take up her entire body without the gnawing inside her that Alice worried her meeting with Lila wouldn't stop. They laughed, longer than was necessary, until the blank sound between them stretched on. Alice could hear her friend breathing, waiting for her to say something.

Alice sighed. "Maybe I should tell him not to come."

"Aww, why?"

Alice bent forward until her forehead touched her knee. "There's so many what-ifs. Neither of us knows if this will turn into anything. It probably won't. And the more I," she gulped, "the more I see him, the harder it's going to be to leave."

"If you only have today, though, wouldn't you want it to be the best day it could be?"

"That sounds like something from one of your books. Not real life."

"So, what if it is? Take the day off from real life."

"I'll call you tomorrow." Alice hung up and went downstairs to the lobby, where Jake sat in one of the hotel's worn leather chairs in jeans and a casual button-up.

"Ready to go?" He offered her his hand, and they walked out to his truck.

"Where are we going for lunch?" Alice climbed into the passenger seat.

She had never been a dreamer. Alice was the practical one, the rule follower. But she tried to embody the confidence and reckless abandon of one of Meredith's sexy heroines, just an average girl who'd happened upon a fantasy.

She tried to channel Rob. When he had disobeyed their parents' rules, he did it with all his might. He'd made it count.

"I thought we could drive around a little bit first, since we have a little time?"

Alice glanced at the clock. Each time she did, she became more nervous. Another hour gone with Jake. Another hour until she would leave and go back to the mess that awaited her in Georgia. Another hour to Lila. To the end of everything she would know about Rob.

"Sure, that would be nice," she said with a smile.

He started the engine, and his hand found hers in the seconds between gear shifts on the slow-moving New Orleans roads. He drove through the different neighborhoods surrounding her hotel and explained the name and history of each. While the damp smell of the air had played with her senses since she arrived, Alice didn't see the water in daylight until Jake drove along the Mississippi River and then to Lake Pontchartrain. He pointed out where the levees were before the hurricane, and which ones had broken in the aftermath.

Alice and Jake made their way to a green space, and when they arrived, he came around to open her door.

"Are you going to tell me where we are?" She tried to allow herself to fall into the predictable unpredictability of her years with Jake.

"The Botanical Gardens."

Although they didn't plan it, they walked through the green-house like a type of timeline. First, they started with the plants native to the southwestern United States. Jake pointed out different types of cactuses from his childhood and recounted memories of football games with his friends in the orange, dry dirt, always on the lookout for snakes.

They passed through the southeastern United States. Alice paused at a dogwood tree to tell Jake about how her mother told her and Rob that the tree's wood was used to make the cross on which Jesus was crucified, and each time she passed one, Alice felt the need to say a little prayer.

They laughed at the sunflowers, remembering the many hours Alice had spent pulling off the leaves and counting the hairs for her undergraduate thesis. Jake reminded her that he bought her sunflowers once, and that, when he came back the next day, he had found them in the trash. She tried to hide that she had thrown them away, blaming it instead on Meredith until he busted out laughing.

"I just can't look at them anymore!" she remembered screaming, before joining him in laughter. They agreed to never buy sunflowers again.

They stopped at the colorful plants that begged for attention among thousands of equally beautiful ones in the exhibition on the Amazon rain forest, where Jake pointed to a few of his favorites from his time in Ecuador.

They passed the Asia wing with a large pot of honeysuckle. When she learned in college that the bright-yellow bulbs that decorated the landscape of her childhood were known as *Japanese honeysuckles* and were, in fact, an invasive species in the South, she walked through campus looking at the patches and wondering how something she had considered so much a part of her could be a lie, could be destructive.

She told Jake now about running through bushes of honeysuckle so big, you could hide inside, and how she would always snap off a bunch when she came back from the river with Rob, how they would lick out the sweet nectar, letting the bulbs fall on the asphalt as they walked, barefoot.

Jake reached over and plucked two off the branch.

"You're not supposed to do that!" She laughed, but she took them and showed Jake how to pinch off the bottom of the flower with a fingernail and pull out the string inside slowly. As she brought it to her mouth and licked the drop, tasting the familiar sweetness, she wished this minute would last forever.

They continued out of the greenhouse, hand in hand to the plants of New Orleans. At the end of an enclosed, ivy-snarled pathway, a large oak shaded a grassy area. It spanned out an impossible length, looking like the Tree of Life, draped with a cape of Spanish moss. As they rounded the corner, Alice slowed, seeing the white wedding chairs lined up underneath the tree's shade. The ease in Alice's chest tightened immediately, as if on a yo-yo.

"Amazing, isn't it?" Jake paused with her hand in his. "I always think that if I get married again, I would do it here, under that tree. In the summer, they put lights on it. It's so beautiful."

Her entire arm locked, starting with her fingers in his hand and continuing to her palm, her forearm, the tendons in her shoulder.

"Do you like it?"

She nodded and let his hand drop. She walked on the path away from the white chairs, trying to catch her breath again until she reached the sculpture garden where concrete art deco sculptures stood guard.

In the corner, near the end of the section, Alice stopped in front of a life-size sculpture of a woman. Pink and white flowers surrounded her. The woman sat on a block of concrete so smooth, it looked like marble. She supported herself with one hand on the block, while the other rested in her lap, loosely holding a flower. Her back stood straight and proud, and her face looked up at the sky with her eyes closed, as if she basked in the light of the sun. Her expression was neither happy nor sad, but content. She looked weightless, as if she had decided to let go, to sit in the garden and enjoy the thrill of being alive. Alice admired the sculpture, envying the feeling the woman so easily possessed.

"This is my favorite one," Jake said.

"Me too. She looks so at peace."

"She always reminded me of you, from the first time I saw her, when I first moved here." He let out a little laugh. "I actually used to avoid this part of the garden because of that."

Her chest twisted again. The fear that like Walker, Jake had an impossible-to-achieve view of her filled Alice with dread. Did Alice ever really have the peace of that girl in the garden? Or did Jake only want to see her like that, through his regret over leaving her? Was that image, like the one Alice showed to Walker, a little white lie?

Jake smiled and leaned over for a kiss. She let him, watching as his face approached, still trying to read him.

"Renascence." She leaned in to read the plaque on the sculpture. "Do you know what it means?"

"Rebirth."

She had allowed herself to be consumed by the grief and anger of Rob leaving for so long and only gave herself an out when she met Jake. Jake, who had the solution at the ready. They would, of course, find Rob together, and then live happily ever after. Now, though, Alice realized that even if they hadn't broken up and quit that plan, it wouldn't have worked like Jake suggested: them finding Rob and living a perfect life together, devoid of parents and bad memories. Rob's issues magically solved.

Jake had been her solution for Rob, just as Walker was the solution for Jake, and now again, was Jake only her solution for her problems with Walker? Alice's headache came back. The questions from Jake's bed that morning flooded back to her before she could stop them. What *was* her plan with Jake? What was his plan? Why had she called him? Why had she come here?

Her stomach rumbled, and Jake laughed, unaware of the pulsating under Alice's skin that was slowly creeping to her fingers and toes and the top of her head.

"Ready to get some lunch?"

He reached for her hand as they left the garden.

CHAPTER TWENTY-NINE

When they entered the seafood market, the owner asked immediately how many crawfish Jake needed. He waved toward a table instead, and the man's hand flew to his chest in mock shock. He smiled at them, saying to sit anywhere.

Alice and Jake sat with a roll of paper towels and three different types of hot sauces between them. He rolled up his sleeves, and she did the same. A huge bucket of crawfish quickly appeared on the red-and-white-checkered plastic tablecloth.

"What'd you think of the garden?" Jake said.

He carefully pinched along the spine of a crawfish, then brought the head to his mouth to suck the juices.

"Beautiful."

"Glad you liked it." Jake sipped his beer.

They ate in silence for several minutes. Instead of the chaos inside her mind that only grew louder as the clock ticked on, Alice concentrated on twisting the tail of the crawfish with just the right torque for the meat to free itself from its shell. The cracks, slurps, and clattering sound of empty shells hitting metal rang out from the restaurant, as every table ate in concentrated silence.

Alice cracked the crawfish slowly, eating the little meat inside. She cracked and ate, cracked and ate, cracked and sucked and ate, but still she couldn't shake the emptiness inside her that she wanted to fill and the feeling in her stomach like spinning in a whirlpool.

What had she thought sleeping with Jake would fix? When she thought of her mother, her children, she felt a brief glimmer of guilt about her own affair, but it was only that—a glimmer. She and Walker had never been honest with each other, could never be honest with each other.

Had she not begun her marriage with untold secrets from the first date? She had told Walker, "One brother. We're not close," but now she realized it was a lie. With each minute in New Orleans, her soul recognized something in the place, as if she'd accepted part of her brother inside long ago and that part was coming home.

She had. She had breathed him in just as he promised to do with their mother's guilt. She had let him reside in her head. And he'd called. He'd followed her. He'd cared about upsetting her when Jake found him.

Didn't that show Rob had also made space for her in that cluttered head of his?

She looked at Jake again, smiling at her innocently over his beer bottle. Walker had begun their marriage by telling her what to do, by assuming he should take what he wanted without real consideration for her, saying simply before their first date, "I'm taking you out this Friday." She had been lying to herself all these years, that she was content with Walker because of the Center, the children, because of reasons she couldn't even name, blockages in her subconscious put there when Rob left, or evil forces lodged against her when she lay awake at night as a child, cursing God for yanking Rob away. Had she denied her destiny with the man in front of her, cowardly chosen not to go to Ecuador, just as she had cowardly chosen not to go to find Rob?

No, no. *You're spiraling,* she told herself, *Stop.*

Jake ripped another paper towel off the roll. The man her parents called a "farmer" and asked, "When will he get a *real* job?" The man whose bony collarbone she had kissed, mouth open, when they slept together the first time. She could practically taste its saltiness as she ate, until she reached the bottom of the bowl where the crawfish had been. Her bucket of shells overflowed onto the tablecloth.

Jake studied her and ordered five more pounds. He slowed down his own cracks, but Alice kept cracking and slurping.

A vision of her mother flashed through Alice's mind to say that she shouldn't be eating this way in front of a man. Alice shushed her. She didn't need to worry because Alice already had a husband, from a good family who could provide for her, as her mother wanted. And Alice had let it happen, let her destiny play out, let the Tate destiny play out, the same one Rob had rejected.

She understood now why he thought he was the "great scar." She could see he felt so much responsibility for Alice, for Maura, when in reality, the blame for Rob's death, for his exile from the family, was shared among everyone who refused to remember him, even Alice.

Jake cracked crawfish, assembling them on the edge of Alice's plate like a little tower. Next to them, an older woman sat down, tied up her black-and-white-striped hair in a bun on the top of her head with two chopsticks and began to crack. The woman bounced shells into a bucket as if challenging Alice to a race.

Alice wanted to fall asleep and find Rob in her dreams like she

had the other night, and scream at him: *Why? Why did you leave?*
Why didn't you let Jake take you to me? Why didn't you talk to me in
Athens? Why didn't you call me when you were sick? Why didn't you
write me a letter? Why did you ruin my life?

Why

Why

Why

Why

She wanted to scream at Jake all over again, like she had
last night. She wanted to scream at Walker over Brittani and
everything else. She wanted to confront Jamie and tell him
she knew about the stolen money. She wanted to stand on her
father's grave and chastise him for making decisions while Alice
and her mother slept, for refusing to look for Rob, which forced
his wife to trust the wrong person, for whatever Rob thought
their father could have done to prevent everything that happened after.

She stood up without warning and went to the bathroom.
The blood of the meal was all over her: the splatters of butter
decorated her clothes, and her arms were red up past the elbows
with hot sauce and seasoning. She stuck out her tongue, which
stung with Tabasco, before running the water and lapping it up
like two kittens Jamie got her and Rob for Christmas one year
always did, fighting over the faucet's stream.

Alice looked at herself in the mirror. She saw the woman in the
statute. She saw her mother and Caitlin and the almond shape of
Rob's eyes. They all blended together and fought for the surface.
Alice saw her tear-stained face, not yet thirteen, the night before
she trudged alone in the woods. She saw herself whispering, "I

will not forget. I'll find you, I will" into the mirror in the bathroom she used to share with Rob in her parents' house.

The promise had come easily to Alice. Her mother's grief when
she lay in bed, letting the phone ring, Alice had understood. She
had watched her mother and thought, *Good*.

On Alice's first night back after her stay in the hospital for
the concussion she got while looking for Rob, she woke to her
mother standing over her bed. Alice pretended to sleep. When
Alice heard her mother chanting, "Please not you too," she had
struggled to keep herself from smiling at the pain in her mother's
voice. It was there, Alice realized, deep down, hidden, the pain
she saw so freely now every time she visited her mother, the
strong facade that the brief disappearance of her second child had
cracked. Her mother felt it, too, the emptiness.

Now, Alice looked at her own face in the mirror and saw herself
truthfully: a mother of two, past forty…maybe soon-to-be divorced.
She saw her brother there, too, with his full eyebrows and his careful
eyes, and she wanted him to speak so badly, to give her permission
to leave him and her parents' house and that little purple bungalow
in New Orleans behind, to absolve her from guilt. She wanted to
blame him and scream at him for everything that had gone wrong
in her life. She wanted him to beg her for forgiveness.

She wanted him to explain to her how he had remained himself. In childhood, in Athens, in prison. How had he remained
so squarely Rob? When Alice, in her comfortable house with
her family and her children, constantly felt the rushing water of
expectations and priorities she had never agreed to? How had he
never wavered while she blindly followed the path her parents,
then Walker outlined for her?

Rob, she thought, trying to summon him like she used to in childhood. *Tell me your secret.*

I don't blame you.

She felt a weight lifting through her veins, a release of the bad, of the blame she'd heaped on Rob, on the teenage rage at him deserting, pulsing through her, loosening, leaving—

"Alice?" Jake knocked lightly at the door. "Are you okay?"

She looked back to the door, meaning to answer, but before she could, the wave lifted too far. She leaned over the toilet and threw up.

Jake stayed silent on the other side of the door. Alice rested her head against the dirty porcelain.

Hopefully Jake left, she thought.

"I'm going to get you some gum, okay? Do you want anything else?"

"I think I ate too much."

Her hand went to her belly. When she heard Jake's footsteps leaving, she rose and washed her face. She looked in the mirror, and the other faces were gone now, leaving only her own. She breathed.

Jake came back to the door, and she took the gum from him. She let him drape his arm around her, and she leaned into it as they walked outside.

"Do you want to talk about it?" He opened the door to the truck.

"Just, let's go to Lila's."

She leaned her head on the seat belt as Jake drove, letting it cool her cheek, letting her mind quiet.

He patted her thigh with his hand. "No crawfish tonight, I promise."

CHAPTER THIRTY

Jake pulled up to the house, and she stared at it. She felt she had lived a lifetime since she bounded up the steps yesterday.

"Do you want me to go in with you?" Jake said.

Alice nodded yes.

He came around and opened her door, taking her by the hand. She let him lead her to the house's door, and he walked up and rang the bell. There were no lights on, and Ben didn't pace in front of the window like when she visited the day before. It would start raining soon and the air had cooled. Alice wrapped the cardigan closer around her that she had buttoned up to hide her shirt and brushed at her stained jeans.

The door opened, revealing a woman with a pile of gray-haired braids wrapping around her head. She looked like an older version of the woman from the nude photos in Alice's parents' house. Lila King was about sixty years old. Had Alice let time slip away from her, remembering her brother as a teenager, or was Lila really much older than Rob?

"Alice." Lila grabbed her in a hug. "Come in, come in." Spying Jake, she said: "And who is this?"

"Jake." He allowed her to hug him and returned the gesture more than Alice had.

Lila ushered them in and pointed to the couch before turning to the fridge. Alice approached it cautiously, as two cats hissed at the newcomers from the carpet. Lila handed them beers, and Alice drank in earnest, while Jake took a polite sip before setting his beer on the coffee table.

"I have something for you." Alice handed the letter to Lila, who set it on the counter next to her, but didn't offer to open it. "Were you and my brother…" Alice struggled with how to start.

"He was in my band, and yes, we were together," Lila said, smiling. "Do you believe in soul mates?"

"Well—" Alice said.

"Yes," Jake answered.

They looked at each other. Did that mean Jake thought *she* was his soul mate? Did *she*?

Lila laughed. "He was that for me. We were that for each other, I like to think."

Alice smiled. To hear that her brother achieved such great love in this city full of music seemed to erase all the bad news. "I've been delivering these letters. I found them in my parents' house, and yours is my last one. I'm hoping that you can tell me about him."

"He didn't like to talk about his family," Lila said. "It made him emotional. But when he did, it was always of you and of your mother and how much he loved you. I know he believed that he would see you two again eventually, in this life, then once he got sick, in heaven."

Alice erased her question from the funeral, when she had prayed that Rob had made it to the heaven he imagined. She believed in heaven, hearing that he did, more than she had hearing countless preachers on Sunday, and believed that he really was there.

Jake offered, "Where did you meet?"

"I hired him as a guitar player when I was on tour and my guitarist got sick with food poisoning. Rob was good. He hung around for a couple of months in the band. We had a torrid affair; I was married." Lila smiled. "The timing wasn't right. We reconnected a few years later though. He wrote me a letter from prison, and I went to visit him a few times. We wrote songs on the phone and in letters. And then, when he got out, he came to live here with me."

Alice smiled, thinking of her brother's talent, that he did something he enjoyed. Knowing this gave her a type of peace. At times, they had both been better with objects than with people, Rob with his guitar and Alice with her plants.

"Do you want to see a video? I think I have one somewhere." Before Alice could say yes, Lila disappeared through a doorway. The two cats followed behind her like a stream of cans on a wedding car, hissing the entire way and glaring back at Alice and Jake.

Alice looked around the room. There were more cats than she had realized. A black one curled on top of the television set. At the noise of Lila's rumbling, he lifted his head and looked in her direction with bright green eyes that gave up his hiding place. As if noticing the visitors for the first time, he blinked at Alice, like Rob used to do. She laughed, remembering how silly he had looked, blinking at her like that. Jake jumped when a paw darted from under the couch and tickled his ankle.

Lila returned and put a VHS tape in the player under the television. After she hit the television, which remarkably caused a line down the middle to disappear, she sat on the couch with them to watch.

Someone held the camera, and it wobbled along with his steps as he walked to one side of the stage. The camera focused on each band member in turn. The place looked like a dive bar with a small stage, the background barely visible because of the lack of light. First, the camera centered on Lila who sang "testing, testing" into the microphone. She wore a loose black top and a jean skirt, tattered at the end. The close-shaved hair, like it had been in the pictures Alice found, gave her neck and chin a graceful, hard appearance that contrasted with the sweet lull of her voice.

As she introduced herself, the camera panned to the right where a man stood with a microphone and an electric guitar. He flashed the camera a thumbs-up, and the man behind it said, "We're getting started here!"

On the television, the camera swerved to a woman sitting behind the drums. Her right foot bounced lightly, and through the speakers came the low rumbling of a bass drum in time with the music. Lila started to sing, and the camera went back to her for a few seconds. Her eyes closed, and one hand rested on the microphone on its stand. The camera found a fiddle player as the slow movement of the bow upon a string began.

Then, the acoustic guitar rang out, and Alice's breath caught. The camera panned, but went too fast and missed Rob, before focusing slowly on his face. He leaned against a stool with his legs outstretched. He had gathered his long hair in a ponytail behind his head, and his eyes closed as he swayed with the music. The song sped up, and his fingers became active on the strings, picking out the notes in an elaborate dance that looked so practiced it could have been a machine. His other movements looked too slow though, as if it took all his energy to move his fingers on the strings.

"I think…" Lila said, and the tape leaped forward as Rob disappeared off the screen. Alice reacted with a grunt that didn't quite form the word *wait*. Lila glanced at her. "I think this is the tape…"

The band members walked back and forth along the stage in fast motion, playing speedily. Rob remained seated on his stool.

Then, the stage cleared, and he pulled the stool to its center. Lila hit Play. "Thank you, thank you," he mumbled into the mic.

"ROB-IN-SON!" came the voice behind the camera, so loud that it jostled slightly, and her brother looked back. "He hates being called that," the cameraman snickered.

Rob leaned into the microphone as his other hand reached to twist the knob on the stand: "Whenever he shuts up." The cameraman flashed the bird in front of the camera. When the screen cleared, Rob sat back on the stool with the microphone.

"He was a good singer, too, but had to be in a certain mood," Lila said.

On the stage, Rob picked out the beginnings of a song, familiar to Alice, but she couldn't place it exactly. He leaned into the microphone and sang in a breathy, low voice. She watched him on the stool, so different than the upbeat croons of their childhood, when he favored the Beatles and Elvis.

The crowd swayed slightly to the music, holding beers in their hands. At the end of the song, he stopped the guitar strumming and repeated the last sad words. The audience clapped and screamed, and the band amassed around Rob, but he stayed seated on the stool with his head leaned into the microphone as if frozen. When the drum for the next song started, he straightened and began to play.

"Was that Nirvana?" Jake said.

Lila nodded. "'All Apologies.'" She turned to Alice. "Do you want the tape?" Lila ejected it, and Alice clutched it to her chest.

More beers came, and they exchanged memories: Alice told Lila about the time her brother took over the school's microphone during recess to sing her "Happy Birthday." She told her of the days they spent playing chicken with the waves at Amelia Island. She told her about the plays Rob would write using the stage and sets Jamie bought for inspiration, where he would act out every part, and Alice would introduce him and operate a flashlight as a spotlight. She described games with impossible rules, nights huddled in the tree house, and Saturdays searching along the riverbanks for the green pitcher plants, just to marvel at the flies that would fall in their leaves.

Lila told of a man who spoke through music, who could approach anyone with a song. He could take an instant liking to someone, a homeless man on the street or a record executive in a suit, and turn on his charm. She talked of late nights with whispered lullabies. She talked about nights on the tour bus, dozing to the sounds of cities along the coast, a trip to the west where he saw the mountains for the first time and wept.

When they reached the story of his decline, Lila spared Alice the details, only that he had suffered. He had been clean when he left prison but picked up old habits because of the pain of his condition, his heart weak from years of illness. And an overdose, or "heart failure," as her mother would say, ended his life before the cancer.

"I went up the stairs to the loft one night to grab him for dinner and found him, sitting in his chair with a drink in his hand. When I went in, the turntable was still spinning, but the record was over, and I knew."

Jake put his arm around Alice's and rubbed her shoulder.

"I knew he would die, because of the cancer, and I thought I was prepared. I wasn't though. He was supposed to have more time. He had some boxes he wanted sent different places, some garbage, some to Georgia, some to me. He told me about them, but I kept shushing him off, saying he could explain it later, it wasn't time yet. And, after finding him like that, I didn't want to go back up there anyway. I sent Ben to get them, and I think the piles got mixed up and things went the wrong way in the shuffle."

"So what about the box with the letters?" Alice asked.

"Not sure, sweetie." Lila glanced at her own letter still unopened on the counter. "Maybe he wanted them thrown out, maybe he meant to send them himself or wanted me to send them or wanted them to end up in your parents' house. We can never know. He always had a plan. That he'd share it with you, and that you'd completely understand it, was less likely, but I guess you knew that."

She smiled at Alice, a sad, defeated smile. "I only knew about any letters because he used to sit at that desk, while I was at work." She pointed to the desk in the corner. "I thought he was writing songs, but after he died, I saw that the cabinet was full of crumbled drafts of those letters, all crossed out or covered with ink."

"But the boxes were already gone," Alice finished. Lila nodded.

"I know it sounds stupid"—Alice looked toward Jake—"but part of me thought that these letters, the people, everything, part of me hoped that he would still be alive, somewhere. That he would be in one of these places and he'd come up to the door when I knocked and say, 'Al, I missed you' and hug me, explain everything. When I saw Ben the other day, I even thought he might be Rob, so stupid."

Jake's hand brushed against her cheek, tucking a strand of hair behind her ear. "It's not stupid."

"Al?" Lila asked.

"Oh, he used to call me that." Alice looked back toward her.

"I think I have something for you."

Alice pulled away from Jake and watched Lila disappear down the hallway toward the bedroom again. Jake and Alice exchanged glances as they heard rummaging and boxes being unpacked and pulled down from the closet. The black cat jumped on the back of the sofa and hissed at them.

"You know, I always thought it was my fate to deliver this one day. Somehow, I knew that Al would find his—or, I guess, her—way to me."

When Alice saw Lila holding the folded-up paper, she knew immediately.

Her letter.

She handed Alice the gift. "I think it's the last one he wrote. I found it in the desk. I would have sent it, but it's not addressed."

Rob hadn't forgotten her after all.

For the first time since hearing her childhood home would soon be demolished, the confusion of Alice's life, the stress of the search wore away briefly and she smiled, knowing that her brother didn't forget her, that she wasn't an afterthought, that he had written to her. Her hand covered her mouth as she let out a quick laugh, and her smile showed through. Jake leaned over to kiss her on the cheek, and she turned, pecking him instead on the lips. Lila smiled too.

Alice reached for the letter and ran her hand over the front, with just two letters on it: "Al," and its fancy seal.

Rob and Lila, soul mates. Her brother had that kind of love and passion, and all of a sudden, she knew that somehow, he had led her here to rediscover it herself. With Jake, in this city of water. It was probably all in this letter, his master plan, to restore Alice to herself.

Alice popped the seal, and the anticipation washed over her like a flood and tightened her throat. Then, a terrible thought occurred to her.

"Maybe he didn't want to send it. Maybe that's why this one isn't addressed."

"Or maybe he wanted to deliver it himself," Jake said.

She smiled, unfolded the page, and took a step away from Jake. She wanted to share this moment only with herself. The paper was different from the others, ripped on one side, but covered end to end with tiny script, so small, her eyes strained as she read the first line.

Alice read the letter and her smile faded, and soon each muscle in her body tensed for flight. She willed them to stay still for the end of the letter. She would finish it. She would read what her brother wrote. She kept reading, and as she finished the last word, she couldn't force her feet to stay put any longer.

Holding the letter, she mumbled, "Sorry, I have to go," mostly to the cat, avoiding Lila and Jake's eyes, and ran out of the room, out of the house, into the salty New Orleans air. The rain had come while she talked to Lila and her feet pounded on the puddles, sending water up that wet the back of her jeans. To where, she didn't know, but she ran.

She heard Jake behind her: "Alice, Alice! Wait! What's wrong? You forgot your shoes!"

She had forgotten that Lila asked them to remove their shoes. Almost on cue, Alice felt the pebbles sting the bottoms of her feet.

She slowed, and Jake caught up to her. Alice cried now; she couldn't process her emotions. They thundered past like trains where you couldn't make out the features of passengers, and she stood on the track, helpless.

She reached in her backpack, fumbling for her phone. As she grasped it, the phone slid out of her sweaty, shaking hand and down onto the sidewalk. A sob racked her body and she bent down, looking for the phone.

"I'll get it." Jake reached for the phone, wiped it off quickly on his shirt, and handed it back. "What happened?"

"I… The letter," Alice stuttered. She took a breath. "I have to call Walker. I have to find Jamie. I have to talk to Robbie. I have to, I have to." She thrust the letter at Jake.

She briefly saw a vision of herself, standing in the middle of the street with the phone and the letter and Jake. She imagined how she must look to the people passing by—a sobbing woman with no shoes, her hair probably a mess, her face all red from the tears, her voice loud and shaky, her clothes stained.

They must think she was crazy. She felt crazy. She took deep breaths and tried to calm down. *Robbie's at school,* she told herself. *He's safe at school.* She chanted it to herself like a mantra: *Robbie's safe at school.*

"I have to go home."

ROB'S LOST LETTERS:

Al

~~Mr. Dylan Barnett~~

~~Ms. Lila King~~

~~Mr. Richard Tate~~

~~Mrs. Maura Tate~~

~~Mr. James Hudson~~

~~Mr. Christopher Smith~~

~~Mr. Tyler Wells~~

CHAPTER THIRTY-ONE

Dear Al:

I tell you this story not to upset you, although it likely will, but because putting this story down on paper, the story I was never brave enough to tell, is the only gift I have left to give you. I have a lot of regrets, but that I let myself become a shadow over your life—that's my biggest one.

When we were kids, I knew I had to go. You were too young to explain the reason to you. I always meant to talk to you again, but wanted to wait until I became something, until I could show you that the pain I caused had been worth something.

You made me a better person. I wanted to be good for you, to stay in the lines, so that I could stay at that house for you, at least until you were old enough to go to college. I promised myself I would, told myself to stick it out, even as it became more and more impossible. Even now, so many years later, I find myself asking "What would Alice do?" like others ask of Jesus.

Do you remember the story I used to tell you about the siblings in the forest? I desperately wanted to be that, that boy who was always good to his core, whose mind was full of happy

*dreams and good wishes. "What are you thinking, Al?" I'd ask
then, hoping that some of that would rub off on me, sink into
my own thought process.*

*But, that's not the story I need to tell you. As Virginia Woolf
wrote, "My head is a hive of words that won't settle," a hive
of memories of us as I write this letter, something I can't make
sense of, especially lately.*

But, where were we?

*Our story starts when I was nine or ten. I'm sure you
remember Jamie babysitting us all the time. You probably
wished he was our father. Sometimes I did too. He loved me,
bought us gifts, bought me the guitar I still have now, the one
I'm sending back for you and your kids, hoping one of them
will play it and love it as I have.*

*I wanted it—that's something you need to understand. Part
of the reason I've never been able to say these words out loud.
When Jamie touched me that first time, I liked it. Liked how
it set my skin alive and made me feel like the adult, like the
man, I so wanted to be.*

*Every night when he stayed over babysitting us, he would
send you out to play or you would fall asleep, and we would
stay up, fooling around or having sex. When I got older, he told
me he was my secret boyfriend, and I loved that, a secret only
I knew about, someone for whom I was the most important
person in the world, someone who could hold me and make me
feel safe and wanted and loved.*

*We would play house together, drink beers at first, then
vodka sodas, then vodka from the bottle, sitting in Mama's
parlor like she used to do when she drank her afternoon*

cocktail. I loved that feeling, that silence. I began to crave it, ask for more, beg for more, until I couldn't think about anything but my next night with Jamie.

He told me how talented I was, that if I practiced, he would enroll me in the best arts schools, pay my way, tell Richard to screw off, and I would learn from the greats and play onstage, all I ever wanted to do. I waited, for years, eating up those promises.

Mama, no doubt, thought I was some angsty teen dying to get out on his own with his guitar and his girlfriend. I can't even remember that girl's name now. But, that's not far from the truth. The girl changed things because Jamie hated her. He was jealous and wanted me to break up with her, but I said I wouldn't, and by the trip to Amelia Island, we were at a standstill.

I told Richard I didn't want Jamie to come. He asked me why and I screamed at him, without explaining, because what could I have said? I mostly wanted him to trust I had a good reason, even though I knew he would never choose me over Jamie.

I told him if Jamie came, I wouldn't. Richard had found me passed out a few weeks earlier with an empty bottle of rum and a cigarette that burned a small hole in Mama's favorite carpet. I think Jamie left me there, after a fight, but it's hard to remember now. Richard told me I was coming, if he had to drag me there, and that I needed to shape up and start acting like part of this family. I went.

When Jamie came in that night, like he always did on Amelia Island, he was drunk. He asked if I had broken up *with that bitch yet, and when I said no, he gave me a choice. He told me that this was our chance, that if I went with him now, he would do what he always promised. We'd go to New York, where the best music schools, the best guitar teachers, were.*

If I didn't, he said he would tell Richard that he caught me with drugs. He even took out a bag of pills in his pocket and shook it for dramatic effect. He said this would be the last straw, that he was sure I'd be off to military boarding school within a week. Truthfully, I considered his offer of running away together. It wasn't a bad one. It was what I thought I deserved.

The girlfriend stopped me. She had been nice to me, without expecting anything in return. She had made me realize that the relationship I had with Jamie wasn't the best offer I could get. And I was older than when he first made those promises to me. What did I need him for anyway? But I knew if I tried to leave, he would tell Richard right away, that I wouldn't be able to get a mile before I was found and right back with Jamie.

I needed a distraction. Before I could think, I reached for the lamp on the table and hit him in the head, knocking him unconscious. I yanked the pills and his wallet out of his pocket and put them in my own a second before Richard ran in. He saw Jamie on the floor, bleeding from his head. He screamed at me, asking me what I had done, but his practicality quickly overtook his questions. He carried Jamie like a baby to the car and sped off to the hospital, leaving me alone in the room.

I knew I had to leave. Right then. I said bye to you before

I left, but I didn't have the heart to wake you up. Maybe I should have, but I knew you'd make me want to stay. I would have, if I had known I would never see you again. But, I still thought I'd be back soon. That I would wait for things with Jamie to die down, that I would spend a few months or even a year or two proving to Richard that I could make it, that I was special.

I went straight to the bus station and bought a ticket on the first bus out, ending up in Dallas, and went on a bender it seemed like it took months for me to wake up from.

I blamed Richard. I blamed myself. But, I didn't blame Jamie until later. Once I was older, once I had been clean for a few weeks (though it never stuck) and had time to think about things. Up until the end, I always chose to be with Jamie, but had I? At that age?

How would my life have been different if I hadn't started drinking at age eleven? How might my relationships have been different if I hadn't had sex with a man fifteen years older than me as a child? I don't know. Even now, I have someone who loves me for real, someone I would lay down all weapons for, but the physical stuff is all tangled in my mind like I got my wires crossed long ago and could never figure out how to right them.

I'm sorry I am telling you this now. I'm sorry I didn't before. I heard through the grapevine you were pregnant (nothing creepy, I have my sources). Congrats. It's a boy.

I don't want you to worry. I believe Jamie and I have reached a, shall we say, understanding. But, you should know what he is capable of. Keep your family safe. I'm sorry never to have known them. But let this letter be a testament that even miles and worlds apart, you were always with me, always on my mind.

With love,
Rob

ROB'S LOST LETTERS:

~~At~~
~~Mr. Dylan Barnett~~
~~Ms. Lila King~~
~~Mr. Richard Tate~~
~~Mrs. Maura Tate~~
~~Mr. James Hudson~~
~~Mr. Christopher Smith~~
~~Mr. Tyler Wells~~

CHAPTER THIRTY-TWO

Alice jumped in Jake's truck and rapped her knuckles against the window as he drove back to her hotel.

"Do you think? Your son," Jake started to say. "Robbie? Do you think?"

Alice slammed her hand down on the dashboard's worn plastic. Her wedding band left a dent in the gray. She stared at it, her permanent mark on Jake's life in New Orleans. "Sorry."

"It's all right." He reached over to pat the dent, like he could smooth it out.

"I'm … Can you ever be sure? I don't think, they don't see each other much, Walker doesn't like Jamie. They don't…" Her voice trailed off.

Rob had assured her he reached an "understanding," with Jamie, but what did that assurance mean when Alice was worried about her son? Because despite what Rob wrote in his letter—"I wanted it"—she would never believe that someone Robbie's age could *want* something like that.

Back in her hotel room, she stuffed her duffel bag with clothes, working so quickly her mind grew blank, focused on only getting home. As she closed the door with her bag over her shoulder, Alice remembered her favorite dress, the one she wore to dinner with Jake, balled on the floor from where she had dropped it that morning. She stepped forward, as if to go back for it, but knew she could never look at it without remembering the fear and confusion permeating through her at that moment. She turned around and shut the door, running back down the steps and into Jake's truck.

A group of four college-aged men exited a bar and crossed the street in front of the truck with their arms around one another's shoulders, one tipping into the other, the one on the end carrying a neon pink Hurricane cup. They laughed, happy and carefree. It was how she pictured Rob's days when her mind was filled with anger toward him for leaving. But she didn't know. Didn't know anything.

How funny, how sad that she could grow up in the same house as Rob, share parents, share dreams and fears, feel his blood coursing through her veins, yet this giant nightmare lay between them. This thing with Jamie that she would never understand.

She looked away from the men trudging down the street as Jake raced through the French Quarter—too fast between lights, then slamming on the brakes, creating the illusion of progress. His fingers danced on the gearshift like Rob's had on his guitar in the video. He saw her staring and flexed his hand out once, then gripped the gearshift until his knuckles turned white.

Just as she could see the highway ahead, see the road back to home, they stopped at a police barricade. Another two cars, then three quickly pulled up behind them on the one-way street.

Jake groaned.

"What?"

He rolled down his window to ask the police officer by the barricade where they could pass.

"Street's blocked off right now," he said to Jake. "You'll have to wait a few minutes."

She heard the music through the open window before she saw anything, the slow *da-da, da-da*, like a waltz from her childhood as she danced with Rob before her first forced Cotillion lesson (which didn't last).

"Chest out!" her mother had called to her. Rob spun with his back toward her and stuck his tongue out without breaking perfect dance posture.

A band in black marching hats stomped down the street with their cheeks full of music. Behind them, men in police uniforms carried a dark-brown casket high over their heads, and along either side, people danced left, then right in a slow, mournful sashay. Some carried lace-trimmed umbrellas in different colors. They stepped slowly down the street, followed by an impossible number of people, black and white, and tourists among them, too, some carrying instruments, some carrying umbrellas and masks, some with their hands in the air. They all made their way down the street with those slow, mournful steps.

"What're they doing?"

"It's a second line," Jake said. "It's for a police officer. I saw it in the paper this morning, I forgot. Sorry, I should have gone another way."

She squinted closer and could see posters with a commanding black man smiling with gray hair and a police cap. "Like a funeral parade."

"Yeah, sort of."

Jake and Alice watched through the windows as the crowd entered the iron gates of the cemetery. Police officers lowered the casket into the ground. Alice watched the family humming and swaying along to a hymn that the brass played. She leaned over to take Jake's hand again and rubbed it lightly with her thumb. She thought back to her parents at Rob's funeral, avoiding each other and their pain, everything hidden under the surface. Rob would have liked a send-off like this, with music, where those he loved weren't afraid to look at one another through tear-filled eyes.

The music cut off abruptly and started again, fast and jubilant this time. Alice watched the mourners dance back through the crowd. The band stomped their feet, and the colors seemed brighter, as the crowd followed them back up the street, back in front of Jake's truck. The posters with the man's face jumped up and down.

She watched a little girl and boy twirling with an umbrella, so many times that she got dizzy again herself, and for a second, Alice thought she saw Rob out of the corner of her eye in the crowd. She smiled at the man, with sandy-brown hair and reassuring blue eyes that seemed to promise that it would be all right, and she thought that back at him in return. He turned around and disappeared.

"I know," she said to herself and to Jake. "It will be all right. It will be."

The blockade cleared, and they started toward the airport again, the highways crossing over the water that fed into the sea. Alice listened to her duffel shifting in the truck bed as Jake lurched the steering wheel left and right.

The truck stopped at the airport, and Jake leapt out to reach for Alice's bag, but she had already swung it over her shoulder. He took her hand.

"Alice, I know this is a crazy time for you, but I would kick myself later if I didn't tell you before you go that I love you. I always have, and I don't want to let you go again."

"Jake, I—"

"You don't have to answer right now. It seems like our timing is never right. But, when it is, you know where to find me."

She kissed him quickly on the lips and turned toward the airport's entrance.

She knew he would stand there and watch her go, as she had done in college when she watched him head down the Jetway for the flight that would take him to Ecuador. But she didn't look back at him as he had done then.

———————

When she reached the Delta ticket counter, the person at the counter told her the next flight took off in thirty minutes.

"That's the one I want," Alice said.

"I'm not sure you can make it, ma'am. There's also one in"— he looked down at his computer and clacked on the keys—"three hours."

"The first one."

He was still explaining what to do if she didn't make it when Alice took off toward security.

When she arrived at security, she thrust her ticket in front of the TSA agent. "What's the rush?" he asked.

She rested with her hands on her knees to take a breath, thanking herself for all those hikes through the Center's woods.

He looked at the ticket. "Oh, you better hurry then."

Her legs felt like nothing, gliding on the moving walkway as Alice ran to her gate, away from New Orleans and toward reality, away from Jake, but toward her son, away from one of the worst and one of the best days of her life. When she reached it, the flight attendant called for final boarding.

"Alice Wright?" the attendant said.

Alice nodded.

"Was about to shut the doors."

Alice found her seat, in a thankfully clear aisle. For the first time since she'd read the letter, she let her eyes close and the questions in her mind take over. The memories from her and Rob's childhood glowed at the edges, the glory years she had cherished so much and replayed to keep herself company in the quiet house for the remainder of her lonely childhood.

The quirks in Jamie's personality that made Alice roll her eyes as an adult had enthralled her as a child. He opposed every quality her father took on: He was animated, bombastic, playful. She loved those puppet games and the little stage he bought for Christmas and would set up in the family room when her father visited the trucking headquarters in Memphis. The Christmas Eve Jamie allowed Rob and Alice to unwrap and rewrap all their presents.

Each memory went gray when she fell asleep, Rob still downstairs since Jamie would let him stay up later than her own bedtime. The static of a VCR tape at the end of its movie filled her ears, the screen buzzing with static.

She thought back to that night on Amelia Island, and instead of remembering how she had pretended to sleep while her brother walked out of her life, she thought about the crash that startled her awake, the car that drove away, the muffled screams of Rob, Jamie, and Richard in the basement and Jamie's absence at their house for the weeks after, barely noticeable in the chaos of Rob's disappearance. Her father had sided with Jamie, yes, but hadn't he also been betrayed? Betrayed beyond something he could ever imagine, could ever let himself imagine by his best friend and adoptive brother?

Her father had chosen Jamie, had trusted the wrong person, and that mistake had destroyed her family. She knew that Rob was right, that Richard would have believed Jamie over Rob about the drugs, would have sent Rob to military school. She thought back to Jamie at Rob's funeral, saying that Rob had every chance that Jamie and Richard didn't have and had thrown them away, and shook her head.

The night she snuck out and found Richard drunk outside Rob's door, he had felt responsible, far more than he had let Rob know. Even though she felt sure he hadn't known the extent or even a little of what had gone on between Jamie and Rob. Rob and Richard had played a game of chicken, Jamie stuck in the middle, and everyone had lost.

She tried to replay the times that Robbie had interacted with Jamie. Had they ever been alone together? No, she told herself. Walker's own short fuse with him regulated Alice's visits with Jamie to the Varsity after church and the occasional family gathering. She replayed Robbie and Jamie's every movement from Christmas, which Walker told her not to invite him to. She should have listened. Walker knew, she told herself. He sensed something that she couldn't. What a bad mother that she couldn't even sense that, from someone she knew her whole life? She recited her mantra from earlier: *Robbie is safe at school.*

Alice retrieved her phone and paid for the internet. She scrolled through three pages of Google search results on signs of abuse and what to say to a child who might have been abused, while promising herself it wasn't necessary. The seat-belt sign came back on, and the pilot's voice told the cabin to prepare for landing.

The Atlanta airport's long escalator, that brought weary passengers up from the basement, had always meant coming home to Alice. She loved to watch the mass of people at the top, held back by ropes, waiting for their loved ones, and the antsy passengers fidgeting on the escalator, eager to reach them. Today, though, she stomped up the escalator between annoyed-looking people, like a soldier going into battle. Around her, couples kissed. Daughters held signs and embraced their fathers, dressed in army camo. Grandparents met their grandchildren for the first time. Alice felt nothing but terror looking at the happy people.

When she got in her Prius, though, a wave of calm rushed over her. Calm, because she knew where she needed to go next.

CHAPTER THIRTY-THREE

She sped to Jamie's ranch, listening to her phone ringing in her backpack. The sound only egged her on, kept her concentrated on what she knew she had to do.

A highway. Traffic. The radio playing country music. The windows cracked open, and her chest welcoming the winter crispness. It meant nothing to her.

Jamie. Jamie. Jamie, she thought. All of a sudden, it occurred to her that this was how normal people committed murder. She had always wondered about those wives on the shows that Chelsea and Caitlin liked to watch, curled up on the couch together. *Snapped.* They had snapped. "I don't know what came over me, it was like I was in a trance." Now Alice knew.

The exit came on fast, and she jerked the car to pull over. She drove past the blank fields on the way to Jamie's estate, where she normally meandered, stopping to look at the horse-filled pastures and the tulip trees. She turned into Jamie's compound, her tires spewing up gravel as she stopped in front of the intercom.

She pressed the button, refusing to announce herself. *Let him look at the video. Let him see my face*, she thought.

If he knew anything was amiss, he didn't say so. "Alice! One second," the box chirped back happily.

Her car tapped the iron gate as it swung open, and she gunned it up the long driveway. She climbed from the front seat and banged on Jamie's door with his large knocker in the shape of a dog.

"There she is, Miss America!" he sang, as he swung open the door. "What a nice surprise." When he saw her face, his smile fell. Alice pushed past him into the living room, and he slammed the door behind her.

"Tell me," she said.

"Tell you what?"

"Tell me what happened with Rob. The truth." She circled the room, pacing like an animal about to go in for the kill. She could hear Jamie's dogs barking in the back where they must be in a kennel somewhere, going crazy over the sound of the knock at the door.

He held her gaze and didn't say anything, just crossed his arms over his chest.

"Tell me why he actually left! What *you* did!"

"This is why I told you not to look in that box." He wagged his finger at her like she was a child. "Bringing up this mess again."

A dirty dish from Jamie's dinner rested on the side table by the television, and she picked it up, ready to hurl it at him. A satisfying flash of fear flew across his face. She set it back on the table.

"Don't tell me what to do."

"What is it you want me to tell you?" He circled now, too, opposite her, and they went around the room like two fighters in a ring.

She stopped and started again, changing tactics. "Just tell me, did you touch my son?"

"Robbie?" He stopped. "How could you say that? I would never!"

He seemed genuinely hurt, and Alice froze, a glimmer of doubt passing through her eyes.

"Did you…with Rob?"

"No! Of course not! Rob and I… I *loved* him. We… He loved me. We were going to move away together."

"That's not how Rob felt."

"You don't know! You weren't there!"

"He was a kid though. He was only nine!"

"Do you think this makes me proud? Do you think I'm *enjoying* this conversation? We had plans, and then he attacked me! I was in the hospital for a *week*." Silent tears fell down Jamie's cheeks, over the wrinkles on his face like water droplets along dry soil. "And then he sicced his bodyguards on me like I was some kind of common criminal. They would come into my house and leave googly eyes on my *pillow*, Alice. I couldn't leave my house. I only stopped fearing for my life once Rob died. You think I like that?"

He sank into a stained leather armchair and sobbed into his hands.

"If you loved him so much, why wouldn't you give the PI the money to look for him, like you told Mama you would? Instead of keeping it?"

"He found Rob in two months. I went to talk to him and tried to get him to come back, tried to give him money. He wouldn't come back with *me*. Then, he ran off again. I couldn't tell your mother that *I* was why he ran away again. I can't believe you would say I would do that to Robbie. I'm not a monster. Just because you *think* things, that's not the same thing. It's not the same thing. Rob was different."

"Shut up."

"He was different, he *loved* me, I know he did."

"SHUT UP!"

He sobbed, loud violent sobs that turned into hiccups. The dogs barked louder, hearing the sound Jamie made, now more similar to that of an exotic bird than any human sound Alice had heard.

"I need to think, okay?" Alice said. "I need a second. You stay here, all right? Stay in the chair."

"Stay here and what? Play computer games for a decade like I had to do before Rob died, afraid his *thugs* were always waiting around the corner for me? I like my life." He cried into his hands. "*He* took *my* life. He did. I didn't do anything wrong."

She screamed in frustration. She needed a silent second without Jamie's tears and screams and lack of logic, without the dogs barking, to work out what to do with him. As she went to the door, she saw a box in the entryway, like the ones from her parents' house, her mother's handwriting on the side: "PI files."

"What is that?"

Jamie kept his face in his hands.

"Jamie, WHAT *IS* THAT?"

He looked up, and she pointed to the box. He returned his face to his hands and sobbed.

She grabbed the box just in case and yanked open the door. She went back to the car, plopped the box next to her. She didn't want to think about the box. *How could there be more?*

She lay down with her back on the hood. Like she had with Rob when their mother took them to look at the constellations in the sky one night, pointing out the symbols from the mythology she liked to quiz them on. Jamie had already begun with Rob even then, had already started to twist him, to confuse him, to hurt him. She *hated* Jamie. She did. She had never hated anyone, had never been able to say "hate" as a child—the "h-word" her mother would say. But she did. She hated him.

Revenge. That's what she wanted, but how? Call the police? Tell everyone what he'd done? Tell her mother? Cut him off financially?

None of that would bring Rob back.

She let her eyes close for just a second, let herself pretend like she was still in that moment with Rob, listening to their mother pointing out Orion's belt.

A sound rang out, and Alice bolted up from the hood. She would recognize the sound anywhere—

The sound of a single shot from her father's favorite rifle.

CHAPTER THIRTY-FOUR

Alice rested her head on her car's window at stoplights, leaving a greasy imprint on the glass. The fog of police questioning and ambulances, all to finally tell her what she already knew—Jamie was dead—had filled her previous hours. In between, she read the contents of the box. It was full of fake PI reports, written by Jamie, filled with "sightings" of Rob, meant to string her mother along, convince her they were close to finding him. They made her sick. She left them in Jamie's yard. They were nothing to her.

As Alice pulled into the driveway, she flinched from Buddy's barking, too close an echo to the hours she had spent at Jamie's listening to the same thing. Buddy jumped at the door and spun around waiting for his usual attention.

She opened the door, and mercifully, he stopped barking as Alice petted him. "Where is everyone?" She walked around the dark house's loop, with Buddy following her. They must be at a late dinner, out and not expecting her home a day early.

Alice walked into the kitchen, still wearing her dirty, fishy clothes from lunch. She felt more tired than she remembered in her life. Back in the kitchen next to the phone, she noticed an envelope that she didn't recognize. It wasn't marked or sealed, so she opened it. Inside were two tickets for a week-long trip to St. Lucia, starting next week. Even at the sight of the tickets, much less the thought of a trip with Walker, a powerful feeling of loneliness weighed her chest.

She checked her phone and saw a text from Jake: You don't need to text me back, but wanted to say that I'm thinking about you. She smiled for the first time in hours.

She went back to the bedroom, stripped her clothes, and kicked them into her bathroom trash can. The bathroom filled with steam from the too-hot shower, and she let the water run over her again. Jamie came to her mind. This morning, he had been in this world, and now he wasn't. She didn't grieve him, but the tangled web of her family, inextricably woven together with hurt and secrets and shame, filled her with sadness.

After she got out and dressed, she heard yelling from the kitchen.

"Mom? MOM?"

"In here!"

Robbie ran to her, and she leaned down to scoop him up in her arms.

Walker came into their bedroom, followed by Caitlin. She hugged Caitlin.

"I'm going to NYU!" she said. "Dad and I talked about it yesterday."

"But…" Walker prompted.

"*But* I'm going to come home one weekend a month." Caitlin smiled broadly.

"That's great." Alice looked at Walker, and he smiled back to her, a reassuring smile as if to say he had everything fixed, everything smoothed over for her return, as if their fight had never happened.

"We were about to go watch something in the basement," Walker said. "We even found something we can all watch together. It's a history documentary"—he pointed at Robbie— "about women"—he pointed to Caitlin—"in baseball." He pointed to himself. He reached out to Alice, as if trying to envelop her in a hug, a reward for good behavior.

She leaned down to hug Robbie again instead.

"Mom, you're crushing me!"

She laughed, one tear streamed down her cheek, just when she thought she didn't have any left. She reached to stroke Robbie's hair and kissed him on the cheek. "I love you. I love you so much."

"Mom, what's wrong?"

"I'm just so glad to be home."

She pulled away from Robbie. She grabbed the arms of both her children and looked at them, deep in their eyes, as she would have wanted her own parents to do, as she wished she had done with Rob that night he left when she pretended to sleep.

"Y'all can never do *anything* to make me not love you. Do you know that? Do you?"

"We know, Mom."

She tickled Robbie's tummy lightly and he squirmed. "Yes!"

"You guys go start the movie. We'll be right down," Walker said.

Alice stood and wiped her cheeks with the backs of her hands. Robbie stared at her, still in the same place.

"She's fine, champ," Walker said.

"I'm fine." Alice smiled, and Robbie and Caitlin disappeared down the steps.

"I bet you're hungry." She followed Walker into the kitchen

where he spooned fried rice and orange chicken onto a plate and popped it into the microwave.

"You're home a day early." He came over to her and wrapped Alice in a hug. This time, she let him. "I hope that means you want to make this work. I want you to know I've ended things with Brittani."

"Walker—not tonight." Today had already been the longest day of her life. She didn't want to tell him about Jamie. She didn't want to talk to Walker at all.

"We don't have to talk about it tonight. I just want to say one more thing: We can move, if you want. I'll leave the firm and go somewhere else, if that will make things better. We could start over." He rubbed her forearm with his pointer finger.

"I got you something," he said, and Alice's chest clenched. He handed her the envelope with the tickets. "Before you say no, there's this great resort a buddy at work recommended. We could go next week, reconnect."

The microwave beeped, and he reached for her food.

"Think about it."

She took the plate from him. "I don't need to think about it. I want a divorce." She said it quickly, casually, feeling pounds lighter with each syllable.

He stopped in his tracks, stunned, and she turned to go.

"Alice," he called, and she turned back around.

He walked toward her, fast and puffed out like rangers always say to do with bears, to make yourself seem larger. She stood her ground.

"Let me ask you one thing," he said. "And I want an honest answer for *once* in your life."

"All right, Walker," she said. If she leaned her face forward an inch, her nose would touch his chin. "What. What's your question?"

"I loved you. I really did. Did you ever love me?"

She looked him in the eye. Robbie's eyes. The eyes she loved, but not the way she loved Jake.

"I love what we built together."

"That's not a fucking answer."

"Then, no. I didn't."

He spun away from her, knocked the container of rice off the counter, dodged Buddy as he rushed to lick it, and headed for the door, slamming it behind him.

As she reached into the silverware drawer for a spoon and shut it with her hip, she heard the roar of Walker's car, driving away, driving to Brittani probably. Good. She hoped Brittani loved him, loved him like Alice couldn't. She ate the food, standing in a halo of rice, following Walker's rule of no food in the basement, even without him there. More, though, she wanted one more minute to herself before she joined her happy children.

She got the letter from her bag and unfolded the paper, careful not to look at it until she was ready. She wanted to skip past all the parts about Jamie and only reread the words her brother had written. The ones she wanted to burn into her brain.

You made me a better person.

Even now, so many years later, I find myself asking "What would Alice do?" like others ask about Jesus...

"Mom, Caitlin's starting it!" Robbie skidded to a stop at the rice on the floor. "What happened?"

"Oh, I spilled something. Buddy's working on cleaning it up."

"Are you coming?"

"Yeah, I'm coming, honey."

He turned toward the basement to go but twisted back around right as he took his first step.

"Who's that drawing of?"

"What drawing?"

He pointed to the paper in Alice's hand.

She turned it over, and her chest jumped for the twentieth time today.

On the back was the drawing Rob had slipped from her room that night on Amelia Island, the one she drew of him on the pier in Savannah. It was all wrong, nothing like the artistic drawing he had done of her, yet there was something about the eyes. You could feel them watching you, the way the irises curved toward the center, pulsated out in little strokes, like the sun's rays.

"Oh, it's... You remember how I told you that you were named after my brother?"

He nodded.

"That's him."

He came over to study the drawing with Alice, and she angled it toward him to look.

"Cool," he said. "Come *on!*"

Alice let him take her by the hand and down the stairs. She let Caitlin and Robbie explain the documentary to her. She felt at peace—picturing Rob's eyes in the drawing—the most at peace she had felt since before her brother left.

But let this letter be a testament that even miles and worlds apart, you were always with me, always on my mind.

In a few minutes, she fell asleep with her head resting on Caitlin's shoulder, listening to the sounds of her children around her.

CHAPTER THIRTY-FIVE

A few days later, Alice shook Caitlin awake at 6:00 a.m. on a school day.

"Let's go for a drive," she said.

"I have school!"

Robbie was at Walker's hotel with him, and Alice had already told the school Caitlin wouldn't be coming today. An important family function.

Not for the first time in the last few days, the thought occurred to her how different Caitlin and Robbie's childhoods would be. Caitlin, her parents married (unhappily but married), living in a gated community in the suburbs. Robbie, shuffled between his parents' homes, living with Alice along the lake where she already planned to buy the lot next to the Center, to build them a home there, one with a spire Robbie could climb inside to assemble his puzzles, looking at the water.

How different it would be, yet, couldn't only a sibling understand something like that? A childhood, a divorce? For she knew no matter how many hours she spent awake at night, talking on the phone to Jake about all they missed, she'd never be able to explain to him fully the things Rob just knew about her, the things they had experienced together. No matter how much life they had lived apart.

"There will be coffee! Trust me and get dressed." Alice flipped on the lights as she left the room. She heard Caitlin moan through the closed door.

An hour later, they sat in Alice's car in front of her parents' house.

"I forgot what this place looked like." Caitlin put her Starbucks to-go cup in the cup holder and reached for her phone to snap a last picture of the house she could barely remember.

Alice sipped her own coffee, glancing back and forth from Rob's window to her Prius's clock to the backhoe's sharp shovel and the hard-hatted man inside. They were running late, but none of the workers seemed concerned.

Alice followed Caitlin's eyes as they scanned the scene, jumping over the caution tape in front of their car, past the garage where her father's Jeep once stood, past the window to the right where her mother always put the Christmas tree.

They watched as one of the workers threw a paint-smeared hammer in the air and caught it. He did it a few times, their eyes watching the hammer's ascent, before missing. It dropped into the pristine grass, and he looked left and right to make sure no one saw. Caitlin laughed.

"Why didn't you tell me? About NYU and the video?"

She turned to look at Alice. Alice let the hurt she had been hiding show on her face, and Caitlin's expression immediately softened. Alice returned her gaze until she looked away.

"I don't know."

Alice cracked the windows and turned the car off. The clock she had been studying went blank. Caitlin looked at her hands, struggling to twist Chelsea's class ring around on her ring finger.

Her own, Alice had noticed, was on Chelsea's index finger. Alice leaned back in her seat and waited for Caitlin to speak again.

"It was easy…to tell you I was gay," Caitlin started, looking ahead with her eyes fixed on the middle, second-floor window—Rob's window—or so Alice thought, though her daughter had no way of knowing which was his. "I knew you would still love me. I didn't worry about that."

"Of course, I still love you, honey. Is that what this is about?" Alice rested her hand on Caitlin's shoulder.

"With the video…it was different. I was afraid if you saw it…" Caitlin swallowed. "I was afraid if you saw it, that you would think *I* didn't love *you*." She started to cry. "And I didn't want you to think that. Because I do, and it wasn't like that. I… It's what I felt. I'm sorry I didn't tell you." She wiped her face with the backs of her hands, like she always did as a child when she cried.

"I know. It's okay." Alice reached over the center console to hug her. "But you can always tell me anything. I know you love me, of course I know that."

They held each other, Caitlin sniffling into Alice's shoulder and Alice breathing in her scent, the girl who always had her heart, who always would, so tightly.

She had decided to be more honest.

First, with herself, about Rob and what he meant to her, about all the choices she'd made, and why. Then, with Walker, about their marriage, about the divorce. And yesterday, with Maura.

Although Alice could never tell her mother everything she wanted to, everything she'd learned about Rob, she could do one thing. When Maura had inevitably asked "Where is Rob?"—as she always seemed to now—Alice had told some version of the truth.

"Remember, Mama?" she said, grabbing her mother's hand. "He's in New Orleans, playing his music, living with the love of his life. He's happy, but he still misses us, and we still miss him."

Alice paused, watching to see how her mother would react, if it would result in the tearful pleas that it normally did. But her mother only smiled and sat back.

"You're asking if *I* remember?" she had said. "*I'm* the one who paid for all those guitar lessons. I always knew he had talent."

Alice smiled, because this, too, was true.

Now, Alice let go of Caitlin and breathed deeply, steadying herself. She had one more person to whom she wanted to give the same gift Rob had given her—the gift of the truth, the gift of knowing that the tingling in your veins, your senses, were real, that they reflected some echoing in the universe that all was not quite right.

"I haven't been honest with you either," Alice began. "That's why I brought you here. I want to tell you something."

"What?" Caitlin wiped her face again. She sniffled, recovering.

"You know how I don't really like to talk about my brother."

"Yeah. We don't know like *anything* about him. Besides he was named Robert."

"Robinson."

She pointed, and Caitlin's eyes followed her finger. "See that window? That was his. Since I went to the house, I've been thinking a lot about him. Way before he died, when he was younger than you, he ran away, and Mimi and I didn't know where he was."

"What happened to him?"

"I didn't know. But I decided that I would go try to talk

to some of his friends and find out. That's why I was in New Orleans. Not for work."

Caitlin sat back into her seat.

"I guess he thought we were better off without him. He loved music, and he played guitar in some bands, and then he went to prison for dealing drugs. He got sick. And he died. You may not remember. You were young when we went to his funeral, but I was pregnant with your brother."

"I remember."

"But I missed him so much. Even when I tried to forget him, even when I didn't want to remember him, I missed him. And it was wrong not to talk about him. I don't want to do that anymore. I want to remember him."

"What was he like?"

Alice looked back at the window, struggling for the words to describe Rob. She said the first thing that popped into her mind. "Messy. He was messy and loud and big-hearted. He wore his heart on his sleeve and didn't follow other people's rules, even when he probably should have." The useless images popped into her mind. How much he loved cherries, him reading the encyclopedias like a novel, him yelling in the clearing.

"He made *me* a better person, I think. I know he did. He was a good person, he was a good brother and son, even with his faults. We loved him anyway.

"And smart. He was so smart. When we were kids, he had the best memory. He could memorize entire plays and recite them. And passionate. He fought for what he wanted and never gave up. You remind me of him sometimes. You fill up a room, like he did, the air changes a bit when you're there."

"I wish I could have met him."

"Me too, sweetheart. Me too. But I have something for you, something he wanted you to have."

Alice opened her door and went around to the trunk. There, she popped open the new guitar case, still without a scratch from the shop, and pulled out Rob's guitar, polished and beautiful, like it was when he left with it on Amelia Island. She brought it back to the car and handed it to Caitlin.

"For me?"

Alice nodded. She smiled, seeing her daughter with it, holding it awkwardly, like Rob had in the childhood portrait her mother used on his funeral pamphlet.

Caitlin strummed the perfectly tuned strings.

"Thanks. I love it."

"See here?" Alice pointed to the back of the guitar, and Caitlin turned it over. Rob's initials—RWT—still stood out against the wood on the back of the neck. She'd had the shop add another line—CLW.

Caitlin ran her fingers over the inscription, smiling. She turned it in front of her and ran her fingers along the strings. "What should I play?"

"Think about it, but I'd suggest Nirvana." Alice opened the door. "I'll be right back."

"Mom, where are you going?"

"Stay there!" she called.

She walked purposefully past the workers still standing about, ducked under the construction tape, and opened the door to her parents' house.

Inside, the place had been completely transformed. The

beautiful wooden floors her mother had cherished had been stripped away to reveal the baseboard underneath. The jewel-toned wallpaper took on a dark and eerie quality from the light that peeked out of the remaining windows. The furniture was gone.

Sure, sell everything, Alice had told the estate company. It was better for the environment, more cost-effective, and she had loved the idea of the wooden plank that she ran on with Rob being used in another kids' house. She didn't know it would look like this though.

She stomped up the stairs, straining to see in the light. The doors were gone too. "This antique woodwork is in demand nowadays," the woman had said. She walked into Rob's open doorway, through his empty room to the closet. The little hide-away door where she had crawled as a child was still intact.

She opened it and crouched down inside, just far enough to slip in a single piece of paper, ripped, then taped down the middle. On one side, a strong-eyed little girl looked at her older brother. The boy, loopy around the edges, looked back at her with love. The back had neat cursive on one side, so small you'd need to lean in to read it. The other side sported Alice's all-caps print, large on the page, the short letter going end to end. *DEAR ROB*, it began. She left them there, the brother and sister, the pair, looking at each other, happy and strong, in the home they kept for each other, and skipped back down the steps, shutting the makeshift front door behind her.

"*Now* can we start?" the man sitting in the backhoe's compartment said, and another one made a motion with his hand. Alice jogged, head down, to her car and climbed back inside.

"They were really mad you went inside."

Alice only shrugged, like Rob would have done.

A beeping started, and they looked back at the equipment trampling her mother's flower beds. The backhoe inched up slowly, high above the house. It blocked the sun from Alice's car.

Then, so slowly that it didn't seem like there would be enough force to destroy the house, the claw crashed through the roof and down to Rob's window, splintering the wood and sending bricks flying.

CHAPTER THIRTY-SIX

Dear Rob,

I delivered your letters because I wanted to find out who you really were.

What I realized, though, is that I already knew. I always did.

You taught me so much. What love was. How to start over. That if you keep a box of secrets in your mind, it will only grow to define you. That you can't untangle yourself from those who stamped their dreams, their ambitions, their personalities, and their love on you.

Even though years have passed since we've talked, there are so many things that only you can understand. So much I need to tell you.

So, I know you're right, that we'll see each other again one day. I look forward to it, how you'll come up to me in the tree house like the kids in your story. You'll look at me and say, "Where were we?" And we'll pick up right where we left off.

Love,
Al

READING GROUP GUIDE

1. Describe Alice and Rob's relationship as children. Were they different from typical siblings? In what way?

2. Put yourself in Alice's shoes. If you found a box of unopened letters from a lost loved one, would you deliver them without reading the contents? Would you open the letters first?

3. Rob spent a lot of his adult life secretly looking after Alice, but he never made direct contact with her. Do you think he should have? Why do you think he chose not to reach out, even when they lived in the same city?

4. Rob writes letters to the most important people in his life, either praising or censuring them. If you conducted a similar project, who would you write to and why?

5. Describe Alice's relationship with Maura, her mother. Now compare Alice's relationship with her own children, Caitlin and Robbie. What do these relationship dynamics look like? What are the similarities and differences?

6. After college, Alice finds herself at a crossroads: she must choose between an adventurous life or a safe one. She ultimately picks a predictable route and marries Walker. Why do you think she does this? What would you do?

7. Compare Walker and Jake. They are very different, but in which ways are they similar?

8. Do you think that Jake should have told Alice when he found Rob, or was it better to keep his promise of secrecy?

9. There are quite a few tragic moments in this book. Which one hit you the hardest? Why?

10. Walker isn't a good husband, but he is crushed when he learns that Alice never loved him. Did you feel sympathetic for him during that scene, or did you feel he deserved it? Why do you think he was so blindsided by what happened?

11. After his initial disappearance, Alice's father never tries to find Rob. Why do you think that is?

12. Jake tells Alice that he's willing to wait for her. Do you think that they will ever get back together? Why or why not?

A CONVERSATION
WITH THE AUTHOR

What inspired you to write *How to Bury Your Brother*?

In 2014, just a month after graduating from the University of Georgia, I had a dream. I saw a woman visiting her parents' house after they passed away, desperate to learn more about her estranged brother. The dream stayed with me, and as I left Georgia's creeks and rivers behind for a move to Washington, DC, I kept returning to this woman, her own past in those rivers and the questions she had about her brother. What did this woman—Alice, who became my main character—want to know? Why was her brother estranged from the family?

A few years earlier, my family had lost a member to opioid addiction and overdose. When someone dies under such circumstances, there are so many questions, chief among them: Why? It's the question that propels Alice throughout the novel, and the one with which I immediately identified. As so many families impacted by the opioid epidemic know, there's no easy answer to that question.

The Southern landscape, particularly the outdoors, feels very important in this novel. Why did you choose it as a setting?

I grew up in Georgia, with a childhood that looked very similar to Alice's—though thankfully, with far less family drama!

Like Alice, I spent many days playing outside with my younger brother, at the creek in our backyard and the woods around our house, which we nicknamed Stick and Snake City.

Setting the story in Georgia, where I grew up and had rarely left previously, was a comfort to me throughout the writing process. As I walked along DC's tourist-clogged streets, listening to the blaring motorcades and marveling at the grand monuments of America's forefathers, I knew Georgia waited for me on my computer. When I felt most homesick, I dove into the forests and rivers of my youth, jumping into the canoe right alongside Alice and Rob.

I also had my best friend, Breanna Crowell, for inspiration. I borrowed her career for Alice in the book. Like Meredith and Alice, we were college roommates, and her missives on water conservation, tales from measuring water foam along Georgia's beaches, and complaints about counting leaf hairs on sunflowers, as Alice does in the book, all served as inspiration to me as I typed the story at the Dupont Circle Starbucks, wishing I was soaking in the sun and salt from Georgia's shores along with her.

What was your creative process for this book like?

I didn't plot the book. I had the dream, with Alice in her parents' house, the funeral scene that kicks off the first chapter, and the final letter to Alice, including the revelation inside. That was it though. I tried not to think too deeply about writing A BOOK when I first started. Instead, I thought I would write until I didn't feel like it anymore. But the story kept coming. And coming.

During my years working on the book, the story changed

drastically. During the first draft, I added and deleted characters as I was writing, changed previous plot points, added or deleted characteristics of the Tate family, all with the goal of writing to the end without editing. When I finished the book and dove into revisions, they were extensive. I would describe it as a painful process! Although I write articles often for journalism, I wasn't used to editing one piece of writing for so long. At times, I had significant parts of the manuscript memorized from reading it so many times.

For my second book, I'm hoping to make things a bit easier on myself by doing more plotting before diving in. Still, though, I find my best ideas come from "flying by the seat of my pants."

Each letter gives Alice (and the reader) a glimpse into a different chapter of Rob's life. Was there a certain letter you enjoyed writing about the most?

Since I didn't plot the book, each letter was just as much a surprise to me as it was to Alice. Although we don't see the exact content of Rob's letter to Dylan, that scene was my favorite to write. It's the discovery in that meeting with Dylan, that Rob was in Athens, that really tips Alice's world and shows her that her relationship with her brother wasn't what the perhaps more pessimistic side of her thought. Writing that scene and the secret included in it also showed me that I wanted to keep going, to keep following Alice and see what she would find about Rob.

This book takes a very realistic stance on grief—you don't avoid confronting the damage inflicted by abuse and loss. Was

it a challenge to get yourself in the right headspace to write the more heartrending parts of the story?

Honestly, no. I tend to feel things very deeply and be empathetic, which is probably true of most writers. I summoned my own experiences with grief throughout my writing of the book and could put myself in Alice's headspace pretty easily. While editing the scene where Alice gets her final letter, I almost always started tearing up right along with her. The challenge bigger than getting in the headspace was getting out of it. I would try to skip around in the manuscript so I wasn't concentrating for long periods of time on the book's saddest sections, and several times, my husband (thankfully) encouraged me to step away from the computer and back into the real world for a few hours.

A lot of these characters must live with the consequences of their elders' choices. What drew you to the idea of generational trauma?

In Southern families in particular, I believe the stories you inherit mean more than many other things you may inherit from your family tree. My own family trafficked in stories, and they were the most valuable currency around the dinner table or at family celebrations. After the food had been eaten and the dishes done, everyone would gather over the evening's empty wine bottles to tell stories. Many, the kids heard so many times we could recite them ourselves (those were the favorites), but as we aged, the stories went back further and spanned out more completely, even the tragic ones told in the uniquely Southern tongue-in-cheek way that sneaks laughter into the painful parts.

Real or fake, the stories Alice has heard throughout her life, the stories the family members have told themselves and one another, have devastating consequences. More so than the trauma, it's those that travel with Alice into the future, even without the storytellers there to tell them.

What are you working on next?

I'm working on my next novel, which is slated to come out in summer 2021.

ACKNOWLEDGMENTS

Thanks to my agent, Katie Shea Boutiller, for believing in this book, championing it, and for offering wisdom, kindness, and speedy answers to my anxiety-induced emails.

Thanks to everyone at Sourcebooks who supported me and supported this book, especially my editor, Shana Drehs, who made this book better with each reading. Thanks to Diane Dannenfeldt and Heather Hall for correcting my commas and taking out the AP style I can't seem to shake.

Thanks to my DC writing group friends: Everdeen Mason, Dana Liebelson, Britt Peterson, Julie Zauzmer, Jeff Ernsthausen, and Dana Stuster. Plus, special thanks to our fearless leader, Cat Traywick, and to Stephen Mays for many conversations while walking along the Potomac. Without your deadlines, encouragement, and notes, this book would be an incomplete Word document.

Thanks to the many people who provided feedback on this book during my writing process, especially my mother-in-law, Dr. Sandy Sipe; my grandmother-in-law, Eva Sue Smith; and my dear friends Whitney Wyszynski and Allison Prang. Thanks also to Jaci Shiendling, Brant Moll, Autumn Lindsey, and Maggie Giles. Apologies to anyone I may have missed.

Thanks to Professor John Greenman of the University of Georgia, for believing in big dreams.

Thanks to Patti Callahan Henry for your advice and generosity and for showing me that writing and publishing a book is possible.

Thanks to Breanna Crowell for letting me steal your career, for telling me that honeysuckles were invasive in the South, and for your limitless friendship.

Thanks to Julia Carpenter for your warmth, encouragement, endless readings, and constant conversations about Rob and Alice over glasses of red wine on Seventeenth Street. Those nights will forever seep into my memories of writing this book.

To my family for your support and for raising me to love a good story. To my grandmother, Gertie, to whom this book is dedicated, for withstanding the many hours of my moaning by the computer while you pushed me to perfect my school papers, for your crusade to "culture" me, and for many readings and thoughtful comments on this manuscript. Thanks to my brother, Davis, for the inspiration of many days in Stick and Snake City. To my parents, Jennifer and Jeff, for allowing my childhood bedroom to become cluttered with hundreds of books and for teaching me the importance of empathy. Thanks to my mother, especially, for being nothing like Maura. Your constant support makes me feel like anything is possible.

This book is written in memory of the boy who read the encyclopedias front to back, and of the 130 Americans who die each day from the opioid epidemic. To all the families impacted by this crisis, my heart goes out to you.

Thanks most of all to my husband, Kevin Sipe. For spending many weekends and late nights working together at the George Washington Law Library, for your unwavering (and seemingly delusional) confidence in me and my writing abilities, for treating this book like it was more than a passing hobby from its first word, and for everything you do to make my writing possible. Thanks for building this crazy life with me. There's not a thing I would change.

ABOUT THE AUTHOR

Lindsey Rogers Cook works as a senior editor for digital storytelling and training at the *New York Times*. She is a graduate of the University of Georgia and lives in Hoboken, New Jersey, with her husband and two fetch-loving cats. This is her first novel.